The Powys Deacon

ALLAN JONES

THE CATRIN SAYER MYSTERIES

The Chinese Sailor
The Scottish Colourist
The Falmouth Model
The Carnforth Double
The Powys Deacon
The Stratford Hunter
The Thornham Copyist

The Powys Deacon

"All art is bad, but modern art is the worst. Just like the influenza. The newer it is, the more dangerous. And modern art is not only a public danger, it's insidious. You never know what may happen when it's got loose."

Gulley Jimson in, *The Horse's Mouth* by Joyce Carey

CONTENTS

From Book Four (The Carnforth Double)

Prologue   1

PART 1: TREGYNON

1   Bristol   5

2   Appointment   19

3   Boeing   24

4   Team   29

5   Stoke Heath   38

6   Van Dongen   45

7   Spots of Bother   50

8   Kowloon   57

9   Richards   68

10   Newtown   76

11   Raid   80

12   Marsham Street   88

13   Harbour City   100

14   Tregynon   106

15   Fowles   112

16   St. Deiniol's Church   121

17   The Gorton Gallery Robbery   130

18   Videoconference   141

19   The Cwmbran Kiln   146

20   Donkey Work   153

21   Tompion   160

22   Detour   169

PART 2: BINDLEY WOODS

23   Body   178

24   Insight   190

25   Details   194

26   Edie   200

27   Rubbish   208

28   Gallery   213

29   Confession   222

30   Ingelsby   229

31   Report   237

32   Plastered   241

33   Calipers   249

PART 3: DUBAI AND BEYOND

34	Wedding	257
35	Statement	268
36	Strife	273
37	Scrapbook	281
38	Performance	286
39	Swab	295
40	Dubai	304
41	Consequences	318
42	Accident	325
43	Tregynon	332
44	Farrell	338
45	Barlow	348
	Epilogue	355
	Notes	358
	About the Author	360

FROM BOOK FOUR
(THE CARNFORTH DOUBLE)

Assistant Commissioner Hunt paused, letting Sayer adjust.

"I want you to become my aide and personal security officer. When we first met, you may recall Sergeant Ross had that role and you have met Sergeant Egar more recently. I would like you to take up that position for a while."

Catrin looked thunderstruck.

Hunt continued. "Inspector Ross is now with the Pan-London Task Force. Sergeant Egar's promotion was approved two days ago. He will join the Barking and Dagenham borough at inspector rank. It's a position which generally results in promotion, you see, if you have the aptitude and stamina… and I think you do."

By now it had sunk in. Catrin glanced at Worsley who nodded and smiled.

Catrin said, "Thank you, ma'am, for considering me but… it is not logical."

She paused, trying to find the correct words. "I am targeted; when, where, if ever, we don't know, but… it's not logical. To increase your risk, I mean."

She thought she could have put it better perhaps, but that was the way it came out. She felt more shocked than tired now and realised she should actually mention her decision on Wales, as the relocation choice. After the encounter with Hunt on Friday she expected to be pushed into relocation and a new identity, perhaps with some incentive, at this meeting.

Hunt nodded, as if she knew this would come up. Or it had already done so, with others.

"On the contrary, I think it is very logical for a couple of reasons. First, you have shown capability in protecting other officers under fire at close range. Few of us get that direct experience, fortunately; and it is a position that requires you to be armed.

"Second, and perhaps the most important reason you should accept it, is that it will help to keep you safe. The word about the appointment will go out to China, Malaysia and to triad groups here; we will make sure of that with the help of Superintendent Baksh and others.

"To kill a police officer is bad enough; to be seen to be trying to kill an Assistant Commissioner of the Metropolitan Police or someone close to her is appalling. No triad would survive it very well; their business linkages would be badly damaged or ruined, for one thing and every police service would be driving them over the cliff for years to come. Nam Wu will be told to keep his private vendetta on ice, at least during your assignment period on my team. That is the expert opinion from a number of sources, here and abroad. We looked into it quite thoroughly in the last few days."

She stood up and walked to the door of her inner office, closing it fully then turned to face the two women.

"And I will be damned if I let anyone tell me that my role is so important that I can't stand with my officers if the opportunity arises."

PROLOGUE

The B4363 now led down the hill as he headed west, between the village of Bagginswood and the town of Kidderminster. The driver knew he was finally on the stretch close to his target. During the day the fields and hedges showed gently undulating countryside, a mix of greens and browns, but at night they were a dark wall at the limit of the headlights.

In the variable darkness of a half-moon through cloud, the vehicle slowed as he followed the turn at the bottom, looking for the unmarked side road. Afterwards, as he neared the brow of a hill on the narrow lane, he dropped to sidelights; it was, after all, nearly three in the morning. The driver was being careful; he didn't want the headlights to flash over to the golf club. Just in case.

The entrance barrier to the service track was only twenty yards ahead, just a simple swing bar of galvanized metal hinged at one post, with a padlock on the post at the other side. The lock was no problem for him; he had lock picks and a lot of experience using them. Once his vehicle was through the gap, he closed the barrier and placed an almost identical padlock, one for which he did have a key, on the barrier. Within seconds he was driving into the woods slowly using only the sidelights, unseen from the road.

In the unlikely event that anyone who wanted access to this track in the middle of the night arrived, they would find that their own key didn't allow them to open the barrier. He had things to do and he didn't want to be disturbed.

At the point where he saw the branch he had placed earlier, he switched off everything and waited with his windows lowered. To him, it was the most dangerous part of his plan, in a sense; idle time. But he wanted his eyes and hearing to adjust and he knew that takes time.

When he felt he was ready, he opened the door, got out and went around to the back, taking a deep breath before opening the tailgate door. Balance would be everything at this point. He wanted to do this cleanly and not leave more evidence of entry than necessary. He pulled the cover off the wrapped body and hauled it half-out. A stoop, a 'fireman's lift' and then he re-established his centre of balance... carefully. He stood still, panting from the effort. Rotating his line of sight, he walked slowly into the coppice, counting the paces, as he had earlier in daylight. He saw the log and the small dip just to the left and gladly dropped the load, freeing himself from the weight.

The log pulled free and rolled clear; a seven inch diameter downy birch, rotten at one end and with a number of radial remnants of its broken branches along its length. He pulled out the entrenching tool from its holder on his belt, opened it and started digging methodically. Better than a spade for close work, he struggled only once when he encountered a sizeable stone. He had to work around it to lift it clear.

It was the only hard part of this phase. After the sharpened edge of the tool cut through the thin roots of ground vegetation, the soft humus lifted more easily than the sandy sub-soil. His eyes were on the task but his ears were tuned to the surroundings, listening for the first sign of any intruders.

Half an hour later the body of the man, now unwrapped but still in the clothes he had died in, was laid in the hole and positioned on his back, as he planned it. He added an initial covering of soil and took a breather, walking back to the vehicle to drink some water first, then some of the black coffee from the flask. Idle time again, but necessary; he wasn't the man he once was, he knew.

His final act was to return to the burial scene with the unframed painting, placing it face down above the soil-covered head. While the dead man may have refused to look at it in life, he now had no choice, at least symbolically, in death. He said in a whisper the short prayer he had memorized; an extract on repentance from Deuteronomy.

After filling the grave he carefully pushed back the layer of vegetation debris that had been peeled away initially. Finally, he rolled the log back in place and stood back. There were several spots of fresh soil showing so he attended to those before concluding it was as good as it was going to get.

He first drove forward without lights slowly along the service track for about fifty yards, rounding a bend. He was unable to turn around so he reversed back to the gate as evenly as possible, not stopping. If anyone noticed the tyre tracks, his stopping point in the coppice would be away from the body.

His eyesight was good until he was near the side road, when the flash of headlights from a car on the B4363 in the distance ruined his night vision. But it showed clearly that he was nearing the barrier. By then it was no problem. Windows open and listening for traffic, he exited the path and refitted the original lock before taking off his surgical gloves, allowing his damp, sweaty hands to dry out.

As he climbed back into the driver's seat he felt the first splatter of raindrops, the start of a shower. He hoped it would help to blur the tracks and settle the gravesite.

PART 1

TREGYNON

1 BRISTOL

Sharon Cranwell was in her usual position in the public gallery at Bristol Crown Court, seated next to the two other women who would have no say in the proceedings taking place in the courtroom below them. They had worked out a rota for saving their seats; which one of them would come early enough to do so, ready for when the courtroom doors opened. In fact, among the regulars there now who knew, their seats would have been protected anyway. Officially they had no standing; they were not even allocated reserved spaces with the five other women.

Cranwell was watching the female police officer standing in the witness box below. The uniform she wore was that of the Metropolitan Police Service from London; she was not local. There were slight differences between the uniforms.

The officer was the first witness today after some procedural bafflegab that Sharon didn't follow. It took place before the jury was brought in and she wondered how they felt each time this happened, knowing that aspects of the case were being discussed without them being present. Did they feel manipulated? She would, she thought. There had been a number of these technicalities in the last two weeks.

Sometimes another woman sitting nearby who had been a

law student explained these to her during the break, but the intricacies of the legal process were bewildering; time-wasting mostly, she thought them to be.

This police officer, though, was interesting. Sharon had heard about her role from Inspector Hicks. She was a dark blonde, a natural hair colour, Sharon thought. The woman wasn't a 'looker'; she was someone who you wouldn't notice particularly in the high street if she was in ordinary clothes. But the Met officer had been an art crime detective brought in from London during the investigation, he had told her; and a clever one at that.

Now this detective was in uniform rather than dressed in plain-clothes and she certainly stood out. Not that there weren't other uniformed officers around, but this one looked so smart, as if she had been personally tailored with clothes that were well-fitting and new. Everything about her seemed neat and precise, every tunic button bright and sparkling.

Her voice in response to the questions rang out clearly in the court, firm and confident, with that melodic carrying quality characteristic of the Welsh. As her testimony unfolded Sharon saw the woman's head turn from time to time and she caught the line of light on the left cheek; a two inch scar. She wondered how that happened.

One of her friends here was under the impression that this witness would be on the stand most of the day. The Crown had finished their questions and the defense barrister, Mr. Willard, had just started his cross-examination. This was always interesting, Sharon thought. Not dramatic, as on television, but it was where the disputes came.

~~

Willard said, "Sergeant Sayer, you have spoken at length about elements of several abstract works painted by the defendant, but just so the jury understands, you currently work in a security and administration role. Is that correct?"

Catrin replied, "Yes, I am the aide and security officer to an Assistant Commissioner of the Metropolitan Police."

She was in her best 'No. 1' dress uniform, spick and span, her hair neat and tidy despite removing her hat once she was on the witness stand. She looked good, she felt, having taken a lot of trouble with her appearance this morning. Her last answer had projected confidence in her role and her pride in her job.

"Could you please explain in a little more detail your current role for the jury?"

Catrin glanced over to the barrister representing the Crown, who gently raised her eyebrows. Sayer's job now was totally unrelated to the reason she was a witness and Willard knew that. But she was under cross-examination and, if the prosecution barrister raised no objection, she would have to reply.

What was different about being on the witness stand this time, she knew, was her own mindset. She had spent months in the company of senior staff at the Met; people who were used to being in public view, to media questioning, to 'being visible'. Some of it had rubbed off, she felt.

So she looked at Mr. Willard and took a moment to prepare her response.

The trial of Philip Staley, a 73-year-old resident of Totnes, Devon, an artist and formerly a professor of fine art at Dartington College, was finally underway. He had been charged with sexual assaults on five women, incidents that occurred many years ago. The trial was in its second week. It had taken fourteen months following his arrest to reach the courtroom.

The prosecution was past the testimony of the five victims and the police officer leading the investigation, Inspector Stephen Hicks of Devon and Cornwall Police. The women had given evidence about the assaults. Hicks had laid out the events leading up to the arrest. Two to three decades on, there was no direct forensic evidence incriminating the defendant and Staley had denied involvement in the crimes from his arrest onwards.

The Crown was now submitting information about a series of abstract artworks that Staley had painted during that period of his life, ones they believed were tied to these attacks. A personal record of the various positions of the victims during his assaults had been coded into his abstract paintings; his secret 'souvenirs' of his crimes that could be used to re-stimulate his memories. Catrin had been the first person to see the link during a related investigation in Cornwall. At the time she was in her former role, an investigating officer with the Metropolitan Police Art Crime Unit.

She knew that following her on the witness stand in this phase of the trial, in the batting order of the prosecution, were two experts. Professor Thomas Anders of the University of Strathclyde was an authority on Staley's art. Dr. Paula Ryder, a forensic psychiatrist who had worked with the investigation team, would speak to the mindset of serial rapists and their need for mementos to relive their experiences.

Philip Staley's arrest had been the consequence of a related investigation into an on-line attack on his granddaughter, violent images concocted and shared on the internet to show the student being raped herself. The perpetrator had been one of Staley's own victims, a Marilyn Greaves, trying in a macabre and unhinged manner to force Staley to own up to his own misdeeds. She had been arrested and had then confessed. Now, after her trial and conviction, she had served part of her prison sentence but had been released recently on probation. Greaves had already been called as a witness.

Catrin had seen news coverage of the first two weeks of the trial, during which two of the other female victims said they felt that at times as if they were in the dock, not Staley. Catrin was beginning to feel the same way, but it was to be expected, she knew, being in the witness box.

One woman had been reported to say, "Staley sits there looking like a confused old pensioner. You have no idea of the power he had over me at the time."

To Catrin, from her vantage point, Staley's posture and

demeanor supported what the woman had said; other than the eyes. When she looked at him they were alert, angry or quizzical at times.

Catrin answered Willard's last question.

"I have a dual support role to an Assistant Commissioner who has significant internal and external commitments at the Metropolitan Police. As part of the support team for an executive officer I am involved in ensuring that all goes smoothly; that long-term plans turn into weekly schedules which are adjusted by the day, sometimes by the minute. I - or another duty officer - accompany her to external engagements for security purposes. I am an authorised firearms officer, trained to provide a first line of protection, if needed."

She hoped that was enough for the jury. It turned out, though, that it wasn't enough for Staley's defense barrister.

"Describe a typical day, if you would, please?"

Catrin thought for a moment about what Willard was doing with this line of questions. He is trying to send my mind elsewhere, she thought, to put me off my stride before he takes a punch, despite it sounding reasonable.

She said, "Well, last week, for example. On one day we had internal meetings, then a visit to the home of a victim's family. It was followed by a visit to a borough police station and a media briefing there before an afternoon engagement at a government office, a meeting. I started my duty at 8.00 a.m. that day and I finished my assignment when we dropped AC Hunt - Assistant Commissioner Hunt - off at her home at 7.15 p.m. That was a heavy day, but not too atypical."

She swallowed. The memory of the young sister of the stabbing victim in Southwark had come back. The girl had been whispering to Catrin, away from the main discussion Sandra Hunt and the local superintendent were having with the grieving parents at their home.

The girl said at one point, "If you catch the man who did this to my brother, will you shoot him?"

She had been eyeing the holstered firearm Catrin was

wearing.

Catrin had bent down and whispered back.

"No, we will arrest him; that's our job. Then he will be tried in court."

The girl said nothing more, just kept her eyes on the gun, fascinated. Her older brother had been knifed for a triviality.

Mr. Willard said, "Thank you. To summarize, you are heavily engaged in a range of duties supporting an executive level police officer, with long days, I am sure. And there is the need for constant vigilance regarding security aspects. But none of this has any bearing on art expertise, has it?"

His tone was conciliatory, but she now realised that he had intended to set her up, as she thought.

Catrin said, "No, at present I don't have any responsibilities related to current criminal investigations of art crimes."

He pressed the point.

"So you are no longer an 'art detective' if I may use that term. In fact, you were never part of the Art and Antiques Unit, were you?"

"No, I wasn't assigned there; that unit is part of the Specialist Crime Command structure of the Met. I worked with the Art Crime Unit in Serious Crime Command at the time of this investigation, a different unit."

He pressed on. "But the Art and Antiques Unit is the pre-eminent art crime expertise area in the Metropolitan Police, is it not? Recognized internationally, I do believe. Is that so?"

Moira Langley, the barrister for the crown, rose before Catrin could answer.

"The role of Sergeant Sayer, her position within the Metropolitan Police Service and her assignment by the Art Crime Unit in support of the Devon and Cornwall Police during the investigation has already been established, both earlier in these proceedings and again during this testimony, m'lord."

Judge Julian Creswell, presiding, looked at the defense

barrister.

"Mr. Willard, if you have a point, perhaps you would get to it, otherwise I will agree with Ms. Langley and we will move on."

He was giving him one more kick at the cat.

Catrin had already been on the stand for well over an hour and a half. Most of this time was spent answering the questions she expected from the prosecuting barrister about the sequence of events leading up to Staley's arrest. Willard had spent ten minutes re-visiting some of those points before starting on this new tack around first her current role and now this issue of the Art & Antiques Unit.

The barrister eyed his notes and turned a page, simultaneously saying, "Thank you, m'lord."

He looked at Catrin and paused; then he read from his notes.

"There are twelve staff members, both police officers and civilian experts, in the Art and Antiques Unit. According to our researches, this includes six detectives with art, archeology, history and related highly-specialized expertise. The head of the unit has degrees from Oxford and the Sorbonne. In fact, three members of the team, including support staff, have undergraduate and postgraduate degrees from the universities of Oxford, Cambridge and London; and one other member has a degree from Yale University. The years of experience in art crime investigation in that unit are listed here; it is quite formidable."

He paused, looking up from his notes, a somewhat disdainful expression on his face.

"Where did you study art and what art qualification do you hold?"

Catrin said, "I have a Joint Honours degree in fine art and art history from Aberystwyth University. I received First Class Honours in both subjects."

Willard ignored the answer. His next question was already on his tongue.

"An undergraduate degree, and then you went into the

11

police service. You didn't join an art team then, did you? What did you do?"

Catrin said, "I was a constable, stationed initially in Lambeth and then in Brixton, with general duties at first. Then I was assigned to a team supporting drug squad work."

Willard said, with obvious disbelief in his voice, "If so much of your career has been spent in other police duties, Sergeant Sayer, now and previously, how can you maintain that you have the appropriate skills, experience and qualifications to analyze the abstract paintings of Philip Staley? After all, that is the evidence you gave at considerable length earlier today."

Catrin looked at him, then at Staley. She had expected something like this would occur. Staley was barely concealing his pleasure at this attack on her. So she looked at the jury instead.

"I am an experienced, gallery-exhibited artist in London as well as a trained police investigator. Both the demeanor of the accused during our first interview at his home and the work I saw then, the second of his Series Eight set of paintings, aroused my suspicions. I saw a direct link between the vase motif in the painting and the vase seen in the internet images related to the assault on his granddaughter."

She had already said as much in answering the carefully laid-out series of questions from the Crown barrister; this was simply a reprise for the jury.

Her gaze flicked across to Marilyn Greaves, sitting with the other women victims that were part of the case.

"We now know these images were orchestrated by one of the former witnesses at this trial, Marilyn Greaves. I saw that link in the painting before we interviewed Mrs. Greaves; that is on record. Her independent confession later validated my suspicion and also confirmed the vase was present when she was raped."

Marilyn was nodding. Catrin turned her head to face the defending barrister.

"So yes, I do have appropriate skills and experience - and a good degree."

There was a moment of silence. Catrin had been emphatic and convincing in her delivery of the answer. She looked again at the jury to reinforce her comment on the value of her qualification. She had said 'rape' deliberately rather than use the word 'assault' or 'sexual assault'. She half-expected Willard to take her to task on that, but she had been the one to hear the details first-hand from Greaves; she wasn't going to back down if he came at that point.

Ask away, she thought. Every time you take a shot at my capabilities is an opportunity to restate the case.

The judge intervened, addressing the defense barrister.

"Mr. Willard, we are close to lunch and will adjourn shortly. For my information, do you wish to continue cross-examining this witness after lunch? If so, let us find a suitable point at which to break."

The judge was well aware, in a general way, of the elements of the crown and defence approaches and wanted to keep the testimony as clear as possible for the jury. Judge Creswell had a reputation for 'tidy packaging' of testimony.

Catrin knew that both she and Professor Anders were on the slate for the day but she expected to be examined more thoroughly on the detailed interpretation of the gesture lines in the paintings, the 'incriminating hidden women', as one newspaper referred to them.

Willard paused, looked at Catrin and then said to Creswell, "No, m'lord. In fact, I have no further questions of this witness at this time."

He turned to his junior, passing back the set of documents he had been holding; his briefing notes for her as a witness, she thought. It was clear that he was incomplete; he had pages as yet unturned.

The judge looked at Langley, who made no move to speak, then at Catrin. Keeping his expression neutral he said, "Sergeant Sayer, you may be excused. Thank you."

Then he addressed the court as a whole.

"We will adjourn now for lunch a little early and resume

promptly at two p.m."

The gavel dropped as Catrin realised that she was finished a little sooner than she expected. Willard would, no doubt, arm-wrestle the detailed interpretations of the paintings with Anders and Ryder. He had what he wanted from her, on record; a basis for his claim that she was inadequately qualified. No doubt that would be brought back in his closing comments.

As she worked her way out of the emptying courtroom, Moira Langley nodded to her and smiled; Catrin had done well was the message her face conveyed. The CPS solicitor who had sat behind the barrister, Duncan Ellis, came over and walked out with her.

"That went well, Sergeant Sayer; your last delivery sent Willard scampering. He will go at it with Professor Anders this afternoon, but Anders will be solid, I am sure, and Dr. Ryder is very experienced at this sort of testimony."

Catrin thought back to previous times she had been a witness, particularly the onslaught from Colin Cheney's barrister in Glasgow two years earlier. She had been a bag of nerves each time, worrying about the cross-examinations. This time, it hadn't hit her that way.

She replied, "I wasn't sure where he was going with the academic qualifications issue, Mr. Ellis. Given that the jury is local, slighting my qualification from Aberystwyth could backfire."

Ellis's eyes were acknowledging that point.

"I had the same thought as well. Ms. Langley and I will discuss this aspect and see what he does with Anders and Ryder. We could come back to it in the closing summary, if needed."

Catrin said goodbye and went out, looking in the main hallway for Christopher Treneer, her fiancé. He had been in the public gallery, observing. Chris had taken time off work as a civilian computer expert with the Met to accompany her to Bristol.

The selection of Bristol Crown Court was related to the projected length of the trial. It handled all the longer and more complex trials in the southwestern region of the UK. For Catrin and Chris this venue was fortuitous; they were now going away for a few days; first to Pontypridd in South Wales to visit her parents, only an hour's drive away. Afterwards they would spend the weekend in Exeter and Falmouth visiting Chris's family and friends. Their forthcoming wedding would be the main item of discussion in both places, they knew.

She saw Chris standing outside in the main entrance area with a middle-aged woman, someone she didn't recognize. As she reached them Chris said, "You are finished, so you don't have to come back this afternoon, after all. This is Mrs. Cranwell. We got talking."

Then Catrin recognized the name; Sharon Cranwell was one of the eight women who had come forward when the allegations against Philip Staley had become public, one whom the Crown Prosecution Service felt could not be included in the case brought to trial. They could only go with cases with the strongest evidence, she knew.

She shook hands but said, "I am a witness, Mrs. Cranwell; I could even be recalled. I am sorry, but I can't talk with you about - ."

The woman cut across her.

"No, I understand. I have picked up a lot in the last while about court procedure. I just wanted to thank you. Inspector Hicks explained how someone from Scotland Yard, an art detective, was involved early on, when they told me about... Hearing you just now, I just wanted to thank you for helping, you know. It was Marilyn's case hitting the news that made me come forward. It was a big step for me. But I do appreciate all you did."

Mrs. Cranwell was getting emotional as she spoke, tears in her eyes, but she just turned away, looked back at Chris and said, "Thanks again for the introduction. It was nice talking to you."

Then she was off, heading outside for lunch, trying to regain her composure, no doubt.

Chris said, with some sympathy in his voice, "She told me she has been here every day. She is staying with another woman locally during the week and plans to stay through to the end of the trial. It must be harder in a way, being on the outside, than to be part of the case."

Catrin said, "I am not sure, Chris. Willard gave four of the women a tough time in cross-examination."

The fifth woman now suffered from early-onset Parkinson's disease and, media-savvy, the defense barrister had been very brief and easy-going with her.

~~

They were driving along the M4 passing Newport when Chris said, "Still musing on it?"

Catrin responded, "Just what he said about the Art and Antiques Unit, funnily enough. In trying to discredit me, the defense had pulled out all the qualifications of the A&A mob, would you believe it? I knew DCI Coltrane had lived in France and, given his wealthy background, he had probably been to Oxford or Cambridge. But he had studied also at the Sorbonne, it turned out."

She laughed. "Willard was parroting this list of Oxford, Cambridge and London; even bloody Yale. I knew when I applied back in Brixton for the Art Crime Unit that A&A was an elitist lot, way off my radar. But this just confirms it."

Chris said, "Well, you can look down on them - and me and my e-crime lot - from the top floor, now."

Catrin thought, yes, in a sense; for another year or so. She was enjoying her new role but had been told that aides to Sandra Hunt were generally a two-year appointment; her boss used the position to develop people she had an eye on. Catrin wasn't sure what she would do next. The only thing, she thought, was that she wouldn't be joining the Oxbridge mob in

A&A; she would fit in better back in Brixton than with that team.

Apparently reading her thoughts, Chis said, "I thought you liked Coltrane? You have worked with him from time to time on cases and he helped out on the Glasgow issue, when PIRC went after you, you told me."

Several years ago Catrin had been subject to an internal enquiry; allegations made during a case in Scotland. The police review commission there, PIRC, later dismissed the allegations, but Neville had gone to bat for her at the time.

She said, "I do; I like him, I liked to work with him, the times it happened. Coltrane may be wealthy and upper crust, but he is easy to get along with, I found. And he is so knowledgeable about art. It's just... the old animosity between the ACU and A&A, I suppose. And working with Keith. He always said DI Caldwell and some of the others were real snobs."

Her old unit, the ACU, wasn't likely to have an inspector-level vacancy unless DI Keith Marshall quit, retired early or died. He was happy in the role, she knew, and didn't want promotion or a move. The Art and Antiques Unit may chase the stolen art internationally and have the big reputation, but the ACU mandate was to provide art expertise support to police services across the UK. It focused primarily on catching criminals, particularly those people involved in violent art-related crime, not in the recovery of art.

But she wanted the promotion that was expected on completion of this assignment; at least, the one that most of her predecessors had received, the rank of inspector. But where that would take her in the Met, she had no idea.

A year later, she was to remember that trip and those thoughts.

~~

Two weeks after her appearance as a witness at Bristol Crown Court, Catrin was sitting next to Assistant

Commissioner Hunt in the back seat of Hunt's official car. They were heading to another appointment in London. Her phone beeped; it was an email from Tony Johnston, the Met communications director.

'Thought you would want to know; Staley jury just came back; guilty on all five. It will hit the news now.'

She looked across to her boss who was, unusually, lost in thought looking out the window. Normally she was visibly active when travelling; reading documents or correspondence, talking on the phone or writing emails on her smartphone.

"Ma'am, Tony Johnston just informed me; the Staley trial in Bristol, the case I assisted on while with the ACU, now has a verdict. Staley was found guilty on all five charges."

Hunt just nodded, acknowledging the fact.

Then after a moment she said, "Let's see what the sentence is. He will serve some time inside, but for how long? Well done, though, Catrin."

George, their driver, who had been on Hunt's team for years, commented, "Whatever it is, it won't be long enough."

He had two daughters, both now married, Catrin recalled.

A week later Philip Staley was sentenced to three years and four months, to be served at Dartmoor prison. He would be out in about a year, Catrin expected, given his age and no evidence of ability to re-offend.

2 APPOINTMENT

In the end, the decision was made by the churchwardens; they swayed the rest of the selection committee. Reverend Crouch had made his position clear. While the man was not a typical candidate, he was a true humanitarian filled with the love of Christ and his message; his ministry was important. Crouch wanted him to be based at St. Deiniol's but he withheld his view; it was the church which needed to decide, not him.

If the last deacon assigned to the church, now ordained in a full priesthood position elsewhere in the diocese, had not been so wonderfully academic and gifted at speaking it might not have been such a contrast. Estelle, the People's Warden, was full of the plusses of the predecessor and how the church should be looking for someone with similar qualities. The now-Reverend Withers and Estelle had each been on holiday trips to the Holy Land and talked about it too often, Simon Crouch thought.

John Farrell, on the other hand, if he went anywhere for holidays, was more likely to be on a pilgrimage to visit homeless shelters in Cardiff Bay, getting soaking wet rather than sunburnt.

"Why us? Shouldn't he be in a bigger city location somewhere?" said Estelle.

"People in need aren't just located in Swansea or Cardiff," said Hugh.

"I am concerned that he doesn't have aspirations for the priesthood," said David, clearly aligned with Estelle, "He wants only to remain a distinctive."

Here Reverend Crouch felt he must intercede. "Serving Christ in the ministry is not solely a priest's role. Remember Margery Johnson, bless her? Distinctive deacons and deaconesses are important members of our clergy."

Deacons could be transitional, a step to the priesthood, or vocational in their own right; 'distinctive', as David said. Deaconess Johnson had been well-loved by the communities across the diocese.

David persisted. "Why not Newtown at All-Saints, perhaps; or a cathedral? This is a small village."

Reverend Crouch smiled. "We have a vacancy; Farrell has just been ordained. The bishop put him forward to us knowing the man and our needs. There are fewer and fewer joining the ranks of the clergy, as you know."

"But... his past?" Estelle said, finally raising the core concern of the objectors.

Gordon Lewis, the oldest person there, the Rector's Warden, had been quiet through most of the discussion, waiting to pounce.

"I know; it's wonderful," he said cheerfully. "Christ in action, don't you think? We should each of us be so fortunate to be moved by the Spirit to change our lives. And I think we should feel very privileged, very privileged indeed, to welcome him to St. Deiniol's."

He knew that this issue would come up at some point and wanted to stop it in its tracks. A man with a criminal past finding God and wanting to work with people in need should be praised and welcomed, he thought, not shunned or mistrusted. The last thing he wanted was another conversation with a deacon 'on the rise' about picking hotels in Jerusalem and how much airfares cost.

~~

Deacon Farrell settled into his appointment; not without quiet criticism from some members of the congregation, some puzzlement from others and, out of left field, strong support from some unexpected quarters, particularly two rebellious teenagers who suddenly stopped causing trouble, turned up to youth group regularly and started bringing friends. He was active, both in the parochial work of the parish and his own mission, working with people released from institutional life, including prisons.

His first major 'black mark' with some members, though, was his the failure to represent the clergy at the Refugee Committee meeting, though he knew Reverend Crouch was on holiday, visiting relatives in London.

"The deacon is supposed to be very supportive of people in need, yet... where is he?" asked Mona, a friend of Estelle Owen. They had formed a camp of discontent over the appointment.

It was Seren Fowles, a late arrival at the meeting, who answered that point after she walked in and sat down.

"Apologies from me for being late and also from Deacon Farrell; he won't be able to make it."

"Really!" said Mona. "What did I say?"

Seren said, "He is working with someone who needs him, at short notice. My boss contacted him, so he was at the station when I saw him. He presents his apologies, as I said, and asked me to pass them on."

Seren was in her twenties and had been at St. Deiniol's all her life. Everyone knew she was now a police officer. She knew how to cut through the guff.

"Is there anything we should do to help?" asked Tim.

Seren knew that, beyond the offer, was the desire for Tim Littleton to know more; he was helpful but was also a gossip.

"No thanks, Tim. I am sure he can cope."

Deacon Farrell was at the Willoughby Farm, she knew. Cecilia Willoughby's brother had died of a heart attack suddenly in Altcourse Prison, near Liverpool. Cecilia was related to Carole Meredith, Seren's station inspector, and had called Meredith to ask what would happen now. Inspector Meredith had thought of John Farrell; he had been several times into Newtown station since he started at the church and had been open with them about his background.

In fact, Seren knew he had visited every police station in the diocese and all the shelters. He was also involved with the local NACRO crime reduction groups assisting people coming out of prison. But none of that was for sharing here. She was, after all, a police officer.

At the coffee chat afterwards, Gordon Lewis said to Seren, "At least Mona didn't comment about John never wearing his suit these days."

Mona had mentioned it at a previous meeting. Farrell had been well-dressed during the first weeks of his service at St. Deiniol's. Seren recalled him in a suit the first time he had given the sermon at a Sunday service. People had expected something based on his past, or his mission; helping people in need coming out of institutions, people often alone or unwanted.

But he spoke about ecumenism, events that brought church communities together in the service of God and, woven in there, the need to reach outside our normal boundaries. He had mentioned that his first encounter with a spiritual adviser had been with a chaplain, a rabbi, in a multi-faith community. He didn't say where, but Seren had noted previously that the label on the suit jacket had been a Jewish tailor in Liverpool. She wondered about that; about the person who had sprung for him to have a hand-tailored suit. Farrell didn't have much money, she knew.

These days he was often seen around the area in a sweater, jeans and an old anorak. The only thing he was consistent about was always wearing his clerical collar. She heard from other officers that he was about at night, too, talking with people on the streets, in the hostels.

DS Pryce had told her Deacon Farrell had been seen by PC 'Collie' Collins talking with Tessa Southwell, a young woman well known to the police, one with a lot of problems. Pryce said the encounter was outside the Albion pub. Two men Tessa hung out with had come out of the pub, half-cut, as they were talking.

"Collins was about to stop and get out of his car; go over and head them off, but for some reason they left Farrell alone," Pryce said. "Collie said that anyone else and they would have given him a right bollocking, or worse. It must be the dog collar."

Seren said nothing; she knew Farrell a little now. The clerical collar may be part of it, but she thought he had a toughness that, if unleashed, could mean he could hold his own with the likes of the Albion crowd, if he wanted to.

3 BOEING

Catrin was in aisle seat 10J facing forward, able to see from her place in the front row of business class directly into the first class section on the British Airways Boeing 777. Through a short corridor her boss was in front of her, the next 'real' row of seats; more accurately, the mini-suites of first class.

Her other travelling companion, Chief Inspector Graham Creedy, who had coordination responsibilities for the Met with their Commonwealth country counterparts, had the companion rear-facing seat next to her; 10K, a window. It wasn't a question of fighting for window or aisle placement; it was policy. Sayer was the security officer and should have the line of sight of their boss, even while unarmed on a Boeing 777.

The cabin attendant came towards her.

"Miss Sayer?"

No ranks mentioned on board, in civilian clothes.

He bent down, close to her ear. Catrin was just sipping some juice, having returned to her seat. She had woken up a little earlier and immediately headed to the washroom to clean her teeth and freshen up, picking the juice up in the galley on her way back. Experience had shown her to use the washrooms as soon as possible after she woke on a night flight, before the lighting level in the cabin was raised and people started surfacing. Any time after they crossed Ireland it would be a lottery, trying to get time in there.

"The passenger in 4K would like you to go forward, if you would. She asked me to look out for your availability, but without disturbing your sleep."

Catrin thanked him and pulled a pen and notebook out of her bag before standing. He led her past the closed curtain to the First Class cabin, to Assistant Commissioner Hunt. The cabin was also darkened still, but several suites had reading lights illuminated.

Sandra Hunt waved her into the neighbouring empty seat without ceremony or pleasantries. "Graham still sleeping?" she asked quietly.

"It appeared so, ma'am, as I got up."

Only Chief Superintendent level and above merited first class travel on British Airways. The three officers were returning from a security conference held in Ottawa, attended by the senior police staff of large metropolitan areas of a number of Commonwealth countries. They had changed planes in Toronto to catch the British Airways flight.

Hunt passed over her iPad, saying only, "Read the mail string, not just the top email."

The most recent email in the sequence was Hunt's own response, sent, it appeared, in the Executive Lounge in Ottawa just before boarding.

'I will check with her; I support it; timing is about right, but it's her call. Hunt.'

As Catrin read through the chain of texts, she realised this correspondence had been going on for about a week, starting with a note from DCI Coltrane, the head of the Art and Antiques Unit, to his own boss, Chief Superintendent Robert Matheson. DI Philip Caldwell in Art and Antiques, who Catrin knew was near-retirement, was suddenly bringing forward his departure date.

Catrin had worked with Caldwell on her final case with the ACU nearly two years ago, chasing two stolen paintings by George Stubbs. Some of the chain of correspondence she was reading referred to keeping whole Caldwell's pension; his wife had contracted cancer, had been in remission, but now it had returned. She wanted to live out her final time with their family in Australia, in the town in which she was born. Caldwell was packing up and leaving as soon as possible.

Then near the top of the email flow was a brief message from Matheson to Hunt:

"We want to re-flag Coltrane's request for consideration of Sayer for Caldwell's replacement. We expect other internal and external candidates, but it would be both Coltrane's and my preference to appoint someone from outside the existing team with art crime investigative expertise, to bring in fresh blood, given the structural changes about to occur. Coltrane is particularly interested in Sayer, given her experience and abilities, if it sits well with you and she is interested. Matheson."

It had taken Hunt two days to reply. Clearly she had been considering her options. As she looked up from the iPad and passed it back she saw that Hunt was watching her with an enquiring expression.

"Well, Catrin?" she asked softly, "I am not pushing it. There will be other opportunities arise for you, I guarantee it. But it is a key art crime role. You have shown that you like that sort of work and have an aptitude for it. And you can handle international travel, I know; some can't. It will be part of the job."

Catrin had no hesitation. Caldwell's team concentrated on art theft and fraud and had an international liaison mandate. This was the key front line position in 'Fine Art' crime in the Metropolitan Police. DI Barnes would be her counterpart in the Antiques Team, she thought at the time, having missed the significance of the 'structural change' cryptic comment.

"Yes, Ma'am; I would be very interested to apply for that

position, if it works out. Thank you."

She wondered what to say to her boss briefly; it was too public an area, even in First Class.

"I know it is coming up to time in this position - ."

Hunt raised her hand, silencing her.

"Later," she said.

Then she added, "I'll let them know. Not bad, becoming a DI before thirty; you are on track. Good decision. A&A are a closed shop, so you will have to sort that out and you know the timing is not going to be easy; they are losing headcount at the same time. But Neville's right; they need new blood."

She smiled.

"But if you have learned anything in the last two years it's not to let people intimidate you."

Then she turned serious again.

"You won't keep AFO status, though; it's a factor. There has been nothing substantive from Malaysia to close the threat file during the last two years. Nothing on the wanted man; what was his name?"

Catrin responded, "He is called Nam Wu. The Malaysian sergeant who was also threatened is called Farra. And it's a long time, Ma'am. I am OK with that aspect now."

Two years since the death threat, they meant. The change in job would take Sayer out of a role carrying a firearm; an Authorised Firearms Officer. Catrin had never mentioned to anyone other than Chris the news she had received from her friend Jian Li Yeung shortly after her appointment; that the threat against her was over with, a result of triad politics.

Hunt nodded, apparently accepting Sayer's remark. She said, "Now go and get your breakfast. We have a busy day ahead."

"Yes, ma'am, I will. And thank you again."

As she walked back to the business class section, Catrin she felt that she was two feet off the floor; promotion and the chance to go back to art crime investigation, this time with the Art & Antiques Unit and its boss, DCI Neville Coltrane. Years ago, early on during her time in the Art Crime Unit, DCI Jane Worsley had said Coltrane had his eye on her.

"He will want you chasing stolen Goya's in the future, Catrin."

At the time she took that as a joke; her loyalties to the ACU were very strong and she was a rookie. But now, after nearly two years of seeing the broader world of the Metropolitan Police in the slipstream of one of its Assistant Commissioners, she was ready. But the issue of the 'closed shop' nature of A&A would have to be addressed and Hunt's comment 'on track' played on her mind; on track for what?

Then she recalled her conversation with Chris after her testimony at the Staley trial, on the drive from Bristol to Pontypridd; she would never be working in the Art and Antiques Unit. She laughed to herself as she reached her seat. Her colleague was sipping juice, his breakfast tray already served.

"Sayer, you are in far too good a mood for this time in the middle of the night, even if the dawn outside is lying to me. The AC is up and about, I take it?"

"Yes sir. She's wide awake and at it."

Creedy yawned. "Why am I not surprised? Watch out; here comes your breakfast!"

His eyes had moved from her to the two attendants now moving the trolley back along the aisle.

As she sat down and refastened her seatbelt, Catrin thought that it will probably not be the last time I am absolutely sure about things that will then turn through one hundred and eighty degrees. But it is a lesson.

4 TEAM

It had been quite a month for Detective Sergeant Mark Harper. But the fact he was so caught out feeling stupid this Monday morning was less to do with the events of the month than with a call from his brother in the early hours, wanting a place to sleep over. He had spent Sunday having another row with his fiancée, it seemed.

"I could drive and wing it," said Dylan.

"No! I will collect you. Stay right there," replied Mark.

Dyl had drunk too much, either before, during or after the row, or all three, but from the state of his voice Mark knew that Dyl shouldn't be driving,. If he could fool himself he was sober enough to drive, he would argue about the cost and effort of taking a taxi. That had been at 12.30 a.m. It was 2.00 a.m. by the time Mark got him back to his flat and settled on his sofa.

He then lay in his own bed trying to sleep, wondering why the engagement, a milestone to marriage, had erupted in more discord than harmony between the lovebirds. Perhaps reality had set in.

Mark staggered through his early morning ritual as he prepared to head over to New Scotland Yard, leaving Dylan stirring and grumbling about his hangover.

If his brother was late for work, so be it.

~~

Three weeks earlier, also a Monday, the Art and Antiques Unit had started as usual with a team briefing by Detective Chief Inspector Neville Coltrane. He began by addressing head-on the 'elephant in the room'; the news at the end of the previous week about the sudden retirement of Harper's boss, Detective Inspector Philip Caldwell. That Caldwell was thinking of retirement was long known; he had the time in. It was the suddenness of its arrival - his quick gathering of Harper and Detective Constable Isabelle Howlett, his direct team, a day earlier; the news of his wife's cancer returning and their decision to move to live near family in Australia.

Harper's first thought was, ironically, how Caldwell would adapt there. As the head of the Art Section of Art and Antiques, he had travelled extensively internationally. But living permanently abroad was a different kettle of fish; Harper had experience of that. He couldn't see his old boss lolling around on Bondi beach or getting fired up about things Australian, other than cricket.

The following day had been Caldwell's last one in the office; a Friday lunch together, clearing out his desk and his departure soon afterwards. The week had finished with Harper dealing with Isabelle Howlett looking bereft. She had worked with Caldwell for a long time, much longer than he had. Mark had gone out for a drink with Isabelle after work before they went their separate ways for the weekend.

DCI Coltrane's comment to the collected A&A team at the following Monday briefing had been straightforward; Caldwell's post was open and approved for filling; it would be processed quickly and applications inside and outside the area would be considered.

Then he added, "Let me also be clear. There are likely to be other changes in our unit. We are still working on those. Art crime may be near the top of the heap in economic impact, but the world of policing priorities is changing rapidly. Resources are finite and the Met has to adjust accordingly. We just need to keep our focus on the cases before us.

"Harper, you will take over the following files with DC Howlett; sort out what you can actively work on and get back to me on it."

'Keep working while our world shrinks a little; we'll let you know," was Howlett's muttered comment, a little later.

During the week and a half after the briefing, things had settled down. Internal and external candidates went in and out of Coltrane's office, including Harper, who felt that his whole interview was somewhat *pro forma*. He knew that with less than two years as a detective sergeant he was not a frontrunner. Nevertheless, he thought he had performed reasonably well.

That DI Barnes was a likely appointee was understood by everyone; he wanted to change over from Antiques to Fine Art, he had made that clear. So it was a forgone conclusion, until the next Friday, when he announced the news of his transfer to manage a much larger team in the Fraud Squad.

"What I hoped for was a change; it is just not where I wanted it," was his comment later in the pub, there for his farewell drink.

"Did you apply there, then?" Howlett asked directly, the question that others had wanted to ask.

Her look said he wasn't going to get off the hook without a straight answer.

"Put it this way," said Barnes, "someone read my palm for me…"

Howlett said, "Next week they will transfer me to Keston as a junior dog trainer."

The training establishment in Keston in Kent provided a range of canine training services for the Met.

"You don't like dogs, you're a cat person," quipped Mark.

"They don't have a cat training school; if they did I would apply, given where this place is going," shot back Howlett.

So the rumour he heard a week later that his new boss was someone now with Authorised Firearms Officer status who would be coming off the Firearms list made him wonder what was happening. The last gun DS Harper had held was an eighteenth century Madrid-lock officer's pistol brought in by a courier, an item of evidence. He signed for it and passed it on to his counterpart, DS Madder in Antiques, when Madder returned from a meeting. The Art and Antiques Unit was a long way away from any tactical firearms work and no-one else there was a firearms officer.

But it was a Friday, late on. There was no-one around to talk to about it other than Laura Bainbridge, the civilian 'stamps and collectibles' expert.

"Have we had anyone here AFO, Laura? You have been here since the flood."

The philatelist half-closed her eyes as she thought about the question.

"Only one I recall was DS Keith Marshall, now DI Marshall with the ACU. Keith had been a firearms officer earlier on in his time, I believe."

Harper nodded. He concluded that DI Marshall was returning to Art and Antiques now that Caldwell had retired. He had heard that there was some bad blood between them from way back. But, other than Bainbridge, Harper's colleagues were either out on cases, heading home early or hiding away in pubs, speculating on the next axe to fall on the Art and Antiques Unit.

~~

So on Monday morning after a sleepless night, Mark's world changed again. First, Derek Nkrumah arrived, an officer from the borough of Hammersmith who had been in and out of the Art and Antiques Unit during the last few weeks, liaising on the Marley case. He was looking happier than he should be for a Monday morning.

Then Neville Coltrane bounced in wearing what seemed to

be yet another new suit, just in front of a slim woman with dark blonde hair. Harper's first thought was that it was unusual to have a visitor during the Monday, first thing; there was the briefing. Coltrane always liked that to be just the team. Nkrumah had sat in a couple of times recently, though. Harper was looking out for DI Marshall to suddenly appear.

It was the expression on the woman's face that jolted him fully awake. She was surveying the people and the area, assessing them. She looked hardly older than Harper himself, he thought; average size, not eye-catching but nicely dressed. He was eyeing up, he concluded somewhat belatedly, his new boss; DI Caldwell's replacement.

As they were introduced, Harper caught the lilt in her voice, Welsh with little or no modulation by the years in London, he thought.

"DS Harper and DC Howlett are your art team, DI Sayer," Coltrane beamed, "You can meet each other now and do the round of the others afterwards. First we have the Monday briefing."

He headed for the meeting room with Sayer having only time to shake hands and say hello.

As the seated themselves, Howlett just raised her eyebrows at Harper and whispered, "A female DI. We can talk about knitting; it will bore the pants off you, just like Caldwell and you did with me about cricket."

She gave him an evil look. Harper was wondering how his network of contacts had not been able to give him a 'heads up' so he could have found out more about this DI Sayer before she arrived.

Coltrane went straight into it after other team members came in and sat down, most into their habitual seats.

"Before we review our caseload and status, let me announce some changes and welcome formally two new members of our unit. DC Nkrumah has been in and out of our hair on the cold-cast bronzes fraud in Hammersmith over the last few weeks, so he is hardly new. Derek is now formally seconded to us for the next six months, but will remain on the borough headcount. They want him back, I understand, though I can't think why. He will continue to work with the Antiques team."

Coltrane was smiling at the young officer as he spoke, clearly pleased with the transfer. There was a round of applause and some comments, warm or humorous, for the beaming young man. Harper realised that this assignment now gave equal police officer workforce strength to the Art team and the Antiques team, at least for the period of Nkrumah's secondment. The civilian staff, four of them, supported both teams. If Kit Madder was promoted to team leader for Antiques, they would be back at their past strength for the half-year.

Uncannily, that was exactly Coltrane's next point.

"DS Madder is now going to lead the Antiques Team; it is an acting position, not permanent - at present, that is. We will have to see if Christopher can keep your noses to the grindstone, particularly with our activity in Acton this week. There will be a lot to do."

Only Coltrane called Kit by his given name, Christopher; he wasn't one for nicknames, it appeared. Again there was applause and some comments. A loud, 'he'll be a bloody slave-driver' came from down the table. Coltrane, still smiling, turned his attention to the real newcomer.

"Detective Inspector Catrin Sayer will be known to some of you; she was previously in art crime work with the ACU. More recently you may have seen her in uniform, a step behind Assistant Commissioner Hunt, where she was her aide and security officer for the last two years. She is joining us to lead the Art Team. Please welcome her also."

There was applause; polite, shorter, fewer hands, but only Harper and Bertie Wells, the forensic expert, could be heard to make welcoming comments.

The contrast in response to the announcements was noticeable and Coltrane's face clouded over. He looked as if he was about to say something when the newcomer spoke.

"Thank you, DCI Coltrane. I look forward to working here."

Coltrane went straight into their case list and assignments. But the opening salvo had been fired.

~~

Later, Sayer sat down with her team to catch up on their assigned cases. All of their workload was continuing work, including a big item for the whole unit on Tuesday; a raid on a warehouse in Acton.

In reviewing the cases and looking at the plans for Tuesday, Sayer said, "This looks like it could be big; it will involve us a lot after tomorrow."

Harper said, "You are right, ma'am. The foundation of this goes back a while."

Sayer asked, "How come these two - the Nahigian brothers - have been below the radar for so long, then?" she asked.

She meant the owners of the warehouse.

Howlett said, "We heard that it has become a bit of a slanging match between Immigration, Interpol and us, ma'am, ever since someone in Lyon pointed out to DCI Coltrane that there are relaxed procedures on EU nationals moving between countries. We could hear him out here, shouting down the phone that Armenia wasn't in the EU or Schengen communities."

Catrin kept her face impassive though the image amused her. At this stage, she didn't know her team members.

She said, "Still, to find that two men operating a shabby little electrical supplies warehouse are not actually Polish; they are Armenians with a track record in theft and smuggling of antiques. Something fell through a very big crack somewhere."

At the end of the case review she said, "So you are Isabelle, I've seen you around before. And it is Mark, right? No preferred other first names?"

They both shook their heads.

"You are from London, Mark? Did you study here?

"No ma'am, I went to Yale. My father is American. Well, I mean, he is all over the place for work but he is based here."

Catrin was getting used to Mark Harper's accent; somewhere between 'Received English' and a broad London accent; people from money.

Catrin said, "So did DI Caldwell include you in any US liaison work? Make use of your American experience, so to speak?"

Harper replied, "Well, my father has spent more time out of the USA than in the country, over the years, and his base is London, with my mother; she is from here. So I hardly spent any time over there as a child. And Yale isn't typical of the USA, believe me. It was my father's college, and his father's, but... I doubt it would give the FBI a warm rosy feeling about me, to push it as a selling point."

He smiled, hesitating before the next comment.

"You are a better fit, ma'am, to be honest. They will love your Welsh accent and you can talk firearms with them; go down to their range, shoot a few targets, ogle the old Winchesters, whatever they do."

Catrin could see he was trying to warm up; take a risk at humour with her. She smiled.

"And you, Isabelle, you aren't from London?"

"No, ma'am, from Oxford."

"You studied there?"

"No, I studied here, at London University. I was born in Oxford; town not gown."

Catrin asked, "Just so I know, and I think I get the drift from the files we have just covered, how have the work assignments generally been allocated in our team in the past?"

Harper and Howlett looked at each other, checking who was going to answer first. Isabelle Howlett was a good bit older than either her boss or her sergeant, so she spoke out.

"Well, generally I do the documentation work and reports, the support work and some of the minor cases. Mainly from here."

Harper said, "I usually worked with DI Caldwell on the bigger cases, unless he was off with DCI Coltrane or… in any event he used to handle the international liaison himself. It takes time, that aspect. But there is a limited travel budget, as you can imagine."

Catrin said nothing, waiting for more.

"Put it this way," said Howlett, "If it is something like the recent Eastbourne case, the alleged theft of a Howard Hodgkin abstract, we handle it."

She pointed unselfconsciously at Harper and herself.

"Well, me; I handle that sort of thing, mainly. If it involves the Art Loss Register level of artwork, items that are worth a bit, or it involves people outside the UK, then DI Caldwell and Mark mainly handled it - and Mark worked between the two of us, leading me sometimes on a case, assisting the DI with others. Like that."

Catrin said, "The Hodgkin painting theft - what happened? I don't think I heard about that one."

"No," said Howlett. "Sussex Police called us in to look into it. The owner, an older lady, had actually sold it four months earlier to a dealer in Bath."

Harper added, "Undiagnosed Alzheimer's. But she was very emphatic it was stolen, wasn't she?"

He was looking at Isabelle.

"I see," said Sayer. "We'll have to see how the caseload assignments work out now, won't we?"

She had the totem pole of her predecessor figured out now.

After they separated for their assigned work, Howlett whispered again to Harper. "I keep getting flashes of choir music; it must be the voice."

Harper smiled. He, too, had been thinking about their new boss's accent and her turns of phrase. She wasn't the formal sort that Caldwell had been, early on.

5 STOKE HEATH

"Is that him?" asked Kevin.

He was walking with Gary along the exit corridor, looking through the glass doors at the people waiting outside Her Majesty's Prison, Stoke Heath, near Market Drayton.

"Yes, that is Deacon Farrell, your ride home."

"He looks - ."

Kevin broke off. The man outside was tall, big-shouldered but was hunched over slightly, in a stance of stoic acceptance of the world around him, it seemed. Other than the black and white at chest and throat, Kevin thought he looked more like someone he would see outside the pub, hanging around waiting to cadge a smoke. He didn't look - a professional man; or soft.

"He looks like he is waiting for you," said Gary.

Apart from the icon of clerical garb, the middle-aged man standing by the car outside the entrance did appear a little rough and down-at-heel. John Farrell was in his late-forties and had a ruddy complexion, weather-beaten from long hours working outside, with streaks of grey and white in his dark, close-cropped hair.

He was wearing a winter waterproof with a lining today,

given the chill in the air, but it was in a style that was too young for him, one with Nike motifs popular about five years earlier. John's hands were stuffed into the side pockets of the coat as he stood there waiting for people to come through the glass doors. He saw Gary Roche and Lisa Stott's boy, Kevin, approaching. Kevin Stott was looking at him suspiciously.

In fact, Kevin was taking in this stranger who was going to drive him back to Newtown, seeing intuitively that the old guy was wearing a 'cast-off' coat, probably from a re-use centre or the Salvation Army. Kevin had experience of both.

Gary said, "This is Mr. Farrell, Kevin, a deacon at a church near your home, the person I told you about. He works with people on release, knows the ropes. Remember what was said inside in the wrap-up, and take care of yourself now. I don't want to see you back."

"I don't want to come back, Gary. Thanks for seeing me off. You have been good to me, helping me see things different, I mean. You know."

Kevin shook Gary's hand formally; too intimidated to be more expressive with this part-time worker, part of the multi-faith chaplaincy at the institution.

Roche then shook hands with the deacon. Kevin saw that they obviously knew each other well.

"God bless, John. Thanks again."

In two minutes they were on the A53 heading towards Shrewsbury in Farrell's six-year-old Vauxhall Astra.

John Farrell drove in silence until the young man gave a sigh; relief at getting out, perhaps, or the boredom of being with a clergyman for the drive home; which he wasn't sure.

Then he said, "How are you? About being out?"

Kevin replied carefully, "I told people back there I was great, but Mr. Roche knows that part of me is scared stiff, in truth; he probably told you. I would have said something else but he said you don't like swearing. And I can't ask to smoke in your car, either."

Kevin was already fidgety.

John said, "At least that is honest of you. It is actually healthy to be a little scared about now. We will stop in ten minutes or so, get a coffee and you can have a smoke. I don't myself now but I have some with me - Player's."

"Great, thanks."

Kevin's face lit up at the prospect of a free smoke and a coffee.

Farrell added, "And no, Gary didn't tell me. He just asked if I would help you start out today."

Kevin said, "He told me that you have been helping my mum and our Sheila. Well, Sheila said that, too, once; she mentioned your name early on, when she came to see me, but I forgot. It didn't register until now, when Gary said you would collect me."

"Yes, I have been seeing them. They are part of a group I help. Your mum is a very nice person."

Kevin said, seriously, "Yes. I don't know how she will be, though, with me back in the house. Sheila said it was OK; she said I could come home. They don't want me going back to my mates."

John Farrell wasn't going to tell him yet, but the 'best mate' that he used to stay with was now in remand; a repeat offender arrested three days ago in a drugs bust. He knew that Kevin would have been told not to associate with his former friends.

He saw the roadside café approaching. "How do you like your coffee or tea?"

Kevin said, "Coffee, milk and sugar, please."

"Have your smoke outside and I will go in and get them and find a table. But don't be too long or, if you do, don't complain if the coffee is lukewarm."

Kevin smiled to himself.

"Any coffee on the outside is better than on the inside, Mr. Farrell. Or do I call you deacon?"

"You call me John. Unless you give me lip; then you will call me whatever I say."

The young man smiled again.

"Right then, John. And thank you again; for everything."

After he got the coffees, Farrell watched the young man through the window. Each movement was jerky, bringing the cigarette to his mouth, the drag, the shake of the head to keep the smoke from his eyes. What he saw was himself, years ago, trying to tough it out after the first stretch. 'Look, I am cool; alright? No sweat, life's great, I am out, see?' Even then he was dying inside.

He watched Kevin take his last drag, went to squeeze the end of the cigarette, keep some for later then, instead, threw the butt away. He almost ran inside, over to the table, picking up the coffee and taking a big swig.

John said, "We are going first to Newtown centre, to your probation office; you need to check in with Mr. Kareedi there, your case officer. You already know him from his visits. I will wait outside when you go in, then I will take you home. He says that this meeting will be about twenty minutes. Your mum has asked me to be at your home for the first meeting between you both, as Sheila will be at work. Just at the start, all being well."

Kevin nodded, understanding.

"I'm nervous about it, too."

"And a man called Donald Tring will collect you this evening at seven; take you to your first AA meeting on the outside. He will introduce you to someone he knows to start you off in NA, too. I suggest you treat these people and their meetings like your parole appointments; you future freedom is going to depend on them. Your sentence isn't over yet; you know that."

Kevin was dually addicted, booze and drugs. 'Speed' - amphetamine sulphate - was his drug of choice and Narcotics Anonymous could help there, but alcohol, once he was drinking, would send him straight back to his dealer and his old life, they knew. He had cleaned up in a detox as part of going inside - and had managed to stay clean in there - but he had to stay off alcohol too. That was a harder proposition on the outside.

John Farrell knew there were more meetings of Alcoholics Anonymous than NA in the area for him to attend. Whether AA or NA, he had to live by the principles of recovery; there was too much against him if he didn't. Kevin Stott could sink again fast if he mixed with the crowd he used to hang out with.

The young man looked serious, contemplating the new reality of his life on the outside.

"And do I meet regularly with you then, John? Do I have to go to church, too?"

He was looking at the clerical collar and his voice had a dual context; beneath the light taunt could be heard a serious question.

Farrell answered, "Absolutely; church once a day for the first year, then we will look at adjusting it to three times a week."

He said it straight, waiting for the expression on Kevin's face to change.

"No," he said, "If you want to meet with me, we can talk about it. I have someone looking out for a work placement for you but nothing has come of it as yet. As to church, it's your choice. I think your mum would like it, but it's your call."

Kevin said, "I am thinking about it, that's all."

They finished up. As they headed out, John could see Kevin working things out in his mind. He may be a man by law but to the deacon he acted very much a teenage boy about to break into his twenties.

Kevin asked, "Does my mum go to your church, then? That's why I asked, she wants me to go, I know."

"No; your mother attends All Saints, close to your home; I am based at a church in Tregynon called St. Deiniol's, but my work covers a lot of places in the diocese - the church area we belong to. If you like, we could meet and I can tell you more about church activities you may want to think about. It is not all Sunday morning stuff."

As they set off Kevin asked, "And what is this job thing

you are looking at?"

"I am not sure of anything yet and your probation officer may have something else for you to follow up on anyway; he is looking around with people. But if my contact comes up trumps it would probably be outside work at a golf course; I have contacts in that line of work."

"You are a golfer, then?"

"No," said the deacon. "I used to work in the same job, golf course maintenance, at a course near Kidderminster. You get to know others doing the same job. It's good, healthy work."

As they drove around the Shrewsbury bypass, John Farrell could see all the information playing through Kevin's face, particularly the apprehension of meeting his mother. High on booze and drugs, Kevin had punched her then pushed her downstairs, breaking her leg badly. He had been arrested, pleaded guilty and was rapidly convicted, receiving his first custodial sentence; four months in Stoke Heath for drug use, drug dealing and assault followed by a year of supervised probation.

John tried to be optimistic and these days he turned it all over to God as much as he could. He also knew the real test for Kevin would come the first time he ran into his old crowd of users and pushers; how he resisted that. He could easily be back in prison; probation is not complete freedom.

He knew all about that himself.

"Do you wear your dog collar all the time then; I mean, during the day, obviously? Reverend Harry at the chaplaincy didn't, only during services, he told us. Is it to show you are a deacon? I don't know what the difference is, to be honest; deacon, vicar, priest. We had a rabbi and a Muslim guy working inside, too."

John sifted the jumbled thought-stream emerging from his passenger, wondering where it was leading.

He answered, "I wear my clerical collar a lot. But not to

show off or to be different. It's to remind me I am to be of service to God and to my community. And in some places, some places you know I might add, it may keep me from being done over by people desperate for money."

Kevin thought about it. "Some of those places wouldn't be respectful of religion, John; you may be fooling yourself. Best stay clear. But I don't think you would be one to be taken down easily, frankly."

Farrell may be getting on in years, he thought, but he was a big man and something about him signaled to Kevin he wasn't the sort to be physically intimidated or be pushed around. But the deacon just smiled.

"It's not respect for religion, it is recognition that I won't have anything worth the bother of doing me over for; clergymen aren't flush with money."

"I gathered," said Kevin. "Your coat is not exactly… the latest style."

Farrell laughed. "No it isn't."

Farrell thought, I wear the collar to remind me I am saved, with a life anew. If I told Kevin what my past life was really like, the look on his face would probably not be one of earnest puzzlement; it would be fear, or worse, envy. They told them about the realities of life in category A and B prisons in Stoke Heaton and the type of hard characters they could run into there. Antagonize people like that and your life becomes hell.

John's Farrell's life now was about the precarious road to some sort of heaven on earth, not heading back to hell.

6 VAN DONGEN

The second salvo against Sayer came the same first day into her new job, from DS Kit Madder, now the acting lead of the Antiques section. After lunch, Harper and Sayer were on their way to a meeting at the National Gallery, the first external meeting for Sayer in her new role. No doubt Madder had been hoping not only for confirmation of his 'acting' position with Antiques, but for promotion. That wasn't unreasonable in principle, but the DI position for Antiques had only become vacant with Barnes' departure.

Madder had two Antiques team members at a table as they passed, with several items on it, including an unframed painting.

He said, "Inspector Sayer, a moment, if you can spare it. Would you know anything about this, by any chance…?"

Harper watched his boss look at the painting Madder was holding. He glanced at it then looked at the two people with him, looking on expressionless. Sayer was sizing up the situation, he thought. He looked more closely, seeing if he should find some way to gently intervene. He hardly knew his new 'guvnor' but she was his boss and…

Catrin said, "It looks like a Van Dongen, don't you think? But your thumb is mostly over the signature. A lithograph, a

45

print run of 180 from the number on this side. It could be genuine. Look at the line work; very fine. In a lot of the Van Dongen forgeries the line work is often quite miserable when you get close up. You should get Bertie Wells to check it out, authenticate the signature, I suggest. Even as a lithograph, it will be worth thousands, if genuine."

She continued, "You think it's a fake, though, do you?"

Kit Madder baulked. "No, I am not saying that, ma'am, just asking…"

Her look was sharp enough to stop him mid-sentence. She looked Madder in the face, eye to eye, saying nothing more before turning on her heels and leaving the area.

As Harper and Sayer entered the lift to go down to the parking garage she said, "Did you or Howlett know I was going to be 'inaugurated', for want of a better word?"

"No, ma'am, I didn't. And Isabelle, well, no. If she had, she would have told Madder not to be so stupid, despite him being a sergeant. The only person she pays attention to in terms of rank is DCI Coltrane, really. No, she didn't know."

Then he realised what he had said.

"And you, of course, ma'am, you are her boss now," he added lamely.

Kit Madder was known to enjoy lunches in the Albert pub on Victoria Street, even if they had to stay off the beer, on duty. He and some of his team had been out at lunchtime, Mark knew, welcoming Nkrumah. They were probably mulling over the changes in A&A and had hatched up this stupid test for the new Art Team lead.

She stayed silent until they were in the underground car park, walking over to her assigned car, a new Audi A6, he saw. He then realised, given the assigned vehicle ordering process at the Met, Sayer's decision on the post and her new vehicle selection had indeed been made some time ago.

As Catrin started the engine she said, "That's a genuine Van Dongen that Madder was holding."

Harper stayed neutral in his response. He could tell she was annoyed.

"I hope that you don't make too much of it, ma'am."

Not complain to Coltrane that his colleagues had tried to test her, embarrass her.

She laughed, which surprised him.

"If Madder wanted to set me up, he should have at least checked me out a little more thoroughly."

"How do you mean?"

"Last year I did two ceramic platters with facial imagery elements that included those characteristic Van Dongen-style eyes. They were a theme for an exhibition at 'Liz's Place'; do you know it?"

He nodded. "The contemporary gallery near Harrods; that one?"

"Yes. She asked a number of the artists who sell through her if we would do something thematic, something along Van Dongen lines, for a charity fundraiser. Jean Hughes, the potter I work with, and I agreed. It was quite a success.

"So did you know I was a ceramic decorator?"

She glanced at him as he responded.

"No, ma'am. That you recently worked with AC Hunt and previously you were with the Art Crime Unit; I checked out those points after the announcement this morning. Isobel said you worked with DI Caldwell on the Stubbs investigation; DCI Coltrane brought you in then, she said. I transferred in after that."

She looked at him, serious again.

"If there are some noses out of joint at my appointment, DS Harper, they are going to have to get used to it. I know that people don't like restructuring; but that wasn't my doing. I started out in Lambeth and Brixton in drug squad work with some pretty hard people. I made it there; I will make it here."

"Yes, ma'am. Glad to hear it. I don't need to have my guvnors revolving through; it leaves all the work on my plate in the interim periods."

His voice had moved from sounding serious to being a little amused as he spoke.

As they drove off she said. "Should I expect more like that?"

Attempts to embarrass her, she meant, Mark thought.

"I can't say, ma'am, but... you have the plum job now; head of the Art Team. A number applied internally and from elsewhere, we know."

"Did you apply, Harper?"

"Yes, I did. But I have less than two years as a DS so... I didn't rate my chances to be high. Others did."

He paused.

"But the message that DI Barnes' transfer sent to me was that I need to look around and broaden my own experience, if I want promotion. Not that I want to leave the team now, but I am just flagging it."

She nodded.

"We'll talk about that in time; it is a good attitude to have. But, for now, I know DCI Coltrane wants the new team to stabilize."

They were driving out of New Scotland Yard, their eyes adjusting to the daylight. Harper thought he would add some more insight for his new boss and test her reaction.

He said, "The story is that all applicants went through the interviews with DCI Coltrane. No-one went for a second interview with Chief Superintendent Matheson. Then you arrive this morning; you walked straight in, so to speak.

"You did ask, Ma'am, the background, I mean."

He was looking at her, checking her, making sure he wasn't over-doing it and getting himself into trouble. They were now driving along Whitehall, heading for Trafalgar Square.

Sayer's face was neutral.

She said, "And what conclusion have people come to?"

He thought for a moment, trying to find the right words.

"Spit it out," she said.

"It was a fix, ma'am. Neville wanted you for the position. Or you were foisted on us by AC Hunt because it was time for her to have a new aide. You had the art investigation background with ACU so… she put you here. Either way it is seen to be a 'fix'. Sorry, but you did ask."

"I did, Mark, I did. I wondered if it might be something like that. But it will sort itself out."

Catrin was thinking back to her discussion with Hunt on the flight from Ottawa. Her boss had said A&A was a closed shop, she recalled. It had seemed a peripheral matter at the time. She needed to decide what to do about it, if anything.

7 SPOTS OF BOTHER

Mark Harper was pleased with how the meeting unfolded at the National Gallery.

He had been with Sayer in DCI Coltrane's office when their boss had said, "Sorry to drop you in this on your first day, Catrin, but if I attend, they will think we are taking a stronger interest. The underlying issue is, of course, important for the art world - but not for Art and Antiques. We have to make sure none of the others decide to lumber us with work we don't want."

Several galleries and government departments were concerned about recent developments in the art investment market and the antics of certain British 'super-rich' buyers. Works that were recently worth hundreds of thousands of pounds were now worth millions, with prices rocketing. That was commonplace these days in the art world globally. It was a visible revolution in the investment and art communities, with little relationship to past market values, artistic merit or art history. At times it could be mind-boggling, the speed with which works changed ownership, to be locked in specialized storage vaults; art banks, really. Not even their owners got to see them; they were regarded as financial assets, not art.

Now the grand project was reduced to 'update' meetings held at various locations; this time, the National Gallery. Suspicion of fraud or market manipulation could only be dealt with in terms of specifics, not generalities. The economic crime people at Scotland Yard and the City of London Police were already tracking the potential for transactional anomalies; to them, whether it was art or real estate didn't really matter. They saw no reason for yet another group. The whole thing was petering out.

In the meeting itself, Catrin said little, other than that she was still new in her role and would be discussing the file further with DCI Coltrane and her team, leaving Harper to address the updates. One of the late-comers from the gallery side into the meeting room, Sir John Vale, seemed a little testy on one point, and Mark was hesitating in framing his response. Sayer spoke up, stating clearly the current Art and Antiques position yet again, as given in her briefing notes.

Afterwards, Sir John approached the two officers.

"Congratulations, Inspector Sayer… it's a long time since I saw you last. Still a detective constable then, I think?"

His boss looked happier than at any other time today, Harper thought. She was obviously familiar with the famous artist. Vale was a sculptor; at previous meetings he had given both Caldwell and Harper a difficult time on some items with almost gimlet directness.

"Yes, Sir John, it's very nice to see you again."

"Still actively at it, I see, artistically; I pop in regularly to Liz's Place, to check things out and talk about newer artists with her, so I see your work from time to time. And you are out of your second spot of bother, I hope. Neville told me that time is passing… two years now, I think."

Catrin replied, "Oh, I am still enjoying ceramics. I am married now, Sir John. My husband is a civilian computer expert at the Met, but, yes, I still make time to work with Jean Hughes and love it as much as ever."

"Don't lose that," he said intensely. "Once you do, it is

hard to get back, believe me. You end up doing administrative stuff like this and mentoring others; but it is not the same. Just look at me."

He tried to look pathetic and she laughed.

"Like you, Sir John; with the reins to just about anything and everything in the world of sculpture in the UK in your hands? Fat chance of that!"

From the time she had started as a constable in London, Catrin had been decorating ceramics with a friend from Pontypridd, the co-owner of the Cwmbran Kiln in Spitalfields Arts Market, a boutique pottery. It was a second home to Catrin; or, more accurately, a second work place. There she decorated the pieces made by Jean, ones they designed together. The regular pottery produced by Jean and her partner Melanie sold in the shop; the 'one-off' works by Jean and Catrin sold through 'Liz's Place', off Fulham Road, not too far from Harrods.

She paused.

"And I hope the answer to your second question is 'yes', too."

The three of them talked a little more before departing.

In Sayer's car returning to the Yard, she asked Harper to drive; the Audi was an assigned vehicle but anyone in the Met could drive it. She returned two quick calls on her mobile then sat back, silent, thinking.

Mark said, "You know Sir John Vale well, it seems, ma'am. He always seemed a bit aloof, a very direct man; he pulled no punches with DI Caldwell in the past."

She laughed.

"Not really, and I have not seen him a lot. Three times, in total I think, to speak with; the first time here years ago, at one of DCI Coltrane's gallery 'coordination' meetings. We were drinking coffee standing next to each other, so I said 'hello' and within ten seconds he was interrogating me about ceramic underglazes, in detail, as if my life depended on it. Yes, he is a very direct man."

Harper paused.

"And ma'am, can I ask? His comment, 'Two years from your second spot of bother?' I can go and ferret around; what did you call it earlier, 'background research' that DS Madder should have done? But it is easier to ask. No-one has said anything about the scar to us."

She eyed him up, assessing him.

My first 'spot of bother', as Vale would put it, was a case in Scotland; an arrest which led to this scar. The second, well… A little over two years ago I shot and killed a gang member in Malaysia, part of a triad called 'Ten Dragons'. I was on a 'diplomatic relations' trip tied to someone else's case, ironically, playing tourist with a Foreign Office bureaucrat and an officer with the Royal Malaysian Police. He was shot and badly wounded by the nephew of an old enemy of his that we ran into by chance. I just used his weapon to defend us. There were subsequent death threats, both to me and the Malaysian officer."

She paused, obviously thinking about how much to say.

"It is why, in part, I took the position with AC Hunt when it was offered. It gave me authorised firearms status, for one thing, as well as a very close working proximity to a senior figure. Experts on triad gang activity thought that no-one would go after me if it placed a senior police officer at risk; there would be too big a backlash against the organization from police services around the world."

Harper said nothing. He had heard of the incident anecdotally, but the identity of the officer had never been released broadly, even within the Met. His new boss had covered a lot of ground, he realised. It reminded him that he needed to broaden his own experience, too.

Harper said, "And now you are back with us, downstairs."

Harper had not trained in the use of firearms; had never considered doing so, in fact. He knew, of course, that it required inspector level approval just to take a firearm out on the street in duty time. Holding 'Standing Authority' by police outside Northern Ireland was much rarer, the ability to carry a weapon routinely, a duty responsibility for the aides to senior officers.

He glanced across, assessing his boss's mood.

"Is there a real risk, ma'am?"

"It's not what I think, Harper, it's what Inspector Entwistle with Organized Crime says; he is the triad expert and the link with Malaysia and the Royal Malaysian Police. There is no more news about the threat or the person who issued it for two years, so who knows?"

They drove down Horse Guards Parade in silence, then Harper said, "It all makes the stuff we talked about earlier, the departmental reaction to your appointment, I mean, a little... petty. So let me personally welcome you properly to the Art and Antiques Unit, ma'am."

Catrin Sayer laughed; an easy, friendly one this time.

"Well, thank you, Mark."

She thought about what she had just told her new team member. It was true; they had no closure officially on the threat against her. But she remembered vividly walking down Glanrafon Hill in Bangor, in tears, with Jian Li, her friend from Hong Kong.

She still believed her and knew that Li, through Michael Yau, had information unavailable to the police. Yau was now retired, but he had been a senior member of a different triad group in Hong Kong called 'Four Square' and somehow Li had asked him to intervene. Nam Wu, the person who issued the death threats for Sayer and Farra, was the uncle of the man she had shot and killed. Wu, she believed, was now dead, but no confirmation of this had yet emerged. She was in a no-man's-land on the issue.

But she smiled to herself, not about that, but recalling another walk down the same hill with Li some years earlier, not long after they met. Li was a student at the university, at the tail end of the investigation into stolen Russian paintings and the disappearance of Li's brother. It was the first time she had heard the name Michael Yau.

They were in the pub across the road at the bottom of the hill, 'The Glan'. Over lunch that day, it had struck her how odd it was that Li's father, Daniel Yeung, a devout Methodist who ran a tailor's shop, met regularly with Enlai Lin, a shipping executive, and Michael Yau, a triad boss. Yau and Lin had interfered in the missing person investigation, Li told her in confidence, wanting to find Li's brother or, at least, clear his name of any involvement in smuggling stolen art.

The three men met each week at a Hong Kong bathhouse.

Catrin had said, "This meeting your dad goes to each week, the bathhouse thing; it's like, what? A swimming pool or a bath with rubber ducks?"

Li had burst out laughing.

"It's very sumptuous; a private room with a large communal bath. For some reason the waters are therapeutic, I understand. Perhaps they bring in a masseur at times. That sort of thing."

She watched Catrin's face, still working it out.

"And yes, they are naked; that's the way. They sit around in the bath or in towels or robes on benches talking and someone will bring in tea or refreshments. It's social as much as hydrotherapy for them."

Catrin smiled. "So, if I understand, Mr. Lin, Mr. Yau and your dad have been meeting for years, yet the only time they get together is in the bath?"

Li nodded. "Unless they go to Coulter and Yarrow for clothes, my dad's shop. I think Mr. Yau does. Mr. Lin doesn't. No, they have nothing else in common, really."

Catrin shook her head. She said, "You are right; it's very Chinese."

~~

As they arrived back at the Yard, Harper saw Sayer checking her texts and emails again.

She said, "Back in the office I have to see Neville, it's

something to do with one more assignment for us this week, apparently; something he didn't cover in the morning briefing."

She added, as an afterthought, it seemed, "And we can see what else my new colleagues want to try and trip me up over."

Harper thought, despite the earlier hard-nosed comments about the less-than-enthusiastic welcome, the stunt by Kit Madder had upset his boss more than she would admit. And he wondered what else was being put on their plate. Tomorrow, both teams of Art and Antiques, with a tactical unit, were raiding a warehouse full of stolen art, they believed, in Acton.

They had enough to do this week.

8 KOWLOON

"Jian Li, how are you?"

The quiet voice of Michael Yau came through her mobile phone, jolting Jian Li Yeung fully awake. She was in her apartment reading a document for a meeting tomorrow, but she had been nodding off. It had been a long day and stresses other than her workload as a maritime lawyer were tiring her out these days.

Li was twenty-six years old and currently preoccupied with two worrying issues; her weight gain and the planning for her forthcoming wedding to James Hoi; two elements of her life vectoring together on the wedding day and currently disturbing her sleep at nights.

She had always been big-boned, with a round, 'water' face. As a result, she had long been conscientious about both her diet and her exercise. Now, whether it was too much business travel and restaurant food, or just her body at her age, she felt every gram of her weight gain as her wedding approached. James's attempts to reassure her were to no avail; he was a man and obviously wouldn't understand.

Li worked in the legal department of a large Hong Kong-based shipping company, LinTan Shipping. Her workload these days was heavy, taking her regularly to a number of cities around Asia with important business links for her company.

Her benchmark on the weight issue, she knew, guiltily, was the wedding a year ago in Wales of her friend Catrin Sayer. It had been a pleasure for her to return to the country where she had studied - and a shock for James Hoi, still her boyfriend at the time. It was his first trip to the UK and immediately he was immersed in accents that had proved a daunting barrier for Li during the early weeks of her studies at Bangor University. But Catrin had looked beautiful as a bride, she thought, and hadn't gained a pound in weight from the time they first met.

"I am very well, Mr. Yau. It is nice to hear your voice. And how are you?"

He responded, "Very good. Did I disturb you? I know that you will have work in the morning, no doubt, but I have a favour to ask, if I may?"

Her sleepy voice must have registered with the man.

"Not at all. Well, I was just nodding off, to be honest, sitting here reading a document in preparation for tomorrow. It is good that you called. It woke me up. But how can I help you?"

"I wonder, would it possible to have a small chat this evening, in person?"

"Of course," she said, checking the time; it was 8.15 p.m. "How do you wish to meet, or where?"

Li's apartment was in the Kowloon-side of Hong Kong, not on the island, along Kimberley Road. Like many people in the city, she did not have a car, so her first thought was of the logistics of such a meeting, not its purpose. But that aspect was sinking in and the suddenness of a call for a meeting surprised her.

As a lawyer, she had had virtually no contact with this man. Her last meeting in person with him was at the time of the threat to her friend Catrin, over two years ago, and that had been only on one occasion; a lunch. Now he was calling her out of the blue, in the evening.

"My driver will collect you when you are ready; he should

be there in a few minutes. There is no great rush, so please take your time. He will wait for you outside your apartment and bring you to my location. It is a white Mercedes; he knows you by sight."

The line went dead.

Really? Li's first thought was how this driver knew her. Then she wondered what to wear.

The Mercedes was waiting as Li exited the building. She saw that the man who walked around to open the rear passenger door was the same person she had last seen in Valetta, Malta a little over two years ago. This driver had collected her in another limousine at the airport there as she exited the terminal, planning to take a bus to the city centre. Instead, she found herself in the back seat being chauffeured while having a videoconference call with a colleague of Yau, Emily Yang. Yang had given Li important information; that the death threat against her friend Catrin had been removed. It had been the basis of the subsequent face-to-face discussion between the two friends in Bangor a few days later.

"Good evening, Miss Yeung," was all that the chauffeur said as she entered, before he carefully closed the door.

The combination of the unexpected call and the sight of this driver now had her worried. She was sure he was a member of the Four Square Triad, as were Yau and Yang. Did this mean that the issue of a threat against Catrin was not behind them, after all?

Then it occurred to Li that Catrin's recent news about returning to art crime investigation could be a factor. It would move her away from the senior officer at the Met who, in a sense, afforded her protection. Yang had confirmed as much, when they last spoke.

As they drove away Li had a sense of foreboding.

The journey was about fifteen minutes in traffic - there was always traffic - but not that bad at this time, other than the crush on entering the traffic flow for the Western Harbour tunnel to the island. They emerged on the other side and headed south-west, into the complex of the University of Hong Kong. The car came to a stop at the Run Run Shaw Tower, one of the university's main buildings. For some reason, Li had assumed she would be taken to a restaurant or a lounge of some sort, perhaps in a hotel, downtown.

As they slowed and pulled over, the limo stopped behind an identical vehicle, other than it was black, not white. Both were in a 'drop off' waiting area; neither one, she realised, was being hassled by campus security - and probably wouldn't be. Triads had long tentacles into many Hong Kong institutions.

Michael Yau, a grey-haired, small man neatly attired in a suit, stepped out of the back seat of the vehicle in front on to the sidewalk. He opened the door for Li before her driver could leave his seat. She could see he was smiling. The dark suit was elegant, one made at Coulter & Yarrow she thought. Li was glad she had quickly changed back into the business suit she had worn to work that day.

"Good evening again, Li. I think you know where we are!"

"Mr. Yau, you know my alma mater is City University, not here. But I have friends who studied here, so yes, I know it quite well. It is good to see you again."

Her eyes were sending the message, 'but why am I here'.

"Please," he said, "Come inside with me. I would like you to meet someone."

As they entered the building, Li came to the conclusion that the person they were meeting was Emily Yang - but again she was wrong. As Yau looked around, Li saw a student, a girl, spot them and smile, say goodbye to the group of students she was with and walk over.

"Grandad!"

Michael Yau turned to Li and said, "This is my granddaughter, Miele. Miele, this is Jian Li Yeung, Mr. Yeung's daughter. I have mentioned her to you."

The women shook hands and Miele said, "It is a pleasure to meet you. Grandad says you will be married soon, so my congratulations and best wishes to you and your fiancé for your future happiness."

"Thank you," said Li, a little lost about what this was all about. Michael Yau was beaming at them both.

"Come, we will have tea," he said.

If Michael Yau had gone inside the building with some of his people rather than alone, one of them might have spotted the female student some distance behind the group of students that Miele had left. She raised her mobile phone, held it steady and took a picture of Miele with her grandfather and this new person. As it was, it passed unnoticed in the mêlée of student movements.

Given Yau's role as a member of a triad, albeit retired, one could think that he was being photographed. In fact, the organisation that the camerawoman worked for had more than enough photos of Yau in different locations. It was the businesswoman with him that was of interest. She hadn't seen her before and it was opportunistic. Her role at present was to keep an eye on Miele Yau and her contacts.

As they approached the two limousines, Yau said, "As you can see, Jian Li, we are a two-car family; just like Americans." She glanced at him realizing that he was making a joke; the first she had heard from him and, for some reason, she found it quite funny.

Michael Yau said, "You can both ride in the white one, get to know each other. I will ride with Alex in the other. We go to the Lock Cha."

Li had been there; the Lock Cha was a teahouse not too far away.

Once they were settled and moving, Miele said, "Grandad and his ways. I said I would like to meet you, you see, and I asked him for your telephone number and would he call you to introduce me. I was going to call you up and suggest a coffee somewhere. Less formal than all this. I am a student, not a business executive."

Li said, "Half an hour ago I was dressed much like you, not

like this. Nor do I ride in limousines usually. A call and a coffee would have been fine."

Miele said, "Your father, my *gung gung* and your boss are quite interesting men, meeting each week, don't you think?"

Her look was impish. She had used the less formal term for her maternal grandfather deliberately, Li thought.

Li just laughed again. "The Shep Kip Mai bathhouse lot!"

Miele responded, "Exactly. I know too."

As Catrin Sayer, half a world away, had separately recalled earlier that day, each week her father, her boss Enlai Lin and Michael Yau met at a bathhouse on Shep Kip Mei Street in Kowloon to talk, 'just as men, about families, about life, not business'. It had started many years ago, not long after her father joined Coulter and Yarrow. Now he ran the high-end tailor's business, but at that time he was just finding his feet there.

His first career choice had been a fireman. Before she was born he had been injured at a response to a fire in an apartment block in Kowloon while trying to save the lives of two boys; the sons of Lin and Yau. It was that event which led to her grandfather Shen Yeung meeting Enlai Lin. Enlai, despite his grief over the loss of his son, wanted to help Daniel now his injury would end his role as an active fireman. He had insisted on buying into Coulter and Yarrow for him, to work alongside his father.

Several years later Daniel had started going regularly to the Shep Kip Mei Street bathhouse, as he had discovered how much it helped with the pain in his leg, an unwelcome legacy of his injury. A friend, a fireman he knew with a shoulder injury, had encouraged him to try it. Unbeknown to him at the time, it was also the meeting place for Enlai and Michael Yau each week, a meeting that had arisen out of their common pain of losing sons in the same incident. They became aware of his visits and invited Daniel to join them in their weekly meeting.

While Daniel Yeung said little, it became clear to Li over time that it was simply that her father enjoyed the discussions with the men as much as the therapeutic benefits of the bathhouse. It was a social contact of three people from the most unlikely backgrounds; a shipping magnate, an organized crime figure and a devout Methodist tailor which went on week after week, year after year.

Later, after her brother's death in Wales, Li could tell from the odd comment by her father that the common loss of sons for the three men had cemented the relationship still further; her dad always talked of Han more, she noticed, after a visit to the bathhouse.

Miele explained the reason for her interest in meeting Li.

"I am going to study in London for a year, at the Royal College of Art, and I said it would be nice to have an introduction to your friends Catrin Sayer and Jean Hughes; I love their work, you see. I want to be a ceramic artist too. I also want to be as innovative. I could learn from them."

Li just looked astonished.

She said, "That's what all this is about; the limos, the call out of the blue by your grandfather?"

Miele shrugged and said, "I don't know. Grandad just called about an hour ago and said he thought it might be possible for me to talk to you in person tonight. He said you are a busy lawyer. I had asked him earlier for your number and he said he would let me know when he collected me. I didn't expect you to be here, to be honest."

Li stopped herself from making a comment on Mr. Yau's maneuvering and said instead, "You think my friends are innovative in ceramic design?"

Miele said, "They are very good. Not as innovative as I would like to be, I hope, but they have established some new ideas, some interesting elements. What is more important is that they work collaboratively on new works, as potter and decorator, and have done so for a while. I want to explore that with them."

They were arriving at the tea house, Li saw.

Miele said, "Let's talk inside, over tea, or whatever we are going to have."

Li realised that she and Catrin owed Michael Yau a lot, she knew, so this sudden arrangement was no imposition, really.

As Miele leaned forward to get out, Li saw the black rectangle on her belt as her jacket lifted slightly. It took a moment to realise that it was not a mobile phone case or something similar; it was a pump, with a thin tube curling from it under her shirt. Li had seen one before on a friend; an insulin pump, in a case similar to the one Miele wore.

Inside, they were shown to a reserved table hastily being prepared. Li thought that someone in the vehicle in front of them had called ahead. The tea house was always busy and a number of people were waiting for tables, but the three of them were taken straight in.

As the women continued their line of conversation Michael Yau was silent, enjoying his granddaughter, it appeared to Li. Miele was talking about wanting to work with someone else in a similar partnership as Catrin and Jean. Li asked a natural question.

"Wouldn't you rather set up as an artist on your own, if you have the means?"

It was the only point when Mr. Yau looked concerned momentarily and Miele suddenly seemed lost for an answer.

"It will be better to have a small team; two or three people working together," Michael Yau said, covering the gap.

Later, Yau surprised Li again when they left the teahouse. The two limos were there waiting. He said something to the driver of the black limo, who scurried round to the other vehicle to talk to the other chauffeur.

"Alex and Tak will take you home, Miele. I will drive Li home myself."

Miele said, "It was a pleasure to meet you, Li. And thank you for saying you will give me an introduction to your friends, for when I get to London."

She climbed into the back seat of the other limo as Li suddenly looked a little lost.

Yau said, "Please take the passenger seat; next to me. You can help me work out what to push and pull on these things."

As he took off into the traffic Li had a momentary panic that she was in the hands of an elderly man who never drove or, if he did, it was before cars and electronics were synonymous. Within seconds though, she realised she was in the hands of an experienced and very capable driver.

"My first job, as a young man, was a driver. I used to like to drive. Thank you for meeting Miele this evening at such short notice."

"It was my pleasure, Mr. Yau. And I will talk with my friends. I am sure they would be happy to meet her and discuss art."

She was thinking about why he had gone to such lengths when the answer came to her.

"I know that you accepted the invitation for Mrs. Yau and yourself to attend my wedding."

It was a statement, as her mind worked through the answer.

"So perhaps, if it is possible, Miele could attend also? We should extend the invitation to her. Catrin Sayer will be there, as one of my bridesmaids. It could give them a chance to meet, to talk, perhaps."

She was watching Yau closely as she spoke. It was in his eyes, not his expression; she was right, that was the reason for the urgency of the face-to-face meeting tonight.

What he said was, "That would be very kind of you, Jian Li; very kind. I know, to be frank, that your father was a little surprised that we were invited. He didn't say as much, but I know him and his manner of speech well now."

A Triad boss isn't normally invited to a Methodist wedding, he was saying; even after retirement from the business.

Li said firmly, "You were on my guest list, Mr. Yau; from the first draft."

That too, was genuine; after his efforts to help her family while she was in Bangor and later to assist Catrin, she wanted to repay his kindness.

He smiled.

"And your other friend, the art colleague that Miss Sayer works with? She will be there also?

"No," said Li, "Unfortunately, Jean and her partner can't come. They have a pottery shop in London to run and... well; it is expensive to travel here from England."

"I quite understand," said Mr. Yau.

They were getting close to Kimberly Road and the traffic was starting to thin a little.

Li said, simply because it came to mind, "Miele seems very nice. She is very beautiful, too. Does she take after her mother?"

He nodded. "Her mother was very like her at that age. Very beautiful. But she died early, in her late thirties. So we have all had a part in raising Miele, trying to fill the void, not that such a thing is truly possible."

He glanced at Li then added, "My daughter was diabetic, with other autoimmune problems that... took her early."

Li said, "I am sorry; I did not want to intrude."

He said nothing. Nor did Li. She was thinking back to the glimpse of the pump on the belt; the surrogate, no doubt, for regularly-timed insulin injections by hypodermic. It seems as if Yau's granddaughter suffered from a similar medical condition to her mother. She thought about the steps being taken by the Yau family to assist Miele go a third of the way around the globe to study as an artist. Despite medical advances, there were always risks.

It explained also to Li the wish to find a creative partner for Miele; someone to help carry the load. Li expected that Miele could have 'up' and 'down' phases in her health, during which it would be difficult to do all of the work that ceramic art entailed. She knew the physical demands of life in the Cwmbran Kiln and particularly on Jean, as the potter.

As Li walked back into her apartment, she saw the document she needed to finish reading for the meeting tomorrow still open on the coffee table where she had left it, flagging to her she had more work still to do. She prepared some fresh tea and sat down to finish it, suddenly struck by the unusual events of the evening. But tomorrow's meeting loomed.

Last year Enlai Lin had retired from both the executive role of CEO and from the board of directors; a well-publicized and prepared event. There needed to be no sudden surprises at that level of the company with the client base and markets. His son David Lin had moved on to the board. A new CEO, Stephen Cho Bai, internally promoted, was now establishing his own path forward, one which involved either joint venture or acquisition prospects for a major division of the company.

As a member of the legal department, Li received a small promotion, leading a new junior hired as part of the legal group growth. Her work focus had become one of legal support for the strategic discussions; travel to meet other organizations with business overlaps had replaced her earlier role. Her work now was well away from legal reporting obligations and compliance issues associated with the highly-regulated world of sea freight.

Strangely enough, her dad was more affected by Enlai Lin's retirement than she was herself. Enlai had immediately become involved in board level activity of several charitable and non-profit organisations but he had also leased a small luxury sailing yacht, complete with two crew members. He and his wife Yolande were spending periods aboard in retirement, in different locales in South-East Asia. Li and James, both sailors, albeit of smaller craft, would have loved to see the boat.

Her dad had commented that the weekly bathhouse meeting of the three men was often just the two of them, at present. Enlai and Yolande had been invited to the wedding and had accepted. With Michael Yau, his wife and granddaughter, the wedding might well be one of the next times all three men were together.

9 RICHARDS

Catrin was seated across from DCI Coltrane in his office. He had closed the door after she sat down; a sign that this was not for the rest of the A&A staff, she thought.

At the pre-meeting that morning he had said that, one-on-one, he preferred the use of first names with his direct reports. In all the time Catrin had worked in ACU, Coltrane had generally called her 'Sayer' and she referred to him as 'sir'. She was mentally adjusting to the change as she sat down.

Coltrane began, "Sorry about the lukewarm reception this morning, Catrin. But I had warned you."

She smiled at him. He had been very welcoming in their pre-meeting, saying how pleased he was that she had responded positively to the suggestion that she should apply for the position and that she had accepted it.

"It will work out, in time, I am sure." She consciously omitted 'sir'.

He asked, "All went well at the National, I take it?"

"Yes. Harper seems well on top of the situation. I let him handle it. We saw Sir John there; he is as sharp as ever."

Coltrane nodded, remembering that Vale was on that committee. His next comment made it clear he was moving on.

"Do you recall talking with an aide to Tom Wicklow at the

Home Office a few weeks ago?"

Catrin thought about it. She knew that Wicklow was a Director General, responsible for the staff working for the Minister of Policing and Justice. But she didn't recall any particular aide. Coltrane was obviously referring to something that occurred in her former role. AC Hunt had regular meetings at the Home Office with senior staff and she had come across Wicklow there.

"Not off-hand; nothing that I can think of, Neville."

There! She had crossed the hump, used his first name.

"She talked to you at a break in a meeting. You mentioned your role with the ACU but never got to finish the discussion with her, she said."

Catrin remembered then. "That was the day of the BBC fiasco. Now I recall the person, but not her name."

Coltrane smiled. "Well, the Director General talked to her; she mentioned you, I understand; where that led, I don't know exactly. They need help with an issue with a painting and they asked for you specifically. The Minister of State for Policing, Wicklow's boss, is Welsh, you may recall; Noel Richards MP."

Catrin nodded.

Coltrane continued, "It is bad timing, of course, but it's a political issue between the Met and the Home Office. In fact it couldn't have come at a worst time, with the Acton arrests tomorrow and you just taking over the Arts team. But we have no choice, I am afraid; it dropped on me and obviously now, on to you. We don't particularly want to upset the Minister…"

Catrin smiled. "Ah, the old boy's network."

Coltrane grimaced. "It is a bit of that, yes; or the 'old girl's network', to be honest. Your old boss was involved, not that I would call Sandra Hunt an 'old girl'. But the routing of the request came to her over the weekend, I gather. I half-thought she would have talked to you directly."

Catrin shook her head firmly. "No, not her; she wouldn't do that now. Once I was out of her team she wouldn't undermine the internal organisational structure. She is a stickler for adhering to that. And last Thursday was my final day on her team; I had the Friday off."

He passed over his notes with the contact information.

"You will find out more about it directly from Wicklow. But I think, from what was said to me earlier, you will be on a wild goose chase into Wales - and will have to chase the goose all the way there and back to show due diligence, I am afraid."

Catrin said, "I will call now and arrange a meeting with them following the Acton operation tomorrow."

She laughed. Coltrane said nothing, but his face showed he was asking why.

"My first travel assignment in the international world of Art and Antiques; back to Wales, of all places."

Coltrane saw the humour of it and said, "Welcome aboard. It will only get busier; sorry."

His phone buzzed and he said, "That's it."

Then, as an afterthought, added, "The BBC fiasco? That was the helicopter thing, I take it?"

But she didn't reply; he was already answering the call. She headed out thinking back to the day in question.

~~

She had been in a conference room with Hunt in the Home Office headquarters at Marsham Street. It was during a break in a meeting when she met the aide that Neville Coltrane had mentioned, during a typically busy day for Hunt and her team. Catrin wasn't that bothered by the long days; she still enjoyed the role. While both she and Chris worked for the Met, he generally had more predictable hours, but his own schedule found him working until late evening occasionally or sometimes pulling all-nighters.

The woman in the pale blue suit had stood out in the mix of bureaucrats in shades of grey and officers in service uniforms. During the break she introduced herself to Catrin, two women not directly 'at the table' of meeting participants. They were both standing in the periphery as the principal players helped themselves to refreshments and circulated, either for business or social reasons. She worked at Marsham Street, she had said, in Mr. Wicklow's team; an external communications role of some sort. She nodded in the direction of her boss. He had been at the table all afternoon, as had Assistant Commissioner Hunt.

Catrin, with other aides and juniors, had occupied second and third row seats during the discussions so far, a now familiar role for her. Chief Superintendent Harrison, the expert on the subject of the meeting, standardization reforms across major metropolitan police areas, was at Hunt's side during the discussions and now stood with her at the break. Conscious of her dual role, Catrin had moved to a position where she could observe the room and its exits and entrances more, cognizant of the movement of people during the break.

In answer to a question of what she did before becoming AC Hunt's aide, Catrin said, "I was a detective sergeant, in the Met's Art Crime Unit."

The woman nodded. It seemed she knew the Met structure.

"And you are from Wales, from your accent, so I take it that you speak Welsh too?"

"Yes," said Catrin, idly adding, "Not much call for it, though, now; unless I speak to my parents or friends back home."

Her eyes were on her boss at the time; she was looking around. Catrin wondered if she needed her, but then Hunt smiled at another person she obviously wanted to speak to.

"Yes, art crime investigation was my last assignment," she said, eyes moving between the woman and her boss.

The woman asked, "Any excitement? Close shaves with criminals in that job, I mean. It must be a bit different from regular police work?"

Her eyes were on the scar on Catrin's cheek, inviting her to explain her injury, perhaps, assuming correctly that it was work-related.

Catrin looked at her, assessing the question.

"Not as different as you would think; a theft is a theft. And none that I could talk about, to be honest. If you will excuse me, I see my boss looking around... it may be for me."

Sandra Hunt was indeed looking around, but her eyes then fastened on another committee member, as Catrin moved over. Hunt moved from one small group to another. Catrin, seeing this, moved away, closer to another security officer that she now knew, keeping in her peripheral vision the woman who had sought her out. Security professionals on duty tend to talk only when there is a need; they have no need for polite conversation.

Catrin said nothing more, just watched her boss and the Permanent Secretary of the Home Office; something intense, serious, obviously a side issue to the main meeting.

Hunt had, on average, Catrin now knew, between six and ten external events each week, besides internal meetings at Scotland Yard. Her team did extensive preparation and pre-briefing for each one and Catrin, during the times she wasn't required to accompany her boss, looked after the security links.

It had been the initial big transition for her; to move from an investigative environment, where she had generally a busy workload of cases that had to be balanced and sometime re-prioritized, to a life which was highly planned. Their schedules covered weeks and sometimes months in advance. By the day in question, her boss's daily schedule was generally planned to the quarter hour. With a workforce of 13,000 police officers and another 7000 community officers or civilian support staff, the top leadership of the Met was a Commissioner, a Deputy Commissioner and then four Assistant Commissioners. This latter group, including Hunt, had executive leadership responsibilities in a diverse range of police activities.

Sayer's job was not to organize security for the meetings; simply to know what was in place, to be aware of the security implications for each event and to fit into the arrangements. Her sole role, in that sense, was to protect Hunt. Which she was doing right now, watching the people they were with and the entry points to the room.

As the break came to a close, her mobile had beeped at the same time as Hunt's, by the sound of it. She pulled it out and saw the code from Anne De Villiers, Hunt's personal assistant, and walked over to her boss as the AC glanced at her own message on her mobile.

As Catrin reached her, Hunt said, "I am sorry, Mr. Leiss, but I am wanted elsewhere rather urgently."

She looked around, saw Sayer and nodded, then caught the eye of the chair of the committee.

"Chief Superintendent Harrison will speak to our remaining item after the break. Gerry?"

Gerald Harrison had noted the alert and was apparently unperturbed about taking over the Met lead in the meeting. Catrin caught Hunt's eye and walked ahead towards the door, keying an acknowledgement back to Anne, after which she called George, who was with the car.

"George, same door ASAP. OK?"

"On my way, Catrin, I got a call from the office, too."

As they set off along the corridor, Catrin could hear Hunt on her mobile already in conversation with the commissioner. From her responses, it appeared to be key messages she had to deliver.

As Hunt closed the call, she said, "The BBC; the Commissioner is stranded at the Brighton conference; a helicopter malfunction."

She gave her the details of the sudden re-assignment.

Catrin said into her mobile, "The BBC, George, and get some clearance ahead; the AC is now taping a Panorama interview within ninety minutes, for tonight's release."

By 'clearance' she meant a brightly lit-up police vehicle clearing a path through the traffic on Whitehall and Regent Street.

She led her boss out of the building, eyes on the surroundings. Once in the car and moving, she called Anne. "Can you get a uniform to collect the AC's and my topcoats from the Home Office secure cloakroom and have a car bring them to the BBC, please? They locked the cloakroom up once the meeting started and we didn't have time to wait. We will freeze to death going home later otherwise."

When she finished, she texted Chris Treneer. "Change of plans; will let you know when."

He would understand; it was a message that both of them sent these days. He came back by text just as Hunt closed her call, but Catrin had no time to look at it. Hunt had just said, "George, there will be security looking for us at the BBC; they know our car registration; apparently there is a protest going on outside, about something."

Catrin nodded, letting her know she had caught the meaning also. They were in uniform, would be driving slowly past a crowd with potentially hostile participants, so vigilance would be needed.

When she looked at Chris' text, after Hunt had been led over to the green room prior to the interview, she saw his message. 'No worries. Should I go ahead with the call with James and Li?'

Damn, she remembered; they were talking with their friends about the wedding plans this evening. She might still be home; it should be late enough. If not … She texted, 'Go ahead anyway. I trust you, LOL."

She positioned herself away to the side with other aides of people on the panel, but with a clear sight of her boss inside the studio. Sandra Hunt was talking about the Metropolitan Police role in allegations of failure to respond to 999 calls as if she had been preparing for this session all day. She hoped that afterwards, Hunt would call it a day and head home rather than go back to the Yard. Then she and George could do likewise.

A studio assistant approached her and passed over a small note. It said, 'your coats have arrived'.

Later, at home, she was just in time for the agreed call with Li. In the rush of events, it was easy to see why a quick chat with an aide to Tom Wicklow was forgotten.

~~

Catrin called Wicklow's office to set up an appointment for late Tuesday morning. She then started catching up on her growing in-tray.

Around seven that evening she walked into their flat in Spitalfields and put her purse down on the side table in the narrow hallway. Her husband appeared from the kitchen.

"Supper is prepared. How did it go today? Your text earlier wasn't exactly full of joy."

Catrin wrinkled her nose.

"It was mixed, really. My team seems OK, but as to the rest... they see it as a fix. Half of them think I am Coltrane's piece on the side, it appears. The rest think I was pushed out by Hunt to make room for someone else. I can't say they were very welcoming, to be honest."

She tried to sound upbeat about it, but he came over and hugged her.

"It was a fix. Neville Coltrane wanted new blood in the unit and you were the best available; he knew that."

She said, "I know he wanted me for the role but... one of them tried it on; tried to fool me with a painting. On my first day, would you believe?"

Her husband smiled. "Tea, with a slice of lemon; I already have one of my beers opened to nurture the chef. But the solution is obvious."

Catrin didn't drink alcohol. Her mother was a recovered alcoholic and Catrin felt, rightly or wrongly, that she took after her; she didn't want to risk it.

She looked at him.

"Go back to the armoury and grab a gun. Shoot the one who did it in the kneecap; the rest will toe the line. I saw it in a western once. Do you want to eat right away?"

She smiled. "Yes, that would be good, I am famished. The best part of the day, to be honest, was the surprise I had seeing Sir John Vale at the National Gallery."

10 NEWTOWN

The Dyfed-Powys police station in Newtown is located on the west side of the town centre, just south of the River Severn. It has responsibilities for policing the town, a cluster of outlying villages and the surrounding rural area. In the normal mix of issues that are dealt with there, from traffic diversions due to road works, local crimes of various sorts and, at present, a rash of school vandalism concerns, the email Inspector Meredith was reading from her boss stood out as unusual.

She said, "Fowles, it looks as if we need to flag a status change for a home in Tregynon."

PC Seren Fowles was currently station-based; she had been on a training course in headquarters recently to implement an information system upgrade. The consultants involved had later whirled into Newtown, uttered mumbo-jumbo, Meredith thought, and whirled out again. As a result, Seren was currently the 'go to' person in the station when others found problems with the system.

Meredith continued, "The home will need to come off the AR list - it belonged to Judge Richards, who died recently."

She looked at her junior officer critically, expecting a response to her statement.

'At Risk' list; persons flagged in a database, which itself was linked to the 999 Emergency Response system. The list included senior police officers, judges, lawyers, probation officers, doctors involved in pregnancy termination and the like.

Seren Fowles said, "Yes, ma'am, I knew she had died; she was a member of the congregation at St. Cynon's. But I didn't think about the AR list."

Her boss smiled. "It's not your job to do that; it comes through the system when the change is notified."

Just then Detective Sergeant Pawl Pryce passed in the hallway.

Meredith called out, "Pawl, one for you, too. A flag on a judge's home is off - Judge Richards - she died. But there is an issue of some sort connected with it. The Chief Superintendent has asked us - kindly, I might add; note that - to co-operate over something to do with a painting found at the house. Not sure what it is about, but there will be an art expert coming up from London, I gather."

Pryce had been a local detective for nine years and had a formidable memory.

"Nothing rings a bell about a painting associated with Judge Richards in my time, Carole. Is it to do with a theft - or what?"

The inspector shrugged her shoulders.

"I have no idea. We have been asked to support, as appropriate. Whoever they send up will call in here first; I expect they will know. I will let you know when I do."

Fowles said, "Miss Richards has, I mean had, connections; the family. Is it to do with that?"

Meredith looked at Pryce then back at PC Fowles.

"You are not suggesting, Seren, that his Highness in Carmarthen is bowing to political pressure of some sort, making the request, are you?"

The young officer smiled then said, "Actually, I think I am, ma'am."

Pawl Pryce chuckled, shrugging his shoulders as he moved on, his voice carrying behind him in the corridor, "I don't see why they have to send an art expert all the way up from

London. We must have some of those just down the road in Aberystwyth at the university. They could be here in an hour."

He looked up the corridor, seeing the familiar figure of John Farrell, the deacon at St. Deiniol's, standing just inside the entrance. Presumably he had been allowed in by the desk officer. Farrell was in and out these days, working with people getting themselves into trouble, one way or another.

Pryce knew his record; he had looked it up shortly after the man had appeared in Newtown a few years ago. But quickly he became convinced that he was a reformed character. It was all in his demeanour and actions, not in his talk; in fact, he never talked about his past with Pryce or his colleagues other than, Pryce knew, his first meeting with Inspector Meredith, behind closed doors. She had come out of that and told Pryce and others that, despite Farrell's record, they needed to give the man a chance.

"Hello, John; what brings you here?"

"Noah Weaver, Paul; Ivor Weaver's son. He was brought in last night. They are bringing him up from the cells. I have his brother in my car and we are taking him home. I will talk to him - again."

Farrell's accent was from further north. He was born near Ruthin, Pryce recalled, but had spent his misbegotten years in England, mainly Liverpool and Manchester.

"At least he was only D&D this time, I see," Pryce said.

Farrell nodded but didn't say anything about the 'only' bit; he knew people who had killed while being 'drunk and disorderly'.

"I collected Kevin Stott from Stoke Heaton last week. He seems to have taken the message at last, thank God. I hope so, anyway."

Pawl smiled.

"And no small thanks to you, I bet?"

Farrell shook his head then smiled back.

"No; well perhaps a little. I didn't deal with him during his time in prison; it was others in the network. I just drove him back home and sorted out some of his contacts."

They were interrupted by the appearance of a uniformed officer with a dejected young man; Noah Weaver.

Pawl said to him forcefully, "Noah, you listen to this man; it could save you a lot of heartache; hear me?"

He nodded at Farrell and turned away, heading back to his desk. It crossed his mind that John Farrell would have overheard the conversation with Meredith and Fowles. The fact it related to the deacon's small village disconcerted him for a moment; confidentiality was important. Then he thought, even if he did hear, Farrell is a priest - almost; whatever a deacon means. It didn't really matter.

But as John Farrell drove away from the station with his passengers, he was clearly distracted by something other than Noah Weaver and the young man's apologies for his drinking escapade; he almost missed stopping at a red light.

11 RAID

If Andy Lehman hadn't retired early, the Metropolitan Police may not have discovered the Acton warehouse operation. Andy always claimed an unfulfilled passion for astronomy but shift work plays havoc with hobbies. In retirement he had started a course at the Open University in Astronomy and Planetary Science. It fulfilled a dream to take his interest in the stars to a new level and, with more enthusiasm than practicality given the urban night sky of London, he had arranged for contractors to put a skylight window in the attic room of his home. Then he invested in a quality mirror telescope.

His wife Vera would have preferred that part of his retirement 'lump sum' to have been spent on a winter holiday in warmer parts of Europe, but their marriage had survived thirty-eight years and could survive him turning a minor interest into a new craze.

"It's better than a passion for pole dancers in nightclubs at two in the morning, mum," their daughter Tammy said. "He may get an asteroid named after him rather than some bimbo's kid."

There was a hard undertone in Tammy's voice. Her mother had begun to worry a little about her daughter's marriage and the increasing tensions she was seeing between Tammy and her hard-working son-in-law. He was always 'away on business' it seemed, generally to some place near Frankfurt.

All Vera could think to say in response was, "Pole-dancing is respectable these days, Tammy; there are clubs and competitions, you know."

Afterwards she wondered why she commented; was she subconsciously trying to give her son-in-law the benefit of the doubt?

The Nahigian brothers had set up an approach-based security floodlight system in the area surrounding their warehouse, to identify any people turning up at night. In the trade of knocking off and smuggling antiques and art, they were aware that others could treat them similarly.

What they hadn't taken into account was that the reflected light from the security system would upset an amateur astronomer in his new 'observatory' a hundred yards away.

"Who delivers statues to an electrical supplies warehouse in the middle of the night?" Andy grumbled to Vera, showing her an image on his camera taken from the attic window; the heinous illuminations interfering with his sky watching showed up the statue quite nicely.

It was Vera Lehman who put the link together. She spotted a news article about a theft of a statue of Diana the Huntress, carved in white marble, taken from a stately home in South Yorkshire some months earlier. It looked to both of them to be identical to the photo her husband had taken.

"Perhaps it's a coincidence," said Andy. "These things must all look alike."

The Lehman couple thought about it a while, because it seemed unreal. Vera, thinking of possible insurance rewards and winter holidays, decided to inform the police. Caveats about 'just in case', 'not saying it is the same statue, of course' and 'we don't want trouble with neighbours, despite their nighttime floodlights', permeated the statement she made.

After a visit from a local police officer who was noncommittal, they had a follow-up from a plain-clothes officer in a nice suit. Detective Sergeant Madder was from Scotland Yard, a well-educated person who seemed to know a lot about art and statues, as well as astronomy and even, to Vera's joy, he knew about timeshares in Portugal. He was well-read, an Oxford University sort, they could tell; a good conversationalist and such a nice young man. They were happy to help him out in any way they could.

He came back later the same day with a technician who was far less communicative. He set up in Andy's 'observatory' an interesting-looking camera connected to a couple of black boxes plugged into the power supply and trained it on the warehouse.

"How often do you need access?" asked Andy, thinking the electronics expert could possibly be a closet astronomer and may need to change batteries or something at two in the morning.

The technician said, "Just to remove it at the end. Even if you have a power cut, I can re-set it remotely. If you could keep the inside window clean and dust free - not do anything unusual, but whatever your regular schedule calls for - that would help. And, at night, the room is dark, correct?"

"As dark as I can get it," said Andy.

~~

Art and Antiques, along with the FBI Art Crime Unit, had suspected for some time there was an important holding location for stolen art near London. They believed it was being used for items stolen domestically in the UK and others in transit from Europe. A number of separate investigations vectored on the city in recent months.

The French art crime group had put under surveillance a similar location near Paris a month earlier, one that now had connections back into Eastern Europe. But it was a waiting game largely; collecting evidence through photography, internet tracking and phone taps while coordinating internationally among art crime specialists in various police services.

They knew that transporting stolen goods into the UK was easier than getting them to the USA or Asia, the primary markets for high-end stolen art these days. How they were moved from the UK to those locations was still a mystery.

For the best part of two months they collected information through observation of the Acton warehouse. Their goal was the maximum return of stolen works while building an evidence base for prosecution of the people involved; the thieves, the smugglers and the customers.

With the Acton discovery, this gave the investigation teams involved a good basis for securing operational funding for a much larger, multinational surveillance and evidence-gathering operation. A formal Task Force chaired by the FBI and in which Art and Antiques now participated was established.

Surveillance would have gone on longer, if they had their way. But concerns about a breach of security with a component of a surveillance operation in Munich led Coltrane, with his international counterparts, to call it a day. They decided to seize what they could in the UK and elsewhere and begin the long process of building and solidifying the prosecution cases. Particularly now, they wanted to 'turn' people; persuade criminals caught in the web to make deals, betray other gang members and provide the locations of works stolen earlier. In doing so, it would escalate the economic value of the art recovered through the operation. It was a critical indicator of success.

~~

The warehouse was located in a side street off a main road, The Vale, in Acton Park, not too far from the Wormwood Scrubs prison. The location had a mix of light industry and storage warehouses, a minicab business, some older homes such as the Lehmann's house and even older warehouse buildings now turned into expensive apartments and lofts. The area was moving more and more towards upscale residential use; it was only minutes into central London on the Underground from the nearby Tube stations.

As per procedure, the Art and Antiques Unit worked through DS Madder, as the warehouse surveillance operation had been led by the Antiques team. Coltrane, in overall charge, wanted the acting 'lead' of the team to continue to take the responsibility. Sayer's team was there primarily for any paintings or other fine art found in the haul.

On the Tuesday morning, Coltrane, Sayer and Madder, with the SOCO lead, were liaising with the specialist SCO19 tactical unit commander, grouped together in a huddle at the pre-operation rendezvous, a car park nearby. DC Nkrumah was hovering by them, holding his mobile like it was the Holy Grail; he was assigned to coordinate the raid with a member of the French team. The French police would be hitting the Paris location at the same time.

SCO19 were the armed tactical unit, brought in to secure the building and any suspects inside. The organization that the Nahigian brothers were now thought to be part of had a reputation for violence. Two years ago a police officer in Slovenia had been badly hurt while arresting one of the known gang members. They were taking no chances this time, in England or in France.

Harper was standing with others some yards away from the leaders. He saw that, from the looks they exchanged, the SCO19 team commander knew Sayer. That wasn't too surprising he thought, given she was a firearms officer until recently. It was after the briefing, just before implementation, that she walked a few paces away and said something quietly to the tactical unit commander and he, in turn, spoke to one of his team members.

It registered with Harper. He saw that the commander had now directed three men to the entry through the back of the building, a fire escape access to the top floor.

The operation went smoothly, in fact. When Harper and the Art and Antiques personnel entered, having been informed that the place was secure, they were confronted by three impassive, handcuffed men and an angry, handcuffed woman. She was cursing the tactical officer preventing her from going to the bathroom, it appeared.

Behind them were rows of shelves with an array of electrical components but, through a door into an inner area, they could see crates and boxes, plus two worktables with items that had nothing to do with electrical work at all. Once they looked inside there, they saw a lot more that pleased the eye.

The crates, statues, museum cases for storing paintings and two large safes would need careful review by Art and Antiques and the forensic team standing by.

As the tactical unit formally closed out their role and withdrew prior to their departure, one of the younger officers assigned to the rear fire escape spoke to Sayer. She was standing beside Harper at the time.

"You were right, ma'am, it was a rabbit warren up at the back. Only one of them was there, the shadow you saw, but he wasn't armed."

He nodded at her, smiled and left with his teammates.

Harper recalled DI Sayer standing by their vehicle down the street, looking intently at the warehouse from a distance. Whatever she had said about the disposition of the tactical team had not been rebuffed. That a person with A&A said anything at all on the subject was unusual. She had spent a lot of time assessing the security of buildings in her last role, he realised.

~~

By 10.00 a.m. they were in Acton Police Station, processing the people arrested, waiting for the various solicitors to arrive. DCI Coltrane would be leading the preliminary interviews there with DS Madder; afterwards they would move future interviews to New Scotland Yard.

The SOCOs and the assigned A&A team members were still working away at the warehouse contents; that would take a while but they knew already from the walk around that they had quite a haul.

Sayer made a call on her mobile to confirm something then she brought her team together briefly.

"There appear to be quite a few items that involve us, as we expected, which is good," was her opening comment.

Howlett said, "I should probably head back to the warehouse and work with the SOCOs on…"

Sayer held her hand up, stopping her.

"No. Harper, you will stay here; you do the preliminary interviews on our items with DS Madder and/or DCI Coltrane, as they work through this phase. Neville will bring you in as they talk about any paintings found."

Harper said, "Not you, ma'am?"

Clearly, such interviews had been led by Caldwell in the past.

"No, I won't be here. So you handle it, as you see fit. Pull in someone if you need more documentation support work here, but it is Antique's lead anyway and DS Madder will handle the documentation team. We will work from that once they have an inventory."

Howlett said, trying to be helpful, to steer her new boss along the normal routes of past operations, "I normally help out with that when we have shared responsibilities with Antiques."

Catrin said, "No Howlett, you will be with me; we are heading over to the Home Office in Marsham Street now. And probably, I think, we will be out together tomorrow, in Wales."

Her subordinate said, surprised, "Wales? Go away now, with all this going on?"

Howlett sounded as if her boss was talking about a trip to Antarctica.

Unperturbed, Catrin responded, "Yes. But let's wait on the meeting there and see."

Harper said, "And if I need you, ma'am?"

Catrin said, "Call me on my mobile, but only if you need clarification or there is a major issue you need help on. Otherwise, a brief voicemail update or an email this evening will do; short and sweet. This will be a marathon run; we will all be on it for quite a while."

Howlett and Harper looked at each other. Things were different.

Catrin smiled inwardly. She had picked up a lot in her time working with Assistant Commissioner Hunt. Give people responsibilities, coach them to do the job and leave them to it. The Acton warehouse case was important work for the long haul; she and Howlett had more immediate and politically sensitive matters to address today.

12 MARSHAM STREET

The modern glass building of the Home Office head-quarters was a place Catrin had visited from time to time with Hunt, so she was generally familiar with the building and its procedures. As they entered at ground level and showed their ID to the security staff, they were directed to a higher floor. An assistant to Wicklow met them outside the lift and escorted them to a corner office.

Tom Wicklow greeted them and invited them to join him at a table away from his desk. As he shook hands, pointing at the chairs, he said, "Inspector Sayer, thank you for agreeing to come."

Catrin nodded. She didn't exactly have a choice, she thought.

"This is DC Howlett from my team, sir."

Howlett was quiet. Finding out they were visiting a senior Whitehall bureaucrat had made her realise that they were not simply avoiding the main work on the big ticket item for Art and Antiques this week.

She just nodded and said, 'sir'.

He looked at his watch.

"I will brief you a little then we have a meeting with Minister Richards, as soon as he is available."

He paused then looked at Sayer.

"I asked for you specifically, by the way, not knowing you were back in art crime work. The fact that you are in your new role makes it easier, if anything. You have art crime investigation experience, speak Welsh and, with your recent experience with Assistant Commissioner Hunt, you are aware that certain matters require extreme confidentiality. This is one of those situations, I feel."

He was looking at DC Howlett as he spoke, for emphasis on the confidentiality aspect, hitting her between the eyes with it.

Howlett thought, he's not subtle, this bureaucrat. Doesn't he know that's what we do? We keep facts confidential until we need to use them. We aren't politicians.

He continued, "This concerns a painting now in the possession of the Richards family, the estate of the late Judith Richards, I should say, the Minister's older sister. She was a judge in the magistrate court system. We want you to find out more about it and... do what is necessary; legally correct, whatever that may be, but as quietly as possible. There is mystery surrounding how it came into her possession."

Catrin interrupted. "Is it a stolen item, then, sir? Are we talking about an existing criminal case?"

He shook his head. "Not that we know of; that's for you to find out. The painting has actually turned up out of the blue, so to speak; that's the problem. It was found in the back of a cupboard or a wardrobe, concealed."

It was clear that he was about to launch into the background when his phone buzzed. He frowned and looked at the display then picked it up and listened.

"Of course, Minister," he said, replacing the receiver.

He looked at Catrin. "Mr. Richard's schedule has changed; we are to see him now. It will be ten minutes maximum and I will fill you in on whatever else is needed afterwards."

He stood, making it clear that they were all going elsewhere. In fact, it was simply a move across the corridor, into a suite on the other side of the building and an inner office there. The minister was seated behind a desk, but he got up and moved to his own meeting table as they entered and Wicklow pointedly closed the door as the two officers shook hands with Richards before taking seats at the table.

For a government minister, he was informal in behaviour and dress, at least today; in shirt-sleeves, with his tie loosened a little. Catrin noticed that a sports jacket was on a hanger on a free-standing coat-rack and alongside it, a hanger with a button-through green cardigan with a red motif in Welsh. Catrin had glanced at it as she passed; a golf club in mid-Wales. His complexion seemed to indicate he was an outdoorsman despite spending, no doubt, most of his life in offices and committee rooms.

As Wicklow did the preparatory introductions, the minister interjected, "Yes, Inspector Sayer; I have seen you with Assistant Commissioner Hunt when you were in uniform, of course. Congratulations on your promotion."

Catrin realised that someone, probably Wicklow, had briefed him; she was hardly someone who would be on a minister's radar, even at meetings with Hunt, she thought.

He paused.

"I don't have long, but let me summarise the matter. Our family home, that is my parent's home, and formerly my grandparent's home, is in the village of Tregynon in Wales."

He smiled, then spoke in Welsh directly to Catrin, "It is in the heart of Wales and yes, I am Welsh, but I scarcely visit there anymore, to be truthful; it's not my constituency. My life is here, as is my work. Look, we have baffled your constable and Tom Wicklow already."

Catrin instinctively looked at Howlett, seeing her DC sitting wooden-faced, not reacting. Richards continued in English.

"I had an older sister, Judith, older by eight years; I was something of a surprise to my parents when I came along. She died two weeks ago; a stroke, after a long illness. She was only fifty-nine."

"My condolences, sir," said Catrin.

Richards nodded his acceptance but continued speaking.

Clearly he had a set pitch he wanted to make and time was of the essence.

"Last week a painting was found in her home by my wife Maeve and our daughter Simone with Dilys Peters, the housekeeper. They were just starting the clearing out, dealing with Judith's things. It was in the back of a wardrobe in Judith's bedroom, with a letter taped to it. It wasn't mentioned in the main will, or in a separate list of minor bequests that she left us to deal with also. In fact, she had never mentioned this at all."

He opened a folder and pulled out a letter and envelope then passed it to Catrin, clearly waiting until she read it. She did so then passed it to Howlett.

Dear Noel and Maeve,

As you are my executors and principal beneficiaries, I am sure that one of you will find this painting. It came into my possession several years ago from a source I do not wish to compromise. He says he was not involved with it directly, other than to deliver it to me. I believe him and, you know me, I am a person who can read people.

Tied to it is a story that I also want to keep with me to my grave, one in which I failed in my duty, I think, in hindsight. While I have not looked at it daily - it is quite a frightful thing, really - the message it gave me was that I should seek the good in people and give, wherever possible, the benefit of the doubt. So I kept it. All I will say is that it belonged to a young man called Edwin Ashe, I understand, who once came before me in court. It needs a home; but not yours, I expect.

So I leave it to you to do with it whatever is right and, if you can do so, protect my good name if at all possible. The painting may be worth something, I suspect. I may not deserve protection completely, but I have done my best, as a member of the judiciary and as a human being. That is all one can do.

Your loving sister,
Judith.

Neither the letter nor the envelope gave a date, Catrin noticed, but the paper wasn't fresh. It had been there some time.

When Howlett looked up from reading the note she saw the minister hand over a photograph to her boss.

"My wife sent this, taken with her phone. We printed it here."

The two police officers shuffled a little in their seats to allow them look at the photograph of the painting together. It was a modern art work, a 'head and shoulders' portrait of a teenage boy; his head slightly turned, his expression downcast, the eyes large, looking lost.

To Catrin, beneath the almost brutal brush work there was an inherent beauty to the model and she could see how Judith Richards could find more in it than the crudity of the brush strokes. She was analyzing how the artist managed to convey that as Howlett said, "It looks like a Bratby; or someone like that. More a preliminary sketch, I think; there is not his normal level of detail and there aren't any additional items around the main subject."

Catrin nodded, realizing the possibility a little more slowly than her team member.

She said, "Yes, it could be in the 'kitchen sink realism' style; that would fit."

John Bratby was a modern artist, active in the period 1950s to 1980s, now dead, she recalled. His paintings were gritty, expressionist oils often in crude, heavy strokes. A 'John Osborne, Look Back in Anger' type of artist from the middle of the last century.

They looked up at the two men.

"DC Howlett is suggesting it could be a work by an artist called John Bratby, or someone who paints in his style. The signature is 'Ashe', we see, which links to the letter. He could be a copyist; an artist who ended up in a court case, by the sound of it, either charged with something - or in some other capacity, a witness perhaps. We would need to look into it, if that is what you want?"

Richards said, emphatically, "I do. The letter my sister left makes this very awkward. What does 'failed in my duty' mean, we ask? My preference would be to give away the painting with the items we are clearing out if it was not so much against Judith's apparent wishes. My wife showed the housekeeper the letter and she is as lost as us as to its meaning."

He looked at Wicklow who spoke up, sounding a little exasperated.

"Inspector Sayer, the minister's sister was a lawyer by training, but for many years sat also as a judge. The concern is, frankly, that a member of the judiciary was possibly hiding a stolen painting, or a bribe or... what? People may think... many things. We want, if at all possible, to protect his sister's reputation, but there is also the minister to consider."

Richards nodded in agreement then added, "I am in a position within government that must be above reproach; or at the very least, have no nasty surprises attached; the Minister of Policing cannot be seen to be breaking rules. Hence, no matter where this goes, there is the need for the utmost confidentiality and to keep my office appraised."

Catrin said, "I can understand the concerns, sir. But to be clear; what exactly do you want us to do?"

Richard said, "Look into it, please; that is all. Work with the local police, find out more about this Edwin Ashe, perhaps; see if it is linked to a local theft... but keep us informed. I don't want this formalized within Dyfed-Powys Police, or any heavy-handed approach which could bring in the press. And Tregynon is a quiet community. A barrel-load of strangers rolling through will cause waves. I thought at first that we could ask some art academic for advice on the painting, but Tom is quite correct; there is a need for expertise, but discretion also. You went to Aberystwyth, I gather?"

Catrin said, "Yes, sir. I am familiar with that part of the world, but not Tregynon in particular."

He said again in Welsh, "But you understand. It is not London..."

Catrin nodded; she understood only too well the ways of small towns and villages in Wales. They want me to wrap it up quietly, tie a bow around the file and bury it, Catrin thought. But legitimately.

Minister Richards said bluntly, as his door was opened by another person who Catrin assumed to be a member of his staff, "Time's up, I am afraid. I have another appointment that Gareth over there is hauling me into. Tom will fill in any other details you may need and my wife and daughter will be available for you in the house; at least for the next couple of days, I understand."

He stood. Within moments, Catrin and Isabelle Howlett found themselves back at the table in Wicklow's office.

Catrin said, "Mr. Wicklow, you want a report back, but that will need to be cleared by my superiors, you understand? Investigations have their own procedures. If we find any indication of a criminal act, we must follow due process."

He nodded then passed over a card with his contact information.

"Providing we have no surprises, we can accept that. It's being blindsided that worries me. Anything else?"

"Did you look into this name Edwin Ashe already?"

Wicklow shook his head. "No, no time really with everything else we have on our agenda. Also, we want to be hands off, as a department; the minister must be above board on this. The time was spent finding the right person to do this - you."

"And was Judge Richards married - or has family?"

He shook his head again.

"Not as far as I know, according to the minister. No husband, no children; he couldn't even recall the last time she was in a relationship with anyone. The woman was a workaholic, I gather; it is a disease a number of us suffer from."

DC Howlett said, "But some people still find the time for a family or partners, despite that."

Wicklow smiled, but was less than amused. "But being a workaholic doesn't exactly enhance relationships, does it? I know that myself."

He said it a little tartly. For some reason, Catrin saw, Howlett blushed.

As they stood up, Catrin said, "Why me, Mr. Wicklow? You said that I was specifically picked to do this. Your department could simply have asked the Art and Antiques Unit for assistance."

She came straight out with it. The issue had been eating at her throughout the meeting.

Wicklow nodded, not hiding it. "Dyfed-Powys Police has a large area to cover and a relatively small force. They don't have your sort of expertise in their ranks. And you are Welsh; you speak the language in the heartland, so to speak."

He is not answering the question, Catrin's expression said. But she stayed quiet.

He continued. "So we asked the neighbouring North Wales Police if they had an art crime expert who was local, within the organisation. A Chief Superintendent Morgan there thought about it, said no; then he mentioned your name. He said you were working in the Art Crime Unit at Scotland Yard but would fit in. Fran, one of my assistants, told me after the call that she thought she had met you only a few weeks ago, at a meeting here and I then recalled the name Sayer associated with Assistant Commissioner Hunt."

He smiled.

"So we checked you out. Morgan called us back the following day to say it wouldn't work; you were with the Assistant Commissioner's staff now, he had found out, not doing art investigation. But we were already on it. Now that you are back at Art and Antiques it seemed even more appropriate."

Catrin nodded. So, it boiled down to a communication gaff by her friends at North Wales Police headquarters in Colwyn Bay, it seemed. Morgan had been promoted to a Chief Super, now, she gathered. He had probably asked DCI Dafydd Powys for a recommendation; they had worked together on the Han Yeung case and she stayed in touch with him and his wife.

Dafydd would be buying her a good dinner in compensation next time she was in Bangor.

"I would like a report as soon as possible, DI Sayer," Wicklow said, with the tone that he had every right to order her around. In his job, he probably did, in a sense.

~~

Catrin led Howlett down the road, away from the Home Office, to a Caffé Nero busy with lunch-time business. They lined up and bought coffees and sandwiches and lucked out on finding a table as others finished and left.

As they ate, Catrin asked, "Are you familiar with Bratby's work, Isabelle? It sounds like it."

Howlett nodded. "I like a lot of modern art, ma'am. It's a passion. Bratby is very 'in your face' art, in technique I mean. He called it - "

She paused, trying to recall the term.

Catrin said, "Tubism; applying paint directly from the tube to the canvas, daubing it."

Howlett nodded. "That's it. I always wondered if he was making a pun on 'Tubism' as a style. You know; the post-Cubism movement?"

Catrin thought about it. She replied, "Bratby's life seemed so chaotic; he was a deranged alcoholic, they say. It would be hard to know what he meant unless you were with him at the time he talked about it. He was a real salesman, working every crowd and clientele he could."

She saw Howlett look at her afresh, her face more animated over the coffee cup she held in both hands. It was clear that she would be happy talking about art for hours. But the woman's eyes also showed that she understood that her boss knew something about it too.

Howlett blew gently across her coffee and said, "I have even seen your own work. Mark mentioned that you were a ceramic artist; I told him I already knew that."

"Can I ask if you like it, then?" Catrin smiled.

Howlett said, matter-of-factly, "Some of it. You did some darker stuff at times; I like that a lot more."

She added, "But your work is not as dark as Bratby can be, though."

Catrin thought Howlett must really know her artistic output with Jean. Her ceramics after the incidents in Scotland and Malaysia had been called just that; 'dark'.

Howlett changed back to the subject of work.

"Ma'am, it sounds as if they want you specifically, not our team. So I am not sure I should be doing this with you. Perhaps I should get back to the Acton case? Also, they seem to think we should just go trotting along to Wales. Most of the work will be done on computer or by phone around here talking to experts, people who know the art and can identify this painting. We could use a better quality photo, obviously; but is it really necessary for us to chase up there now, just for that? The locals can produce one for us."

Catrin asked, "Is going away a problem, then, Howlett?"

"No, my neighbour will look after my cat. It's just…"

Catrin said, "Neville said we would have to do due diligence on this; a 'wild goose chase', he thought. I think he is right. This is politics between the Met and the Home office. If we don't go up to Tregynon it will be seen as giving the issue short shrift. You should come with me. You know the art and two heads will be better than one, given the nature of this puzzle. I am not sure where this is going, at all.

"But I do know we need to clear it off the plate quickly, one way or the other. We can then let Neville, or more senior staff, know that we did what they wanted regarding the minister's personal issue and we can report back to Wicklow and Minister Richards. After that we can get on with Acton and other cases that matter more."

Howlett nodded. "If you say so, ma'am, I will, of course. When do we leave?"

I do, thought Catrin; if, for no other reason than to get you out of your comfort zone and make my own mark on this team.

"We will head out tomorrow, an early start. I can pick you up on the way, let me know where. This will give you the chance to do some work on the warehouse inventory this afternoon, which will please the Antiques team, no doubt, and me - I will start on investigating any possible Bratby link... and checking out any copyist of the style with a signature called 'Ashe', perhaps.

Howlett was squashing up her sandwich wrapping; she was done. Catrin had finished half of her sandwich, as she had been doing most of the talking while they had lunch. She picked up her other half and started eating, waiting for Howlett to say something, but her new team member didn't make casual conversation, it seemed; she kept glancing at her mobile.

Catrin asked, "You are interested in art; do you paint yourself?"

Howlett shook her head. "No, I don't have the creative gift, so I don't want to produce derivative work or anything mediocre. I like to see it, to experience the work of others."

Catrin didn't argue, just filed it away. Part of artistic development was a creative desire, but a lot of it was simply the hard work of application of technique coupled with self-confidence to try and improve.

Then Howlett added, "I have training as a conservator, though; I just never qualified."

It hadn't been in her personnel record; Catrin had read up on both Howlett and Harper on Monday afternoon.

She said, "Really; where?"

"I studied at the Courtauld Institute. But I gave up; came back from my unpaid leave of absence, returning to the Met early."

From her expression, Catrin thought that she wasn't going to get more out of her.

Then Howlett said, "Not every job change works out, does it?"

Catrin wondered if she was talking about herself or her new boss. But Howlett changed the subject yet again.

"I was wondering about holiday coverage, ma'am, so I can

plan? We haven't talked about it yet, but normally DI Caldwell ran though it with Mark and myself around now; so we all knew when the others planned to be away."

It was a good point, Catrin realised. She needed to cover that with both of them but Howlett asked her about her own plans first.

Catrin said, "I am taking a week's holiday three weeks from now; going away. It has been booked for a while."

Howlett nodded. "Are you going anywhere nice?"

Catrin replied, "Yes, to Hong Kong, for a wedding of a friend of mine. She is from there, but we met in Bangor."

The expression on Howlett's face was the same as earlier when she mentioned the trip to Wales. It may as well have been a trip to the moon.

She steeled herself before asking. "Where do you go for your holidays, Isabelle?"

She wondered if Howlett had ever taken a train outside London, other than to Oxford, never mind a plane out of the country.

13 HARBOUR CITY

Jian Li Yeung had called Miele Yau the following day, to extend an invitation to have lunch together later in the week. She suggested a Vietnamese restaurant she liked at Harbour City, a shopping mall on the west side of Kowloon. The younger woman was happy to follow up so soon.

Li arrived there straight from work, again in business attire. This time Miele was more formally dressed, too; no backpack and jeans. She was wearing business casual clothes that looked expensive.

As they got to know each other more, Miele was probing a little the direct linkage between her grandfather and Li. It took a moment for Li to catch on.

"I have no business dealings with Mr. Yau, Miele, if that is the basis of your question."

Miele replied, "I thought so, but wasn't completely sure. I saw the gold sailing boat you gave to my grandfather; he is very pleased with it, I think. I wondered if it might be a business gift."

It had been a present; a hand-made filigree miniature of a traditional Maltese boat specifically made to order from Welsh gold. It was a 'thank you' gift to recognize Mr. Yau's assistance in removing the death threat against Catrin. But she wasn't going to talk about that.

"No. It was simply a gift; one to him and a similar one to my boss, Mr. Lin. I was on a business trip to Malta and filigree items made like that are a local tradition."

Miele nodded. "Then you need to know that I am not involved in my family's business. And do not plan to be. I am going to be an artist."

Not involved in triad matters; she wasn't tainted, she was saying.

Miele said, "My grandfather, Mr. Lin and your father have been meeting regularly since before I was born."

Li answered, "Yes they have. You lost an uncle, your grandfather a son. My father and Mr. Lin also lost sons; it is a bond between them."

Her face clouded over with the memory of Han, her brother murdered in Wales. Li realised that probably Miele had no idea of the linkages to her - Michael Yau's role in the investigation into Han's death or his more recent involvement to thwart the death threat against Catrin. She reached into her bag.

Miele said, "Your father is very highly thought of in our family; his efforts to save the uncle I didn't get the chance to meet have never been forgotten."

Li nodded.

"Thank you. But shall we talk about your interest in meeting my friends? About your expectations coming out of any meeting with Catrin Sayer and Jean Hughes? It brings me to one of the reasons for meeting you again, to give you an invitation to my wedding."

She passed over the formal invitation in the sealed envelope, reading Miele's face.

"And before you politely decline, that you do not know me well enough, Catrin Sayer will attend; she is one of my bridesmaids. You will get the chance to meet her there."

Miele looked pleased. She said, "I had only asked for an introduction in London, when I go…"

"I know. Also, do you know she is a police officer?"

Miele looked earnest. "Yes, I saw that on the web site. It says she is with the London police. But, it won't matter, will it? It is just about art."

That was exactly what Li had been thinking about; exactly what to say to Catrin, or what not to say. And she didn't have an answer to that yet. In fact, part of the reason for the face-to-face meeting was to help her decide what to do.

~~

This time it wasn't a phone camera; it was a Nikon with a telephoto lens, capturing video but not sound; they had no time to set that up in such an open and visible restaurant in a noisy shopping mall. But they had good lighting on the two women and someone they could call on to lip read the recording; that would do almost as well. By now they knew quite a bit about Jian Li Yeung.

'They', in fact, were not a Chinese or Hong Kong organization. The information was being sent considerably further afield; to London, to a building on the River Thames at Vauxhall Cross. It was the headquarters of SIS, the Secret Intelligence Service, formerly known as MI6.

If Catrin Sayer had known of this, the first thought that would come to mind would be the phrase 'our slimy friends'; Superintendent Jack Taylor's pet name for SIS. They had popped up - at some distance - in the last case she worked with the ACU, the Stubbs painting investigation. And on a few occasions in the last two years, people from the security services found their way into the higher levels of New Scotland Yard and into Assistant Commissioner Hunt's office. When they did, none of her staff were included in the meeting and the door was closed.

Now, unbeknown to her, they were getting far closer to her own life through Jian Li.

~~

Deacon John Farrell met Kevin Stott's mother, Lisa, at All Saints Church in Newtown during her lunch-hour. She worked nearby and said she would like to talk with him, but not at her home, so they agreed on the place and time.

The reconciliation with her son on his return from prison had been emotional and heartfelt, he thought - and hopefully permanent. Most of it would depend on Kevin and his behaviour now he was home. She had seen his solemn promises evaporate in minutes on previous occasions, but this time she would not tolerate it if he went downhill; she had joined Al-Anon during his time in Stoke Heath and had a support group of people to talk to now.

John had explained this to Kevin after the crying and hugging was over, when he really understood what he could lose. She had asked Farrell to do that.

"Coming from you, John, it will hit home harder. You have that manner about you when you choose to, I know."

Farrell asked, not wanting to, "What 'manner', Lisa?"

She came right out with it, but with a smile.

"Hard. I should say 'no nonsense'; but I mean it well; you can be a hard one, I think, particularly for a clergyman."

He looked at her ruefully. "It's all show."

She shook her head.

"I don't think so. At least, it doesn't come over that way to me. You were a tough one before your went into the ministry, I think."

As he parked further down Commercial Street and walked back to the church, he wondered how it was going with Kevin. It had been less than two weeks since he had taken him home from prison, but he had heard nothing from him.

Lisa was already there. After the opening greetings she got straight into it.

"I am not sure what you and Kevin talked about on the drive home, John, but he is different. In a sense, it's worrying me."

Farrell had expected some news of a drinking lapse or a

row between the mother and son. He said nothing, waiting for more.

"He met some bloke at Narcotics Anonymous, fell in with him, I think. He is Kevin's NA sponsor now."

"That's good, Lisa. That is what is needed in recovery, to find someone more experienced to work with."

She nodded, but still looked troubled.

"It's the rest of it. This sponsor, Ryan, is 'born again' or something like that; not a Mormon, but some similar religious group starting up here, already established in other places. They don't have a church building yet but Kevin is falling in hook, line and sinker, it seems to me. He is talking about repentance all the time, needing to pay God back first; that his life has to be renewed. He is always reading their literature and talking on the phone to Ryan.

"The rest of it; he is up early, making his bed now and looking as smart as he can, generally; it's a big change. He disappears during the day but I know he is going to the probation officer on schedule; otherwise the police would be round. And he is regular in his AA and NA meetings, staying clean.

"One of his old friends came round. I dreaded what would happen but within ten minutes he left. I heard Kevin giving him a hellfire and damnation tongue-lashing about his evil ways. Arnie was out of the house like a bullet out of a gun."

She laughed, but Farrell could see the fear on her face.

"It's not our Kevin. It worries Sheila and me."

John Farrell had the picture.

He said, "Recovery groups, whether for drug users or alcoholics, have all sorts of people and, as they say in Al-Anon too, I know, some are sicker than others. What they mean is that you can't predict the behaviors of people there; it's not a doctor's office, there are no professional standards. But there are many ways to find God, Lisa; you know that yourself. Suffering is one of them. But we can't dictate the path for Kevin, or others."

He answered her original question. "What did I say to him

about religion on the drive home? Nothing really, other than that you went to church; he knew already it would be something that you would like him to do. Other than that, well, he asked a bit about me; what it meant to be a deacon. What I did before; that sort of thing. But he gave no indication of any conversion or interest himself; just a curiosity. I offered to talk to him about that, if he wanted.

"Or, at least, I didn't see it. Perhaps I should have."

Lisa Stott looked at him, searching; she trusted him.

"But is it OK? Is this right for Kevin? At least he is not drinking and drugging, but… it worries me."

Farrell said, "Look, I will come round and talk to him; take him for a coffee."

She shook her head. "God knows what he will have if you take him out. He is 'abstaining from stimulants' he told me; no coffee or tea as of yesterday."

"Still, I will meet him one-on-one; talk to him about it."

He smiled, making it seem as if it was OK.

Deep down it worried him. The change in Kevin was dramatic. It could be for the better, albeit the boy turning into some sort of self-righteous fundamentalist; better than a road back to Stoke Heath. But John Farrell's mind was going back to another man who made a similar transformation in his life. That hadn't turned out too well at all, he thought.

In fact, he used to have a painting in his flat to remind him, but had sold it over a year ago. He would talk seriously with Kevin Stott, he decided; perhaps he could get one or two of the older members of the youth group involved, if it worked out. Kevin needed new friends.

14 TREGYNON

Catrin picked up Howlett outside the Royal Oak underground station the following morning and drove out on the A40, heading for the motorway. She had chosen the M40 rather than the M1 and M6; it was a more pleasant route and only a little longer in time.

In the drive north-west, once they were moving freely on the motorway, she went through the case again and Howlett talked about her own research last night after Catrin had gone home.

"Like you, ma'am, I found no painter called Ashe in the style. Bratby had a prolific output including a lot of portraiture, but I couldn't find the name Ashe associated with it at all."

That had been Catrin's own conclusion, too, yesterday afternoon, she had told Howlett.

She replied, "It could be one of the artist's friends or contacts. We really need a Bratby expert, but let's not jump ahead of ourselves. Let's examine the painting first to see if there is a case at all. The letter from Judith Richards was so... vague. I would like to know more about her state of mind in the period before her death."

Howlett said, "She could have been rambling, or at least, not completely with it."

She paused, reflecting.

"But if she was, I don't think that her brother would have gone to all this trouble. There is something more, he suspects. He knew his sister."

Catrin turned the conversation to Isabelle; trying to find out more about her team member than her personnel file indicated. From the conversation in Caffé Nero she knew about her holidays, but that was about it. Howlett stayed several times a year with her aunt who lived on Canvey Island, on the Essex coast, 'no beaches, but walks along the sea wall; very refreshing' and, once every two years, she and a friend who also liked art 'went on a trip away to see galleries and museums'. They had been to Amsterdam, Rome and Madrid so far. Berlin was eighteen months away it seemed, on this inexorable timetable of working through the world's art galleries.

She hadn't specified whether the friend was male or female.

Catrin now knew that Howlett was divorced, something of a loner, it appeared. She had reverted to using her maiden name; her file had mentioned that, the name change. It had been something she had to consider herself before marriage; to become 'Mrs. Treneer and 'DS Treneer' or not. She had decided to retain Sayer as a professional and artistic name.

Jean had asked her about that aspect as the wedding date was announced. Catrin had looked at her friend, assessing the basis of the question.

"Liz raised it, I guess? We have a visibility in the marketplace as Sayer and Hughes. No, I will be staying with 'Sayer' as an artist; that's decided."

Catrin's conversation with Howlett in the car quickly led to Isabelle's soliloquy about her Burmese cat. It seemed to be her main companion in life outside work. By Banbury, Catrin had heard enough about the cat's life with Isabelle and changed the subject, talking about the area of Wales they were going to.

"It seems in the middle of nowhere," said Howlett,

apparently unaware of her indelicacy on the subject of geography.

Catrin had gained the impression that Howlett's world was a slice of land extending from London to Canvey Island oil terminals and a collection of art galleries inconveniently connected by aircraft rather than the London Underground.

"Well, Newtown and Tregynon are certainly in the middle of Wales," countered Catrin.

"So Newtown is a new town, close by to somewhere old?" Howlett asked.

Catrin shook her head.

"It dates from the thirteenth or fourteenth century; sometime around there. It's a border town, so has a history associated with the Welsh fighting the English. They established it around the time the English killed off the King of Wales and stuck his head on a spike at the Tower of London. It was new around then."

Howlett looked at her as if she was having her leg pulled. Catrin just kept her face straight, enjoying it.

Her team member said, "Hopefully they won't be seeking retribution. I will stay close to you; you speak the local language."

As they left the A5 for the A458 after Shrewsbury however, Catrin let the conversation lapse and both of them were absorbed in the scenery. For Catrin, it brought back memories of living in Aberystwyth and her travels in this countryside. She had been on a volleyball team at university and 'away' games at other universities in the Midlands were part of those memories; coach trips with her team along this road. Driving here gave her the sense of being 'back home', despite their destination being a long way from Pontypridd.

She understood well the term 'hiraeth', for which there was no literal English translation - home-longing came close - and did not suffer from it herself. She knew people who simply couldn't live anywhere else; they had to be... home.

For Howlett, it was her first time in mid-Wales. As a child, her parents had once had a family holiday in Pembrokeshire, she said. Sheep, pastures and road-signs in an unfamiliar and unpronounceable language caught her eye when she wasn't checking updates on the Acton developments on her mobile.

They had been booked into the Maesmawr Hall Hotel near Tregynon overnight, a small, country house hotel that had been recently renovated, Sayer told Howlett. The Newtown station of Dyfed-Powys Police was on Park Lane, adjacent to the County Council offices, she said, when they were about fifteen minutes away.

"No Hilton in the city centre, then?" Howlett asked, straight-faced.

"Maesmawr Hall dates from the sixteenth century; a little earlier than a Hilton… and it is a nice country hotel, I recall."

She looked at her satnav. "It seems we turn just ahead and we should be on the road to the local 'nick'. We are to ask for an Inspector Meredith."

~~

Inside the Newtown Police Station, Sayer and Howlett were shown to Carole Meredith's office.

After introductions, Meredith said, "We are at the other end of Powys here; headquarters are in Carmarthen. I had an email about this matter from HQ and have asked DS Pawl Pryce to assist you. What on, though, we are not sure. I will call him so you can explain what you need from us."

They were joined by a male police officer in plain-clothes; perhaps five-eight, five-nine, in his early forties, Catrin judged. No smile, just a studied look as he came in and shook hands during a round of introductions.

He said, "I am on an investigation into a hit-and-run at present so may need to break away, but if we can help, we will. What is the case and what assistance do you need, ma'am?"

Catrin nodded, understanding. He was straight to the point. Nevertheless, they too had been hijacked into doing this and had driven half-way across the country this morning. He wasn't going to get much sympathy. She wondered how to play this, given the start. Straight out with it, she thought.

"We don't know if there is a case. We have been asked to investigate the origin of a painting in the possession of the Richards family in Tregynon, part of the estate of the late Judge Judith Richards. Until we have seen the painting and find out more about it, I can't be more precise.

"If there are any records related to cases involving Judith Richards and a person called Ashe, any thefts of paintings locally in the last five years, or any knowledge of an artist in the area with that name, we would appreciate it. Or if you have any records of thefts involving paintings by a list of artists DC Howlett put together as we drove up here; these could have the signature altered to the name Ashe, perhaps."

She looked over to Howlett, who handed over a notebook page with a list of about ten names. John Bratby was at the top.

Howlett added, "Also, if the name 'Edwin Ashe' is featured in any criminal records in the region it could help us, perhaps."

Catrin continued, "We have been asked to review this issue, right in the middle of a major case of our own, and had to drive up from London without a crime identified, a victim or a perpetrator."

Pryce said, "Can I ask by whom? It wasn't by us."

"By my boss, DCI Coltrane," she said.

She wasn't going to say anything about the Home Office connection. Doubtlessly, being local, they would know that Judith Richards was a judge and that the Richards family had a member who was a senior government politician. But it wouldn't come from her. Nevertheless, the expressions on everyone's faces showed that they knew Noel Richards was involved.

Catrin said, "We were asked to examine the painting and report back to my superiors what we learned."

Pryce grimaced.

"So, in reality, you know no more than me?"

Howlett shook her head and Catrin avoided the question.

She just asked, "Can you help with the database searches, then? We did a quick check on-line but it didn't help. Nothing in the major crimes database showed up. It needs a local eye on it and a check of local records."

He nodded.

"We can do that; at least, I will work on it here with someone. Although I recall Judge Richards actually worked in the courts around Birmingham, so you would need to check with the Midlands Police as well. Will you be going to Tregynon to see the painting?"

Catrin nodded.

"It's at the house. The family is expecting us around now, we understand. And the sooner we get through this, frankly speaking, the sooner we can all get back to other work."

From his expression, he clearly agreed with her.

"Do you want me to come along?"

Catrin shook her head. "No need. We have a satnav and can find our way…"

Inspector Meredith interrupted.

"If you don't mind, we will send someone with you. It is our patch… and if anything arises which starts a formal investigation I would rather know directly from my own officer."

Catrin said, "That would be fine. In fact, we appreciate it."

Pryce said, "And I will have someone start work on your shopping list while you are over there."

15 FOWLES

A PC Seren Fowles was assigned by Inspector Meredith to accompany Sayer and Howlett. As they were introduced, the station commander said, "Seren is local, she knows Tregynon; just in case it helps."

The young constable just nodded and smiled.

Though Catrin was watching the road as she drove, listening to the instructions from PC Fowles sitting in the front passenger seat, she could see Howlett's face in the rearview mirror, eyes fixed on her mobile. More messages about Acton, no doubt.

"You live in Tregynon, then?" Catrin asked.

Fowles replied, "Not now; I grew up there and my mother lives there still; my dad is dead. So I know a lot of the local people."

"Did you know Judith Richards?"

"The constable nodded. "Oh yes. Not as a judge; that was away from here. But as a member of the church - Yr Eglwys yng Nghymru."

The Church in Wales, part of the Anglican Communion.

"I haven't been in her house, though. She always seemed a bit distant, but I think she got on well with the clergy in the diocese. She went to St. Cynon's Church, close to her."

Catrin smiled. "She was probably a good supporter of the church."

Fowles said, "The Richards family always has been, so yes."

There was a pause, a silence for a minute. Then the PC said, in Welsh, "Turn left at the junction. It will be the fourth house along that stretch of road, on the left."

"Right," responded Catrin, in the same language.

Fowles realised she had cut Howlett out of the conversation flow.

She said in English, turning her head, "Sorry, it's her accent; I can't help but think DI Sayer is from around here, not London."

"That makes two of us," said Howlett.

The Richards' house was further along the rural road on which Gregynog Hall was located; a large, impressive, black and white Tudor-style hall set in extensive grounds.

"Well look at that!" said Howlett, forgoing her emails, sitting up and turning round to take it all in as they drove past.

"It's now part of the University of Wales and is used as a conference centre. It dates back about eight centuries, I believe," said Catrin.

"That's right," said Fowles.

"To think, a building as grand as this, in the middle of nowhere," said Howlett.

Catrin and Seren Fowles exchanged smiles.

Fowles said, "It's quite famous, probably the most famous thing around here."

As they passed the mansion, Catrin thought about how she would like to be here with her friend Mason Carrington, her sister-in-law's partner. He was a well-known watercolourist. She could see them painting the scene together, him talking away, her getting his input. She had no idea where he was this week. He was often abroad teaching art classes if he wasn't painting his own works back home in Cornwall.

The Richards' home was a small, more austere building; a nineteenth century redbrick house with steep gables. After parking in the drive they knocked and, as the woman opened the door, she recognized PC Fowles and started talking to her in Welsh.

"These officers are from London, Mrs. Peters," Fowles said, in English.

The woman said, "Oh yes, you are expected. Mrs. Richards is inside."

They had started with tea, at the insistence of Mrs. Richards (I'm Maeve, this is my daughter Simone. Let's have some tea or coffee, Dilys). The Home Office minister's wife was friendly, but she was looking harassed or frustrated by the significant array of clothing and possessions in boxes and bags.

"Since we talked to Noel and he said the police would look into it, we have sorted things but not given anything away yet or thrown things out, I am sorry to say. It is difficult to make progress."

She looked at the officers.

"I hope you will let us get on after this. Simone and I have to go back to London tomorrow, DI Sayer. So if you need anything further from us, you can contact us at home. If you need anything more from the house, please call Mrs. Peters. She will do whatever is necessary. We are finished here, at least with Judith's personal possessions."

Catrin said, "What will happen to the home and furnishings you choose not to dispose of, may I ask?"

"Oh, they will stay in the family; we just haven't worked out yet what to do. Living in London, with my husband in his position, it is not really practical for us at present. But it won't be sold, I think; it has been in the family since Noel's grandfather's time. It was bought as a wedding present for him and his new wife."

A family with hereditary wealth, Catrin thought.

"Nice wedding present," said Isabelle Howlett, not quite keeping the irony out of her voice.

Maeve Richards let the comment go by.

She said, "With Judith being older than Noel, we thought

we may have to deal with this sometime; but not so soon."

Catrin turned to the subject of the painting.

"So, can we see this painting that has created this puzzle for your family - and now for us?"

Mrs. Richards said agreeably, "I am sure you have better things to do than chase after this mystery... it is on the dining table."

Catrin saw Howlett and the daughter nodding, smiling to each other.

Maeve Richards asked, "Is it me, or is it ugly as sin? Are you sorry you drove all the way up, now?"

Catrin said, lost in the painting, "Not all portraits are realistic. This one is certainly not, is it?"

The sketch was not large; a commercial pre-stretched canvas measuring eleven by fourteen inches, excluding the frame. On examination Catrin saw it was, or was similar to, the portrait work of John Bratby, as they thought. A gritty, expressionist oil sketch of a young man in crude strokes, the paint uneven, roughly applied. She looked carefully for any signs of layout charcoal, pencil or re-work.

The two officers turned it over carefully and examined the back and the frame. Catrin couldn't see anything special to help them; no dealer marks or stamps. She glanced at Howlett, who wrinkled her nose.

"The frame seems nothing special, ma'am, but can I look at this signature more closely?" was Howlett's comment.

They turned it back over.

Catrin pulled out her tablet. A search page for Bratby portraits was already loaded.

Howlett was looking at the work again. She said, "Tt seems to me to be similar to Bratby's portrait of Brian Aldiss, the writer, in style and colours, but as a preliminary sketch, not a finished work. Can you find that one, ma'am?"

As Catrin looked at the work and zoned in on the request, she could see the reasoning behind Isabelle's comment.

"You are right, Howlett. Good catch. Look at the colour

selection and placement for the forehead, for a start."

Howlett nodded. Then she searched through her bag and pulled a small folding loupe, or magnifier, with its own frame designed to position it at the correct distance from the object. It was a heavy brass antique in a worn leather case. Howlett opened it and positioned it above the signature area, then bent over to view the detail, lost in the painting. Catrin had to hide a smile; Isabelle looked like a parody of Sherlock Holmes, the intensity of the gaze through the lens. She knew it was unfair; she had her own, and much newer, folding jeweler's loupe in her briefcase. At times the joke could apply to her.

Howlett said, "The signature box is quite crudely over-painted. I can see gaps in the brush strokes and beneath them a background colour slightly different to the one in the original work.. The signature area looks to be oil paint but amateurishly applied, unlike the main painting."

The detective went rummaging through the bag again, pulling out a small wooden box containing screw-top vials of clear fluids and a pack of precision swabs; flexible plastic sticks with small cotton cloth heads. She opened one bottle, dipped a swab, shook it off and gently applied it to a corner area of the signature box.

"Not water soluble. Let's try to see if it is oil, and if so, how it tests against the original."

She repeated the test with a solvent on a swab in the same area, counting the number of light strokes until she saw a trace of colour on the swab head. She repeated the test with a small area of the main painting of similar colour, to the side. Then she examined her swabs with the lens.

"It is oil paint, ma'am. From a quick check on the mobility of the paint, the sample from the signature is a poorer grade material, by the look of it, and it was applied more recently than the main area. I think we will find the original signature underneath, if there is one. But that would require proper work in a laboratory."

Catrin was quite impressed by the technical capabilities Howlett possessed and her confidence in tackling the issue head on.

She asked, "Mrs. Richards, where was the portrait found? What was it stored in?"

"Ah," the daughter answered, "you had better come upstairs."

They followed her up the staircase into a large bedroom. It contained furniture which could be original, Catrin thought. Dark, ornate woodwork, finely made pieces that were probably impossible to re-sell these days, unless it was a collectible item. In the corner was a mirror-fronted, large wardrobe.

"At the back of this. In that."

She pointed at the layers of brown wrapping paper and thin card, taped along its length, one end opened and worn. It looked to be a transport cover for the painting, re-used as a protective sleeve afterwards.

"And I take it that all of you have touched this?" Catrin asked.

Mrs. Richards said, "Yes, I think so. Simone retrieved it."

The daughter spoke up.

"We took it out with other waste at first. When we found the note, I went and brought the wrapping back. I thought it might be needed for forensic work, for fingerprints or DNA testing."

Catrin nodded appreciatively.

Mrs. Peters said, "It was at the back of the wardrobe on one side, partly hidden by the dresses hanging up in front. I can understand that; I wouldn't want it on my bedroom wall. Actually, on any wall. It's a bit creepy. Is it worth much, do you think?"

Maeve Richards said, "I don't think the police do appraisals, Dilys."

Howlett answered her.

"If it is a Bratby, it would be quite variable in sales value at present, I think; some sell for around three thousand pounds, some of his major works go at auction at twenty thousand or more. But I don't think this one is catalogued. As Mrs.

Richards says, it would need appraisal."

Catrin asked, "The signature 'Ashe'. Does it ring any bells?"

The three women said no or shook their head.

Dilys Peters mused, "No. No-one local by that name, I can say that. If it wasn't for the note that Miss Richards stuck on it, the painting would be in the jumble sale by now, the way we were going through stuff. We were making good progress."

Catrin looked at the housekeeper.

"How long did you work for Miss Richards? And have you seen it before?"

"Not me, no. I have worked here two years now, but I never went into the back of the wardrobe. I would just hang the dry-cleaning there and put away the clean laundry in the dresser.

"Miss Richards became sick soon after I started, then she retired. My aunt, Belle Thomas, was the housekeeper for her before that, for a long time. She now lives with her son and daughter-in-law on a farm near Machynlleth. They made a little flat for her there at the side of the place.

"She worked here until she was seventy. I would have to ask her, but she is not doing too well at present, I heard last week."

"Is that close to here?" Isabelle asked, recognizing that Dilys Peters' aunt may be the only first-hand witness to the arrival of the painting at the house. "I can't even say the name."

Catrin said, "It's near the coast, about thirty miles away."

Simone Richards looked at her. "You are trying to decide if it was deliberately hidden or if the wardrobe was just a convenient place to store it, assuming she didn't want it on display, I suppose?"

Catrin said, "Yes, Miss Richards. Exactly. Are you planning to become a police officer, by any chance?"

The girl laughed.

"No. I have just been accepted at King's College, London to do law. It was where Aunt Judith studied so, who knows?"

It was nearly four p.m. Catrin felt they had a good picture of the discovery of the painting now, so she said they would be leaving. They left them their business cards, saying if anything else came to mind, they should call her or DC Howlett.

Maeve Richards reminded them that they were returning home tomorrow.

Catrin asked, "Can we take the painting back with us, have it checked properly? It will be returned, assuming there are no complications."

"We wish you would," said Maeve Richards and Dilys Peters, almost in unison.

"Then we can get on with the rest of it," said Dilys.

"And I will talk with my husband," said Maeve, "Even if you find no owner, we won't want it back. It should go to a charity fundraiser of some sort, given Constable Howlett's comment on its possible value. I am sure Noel will agree."

On the short drive back to Newtown Police Station, Catrin said to Howlett, "I like the loupe. You came well-prepared. It looks quite old, though; at least the case appears that way?"

Howlett answered, "I bought it secondhand, for my conservator course. It's heavier than a modern one, but I like it."

As they turned back on the road to the station, PC Fowles said, "What now, ma'am? Do you need me further?"

Catrin said, "No, I think we can call it a day. We had the drive up and... we will be here tomorrow, hopefully, to see anything DS Pryce's data search turns up. We will drop you and head over to the Maesmawr Hall Hotel. Do you know if the restaurant there is any good? Or do you have other suggestions for places to eat around here?"

Fowles said, "Yes ma'am. It has a good one but... I was just thinking. We have a women's supper at my own church, St. Deiniol's, tonight, a fundraiser. There will be plenty of home-cooked food and it might be a bit more relaxing. If you want to, that is."

Catrin was looking at Howlett's face in the back seat as her

DC responded first.

"That would be nice, I'm sure. I would like that but... ma'am?"

Better than being in a one-on-one situation all evening with her new boss, was what Catrin read on her face. Isabelle Howlett was a very private person, she realised.

She said, "That is very nice of you, Seren, if it works for you."

Fowles responded, "It's actually not far from your hotel, as well. But I would like to change out of my uniform at the station, ma'am; that was my plan. I could lead you from there in my own car."

16 ST. DEINIOL'S CHURCH

As they waited inside the station for Seren Fowles to change, a constable in uniform complete with a stab vest and an equipment belt came up to them. He was ready to go out on shift, it seemed. He introduced himself; a PC Morrissey.

"PC Fowles says you are joining her at the supper tonight, in Aberhafesp."

"Yes," said Howlett, answering first, "A very kind invitation. Wherever that is."

He said, "You will enjoy it, I'm sure; the food is good. Seren and I are engaged, by the way; that's how I know."

He paused. "I wonder, can I ask a question? Did you both start out in general duties and make the change to headquarters in Scotland Yard?"

Both women looked a little surprised at the question, so soon after meeting the officer.

You see," he went on earnestly, "I, I mean we, are thinking of applying for a transfer to headquarters if positions come up and... it is always good to know what works and what doesn't."

By headquarters, Catrin realised, he meant Dyfed-Powys Police headquarters in South Wales. She saw the seriousness of the request, recalling her own anxieties in this area years ago when first deciding to join the Met. She answered him patiently.

"I have a degree in Fine Arts and Art History from down the road, Aberystwyth University. When I joined the Met I started in Lambeth as a probationer and then served in Brixton, at the borough station there. As simple as that. I once told my inspector there, offhand really, that I didn't think I would get to do anything in a place like Scotland Yard. He told me not to close doors in my own face; to look out for opportunities and give them a try. Others will close the doors if it isn't going to work. It was good advice. I still follow it."

The young man nodded.

Catrin looked at Howlett inviting comment. She said nothing, but her face clearly showed she had taken in the snapshot of Sayer's work history.

"Is he pestering you, Inspector?" asked Seren Fowles as she approached in street clothes. "He does that. Very serious, is my fiancé."

Catrin said, deadpan, "He's a terror, interrogating me and DC Howlett."

The man got out a half-formed denial when Fowles said, "Anyway, he doesn't want to be late for his shift and we should go, so…"

She looked at Morrissey, who took the hint.

"Thanks, DI Sayer, for the advice. I had better head out."

Morrissey walked away, with Fowles smiling after him.

Catrin said, "Your fiancé is keen, Seren."

"He is that, ma'am. Good to have ambition, I say, and he has more than enough for both of us."

Catrin had noticed earlier the engagement ring on Fowles' hand.

As they left the building, the local officer said, "We are in good time to stop by the hotel and check you in first. Then let's go together in my car from there and I will drive you back afterwards."

~~

The conversation was local, in Welsh mainly, at half-a-dozen or so round tables set up in the church hall. Catrin and Howlett found themselves in a cluster of women during introductions and Howlett ended up sitting at a different table than her boss. It appeared she had steered herself that way as they sorted out the seating.

Catrin was at a table with Fowles, enjoying the discussion and the meal. They had been introduced just as 'colleagues, visitors from London'."

One older lady said, "You are Valley Welsh though, not London, correct?"

"Yes," said Catrin, "from Pontypridd."

The woman called across to another table. "Lil, there is another one like you here, from your home town."

The response was, "Another sane person? I can't believe it!"

She came over and said hello.

They served themselves from a plentiful buffet, Catrin absorbing the conversation of village life, the work of the church and the purpose behind the fundraiser. She had already put a donation into the basket by the food area. Nearby were various handicraft items made by the Women's Guild also being sold as fundraisers; jars of jams and preserves in one area, handicrafts on the other side, mainly crochet and knitwear, woven bookmarks and some handmade small rustic crosses made from local wood.

As they started eating, a clergyman came in and joined the group, slipping into the one remaining chair empty at Catrin's table, to be warmly greeted by the women there. Seeing the new face, he stood up, came round and introduced himself.

"I am John Farrell, a deacon here, one of the few males allowed at this gathering, other than Reverend Crouch; and he is tied up elsewhere tonight, unfortunately."

Carin saw he was middle-aged but had a rough and ready look about him; he could get by in Brixton as easily as rural Wales was her first thought.

She replied, "I am Catrin Sayer, from Pontypridd, the other sane person in the room, I gather."

He laughed.

"That's Lil's claim too, I know."

Fowles said, "Inspector Sayer is a colleague from London."

"Oh," said Farrell, "are you here on a case?"

Before Fowles could respond, Catrin said, "On police business, yes. It was good of Seren to invite us this evening. My colleague with me is there, at the next table."

She pointed out Howlett then gave a glance at Fowles, just to make sure she understood; whatever they were here for was police business only.

"Deacon Farrell's mission is working with the disadvantaged, particularly with the rehabilitation of people," said Anne, a young woman at the table, a little later. From her body language earlier, Catrin had seen that she didn't appear too comfortable being at a table with the police officers. The politics of church life, she thought, or past misdeeds, perhaps.

The deacon smiled. "Yes, people coming out of institutions of all sorts, helping them with readjustment. With the expansion of prison populations, released inmates and their families have been a focal area for me. The prison population has doubled in the last decade. But you know that."

Fowles said, "John says he is busy with his duties, Catrin, but I think he spends half his time behind the off-licences or pubs - or in them. That's often where I see him."

He smiled at the taunt.

"I am a distinctive deacon, aren't I, Seren, very distinctive. Can't go anywhere without being spotted."

Catrin knew that deacons were either transitional, on their way to full ordination as a priest, or vocational, a member of the diaconal order.

She asked, "A vocational deacon?"

Farrell replied, "Yes; you know, I see."

Anne said to Catrin, pointedly, "So you and Seren lock them up; John helps them when they come out."

Catrin began to see now the basis for the woman's discomfort but Farrell shook his head emphatically.

"No, Anne. We lock them up; all of us. Not the police. They bring in people they think have committed crimes. It's the courts and the laws which lock people away. And they are our laws, at the end of the day."

Catrin glanced across at Farrell as she nodded her approval of the rebuttal. She saw also that Seren Fowles thought highly of the deacon; it was on her face.

Catrin said, "I used to work in Brixton, on drug squad issues. I came across a lot of people in church communities there, sometimes around betting shops or pubs, or under bridges. People in trouble need help, then and now."

"They always have," John Farrell said. "The church tries to help. People from the Howard League and Elizabeth Fry society have been helping inmates and released prisoners for many decades. We often see apparently tough and hostile young men and women, but deeper down they are just people who have been institutionalized, frightened of being out in the world again. How to make it? What will people say? Will they get work? And some carry scars inside of their experiences during incarceration or institutional care."

He was passing a dish to another person as he talked and Catrin saw he had a scar on his thumb; a deep permanent groove. She looked up and saw that he had noticed her gaze. Then he too looked at the scar on her face. They said nothing, but they understood each other's looks; wondering how the other person received their wound.

He continued, "My most important role is one of love and relationship; tough love sometimes. It is explaining those words, living those words to people who think love equates with sex and that relationship means 'who is more powerful in the hierarchy'. If we can do that, there is less chance they will re-offend. And if there is no re-offence, there is more likelihood of the person having a meaningful life."

"Getting their life back together," chimed in Anne, in support, still looking as if all these problems were caused by the police.

"Sometimes it's their first real chance of a meaningful life," said Catrin.

Farrell smiled at her, nodding. She too, he could tell, had met some of the same people he worked with.

Later in the meal an older woman came around with a dish on a tray; a homemade lasagna.

"Anyone for some more… while it's still hot?"

Catrin realised she was really hungry so indicated she would accept a small portion.

"Where are you from?" the server asked, as the large spoon moved towards the plate.

"London," said Catrin, automatically, seeing a woman across the table raise her eyebrows and shake her head slightly.

"Well, said the server, "I was in London once…."

The spoon was left hovering around while the story of Irene Meadow's week in London in 2003 unfolded. Irene had a thick accent in Welsh; Catrin had to concentrate and wondered what she sounded like in English.

Anne said, "You should serve that, Irene."

The suggestion was ignored; Irene was focusing on her story. The finale was, "I never went back; I couldn't understand them, all those Cockneys. You should come back to Wales, love, you sound Welsh."

The spoonful of inviting-looking lasagna, now well-fanned and cooled, was added to Catrin's plate.

"Anyone else?" asked Irene.

There were no takers.

After she left, Anne said, "While it is still hot, indeed. You should have said Pontypridd; she doesn't have a life story from there."

Farrell, said, "She means well…"

Another woman said, "Irene can't do two things at once, that's the problem."

As Irene went on her mission to the next table Catrin noticed that Isabelle Howlett was deep in conversation with women she was seated with. There had been occasional chuckles coming from that group throughout the meal.

Deacon Farrell talked a little about the church, the activities there, its history, for Catrin's benefit. Catrin could tell his Welsh accent was not local but from further north.

"Deiniol was a monk in the sixth century," he said.

Catrin nodded. "He was the first bishop of Bangor, I recall."

Anne brightened at the observation. "Fancy that! A police officer from London knowing about Deiniol."

Catrin smiled. "I had a case once in Bangor for a few weeks; somehow I picked it up there, I think."

As they wrapped up, the people bustling around insisted that neither Catrin nor Isabelle should help clear up; they were visitors. Deacon Farrell went over to Howlett to introduce himself as Catrin moved across to collect her team member.

Lil, Catrin's 'sane' Pontypridd counterpart, was standing with her, and said, "Miss Howlett is an art detective, Deacon Farrell. She knows so much about the subject of art; it has been very interesting."

He smiled; a pleasantry it appeared, but then he glanced back at Catrin, registering the comment. There was a look on his face that she couldn't quite read, as if he wanted to talk more on that subject, but also a tinge of fear or apprehension, she thought. As she registered it, his face changed to a smile, albeit forced.

Catrin said, "We had better be going, Isabelle."

As they left, Catrin said, "Thank you, Seren. It was great."

The PC looked at her suspiciously, then saw that she was being honest, and smiled.

"It's a good group. I am glad I asked you both."

Howlett surprised Catrin. Her response was animated and sounded sincere.

"It was really nice, I thoroughly enjoyed it; such a nice group of women to talk with. Thank you."

Outside Catrin looked up at the bell tower.

"I like your church. It's a beautiful building, so I am glad I came for that, too. I actually go to St. Paul's Cathedral. I find it peaceful; restorative somehow."

The younger woman nodded.

"I like being here, for the same reasons. It's mine; I grew up in its family so I know everyone here. Which is not always an advantage, I might add. Not when you are driving home one of their kids found out and about and up to no good in the early hours. But Jim and I will be married here."

She looked back on the view of the building in the fading light.

"Do you paint, either of you?"

Howlett shook her head. Catrin said, "Yes. I decorate ceramics with a potter friend in London; we grew up together."

"In Pontypridd?"

"Yes. And sometimes I do watercolour painting now. My sister-in-law has a partner who is a professional watercolour painter. He dragged me kicking and screaming back into it."

Isabelle asked, "Would I know of him?"

Catrin smiled, "Given your interests, I am sure you would; Mason Carrington."

Seren said, "I do too, I have heard of him. He was on television a while ago."

She looked at the church, now a silhouette. "I should learn. I would love a proper painting of St. Deiniol's. I have photos, of course, but it is not the same."

Catrin said, "You should try. You know, most people have more artistic talent than they credit themselves with and it is 'practice, practice, practice' that is needed. You could have your own painting to look at."

She avoided looking at Howlett as she spoke, but the comment was directed to her, as well. The younger woman nodded, but said nothing as she unlocked the car for the short drive to the hotel.

~~

Reverend Crouch had been attending the death of an older parishioner that evening and into the night. His route home in the early hours took him past the church, so he was surprised to see a light still on inside St. Deiniol's.

As he pulled into the car park he saw John Farrell's older Vauxhall parked, so knew he would find him inside. As he entered, he saw the deacon sitting on the first pew, bent forward, apparently in prayer.

"John," he said, gently, wondering if he had dropped off to sleep.

The deacon sat up, clearly unaware of his entry, looking surprised.

"How was it, with Ted and his family, Simon?"

"Peaceful at the end, thank God. But what are you doing here. How did the supper go?"

"Very well; it was a good turnout. Seren Fowles even brought visitors. Other than we have to stop Irene serving food; her mind is always elsewhere and the food gets cold."

He looked at the priest, who was ignoring his deflecting comment about Irene, seeing from his eyes that he was still wanting to know why John was still at the church.

"The visitors were police officers from London; art detectives, it seems. I have been praying."

The priest looked at the deacon, concerned.

"Is it something we should talk about, John?"

The priest knew his deacon's history, in general. The man was troubled by his past at times, he knew, and had opened up only so far with him to date.

17 THE GORTON
GALLERY ROBBERY

At breakfast the following morning, Catrin came into the dining room at the time they agreed to meet. She found DC Howlett already well into a full English breakfast. No muesli and low-fat yoghurt for her.

Catrin was feeling good, having gone out earlier for a run in the post-dawn light and misty rain. The sights and smells of the countryside had made her feel happy to be back in Wales. She had passed a car stopped outside a house, the people inside it talking to a local man leaning over a wall. They had stopped talking momentarily and looked at her as she drew closer, then when she called 'good morning' in Welsh, they had opened up the conversation. It had taken her another two minutes to get away and on with her exercise.

She served herself from the buffet; scrambled eggs and a slice of toast with a bowl of fruit salad.

Howlett said, "I didn't sleep well in a strange bed, so I came down early. I checked with Colin Truman in Antiques; he is always in the office early, to beat the traffic."

Catrin sat down as the DC spoke. "And?"

"They now have twelve paintings and six fine art sculptures, including a Gertrude Hermes bust, and still have other cases to open. Antiques now have the two safes open, and are happy to find a bunch of jewelry and a rare stamp album. Do you think we will be back today? It's building up, ma'am; the workload."

Catrin could see that Howlett's mind was heavily into the warehouse raid aftermath.

"Probably, Howlett. But we are here for part of the morning at least."

The DC nodded. It was evident that she wanted to get back to London, to her regular role.

They were in the Newtown police station at 8.45 a.m. and by 9.15 had read the report with the additional information obtained by DS Pryce. It wasn't much; in fact, it was disappointingly small.

"Ashe or Ash is not that common a name around here," said Catrin.

"This is Wales, ma'am. I expected everyone to be a Jones, Hughes or Parry," responded Howlett.

Pryce came in about fifteen minutes later and joined them.

"Didn't look too promising, the information we found, did it?"

"Nothing seems to be relevant, we agree," Catrin said.

"Particularly a fifteen-year-old arrest for sheep-stealing; a Lawrence Ashe of Brynmelyn," said Howlett, pronouncing the place name as 'brine' and ending with 'line'.

"Brynmelyn," said Sayer and Pryce correctly, almost in unison.

Howlett looked at Catrin balefully.

"You said you would protect me, not join them. I am lost in a foreign land."

Catrin replied, "It was only if they were going to hang you, Isabelle, in retribution for spiking Llewellyn's head on Tower Bridge. Mispronouncing Welsh names is a far worse crime. You are on your own."

Her mind was suddenly carried back to a day driving Jian Li to Aberystwyth from Bangor, years ago, when they had played a game of place-name pronunciation. She quickly brought her mind back to the case.

"Nothing on an Edwin Ashe, then?" Catrin asked.

Pryce said, "Not in our records. Is that the name of the painter?"

"It could be, or it could be the subject," said Catrin.

"You should try in the Midlands, nearer Birmingham, where Judith Richards worked," he said.

Right, thought Catrin, we should. They hadn't even looked at which courts Judith Richards worked at yet. Even approaching that would need some care.

"Pawl, we are wondering about the housekeeper's aunt at the Richard's place, a Belle Thomas. She was the previous housekeeper until Dilys Peters took over and would have been around when the painting came into Judith Richard's possession, perhaps. Peters said she is in Machynlleth."

Pryce said, "I will give Dilys Peters a call and check it out. Unless you want to do that yourself today?"

As they watched him dial, Catrin's mobile rang. It was Mark Harper.

"Yes, Harper?"

"A twist in the Acton case, ma'am. Five paintings from a robbery two years ago in Old Bond Street, the Gorton Gallery theft, were found just now. But the big thing is that the other painting stolen at the time was called 'Seal Island', by Alfred Bierstadt, from the USA; it is worth a great deal. But that one is not at the Acton site and nothing there gives us a lead, so far.

"DCI Coltrane and I are going to interview the Nahigians again later, but I doubt we will get anything from them. Are you heading back today?"

She answered, "Yes, I expect we will be heading out soon."

"Then you may want to have Isabelle give you the background on that theft; she was on the investigation, not me; it was before my time. But it is a big item for us as part of this haul, DCI Coltrane says; and it will be a big question for the Task Force now."

"Thanks, Mark, for the heads up. I will do so."

As she put her mobile away, Pryce finished his call.

"Dilys Peter's just gave me the information on her aunt. She called her brother after you left. Belle Thomas has been having rough nights, not sleeping lately. The brother suggested afternoons, or around supper time, to talk to her."

His expression said, 'What now?'

The news from Harper was playing on her mind. They had gone far enough on this one, she realised.

"We will take the painting with us for analysis, as we have Mrs. Richard's written permission to do so. At present we have no crime, no understanding of the linkage of the painting to a crime, no victim, nothing really; just a mysterious letter with hints.

"It's time for us to go home and you to get back to your hit and run. But if you could pop over to Machynlleth…"

Pryce said, "We found the driver last night on that one. But I do have lots more work. I can go over, talk to the aunt later, or, if not, in the next day or so."

"That would be much appreciated, Pawl; thank you."

As they left the station they said goodbye to Inspector Meredith, giving her the gist of the situation and, in the corridor, they saw PC Fowles.

"Thank you again, for dinner, Seren. It was very nice of you."

"You are very welcome, DI Sayer. Come back and visit sometime. And you too, Isabelle."

Ten minutes later they were on the A483, heading south.

"We will go back through Leominster," said Catrin, "Show you some more of Wales on the way."

~~

Sayer waited until they had turned east on the A44 before raising the subject of the Gorton Gallery.

"Mark's call; it was to tell me that they found five paintings taken from the Gorton Gallery theft. You were on that investigation he said."

"The 'Hackney Heist'? Yes, I was. But five paintings? There were six stolen, I recall."

Catrin realized that she knew a little of the case from the newspapers; Mark had not used the nickname given to the robbery by the press. Catrin would probably have known more about it if she had still been with the ACU, but it coincided with her starting work with Assistant Commissioner Hunt. She had been immersed in her new role.

She said, "The painting still missing is 'Seal Island' by an Alfred Bierstadt. Can you give me the story on the robbery?"

Howlett took a moment to sort out her thoughts.

It had been referred to at the time as the 'Hackney Heist' in the tabloid press, a name sneered at in the upmarket media; they thought it was a quite unsuitable name for a Bond Street art robbery; it lowered the tone. There again, though, it was not an elegant crime, nothing high tech; no clever entry to the gallery during the night or over the long holiday weekend before the robbery, which took place on a Tuesday morning. If it lacked refinement, it made up for it in damage and shock value, so perhaps the name was not too inappropriate.

Added to that was the battle between the angry 'sound bite experts' among the anti-seal hunt activists and the more measured protested innocence of the sealskin industry, a subject always a lightning rod for media interest. Three of the paintings stolen did not even belong to the gallery. Two of these were recent paintings of seals in the Orkney Islands by a wildlife artist from Dundee, Cheryl McKinnon, and had been donated by the artist for a fundraiser. They were to be auctioned, the resulting funds to go to the International Fund for Animal Welfare, a long-standing anti-seal hunt environmental group.

Jocelyn Gorton, co-owner of the gallery with her brother Russell, was a close personal friend of the president of IFAW.

She offered to display the works for a month to increase the visibility of the auction and also have collection boxes there, where smaller donations to IFAW could be made.

It turned out that she was also an acquaintance of the wife of an American diplomat, John Herron, from a wealthy family that owned the Bierstadt painting, 'Seal Island'. Over coffee, tea or something stronger in some social setting, the plan was hatched to loan 'Seal Island' to the gallery and display all three together, using the rarity of this particular Bierstadt as an additional 'pull' for the campaign support.

The CCTV footage, some later released on television, showed two London taxis driving down Bond Street. About twenty yards from the Gorton gallery, the first taxi sped up and veered to the far side of the road before turning hard, wheels squealing, to accelerate into the gallery plate glass window.

Two men with ski masks came from the taxi behind as it pulled up. They ran over, one into the gallery, the other to pull open the side rear passenger door. The taxi had been modified; there was no screen between the driver and passenger sections and the driver of the crashed vehicle came out that way. One man threw a smoke bomb into the middle of the north side of Bond Street, the wind carrying the black cloud released in the same direction, causing confusions and chaos in the traffic and the crowd. All the men except the driver of the second vehicle went into the gallery.

Thirty seconds later, witnesses caught glimpses of the men exiting, carrying paintings as they climbed into the undamaged taxi. It was also partly caught on CCTV cameras; there were no lack of them in Bond Street, but the smoke plumes meant that visibility was hindered until the wind moved it along the street. The taxi took off leaving people in shock or helping others get out of the smoke.

Cameras also saw them turn left into Piccadilly, hurtling along past the Ritz. The taxi was then hidden by bus traffic and, for a crucial time afterwards, was lost from view. It took twenty minutes to work out that the escape vehicle had made a

U-turn and had headed back along Piccadilly. It turned on to Stratton Street and entered an underground private parking lot, one which required an access key card. That was where the abandoned taxi was found, neatly parked. It had many fingerprints; none appeared fresh, nor did they flag any 'person of interest'. They had all worn gloves, anyway; that was evident from the CCTV.

A search of the area took place and detailed analysis of CCTV coverage was conducted. A more focused search of the building and the neighbouring areas took somewhat longer, but nothing was found to help the investigation. The taxi, despite the circuitous escape route, had been dumped no more than a few hundred yards from the scene of the crime.

Media coverage over the next few days highlighted that there was a suspicion of deficiencies in the gallery security equipment. Also, a known sealskin couturier had been shopping in Bond Street at the time (he later said that was all he was doing; shopping) and an article about even 'coins from children donated towards saving baby seals' were stolen.

It was true that one of the collection boxes was grabbed during the raid; but it was dropped during the exit and left in the rubble. Whether or not it contained children's coins was not the point; the loss of the far more valuable works, particularly the Bierstadt painting, was the issue. Accusations that the theft was not about owning or re-selling stolen art, but about thwarting anti-sealing activities dominated the story in the media.

Howlett said, "We never found anything to help. The taxis were stolen, but we couldn't get any leads there - and nothing from the gallery. What came out of the investigation was that, chaotic as it sounded, everything was carefully orchestrated, down to the way they carried the paintings out and their re-entry sequence into the escape vehicle.

"DCI Coltrane said that discarding the collection box outside the gallery was a deliberate diversion, designed to give the media the sort of sensationalism they like. The operation was as smooth as a circus routine.

"We got nothing from forensics, nothing from the CCTV, nothing from anyone's informants that proved to be useful. The outcry was largely about the audacity of it all. And the seal debate."

She paused.

"There was the loss of the paintings for sale at the gallery and those for auction, but the big loss was the loaned item, the Bierstadt painting, worth around three million dollars according to insurance estimates. It wasn't for sale; it is a family heirloom, brought over from the USA while Herron was Deputy Chief of Mission there. A goodwill gesture, I gather, that didn't work out too well. DCI Coltrane said that Agent Klintz with the FBI was put under some pressure 'to assist' at the time, which he couldn't really do, of course. Not his jurisdiction."

Catrin said, "And now five paintings have turned up. But we know nothing of the whereabouts of 'Seal Island'. DCI Coltrane and Mark are interviewing everyone taken in yesterday again specifically about these items."

She sighed. "And now the American interest will be re-awakened, no doubt."

Howlett said, "You can count on it. And you have your first Task Force conference call this Friday; with David Klintz in the chair."

They drove on a bit further in silence.

Catrin said, "I may know about Bratby, but I know nothing about this artist Bierstadt; what about him?"

Howlett said, somewhat mechanically, "Neither did I before the case. An American-German artist, nineteenth century; quite popular in the USA, actually. Known mainly for his romantic landscapes of the Great Plains, Rocky Mountains, that sort of classical artist. Very popular with people who like that sort of thing."

Catrin looked at her, checking Howlett for humour, but she

saw none.

She said, "A long way from Bratby then…"

Howlett chuckled. "In art, in price and in political pressure. Not 'kitchen sink'. Think more of Teddy Roosevelt at camp, at sunset, in the Grand Canyon. Or in this case, on the west coast of the US. Bierstadt did a number of sea paintings there, some involving seals. But not a Corn Flakes packet or a beer bottle in sight."

Catrin mused, "Bratby, Bierstadt, I'm starting with the 'B's…"

"Working your way down, ma'am, to Warhol and Zox. Career progression."

After a few minutes Howlett said, "It's ironical. Bratby turned up during that investigation too, come to think of it. A work that is still there, in the Gorton Gallery; the thieves left that one alone. It had been given by the artist to the original gallery owner, the father of the current owners. It was always on display there, we heard. Not valuable then, of course, and relatively speaking it still isn't. It looked quite out of place with the other works they had, but the old man was proud of it, particularly when there was all that fuss about Bratby's murals in the film years ago."

"Oh, right," said Catrin, "The Alec Guinness one…"

Howlett said, "About the eccentric artist Gulley Jimson, called The Horse's Mouth; a lovely old film. Bratby was a real showman, promoting himself back then. I haven't had a case involving a Bratby painting since the Hackney Heist until now."

"We haven't got a case, really," said Catrin, "just enough to report back to Noel Richards that his sister isn't involved in a theft, it seems, and the family may have a Bratby that someone has tried to falsify the signature on, for some weird reason. Let's talk to Mark if he is at his desk."

She called Harper on the speakerphone.

"Mark, Isabelle has clued me in. During the prelim interviews with the people we arrested on Tuesday, did you get a read on who is most likely to talk?"

Harper said, "No-one said anything ma'am; it was a waste of our time and the solicitor's time, as expected. The third man is just a warehouseman. If he can recall any names, that would help. He is not too sharp, but we may get something useful from him if he can be persuaded.

"The woman might be a better bet. She is as shrewd as the other two men, the brothers, but very temperamental. DCI Coltrane thinks that stirring it up a bit might get something from her. He said he may want you or Isabelle with him in the next round with her, tomorrow."

Catrin said, "Thanks Mark. We are heading back now. We should be in the Yard later."

~~

"This signature issue."

They were looking at the painting with Harper, now they were back in the office.

Howlett said, "When I did my quick test I thought it might be something else, perhaps enamel or another type, even household paint. It isn't; the signature is oil paint but as I said, it is not recent."

Catrin nodded.

"Well, let's get Bertie and his people to have a look; see what comes from that. What do you think, Mark?"

He shook his head.

"Hard to say, ma'am. I mean, with the amount of stuff out of Acton and now the Bierstadt; it's a lot to do. We haven't even contacted the original owners yet of the pieces we have found. Even if it's a Bratby, it is hardly big money... and not even a case. Sorry, but you did ask."

He glanced at Howlett and Catrin could see they were of a similar mind.

She nodded, convinced.

"I have one more stop on this; Wicklow and the Minister; then it's done."

Later, as she checked her email, she found that Pawl Pryce had been good as his word.

"I went to see Belle Thomas at her son's place. She was trying to be helpful but didn't give us anything useful, just a loose list of people she recalled who visited Judith Richards and may have brought things at times - mainly village and church people; very vague. But she couldn't recall any strangers carrying a painting into the house. Anything else you need?"

She emailed back.

"Thanks, Pawl. But no, we see no further avenues to pursue at present. Sayer."

18 VIDEOCONFERENCE

"Ballard, watch your... too late!"

The man at the head of the conference table on Screen 3 was remonstrating with his colleague, FBI agent Walkley Ballard who, in leaning forward, had allowed the corner of his holstered service weapon to knock over a coffee cup. Catrin watched the liquid run across the table surface in the room in FBI Headquarters and down a slot through which cables and power bars were gathered. The FBI had as many people attending the videoconference in their location as the total present from the police services in Europe, it seemed.

She wondered if Screen 3 would blank out. It didn't. Various comments to Ballard, some helpful, others colourful, from people gathered in the Washington conference room were heard in the background.

The man at the head of the table, David Klintz, looked up at the camera.

"Pardon our French, folks... Walkley, get some paper towels; your pack of tissues is not going to cut it. Give us a moment. These... lumps of iron."

From his face it appeared that there would have been various epithets added to his last sentence if he wasn't on screen in an international meeting.

There was silence on Screen 2 from the Germans; the chuckles and comment from the French on Screen 4 were related to Klintz's use of the phrase involving their language, Catrin heard. She knew none of them yet, but the French officers seemed pleasant; less 'officious', if you can use that term in a group like this; they were with the O.C.B.C.; the 'Office Central de lutte contre le trafic des Biens Culturels'; the equivalent of Art and Antiques.

The only person she had met internationally in the art crime world so far was an Italian policeman, Major Vittorio Cuoco, during a visit to Rome over two years ago, at the start of the investigation into the recovery of the paintings by George Stubbs. Coltrane had not yet explained how the Italians escaped being involved in this Task Force.

It was Friday. The videoconference call of the Task Force included the USA, UK, Germany and France; all areas with active investigations linked to the same art crime file. It had been meeting weekly for three months now; early Friday morning Washington time; early afternoon European time.

It was Catrin's first time participating in this meeting, but she had past experience of multi-site videoconference calls over the two years with Hunt. She knew that every call began with chaos; each group doing its own thing until the chair called the meeting to order, after which silence and meeting discipline came into play.

FBI Senior Agent David Klintz was a legend in the art crime world. For Catrin, being included in the Task Force discussions not only brought her into contact with this art detective, but made her realise just how far she had come in her career. He was credited with closing down several large international art fraud operations and had recovered major art stolen from museums on the east and west coast of the USA.

Klintz was also known to be very vocal about his dislike of firearms in general, in civilian use or for routine law enforcement; one of few police officers in the United States to speak out so, she thought. It was a pity for Ballard that it hadn't been his elbow that knocked over the coffee cup; a weapon involved made it a more heinous crime in the senior agent's eyes, no doubt.

Klintz said, humorously, "Neville, what are you smiling about? You are to kick off, I think?"

Catrin thought that, although she followed the French team's mutterings, Coltrane was fluent in French and Italian; he was probably following every ribald nuance of their sotto voce conversation.

Coltrane said, "I was just thinking how the holster that DI Sayer used to wear seemed more chic than Agent Ballard's, David. Walkley's looks more like a high-tech fracture splint than a holster to me. But let me - ."

Klintz interjected, with feigned shock, "You are armed, DI Sayer? The Brits are arming their art detectives now. What has the world come to?"

Catrin smiled. "I was, sir, in my last role; but not now."

The FBI man responded somewhat sarcastically, looking slowly around the table at his gathered team. "Well, come on over to Washington, Sayer, you will fit right in with this lot. But sorry, Neville. Walkley... are we ready to go at our end now, or what?"

"We are ready to go here, David," said Coltrane.

"Fine," said Klintz, "Let's do a role call around the links for the minutes that Walkley will take. You can formally introduce your new team members."

Coltrane, Madder and Sayer were at the London end, in a videoconference suite at Scotland Yard. Coltrane referred to notes as he addressed the UK update, the first proper agenda item.

"To summarize the progress at our end. The close-out of the supply line side through the Acton warehouse is pretty much complete, with two major gaps in high-end items. This is offset by some other finds; unexpected, but ones we were pleased to have. All the antiques impounded are accounted for, including some unexpected antiquities we will need to take up with the authorities in India separately.

"The jewelry haul is more hit and miss. We have identified about sixty percent of the items and note particularly some items taken from the same theft of the Ansell necklace in Knightsbridge; but the necklace is not with the other items.

"Not too bad, as a number of the jewelry items are clearly off the radar; they are not registered anywhere. And we are making good progress on the fine art identification.

"In terms of paintings, we have a Bruegel copy that Gerhardt's people will want back in due course, plus a number of smaller works. The big gap is a Bierstadt painting. I know that will be a particular disappointment to your team, David.

"Everything that we know to be of non-UK origin, in terms of the original thefts, has been flagged to you and DC Colin Truman is coordinating that. He briefed me that the coordination with your teams is going well."

He paused.

"I will take any questions."

Klintz said, "So we are still left, I take it from your 'major gap' comment, with 'Seal Island' unaccounted for?"

"That is correct, I am afraid. We will continue our investigations."

The lead for the German team, Gerhardt Amsel, spoke up. "It is worth more than two million euros, Neville. That would increase significantly the haul if we could track it down. We have all incurred considerable costs in this operation to date."

"I am well aware of that, Gerhardt," said Coltrane, a little frostily.

"It would be even more valuable to us politically, of course, but it sounds as if Neville's team has done well," said Agent Ballard.

He left unsaid that the wealthy diplomat, the owner of the work loaned to the Gorton Gallery, was a now stationed back with the Department of State in Washington.

High expenditures on an international investigation need to be connected to successful recovery of valuable art. Catrin was still settling into this aspect of her new role. Investigations at the ACU earlier in her career had always been focused on the criminals and, while the art value was a factor, it was not as primary a focus as she was seeing in the discussions of the Task Force.

The German couldn't leave it alone, it seemed.

"Six paintings were taken that day. Without 'Seal Island', it will weaken any prosecution case considerably for the others."

Klintz in Washington was nodding, in agreement. Coltrane knew it was correct; he was just kicking back at the German. The Gorton Gallery robbery was in London, not a German city, even if the artist was of German-American origin.

Coltrane moved on; he first invited DS Madder to talk briefly about the interview 'non-progress' and then asked Catrin to give an update on the work plan to re-interview witnesses to the UK thefts, to see if any new information turned up. He had briefed her that she would be leading that, starting next week.

Both kept their comments to the minimum. It was *pro forma* stuff and there were no questions at the end.

Agent Ballard said, "DS Madder and DI Sayer, welcome to the Task Force. I think I threw Agent Klintz off his stride to do that by pouring my coffee on the table. By the way, I love your accent, DI Sayer; Welsh, I understand."

Coltrane let out an audible sigh.

"Over to you, Eric," addressing the French lead, "then we can love your accent, too."

Coltrane looked at his watch. Another two regional updates from Europe and forty-five minutes to go on the conference call. The weekend loomed.

19 THE CWMBRAN KILN

"So, do you like your new job?" Liz Marshall asked.

Catrin was putting a finishing touch of decorative elements on a vase that would receive its final firing overnight.

It was the following day, Saturday, in the Spitalfields Arts Market, a day when Catrin usually spent some time at the Cymbran Kiln, designing or decorating ceramics. Jean and Catrin worked together on the concept for the piece, Jean then did the structural work in clay and Catrin did any decorative finishing. In comparison with the regular output of the boutique pottery, every Sayer-Hughes work was unique and was sold exclusively through the gallery 'Liz's Place'.

Liz was picking up two new pieces that Catrin and Jean had made in the last few weeks; together they formed a single work for sale. Jean's partner Melanie was packing the pieces for Liz in a box as the gallery owner continued talking, not waiting for a reply.

"After you became Hunt's aide, you and Jean were more consistent in your output. When you weren't away for work, that is. I don't know what it will be like now you have joined Art and Antiques. Not as bad, I hope, as when you were working in the Art Crime Unit with Worsley and my brother, the slave-drivers."

146

Detective Inspector Keith Marshall had been the original link between Catrin and the gallery, flagging their work to his sister.

Catrin said mischievously, "We will have to find out, won't we, Liz? My new job could take me away to places, just like with Hunt; a lot of their cases have international dimensions. Why, I was back in Wales for a couple of days this week."

Liz said, tartly, "Wales is international now, is it?"

Then she added, "Hunt always likes to be back for the weekends, wherever she goes. You told me that. She lives in St. Paul's Cathedral at the weekend, you said, with all her commitments there."

She wrinkled her nose, thinking how to bait Catrin further.

"I am not so sure now. You will swan off on international art crime work, lying on beaches sunning yourself and picking up strange men. And you still haven't said if you like the change."

Catrin looked over at Jean and raised one eyebrow, looking for sympathy and getting none.

She said, "And coppers are supposed to be the ones giving people the third degree treatment? I am still new, settling into the job, Liz. The furthest abroad I have been yet in this role is a conference call with counterparts in other places."

Melanie said, "There, you got the answer; deflection again. Clearly it's not going well. She used to say how snobby that lot is."

Catrin said, defensively, "I did, I must admit, but it's not that; it's just not the easiest transition. I thought it would be back to case assignment work, you know; a priority case or two, others to work as you can, just like with the ACU but... less chaos. In fact, it is more chaotic. I barely start one thing and find myself on another. I almost miss being in Hunt's office, with its careful plans and scheduling reviews."

Liz came closer to Catrin's work bench, squinting as she inspected more closely the vase being decorated.

"Give up the police rubbish and do this full time. Have more fun and increase my profits."

Jean looked up from a platter, one of her regular items she was making, and burst out laughing at their gallery owner's banter.

Liz Marshall said more seriously, "So what did you like most in the last job, with Hunt, now you are back to art crime work? No. Answer this; what have you learned from it?"

Catrin thought a moment then listed off her thoughts.

"Airs and graces are nothing. Authority, decision-making capability and good manners are everything. People are nice or not, but that's nothing to do with you, so don't ever be intimidated by others. Put that lot together in the right mix and you can be comfortable in a hard environment like the Brixton nick or in Number Ten Downing Street. That's what I saw each day in Sandra Hunt's behaviour."

Liz nodded. Her husband William was a member of the aristocracy, they all knew, and yet he hated the thought of pompous airs and graces. Good manners and good friendships were everything for him.

Melanie had been listening. "You hadn't said you have been to Number Ten."

Catrin smiled, "Twice now."

Then she said, "Superintendent Taylor, Worsley's boss, had it right when he spoke to me when I changed jobs last time."

They were looking at her, waiting.

"Go to the bathroom before the speeches start and don't spill gravy on your uniform."

"Speaking of which," said Liz, "That maroon stain you are applying; there is a spot on your apron; don't shake your arm as you are talking."

"It's what it's for, Liz. And if you weren't pestering us, it would be quiet in here."

"And two very tiny spots on your pants leg need attention," Liz added, "courtesy of my eagle eyes."

"Damn," said Catrin, reaching for a rag.

~~

It was after Catrin left the workshop and Jean and Melanie were closing up for the day that a neighbouring shop-owner in Spitalfields Market popped into the Cwmbran Kiln. Cassandra Seaton was co-owner of 'Silk Creations', a hand-painted silk garments shop. Melanie knew that Cassandra and her sister had opened up the business together just four months ago, when they had come along and introduced themselves to other shop owners.

She remembered the sister's comment from that meeting.

"You have been in business eight years here? My God, that's success! It's a real struggle to get going. There is a big turnover in art boutiques, we know."

Meaning at the Spitalfields Arts Market there were lots of great ideas and innovations starting as businesses, but the rents were not low and, if the products didn't catch on, lack of sales revenue led quickly to businesses going under.

"It's a real struggle, whether you are here for weeks or years," said Melanie. "You have to work to the seasonal peaks and prepare your stock levels accordingly. For example, the late spring tourist flush can sometimes surpass the expected mid-summer sales levels in some years, we have found. There are less people walking through, but they spend more."

The Seaton sisters were showing a lot of enthusiasm since they opened, Melanie had noted.

Cassandra said to her, "We had this idea for a focal display unit for the boutique; a ceramic and wood unit in the front centre of our shop to drape our silks on. We wonder whether you would be interested in helping us build it."

She pulled out the drawing and the three women clustered together, Jean immediately asking questions and pointing out what would work and what wouldn't technically.

Melanie, ever the businesswoman, said, "We would like to help, to do something like this, but it can't really be a freebee; we have our costs, too. It would be quite a bit of work; particularly as you want two of these elements and they are similar, but not simply duplicates."

"We don't have a lot of free cash, to be honest," said Cassandra.

"Tell me about it, we know," said Melanie. "And we like silk scarves, but don't need a drawer full of them. Well, another drawer of them. What we really need is a clear-out."

She eyed her partner accusingly. Jean was not known for letting clothes go; in fact, she would keep everything forever, if she could.

Cassandra thought for a moment, or appeared to. Melanie thought that the proposal that emerged had probably been in her back pocket during the discussion, ready to play at the right time.

"You know I am full-time here; Natalie is part-time. She works in Joachim's, the travel agency in Holborn, and she gets freebees and discounts that are transferable to friends and relatives. You don't fancy a holiday or a trip somewhere? You would only have to pay the VAT. We could fix a good deal that way."

She looked at the two owners of the Cwmbran Kiln and from their faces knew she had a deal in play. She wondered where they wanted to go, and whether it would be worth enough pottery elements to build three units, rather than two.

~~

On the Sunday afternoon, Catrin went along to watch Chris's five-a-side team play a visiting team from Chelmsford. The visitors were a police team, on a series of games played around London for a week as a fundraiser for charity, so he had persuaded her to come along to show support.

"It will take your mind off things at work; cheer you up. And it's a team of people in the job."

Their job, police work, he meant.

Catrin didn't often go to watch Chris play - he was good, she knew, and passionate about the game, but his matches were normally on Saturdays and, by mutual agreement from the outset of their relationship, Saturdays were 'art at the Kiln' for her; football for him. Sundays were their day together. Chris would sometimes accompany her to St. Paul's Cathedral for the service, if she went, but more often than not he chose to do housework, catch up on laundry in the morning.

Catrin found herself watching the match, but her mind kept slipping back to the last week and the changes.

"Not interested? Neither am I, really." A voice next to her penetrated her thoughts.

From the woman's accent Catrin could tell she was with the visiting team.

"Which one is yours?" Catrin asked.

"The big lug in goal, my husband. And yours?"

"The forward on the left, my husband, too."

Catrin looked at the woman and instinctively she knew from the hair, her clothes and her demeanour that she was a police officer.

"You are both in the Essex mob, then?"

The woman laughed. "Yes both police officers, you spotted that one. And you?"

"With the Met; so is Speedy Gonzales over there; a 'civvy'."

She laughed again. "And this isn't a police team, Ed told me."

"No, it's coincidence. Chris told me your team was and he persuaded me to come along. What do you do?"

"For work, you mean? A sergeant in the headquarters, in Chelmsford; traffic logistics now. I used to be at the old Maldon station, on the Blackwater, a beautiful area. Community policing, then. I miss that really, but I wanted the promotion; Ed and I have a mortgage... And you?"

Catrin said, "Just been made DI at Scotland Yard. Worked there as a sergeant and as a DC. Now I am back investigating art crime."

"That must be interesting! More than traffic logistics."

Catrin said, "It is, but I know what you mean about missing being at a station. I started in Brixton. Not a nice area, like the Blackwater but... everyone knew everyone in the station. I miss that sometimes. People stopping for a chat."

Clearly the two women understood each other. Catrin thought, this was supposed to take my mind of work. The standoffishness around Art and Antiques was a big contrast to the collegiality in Hunt's team and the camaraderie in the Art Crime Unit. She couldn't really decide whether it was because she was an 'outsider' or whether she was now holding inspector rank.

There was a cheer as the visiting team scored and Catrin saw Chris grimace. He had missed an interception and the visitors took advantage of it. Catrin smiled to cheer him up, she hoped.

~~

The email to Catrin and Li from Melanie two days later said happily that she and Jean would be able to attend the wedding after all; they had a windfall; a package deal organized to get them to Hong Kong, including three nights in a hotel. They had traded some work with another shop and their part of it was the holiday.

20 DONKEY WORK

It was the following Monday, early, that Howlett came into Catrin's office with the final results of the search of the names 'Ash' or 'Ashe' linked to Judge Richards.

"I came up with four names after some careful enquiries. Her former clerk in Birmingham was very helpful. I told her we were following up on an old enquiry in which both the names Ashe and Judge Richards appeared."

She looked at her list.

"A John Ash, a long-time court police officer, retired five years before Judge Richards left. A Robert Ashe, a solicitor in Birmingham, who had appeared before her numerous times. We could chase him up, if you have the money."

"Money?"

"He retired to Florida. I asked if she knew him at all. She said, a bit, like the other regulars among lawyers and barristers. Did he have an interest in art, I asked? She roared with laughter. Only if rugby union is an art. That was all he liked, she thought, that and his family. She was surprised he moved from England."

Catrin said nothing. Howlett looked at her notes.

"A Corinne Ashe, female. She was convicted of driving while intoxicated. Finally, the name Edwin Ashe, as per Judge

Richards' letter; a male age thirty-four, a bail hearing on a fraud charge seven years ago. That was the only time he appeared before her. Bail was denied. And he has no links to any of the others, as far as we can tell."

Catrin thought about it.

"Nothing leaps out, does it?"

"No, ma'am. I can't see a bail hearing as anything that would link back to a judge. A ten year sentence when a six was likely, well, there could be a grudge, which would tie in with Judith Richard's note. But not a bail. And she wasn't a high court judge, wouldn't be dealing with longer sentencing terms. The clerk said the man got bail at the next remand hearing anyway, the following week."

After a moment Catrin said, "File it, Isabelle, we have done due diligence. Thanks for seeing it through."

Howlett said, "Thank you too, for taking me along to Wales. That meal at the church was worth it."

Catrin looked at her watch. "Time for the briefing."

~~

Neville Coltrane was summarising the situation and his work plan for the Art and Antiques Unit on the Acton case.

"We now have the Nahigian brothers and their assistants on remand for a week before they all go back for bail review. We need to find something to make at least one of them talk or provide leads back to the UK thefts; anything to keep all of them in custody. We will be able to hold Kristoff without a problem; he is the legal owner of the warehouse. His brother Jorge - perhaps. But Eniel Smyth, the warehouseman, and Julie Malkovich, the 'office assistant' as she referred to herself, I doubt it. And we may get more from them than the Nahigians, if they break."

He took a breath.

"I want information on what we didn't find and, given the haul, what should have been there; particularly two big ticket items, the Ansell necklace and the painting 'Seal Island'."

Coltrane was addressing his whole team and the three uniform officers drafted in for the duration; they had particular experience in documentation and records, something there would be volumes of, given the number of stolen items found at the warehouse. Howlett's expectation that she would be immersed in that aspect was now history; the team's detectives would have a plate-load of more appropriate investigative work to handle.

Bail had been refused for all four people arrested at the Acton warehouse. They were now charged with a range of offences related to receiving and handling of stolen goods. DCI Coltrane had taken the unprecedented step (for him) of attending the bail hearings.

He said nothing there, but the Crown prosecutor made it clear that the police had significant concerns about both flight risk and the possibilities of violence 'to render the accused unavailable to assist further the enquiries into the case'; the barrister's polite way of saying they could be intimidated or eliminated. It was the only occasion that the older brother, clearly the leader, spoke at all to his defense counsel, who then jumped up.

"My client assures me that he and his colleagues have nothing to fear in that regard, your worship."

Provided they don't talk to the police, Neville thought. He noted that it would have been more beneficial for his clients if the solicitor had addressed the issue of flight risk with the same level of confidence; but he hadn't.

"DS Madder and his team will handle the interviews with the Nahigian brothers and Smyth and the identification of items found that, as yet, have no known owner. The interviews, I expect, will be one-sided and boring, but it is necessary work for the preparation of the case. Sayer, you and I will talk with Malkovich; see if we can get through to her. Truman, you will continue to be the liaison coordinator with items known to arise from thefts overseas, feeding whatever is needed to others on the Task Force as they pursue their own local enquiries. The rest of DS Madder's team will work on the customer end; the people we know to have received stolen items in the last two months. Start the evidence preparations for warrants for our next set of arrests.

"Are we clear so far?"

He looked up for the nods and murmurs of 'yes' and 'sir'.

"DI Sayer and her team will handle the follow-up with the original owners of items of known UK origin, independent of whether they are art or antiques, particularly to see if fresh eyes on the original cases throw up any new information which will crack open new leads, new charges."

He surveyed the room.

"I know it is putting on one side the normal divisions of work, but this is one big case, one of the largest we have ever had, so we are one team on this one. A lot of going back over information; the donkey work. But it is crucial. Don't miss anything. And I want you all working well together."

His eyes fell on Madder as he made the statement. One of his team members who had been at the Van Dongen 'test' on Catrin's first day blushed, she saw. Coltrane must have heard about it in her absence.

Then he added, "Sayer, the most important things for you in this lot is to re-visit the Gorton Gallery case and the location of 'Seal Island'. Secondly, any information you get that may bring new light to the investigation you should feed directly to Madder's team for use in the interviews. If you can find things to make them crack open it will be a breakthrough that we really need."

After they separated to start their assignments, Catrin signaled to Harper and they walked over to Kit Madder.

She said, "Is there any particular recent case in this list with actual witnesses to the thefts? People who may be stimulated to recall more information from a second interview? You two have the background here."

She made sure she was sounding friendly, collaborative.

Madder kept his expression neutral but she didn't sense any hostility. He looked at DC Stephen Corrigan, one of his team members.

"Offhand, I would say the Thomas Tompion clock theft, ma'am. Steve?"

The DC nodded. "I agree, Sarge. We left that one feeling that if we had more time and something to trigger the owner's recall, they could have told us more. I would go back to them early on, too."

Harper said, "I will have to give it some thought, ma'am, regarding the paintings; nothing springs to mind at present."

Madder continued, "We found Jorge's prints on the clock yesterday, not only on its travel case. They could be there from when he stole the item, if he did, but his solicitor will argue the print occurred in the warehouse, of course."

Catrin nodded. "We will look into that first, then. Thank you."

~~

Once they had wrapped up, Coltrane asked Sayer to stay behind.

"Minister Richard's issue; what's the status?"

She brought him up to speed.

"Bertie checked the painting yesterday afternoon. It is a John Bratby painting, after all; his signature is underneath the 'Ashe' signature. Howlett looked into any links between people with the name Ashe and Judith Richards, in her professional capacity as a judge or as a barrister previously; her legal staff, cases tried, that sort of thing. The closest link was a man with the same name, someone whom she denied bail seven years ago, but he was only in remand for a week. Other than that name, it's the end of the road, at present. There doesn't seem to be a crime associated with her ownership of the painting, despite her note.

"I need to tell Wicklow or the Minister, I think, seeing as they asked for me specifically. I prefer to do that with Richards himself, to make sure he is happy about it."

Coltrane replied, "I agree. Do you want me to be there when the news is conveyed?"

"Not unless you want to be, no. I think it would be best one-on-one, if the DG allows that; he is all over this one."

Coltrane said, "I don't want to be there, particularly with this lot going on. When will you do it?"

"When he fits me in; he is the minister. I will work it in around the other assignments but as soon as possible really. It was a blip on the main work as I started here. If I finish it off, even in the state it is in now, I would be happy."

Coltrane nodded. "I will call Tom Wicklow; it will probably be squeezed in later this afternoon or this evening, if the minister is not in the house for some reason. If he is, you may end up briefing him there. I take it you will tell him that we will log it? There may be other paintings treated the same way out there."

"Yes, we have already put it in the system, but I won't hold my breath. The whole thing is too weird; it is likely a one-off."

She smiled. "I will tell him it seems to be a part of the inheritance. It could be restored easily enough, Bertie said."

~~

DCI Coltrane was not far off the mark. Catrin ended up in the Houses of Parliament that evening, being kept waiting for over half an hour for the Commons session to finish and eventually seeing Noel Richards alone in his parliamentary office.

When she informed him of her visit and the developments, he said, "So what happens now, DI Sayer?"

"Not much, sir, to be honest, unless some linkage between your sister and this man Ashe emerges, leading to any on-going concern. Your letter and painting will be returned to you; they form part of the bequest. You could get it restored.

"We have flagged this issue of a Bratby being over-signed by the Ashe signature in the national crime database, but without attribution, other than its discovery in a set of household belongings in Tregynon, to protect confidentiality."

He nodded, seeing it was going nowhere and that nothing new was likely to develop.

He mused, "Judith was not a person to break the law. Whatever the reason was, it was not about possession of the art; it was something else."

Catrin nodded.

He added, "I don't want it back. If it can be restored and sold to a collector and the funds go to a charity, I think that would be best. I will ask Maeve what cause she would like to suggest and between us, we will pick one and let you know. Could that be handled by someone knowledgeable, do you think?"

She thought about it.

"I don't see why not. There would be some paperwork to transfer it to whomever. If it's for charity, I will see if I can get the restoration work completed for free or at minimal cost. Do you want the recognition of the gift to be attributed to you?"

He laughed. "Politicians always seek positive limelight, don't we? Well, in this case, no. Make it anonymous. It was the way my sister set this up, in a sense, and if it goes to someone who likes the art and a charity benefits from it, that is as much as I can do, I think. I am just happy it wasn't linked with any criminal activity."

Catrin was quite impressed by the comment and the tone of the man.

"We will see what we can do.. I will talk to DCI Coltrane; he is well-connected in art charity activities and could handle it, I am sure, or get someone else to do so."

Within minutes Catrin was walking out through St. Stephen's Hall into the night, passing the clock tower of Big Ben as she headed for home. She was glad to have cleared that one from her slate; or so she thought.

21 TOMPION

"Our clock; it has been found? Oh my goodness! After all this time!"

Mrs. Newbold was clapping her hands as she heard the news. Her husband was looking at her as if she had gone mad. Catrin and Harper just waited.

Catrin was struck once again by the vagaries of the art world. A fusée mantle clock by a seventeenth century English maker, Thomas Tompion, now worth probably the best part of one hundred thousand pounds, had been stolen from this ordinary-looking old house in New Barnet. The house was worth a lot more than Chris and Catrin could afford, of course, even if they had set their sights on this 'posher' London borough. Nevertheless, it was not a palatial home; not one of the stockbroker mansions people read about. The file said the timepiece was a family heirloom on the wife's side.

After hearing the news and the officer's request to remember what they could about the robbery, the couple took them from the drawing room where they first talked into a room across the hallway. They were now in a large front room, turned into a surprisingly modern-looking studio apartment with a single bed, a work desk, contemporary wall art and modern lamps. Ikea mainly, Catrin thought, but nicely mixed with personal items and some antiques, probably family items. It was a surprising contrast to the classical drawing room they had first been led into, to break the news.

Mrs. Newbold said, "The mantelpiece was over here; it has now been blocked and boarded-in properly, to make the alcove sides for Bernice's shelving and bookcase units. This is her room now. But the clock sat there. We were very proud of it."

She was waving vaguely in the direction of the middle of the wall.

"The insurance people said afterwards it was probably contributory to the theft; it was too visible from the road, even allowing for the front path and garden, they claimed. They used it as a 'mitigating factor' in the settlement. Martin wasn't pleased, were you?"

Martin Newbold had said virtually nothing so far, leaving his wife to answer the questions as the detectives tried to re-visit the crime.

"Shysters," said the husband.

His look said that was enough on that.

Cynthia Newbold had mentioned that since the robbery, their niece Bernice had moved in with them. She was a student at Woodhouse College, a sixth-form educational establishment, and Mrs. Newbold talked about how much they enjoyed her presence livening up the house. Catrin had noticed the ramp in the entrance hall, the widened doorway to the downstairs lavatory and what appeared to be an adjacent cupboard extended and converted to a shower unit. In the corner of the modern room was a small wheelchair.

The Tompion clock was ornately characteristic and numbered. The family still had the purchase receipt made out to Cynthia's great-grandfather. Tompion had been the first English clockmaker to uniquely number his works, so the ownership was indisputable. It was also one of the few items where an identification of the burglar had been made, albeit vaguely; which is why Catrin, as part of their assignment and with Madder's advice, was paying them a visit.

The night of the robbery, Mr. and Mrs. Newbold had come home early from a social function. Every Thursday evening, October to June, they were at the Hillingdon Choral Society choir rehearsal. Both were members. Martin was a baritone and Cynthia a contralto. Catrin hoped that Martin was more vocal when he sang than when he answered questions.

Mrs. Newbold recalled the event for them.

"As we turned the corner of the road I saw the man coming out of our garden gate and by the time Martin had parked he was in the street about twenty yards off, walking away, carrying a case of some sort. I got out and called after him, 'Hello. Are you looking for us?' as I thought it was a delivery or something. Sometimes people receive a letter or parcel in error and find it's addressed to someone further along the road, so they drop it off later.

"He turned round and looked at us briefly then turned back and walked on. When we looked, the front door was pulled to, but was still slightly open. That was when I realised. I called after him to stop but he ran then."

Mark had led them back through the sequence of events. The answers now didn't differ significantly from their statements at the time of the theft. They tried to get from the woman her recollection of the man and his face but Catrin saw it was not going to help them.

"Even if she sat down with a sketch artist, it doesn't seem she will recall anything useful," Harper whispered to Sayer at one point, as Mrs. Newbold fussed with tea things.

They were on the point of making their exit when the front door opened and Catrin heard the wheelchair come in.

"I'm back." A young woman's voice that came down the hall.

As she stood up, Catrin saw the young woman propel herself through the doorway, closing it behind her effortlessly as Mrs. Newbold said, "We have visitors, Bernie, police officers. Our clock, the one that was stolen, has been found."

The voice called out, "That's great news. I'll just change

chairs."

Catrin looked at Mark Harper who was poised to go, her eyes indicating they should stay. You never know, she thought.

In a couple of minutes, minus coat, Bernie wheeled herself into the drawing room in the smaller inside chair they had seen in the front room. They went through the introductions.

You weren't here at the time, I understand," said Harper.

Bernie smiled at him. "I would have been pretty hard to miss, wouldn't I, if I was?" she said, impishly.

"Right enough," came back Harper instantly. "We always spot the lookers; they are usually the villain of the piece. It would have been noted in the file for follow up. You would have got the third degree treatment."

They all laughed. Catrin liked his recovery.

"We had better be going, ma'am," he said, just as Bernie wheeled over and picked up the photograph of the clock, examining it.

"Do my aunt and uncle get this back now or do you need to keep it for evidence?"

Catrin said, "No, we have it documented. We mentioned that your family can arrange a secure collection of the item and inform the insurers."

She looked round the people in the room. "Well, goodbye."

As they moved down the hall with Mrs. Newbold leading, Catrin was behind Harper when she heard Bernie say to her uncle, "It doesn't look as big and heavy as I thought it would be, given what you said about him running away."

She stopped. Clearly in whatever Mrs. Newbold was saying to him, the comment had not registered with Harper.

"One moment," she said, pointing back to the room.

Once inside she spoke directly to the student.

"Bernie, what was it that your uncle said, about the man running away?"

Then she fastened her eyes on the taciturn Martin Newbold.

~~

Sayer and Coltrane watched as Harper and Madder interviewed Jorge Nahigian.

Neville said, "Harper said you spotted it; it didn't register with him."

Catrin said, "I am not surprised; he was closer to Mrs. Newbold. She never stopped talking and Martin Newbold never said anything, I realised. I was behind them as we left and heard the comment from the niece, so the effort to re-interview may have been worth it. More could come from the other follow-ups, Neville, so we will keep on it."

They could see the interview was coming to the critical stage so they stopped talking. Harper had been leading the questions, again getting no comment from Nahigian.

He asked him, "Would you care to tell us more about your whereabouts on the day?

"No comment."

"Then Mr. Nahigian, we are adding to your charges. Burglary, theft and forced entry of premises on Fitzjohn Avenue in High Barnet to steal the Thomas Tompion carriage clock found on your premises. You see, we are starting to move beyond the charges of receipt, storage and smuggling of stolen goods. The charges will only grow.

"And we will continue to oppose bail - for you. A new charge should help that."

They knew the brothers were close. The strategy going forward now was to separate them; one free on bail, the other in remand. They would also keep the woman in if they could, too, making it clear to her that Smyth, the warehouseman, had been released on bail; see if her volatility extended to resentments.

For the first time Jorge Nahigian broke stride in saying 'No comment'. He said nothing, thinking it through. Then he said the same words.

Cardew, his solicitor, said, "You have a basis for adding these charges at this stage, I take it, Sergeant."

Madder said, "We have a witness."

Nahigian looked at him as if he knew what Madder was talking about it, but didn't believe it to be credible.

"Your walk and run, after the car drew up, Mr. Nahigian; it is very characteristic, you see, having one leg slightly shorter than the other."

Nahigian looked at his lawyer, who said, "I think my client and I need more time alone, gentlemen."

"No," said Nahigian suddenly. "I don't. No comment."

They paused for a moment then Madder formally charged the man.

Catrin was looking on, grimacing at the outcome of the gambit.

Coltrane said, "I am not surprised, Catrin. But it is a crack, the start of something. Kristoff and Jorge are very close and neither one of them will squeal on the other. They decide things together. One taking a longer sentence than the other will make them think."

~~

The Facebook message from Li simply said, "It's a routine week for me, despite the preparations. Any chance we can talk on Wednesday evening, my time? Just you and me?"

Catrin thought about it a moment, realizing the significance of the innocent request. On Wednesdays, usually, Li had dinner at her parent's home. It had been there, calling from the Cwmbran Kiln, where she and Li had talked about the role that Michael Yau had played, at Li's request, to interfere with the plans for the attack on Catrin by the triad member Nam Wu.

She was a police officer and Li was a lawyer. Both of them were in positions where they should not be communicating with organized crime figures, even with a retired old man from a triad totally unconnected with the one that threatened Catrin. The 'just you and me' phrase signaled, though, that Li wanted a similar private, untraceable conversation.

She sent back, 'Sure, I will give you a call. I have to stop off before work anyway'. She didn't say where, but the phrase would be understood by Li, she knew. The time zones for Hong Kong and London worked out that way. And it told Li that she would call Li's parent's home from the Kiln, not on her own phone.

On the call, after Li explained the request from Yau for an introduction to his granddaughter, Catrin thought for a moment.

"Do you think she is involved?"

With the Triad; with organized crime.

"No, I don't," said Li. "I met with her separately. She raised the subject knowing, I gather, that I was a lawyer. She is smart. And I believe she really is into art; she talks about it and her goals convincingly. Plus, she sounds just like you and Jean talking about your works. You know; dedicated."

Catrin said, "Well, I don't see a problem, really. It is probably best if I meet her outside the wedding event itself. It's going to be a busy day and who knows when a discussion like that would fit in? But something else is bothering you about it, I can tell."

"Yes," said Li. "You know how interfering Mr. Yau and my boss were in Bangor, during the search for Han? I am just concerned that he raised it with me and, two weeks later, we get the email from Jean and Melanie that they can come to Hong King after all. Am I being too suspicious, do you think? It means both you and Jean - and Melanie - can meet with Miele during the visit."

Catrin said, "It was a neighboring shop, a deal; some work by Jean in exchange for the trip earned by one of the sisters, I gather. One of the women owners is part-time there and part-time in a travel agent, with benefits. Hardly a mysterious gang member dropping airline tickets through the postbox of the Kiln. But I will check. Anything else?"

Li paused.

"Not about that. About my dress and - I will probably find myself getting re-fitted the same time as you. Despite my best efforts I am gaining weight. And I am not eating any more than normal; trying to exercise… I am up and down like a yo-yo. Catrin, it is quite worrying."

Catrin smiled. She knew that her bridesmaid's dress was being made locally, to measurements she had supplied. The fitting would be done on arrival. One thing about Li's dad being co-owner of a high-end tailor was his links in the trade. The shop that the wedding dresses came from was owned by a colleague.

"It will be fine, Li. Honest, I know. I went through that sort of worry with mine, too. Once I was dressed, getting ready to head over with my dad, it was not an issue. There is too much else to think about on the wedding day."

Li said, mournfully, "That worries me, too."

Later, as she was leaving, Catrin walked across to the 'Silk Creations' boutique and popped in. A woman was there - Cassandra, the full-time sister, she found out after she had told her who she was.

The woman said, "I saw one of the pieces you decorated in the Kiln before it went off to the gallery. It was really impressive. Are you helping on our project?"

"No," said Catrin, "That is all Jean and Melanie; they are really happy with the travel package that you and your sister offered. It was very generous of you."

She was browsing through the scarves as she talked.

"Oh," said the woman, "That was good luck; we had no idea that they wanted to go anywhere. It was Danny's idea in a sense."

Catrin, attuned, just smiled and nodded, appearing interested. Sometimes a silence and a communication vacuum is the best interrogation technique.

Cassandra continued, "He had talked about a striking display unit probably helping sales and had suggested that something unique, not a standard mannequin, would be an idea; perhaps something that the pottery further along the row of shops had - or could assist with? The design for it was our idea: well, my sister's really."

Catrin picked up a scarf, admiring it. She said, less interested in the question than the scarf, it appeared, "Danny is a business partner, then?"

"No, one of our silk suppliers; we design and paint our own, of course. We have several sources. Danny Nim supplies us with our Chinese silk. Do you like that scarf; I could give a good discount?"

Catrin said, "I am deciding between this one and the darker shade, actually; but how much?"

The woman told her and Catrin selected one, appearing to vacillate between the two. She said, "But still, your sister was generous to give up your free holiday trips; even if it is helping the business."

As she wrapped the chosen scarf in tissue paper and placed it in a bag, Cassandra said, "Yes, but it was a windfall, really, and with the new business, we aren't going anywhere for a while. It was Danny who talked with Natalie. He bought through her a set of several 'open' round-trip tickets to Shenzhen for him and the guy he works with, his new junior buyer. It makes him not only our supplier, but a new customer for Natalie's agency, and a good one, too. His sales are growing, he says, both in London and other boutiques around the UK.

"It gave Natalie a good bonus with the agency. When she told him, he suggested, jokingly, that perhaps the people at the Kiln might want a holiday as payment for helping make the units. He liked the design of our display units and Jean and Melanie did want a trip, it turned out. It was a coincidence, really. But everyone is happy."

"Yes, it worked out well. Sometimes life does, don't you think?" smiled Catrin brightly. "And thank you for the discount on the scarf."

As she left the Arts Market she mulled over the discovery that it wasn't a coincidence, after all. It was Li, not her, who had showed an investigatory 'nose' for something not quite right on this one.

22 DETOUR

The schedule for re-interviewing witnesses to the known UK thefts associated with the Acton warehouse haul was progressing well other than, ironically, the key people in the remaining high priority item; the Gorton Gallery theft. That had been delayed as the gallery owners, Russell and Jocelyn Gorton, were both away at a new gallery venture they had established in Dubai. When Harper and Howlett had visited the gallery on Bond Street they learned the news from the existing staff, neither of whom had been employed there at the time of the robbery.

"Miss Gorton will be back the weekend after next, we know. She plans to be in the gallery the following week. The new venture is taking a lot of Mr. Gorton's time at present, so we aren't sure when he will be back. There is a lot of business developing for us in Arab Emirates."

Howlett was taking in yet again the Bratby painting given to the owner's father.

"Can I take a photo of this, for my own use? I like Bratby, but this one is not an image I found on the internet when I looked recently. Unless you have a gallery notice about it or a print that I could buy?"

One sales person looked at the other, then decided herself.

"No, it's not for sale, so is not in our catalogue. But you can take a snapshot if it is for your own use, I am sure."

Howlett got out her smartphone and did so.

Harper asked, "So is much art being sold by the gallery in Dubai?"

The senior assistant responded, "Yes, that's why Russell is almost always out there now, it seems; it is very busy. Only works from here for which we have export licenses, of course, can go to that location. And we import quite a bit of Middle East modern art to sell, newer artists from the area, sometimes with quite radical, striking works. They have a growing market here these days."

She pointed to several items on display.

Catrin reported the status to Coltrane later that afternoon, but he just grimaced. He was becoming frustrated by the lack of progress on this particular item. After half an hour of discussion between them, she emerged and pulled Howlett and Harper into her own office.

"We are now to focus exclusively on the recovery of the Bierstadt work. Nkrumah and Truman will be assigned to interview the remaining witnesses on the UK art theft list. We are to go back over the robbery completely; review the whole thing from top to bottom looking for 'Seal Island'. DCI Coltrane is feeling the heat from up the ladder. And if the Gorton siblings don't appear by a week on Monday, we may have to go out there to interview them."

Howlett looked serious.

"Timing is everything. It may not be that simple, ma'am. I took a call from the West Mercia Major Crimes Unit just before you got back. I told them you were in a meeting and would be back soon, but they want to talk to you as soon as possible."

Catrin said, "Did they say why?"

"All I know is that it is linked to the Bratby filing we did after the visit to Wales. The caller was a DI Merton. He is a homicide specialist; and he said he wants to talk to you, not me or Mark."

Catrin thought for a moment.

"Get everything on the Gorton Gallery robbery together and make a list of anyone here who worked on it first time round. I will call Merton, clear that away; then we can take it from there."

~~

The number she had dialed direct, a mobile, was picked up on the second ring.

"Merton."

"DI Sayer, Met Art and Antiques Unit. You wanted me to call you as soon as possible, I believe."

"Yes, DI Sayer, I did, thank you. You filed a report recently about a painting in the style of an artist called John Bratby, with a signature 'Ashe', linked to an investigation in Wales. But there is precious little else in the entry. What was that about, can I ask?"

Catrin paused and collected her thoughts.

"It was a case where a painting, an oil sketch, unexpectedly came to light in the possessions of a judge who died recently. The family believed that it did not belong to her or to them and they wanted us to check. We didn't discover any criminal involvement, but did check out the painting. It is an original work by the artist John Bratby and the signature 'Ashe' had been overpainted for some reason. If anything more comes to light now it will be a matter for the local police service involved, Dyfed-Powys; it wasn't anything that happened within the Met area of operation."

She stopped. It sounded as if she had given a thorough answer without giving any details, she knew.

DI Merton sighed. "Yes, the people at the Newtown station are listed in the entry. I think someone is giving me the runaround, to be honest. It was the Powys police, a DS Pawl Pryce, who put me on to you; he said your team was most current on the file. We need to know more."

His voice sounded impatient. She could understand that.

"Well, I am afraid if you need more on that case, I will need to clear it with my boss, DCI Coltrane. I am sorry; but those are my instructions. Can I at least ask why, if I may, and I can talk to him about it?"

There was a deeper silence on the line. He had probably muted the phone to talk to someone else. Then a new voice came on the line.

"Inspector Sayer, this is DCI Hendry. I am more than pleased to be open and co-operative with you, despite all the stone-walling we are getting. I am such a good-natured man, you see. My super isn't, and won't be once I tell him how the Welsh collectively are giving me the runaround, as DI Merton said. You are Welsh I take it?"

"Yes, sir. And I am sorry, but on this one I am under my own constraints."

Hendry said tersely, "Well, see if this loosens those up a little; go talk to your boss. I have a body in the process of being pulled out of a woodland area beside a golf course near Kidderminster and, with it, an ugly sod of a painting with the signature 'Ashe'. But I want some information quickly, not 'soon, not 'next week'. You are a DI; sort it out."

The line went dead.

~~

"DCI Hendry, this is DCI Coltrane, Metropolitan Police Art and Antiques Unit. DI Sayer is with me and she has briefed me. We want to help, of course. The file, for what it is worth, will be provided to you as soon as possible but there are some areas of sensitivity that you should be aware of. What we have factually, I think, will be of little use."

The response from Hendry was still brusque but a little more tempered than his final comments earlier, Catrin noted, listening on the speakerphone in Coltrane's office.

"I think, DCI Coltrane, once I have seen the file, I will be able to decide what could be useful to us. And what is sensitive or not will need to be determined by the course of the investigation. I take it you mean politically sensitive?"

It's my case, he was saying, Catrin saw.

Coltrane answered, "Yes. I am arranging for DI Sayer to deliver the file in person, first thing tomorrow, if you wish. You can have her expertise and our insight regarding the painting we looked into and she can examine the painting you have discovered. It may help. But she needs to be back at the end of the day tomorrow. You have your investigation; I have my own cases to resolve."

Coltrane's voice had a 'take it or leave it' element to it. There was a pause at the other end.

"Thank you. Have DI Sayer email me, if you would. I will send her the location information to meet me tomorrow."

He sounded conciliatory, realizing that he had pushed too hard on Coltrane, as he provided his email address over the phone.

Coltrane said, "Will that be at your offices or at the local station being used as a command centre?"

Hendry said, "No. It is the exhumation site. I will be there first thing, I expect. It is a complicated extraction and they are hardly into it at present. It will still be ongoing tomorrow, the pathologist says, but they should have both the painting and the body removed by then. Thank you for your co-operation, we will try to use her time well."

The line went dead and Neville Coltrane switched off his speaker phone.

"Catrin, you should head up this evening, stay somewhere local; have Vicky make a reservation somewhere. Better than finding yourself searching for some remote lane tomorrow morning, arriving late and have Hendry growling at you."

Victoria Camberwell was his personal assistant.

Catrin said, "Yes, that's a good idea. But I am not happy, given where we are on our own work."

Coltrane nodded, understanding.

"We have to do it this way. First, the file isn't going to help Hendry; you know that. But he will chase every nook and cranny and re-open the link to Minister Richards. If that can be avoided, or at least the ground prepared properly, I know that behind the scenes here it will be appreciated. These days, budgets and politics being what they are, Art and Antiques needs all the appreciation we can get inside and outside the Met.

"Also, if I am right, you can give them some insight on the painting they have found. It is, after all, an enquiry into a suspicious death."

He paused.

"The bigger challenge is not Hendry, thinking about it - it is your old boss. If there is a body involved and art expertise support needed for a regional operation, it is really her bailiwick, the work of the Art Crime Unit. I have been very careful not to tread on Jane Worsley's toes when it comes to jurisdiction."

Catrin nodded. She, too, had thought that this request fell fairly and squarely into the remit of the Art Crime Unit.

"Why don't we both go and see her, Neville?"

"Seeing as it's Catrin on this, and just information on the painting, I will go along with it, Neville," said DCI Jane Worsley. "From what you tell me about the background politics, either I or Keith would need to do this one, if the case was assigned to us."

She added, "Has this been flagged to Jack?"

Superintendent Jack Taylor was her boss.

"No, we came straight to you."

Worsley said, "We are up to our eyes, anyway; something would need to give in our workload, so I should thank you, I expect."

Then, looking at Catrin's face, she added, "I guess you don't have much time for this anyway, with the Acton case."

She came to a conclusion.

"Just keep me in the loop, the highlights. So if it comes back down to me from my line of bosses, I can point to it being an example of good caseload cooperation."

Coltrane said, "Thank you, Jane."

Worsley smiled. "I am not sure you should be thanking me; it should be me thanking you, stepping into the West Mercia Major Crime Unit 'soup'."

Regional major crime units were always more complicated teams for the ACU to work with than specific police services; there were a lot of players involved, from neighbouring police jurisdictions and people from the UK National Crime Agency.

Neville and Catrin stood up, preparing to leave her office. Catrin had caught sight of her former colleague Aina Jinnah through the glass wall of the office; they were exchanging smiles.

DCI Worsley said candidly, while looking at Coltrane. "Is his mob still giving you the cold shoulder, Catrin? That's what I heard."

Her stare was quite blatant; do something about it, Coltrane, was the message.

Catrin ducked the question and said, "I am settling in well with my team, ma'am."

She smiled and then pulled a face at her old boss as she followed Coltrane out the door.

Worsley called after them. "Neville, send her there and get her back quickly; she has sticky fingers for cases she shouldn't be involved in; like the one in Cornwall where she found a husband."

~~

Catrin phoned Chris and told him. "I will swing by home, get some overnight things and head out after the rush-hour. And you?"

He said, "I will be late tonight anyway; I am on duty cover, remember? I am currently working on a smelly mobile phone, searching it. It arrived in an evidence bag and you could smell the pee as soon as I opened it."

Chris Treneer worked one day a week as 'duty cover'; lunchtimes and after the regular working day until 8.00 p.m.

Then once a month he drew 'night cover'; from 8.00 p.m. until 8.00 a.m. Most e-crime technical service support was regular day work, but there had to be emergency coverage at all times.

Catrin had started out in support of drug squad work, so she had an inkling of Chris's task.

"Don't tell me; the mobile was thrown in the toilet as they arrested someone. Will you get anything off it, then?"

"Yes, it jolted on the porcelain, disconnecting the battery. From high end systems to lowly mobile phones, that's us. The battery is fried but the chips are OK, it seems. But I have to get on, sorry love. DI Steadman is next to me, breathing down my neck."

Catrin laughed.

"Say hello. I will call when I get to the hotel. Call my mobile if you need me before then. I should be back tomorrow during the day sometime."

As Chris closed the call, Steadman said, "Is Catrin settling in OK at her new position?"

He had worked with her on the Greaves case in Falmouth.

"So-so; it has its ups and downs," Treneer replied neutrally.

PART 2

BINDLEY WOODS

23 BODY

Catrin took additional footwear, not knowing where the body was located. Her old uniform work shoes were quite sturdy and rubber-soled and she also put rain boots in the car. The forecast was for showers or rain; she wasn't sure which footwear would be best, but she knew that turning up at an outdoor crime scene inappropriately shod was the sign of a novice.

To add to the disruption to her Thursday, she finally arrived late evening at the Gainsborough House Hotel near Kidderminster, glad to get out of the Audi and into her room. The traffic leaving London had been heavy and it had delayed her; the journey took closer to four hours than two. She slept well and had a nice breakfast the following morning.

She found the location provided by DCI Hendry off the B4363 without problem. A police car was parked at the junction to the side road. Once she showed her identification, the officer directed her and she heard him reporting her arrival as she drove down the lane. Near the top of the rise she saw a trail entry point for Bindley Woods, part of the golf course.

Catrin parked with other vehicles next to a SOCO on-site forensic trailer then showed her ID again, to sign in with the

Scene Control Officer. She returned to her vehicle and opened the boot. It wasn't raining at present but the ground was wet and muddy; it was rain boot terrain after all.

A tall man was walking up the forest service track towards her from a SOCO tent just visible inside the coppice, about seventy-five yards away, slightly off the path. He, too, was wearing boots and a pair of blue disposable coveralls. She stood waiting by her car.

"Inspector Sayer? DI Merton, I work with DCI Hendry. We spoke on the phone. The DCI is in the scene tent. I will take you over."

"Thank you; it's Catrin, by the way."

"Then it's Alan. And thank you for coming. Please leave your bag in your vehicle, if you would. We want to minimize site cross-contamination risks."

She nodded, understanding, placing her purse next to her briefcase in the boot before locking the vehicle.

As she turned to walk with him he said, "Mind the holes as you go, we don't want a twisted ankle. You are in art crime work at the Yard, I gather?"

"Yes, that's right."

He asked, "Have you seen a dead body before; I mean, partially or fully decomposed? I am not trying to be awkward; I just want to warn you, in case it's your first time. It's always assumed police officers have, but…"

He let his voice trail off.

Catrin said, "I used to work in Brixton, in drug squad work, so yes, I have; at least some corpses that were nowhere near fresh. And I have seen a body decomposed after six months in the Menai Strait. But it has been some time…"

He said, "At least the smell is not too bad here, we find. It wasn't buried deeply and there is a lot of air movement over the gravesite. We are surprised there isn't greater animal damage than there is. But you will notice the odour inside the tent, nonetheless."

At the entrance area to the crime scene tent, she slipped on the blue disposable coveralls. DCI Merton put on fresh shoe covers and Catrin did the same. He led her inside to the group of people in white, the forensic pathologist and the scene of crime people, standing with the solitary man in a similar blue coverall; another police officer. He was portly, middle-aged and about her height; short for a male police officer. Yet he had the air of authority of being the person in charge.

Merton said, "DI Sayer, sir."

The man looked up from the grave site at Catrin, taking her in, assessing her.

"DI Sayer, thank you for coming. We thought you should see this before it is disturbed further. It will take this bunch most of the morning, they say, to finish extricating the body. They must be milking the overtime."

There were a couple of looks and a grumble about Hendry's comment from the SOCOs that he ignored.

"Then we can go back to the trailer and have a first look at the painting; it was finally taken out not that long ago."

He watched her carefully as she moved forward into the trench area, towards the cluster of white, as they made room for her at the illuminated hole.

The skeleton, with its mosaic of sinew, dried organ shreds, clothes, skin and hair was positioned on its back, face up, she saw. The dark holes of the eye sockets were exaggerated in size by the angle of the lighting. The SOCOs had excavated a trench alongside the body once they had its directional position worked out and were now moving into the cadaver area both from above and laterally. That had taken a lot of time, one said, "despite the complaints from some."

They were looking and recording anything they found, down to plant fragments and stones.

The SOCO continued, "We are looking for decomposition, plant materials and other debris; anything with residence-time factors to let us determine when the body was buried. It is a male, as you can see. Some of the skin fragments have tattoo marks. One could be a classic prison tattoo, according to Holly here. She is into tattoos, aren't you?"

The female pathologist ignored the jokey comment and introduced herself; Dr. Holly Braden.

"See the channel to the left there? It was a run, either small rodents or water channeling. The left forearm, finger and wrist bones were mainly at the bottom of the run; well, most of them. Some are missing. We think it occurred after burial; it doesn't appear to be pre-mortem damage, at this point. The other bones so far still seem to be in place."

Catrin said, "Any idea how long he has been here, roughly?"

One of the other forensic people said, abstractly, "At least three to four years, we think, so far; could be longer."

Braden said, "The painting you are interested in was positioned above his face. A spade or a trowel used by the person who first found the site caught the corner and damaged it, I understand, before the fellow realised what it was. Otherwise, as you will see later, it is mainly intact; dirty and mouldy, but not decomposing too badly yet.

"Then we found the skull beneath it, as if the painting had been positioned for viewing post-death, we think. Unless he was buried alive, which we doubt, at present. There would be more evidence of soil in the skull cavities. It must be symbolic."

Catrin said, "I can see the corner mark on the far side, where it rested, there."

Braden added, "We think initially it was higher, about six to eight inches from the body. Compaction and subsistence movements brought them together."

They stood in silence for a moment, watching her absorb it, thinking it through.

Catrin asked, "How was it found?"

The SOCO joker laughed.

"By accident. Or an act of God. Actually, by a forensic archeology student showing off. One of Holly's students. You tell her."

Braden said somewhat defensively, "He and his girlfriend

were walking here when he saw the log outside. It was over the grave but it had clearly been rotated at some point, he saw, from the position of saprophyte locations on the trunk. Then he realised that the area had been disturbed; the cover vegetation had changed, of course, with a corpse so close to the surface."

She sighed. "So, showing off to his friend, he told her that this was exactly the sort of situation where a body could be buried. That was the good part. The bad part was that he pulled the trunk away and saw the subsistence outline, adding to his suspicion. What he should have done was call it in, but she caught the sense of the treasure hunt and they went back to his car for a shovel. They came back digging and… he was shocked to find it was actually a burial site, after all.

"We are pretty close to being able to remove the body now."

"Apart from the chunk which your student already brought up," said Hendry.

Dr. Braden turned to look at DCI Hendry. "At least he found it and called it in once he realised it was a grave. Then he stayed until your lot turned up. You have a chain of custody on the site from its discovery."

Catrin looked at her.

"Why were they here specifically; did they say?"

DCI Hendry answered. "His girlfriend works at the golf club across there and it's a place that doesn't get many visitors, I gather. Romance in the air."

The SOCO said, "He probably …"

Merton interrupted. "We should go and see the painting in the trailer, sir; they want to get the current evidence set, pre-removal of the body, sent back to the lab."

They made their way out of the coppice to the track, then back to the SOCO trailer by the entrance barrier. A technician was working there, documenting and storing the evidence collected in containers at the site.

DCI Hendry said, "The painting, Janice, if you please. After this, it can go."

He turned to Catrin. "You can see it in the lab also, under better conditions there. Headquarters is at Hindlip, on your way back south, not too far away."

Catrin nodded.

"I went there once, sir, while I was with the Art Crime Unit, with my guvnor then, DCI Worsley.'

He nodded but said nothing.

The SOCO led them around to the sliding side door, behind the passenger entrance. The painting was there, the canvas supported by polystyrene wedges fitted around the frame, holding it firmly in a clear plastic tray. There was a triangular rip in one corner, perhaps where the student's spade had hit it.

Catrin examined the canvas closely then asked the SOCO, "The lower left edge - here - can you brush some of the mud away without damaging it? If not, we can wait for the lab."

The woman nodded, "We can try."

She did so, sufficient for Sayer's purposes.

Hendry asked, "What do you think?"

Catrin said, "At first glance, from the bits I can see, it looks very much like the Tregynon sketch that I looked into, the Newtown case. The signature at the bottom, Ashe, you have seen already. It will likely be over-painted, as it is very similar paint and lettering to the one we have. The Bratby signature, the original artist, is probably underneath. And here - and here; the paint colours, although changed, aged, make me think it is by John Bratby; another portrait sketch of the same male subject, but from a different angle. I have the photographs from that investigation with me, in my briefcase, with the file material for you."

She looked at DCI Hendry.

"That's about all I can say, at present. What you want to know, I am sure, are they linked? I think, for whatever reason, there is a very strong possibility they are. Do you think that the person in the grave is possibly 'Ashe'? I couldn't tell, from the state of the face."

Hendry looked at her.

"It is too early to say. We will need to look into it and do dental record and DNA checks, if we can. Let me buy you a cup of coffee at headquarters. As I said, it is only a half-hour away. A convenient one, this case. I'll lead, show you the best way there."

~~

DCI Hendry said, "So on your first day in the Art and Antiques Unit, you get sent to the middle of Wales? Didn't they know what to do with you or what? Do Londoners get lost north of Watford Gap?"

Catrin smiled.

"No, sir. Case assignments that come up; well, you know better than me how they are given out. And my team was working on other things, obviously. It is just the way it worked out."

She had carefully briefed the senior officer in a way which made no reference to the discussions with a cabinet minister and his staff.

Hendry asked, "So your involvement ended with what?"

"The identification of the painting as a work by John Bratby; that the signature 'Ashe' - the same as found on your discovery - was overlaid, for whatever reason. And, to the best of our knowledge, that the painting was not stolen. The one in Judge Richards' house had been there for several years, we think.

"We found only one tenuous link between Judge Richards and the Edwin Ashe mentioned in her note; a preliminary hearing at which he was denied bail. And, as a former judge, we checked the databases for other people with the name Ashe, including anyone working in the legal system around Birmingham with whom she may have had contact. Nothing stood out from a first glance, but that was where we stopped.

"We gave the information about the painting to Judge

Richard's family, who were in the process of clearing the home. They asked me to look into finding someone who would remove the signature 'Ashe', restore it and see if someone would sell the painting for charitable causes. They didn't want it.

"Once we had your call, we stopped thinking about a restorer; it was a low priority item, anyway. It sits in our evidence lockers now, given your news. Everything is in this file."

She handed it over.

Hendry asked, "Are you sure the Judge died of natural causes?"

Catrin replied, "We didn't look into that. It was not reported as a suspicious death; only that an item had been found."

She was thinking about what to say next.

Hendry said, "It needs re-examination. If there are suspicions, or another body turns up associated with a painting like this, we could have some sort of serial killings on our hands. It would escalate the investigation."

Catrin said, "There was a note found, in Judge Richards' handwriting, which caused the original concern by the family, sir. She received the painting from someone unidentified, but it brought out in her a sense of ... contrition, not fear. It would go against your interpretation, but, again, a copy of the note is in the file."

He thumbed through the slim file and she pointed it out. After he read it, he said, "I am not convinced. If she is feels some guilt, or remorse of some sort, it could still mean a suspicious death. I will get on to Dyfed-Powys. Who did you deal with there - this officer Pryce?"

She nodded.

"Yes, we just checked in locally. An Inspector Meredith runs the local station. I had no contact with Dyfed-Powys headquarters on this one."

He looked around, seeing who was available in the busy area, spotting a DC at a desk. "Wescott, can you look after DI

Sayer; find her a desk to work at and then show her the way to the lab, she may want to see the initial work on the painting recovered."

He looked at Catrin. "Settle in, we will talk later."

Hendry was about to close the file when he stopped, looking at the note again. "Judge Richards. Her beneficiaries are a Noel and Maeve, this letter says. By any chance, is this Noel Richards we are talking about, the minister at the Home Office? Is this the 'sensitivity' that DCI Coltrane mentioned; the one you have been careful not to mention so far?"

She looked at him, blank-faced. "Yes, sir."

He paused.

"Better still, Wescott, take DI Sayer along to the lab as they work on the painting now; DCI Coltrane gave you to me for the day. I may come back with my little knife and try to prize open the clamshell a little more."

He walked off.

Catrin remembered Coltrane's talk of a time limit. It cut both ways. She couldn't really go back yet, even if she wanted to.

In the lab Catrin found the same forensic technician working with another person, obviously in the middle of a transfer of responsibilities for examination of the items. Once they were through the introductions, she asked, "Can I just look at the small area here again; with the signature. I want it magnified, with a light source along the plane of the painting."

They worked with her on it.

"See," said Catrin, "The 'Ashe' signature panel is overlaid. The illuminated edge of the panel is facing out; not created by a mixture of brushstrokes. That is what we found with the similar painting we looked at on our case."

"And where is that one?" the forensic technician asked.

She said evenly, "Currently with Dr. Wells in the Art and Antiques Unit at the Met."

~~

Hendry came back about an hour later, as Catrin was sitting at a desk, winding up a discussion with Harper on the next steps on the Gorton Gallery case.

"DI Sayer, I now see why your face has been so impassive throughout the morning. My serial killer idea has no merit regarding Judith Richards, I now believe. Someone on my team talked to the coroner who signed the death certificate and also spoke to her family doctor. They more than convinced us that there was nothing suspicious there."

Catrin was impressed at the speed with which Hendry moved his investigation. In homicide, time was always a factor.

He continued, "Any more ideas you have buried away, but aren't able to share, officially?"

She shook her head. "I wish. I have been giving it some thought. We got the impression that it was not the art; Judith Richards didn't have similar paintings in the house. It was personal, to do with the altered signature; the 'contrition' element."

She continued, "But why was the name Ashe added? We don't know. A bail denial is not that significant, you would think. She didn't try him for… whatever. Or sentence him; we found nothing on that. So we stopped.

"But we didn't do much with the other three 'Ash' or Ashe' names we found either, the ones we mention in the file. Doubtlessly you will be more thorough. Why would she feel a sense of guilt over a bail hearing? I suppose you need to talk to the family, despite Richards being a Minister of the Crown."

He nodded as she shared her thoughts then replied, "Perhaps - but perhaps not, either."

Catrin added, "The disposition of the painting found in her bedroom implies she knew all about it, wanted to keep it, but store it out of the way rather than have it on display. We found nothing untoward about Judith Richards, but it was a preliminary scan, for obvious reasons."

Hendry nodded again.

"That's all, sir. If your team finds out the identity of the victim perhaps you could let me know?"

He paused, deciding what to say.

"We are a little ahead of you now, in a sense. I looked at the bail denial record and called the arresting officer who was named. Now I am waiting on files from them.

"Edwin Ashe was in Wilson Green prison on a fraud charge, fairly small stuff, but the officer clearly recalled the case. Ashe was held on remand for a week, after which he got bail from another judge and was released. He was supposed to meet with his solicitor the following day but he didn't; nor did he return phone calls from the solicitor's office.

"They found his body in his car in the garage; an overdose of drugs that were self-administered; that was clear. He had a drug habit. The fraud was tied to funding his addiction, it was believed. The case was closed."

Catrin knew that HMP Birmingham, a large, older prison, was located at Wilson Green and went by that name.

He sighed then continued, "What that has to do with this body in Bindley Woods, I have no idea yet, but if Judith Richards felt her incarceration of Ashe led to his death, that could account for the note. But we will be looking into it."

Hendry stood up.

"DI Sayer, you can head home early; I am giving back to DCI Coltrane the remainder of your day. Not for good behaviour, I might add, given the link to Minister Richards that you elegantly bypassed. But I understand you were under orders. Anything new occurs at your end, give me a shout. Is that a deal?"

"Yes, sir; if I am allowed to. And if you want anything checked - names that come up or information on paintings, please let us know."

"Well, thank you for your time and for coming up so promptly - and for DCI Coltrane being willing to let you do so. Please pass that back to him. You have your own workload, no doubt."

He looked at his wristwatch.

"Do you want an early lunch? There is a cafeteria here; but I need to get on with this, so I can't join you."

"Thank you. I will head on back, stop on the way for a sandwich."

He nodded and stood up to leave.

"There is more to this; I feel it. Hopefully it is not linked to the reason Noel Richards brought you in on his sister's mystery painting, that he is involved somehow. So, I mean it, anything relevant turns up, let me know. This is, after all, a possible murder investigation. Goodbye, Inspector Sayer."

He was a homicide detective and didn't really have much time in the day for a specialist on the periphery of the case, she thought.

24 INSIGHT

As she was leaving the Major Crime Unit headquarters area, she saw an older woman, well-dressed and carrying a briefcase, who was heading in towards her at the door. Catrin held it open for her, suddenly recognizing her face but not recalling the name.

The woman stopped and said, "Sergeant Sayer?"

"Yes, ma'am?"

"Is AC Hunt here?"

She was taking in that Catrin was in plain clothes. Catrin recalled the name just in time. The woman was Superintendent Lane, an EMSOU senior investigator, the East Midlands counterpart of the West Mercia lot. She had given reports on two occasions at meetings of the Association of Chief Police Officers, which Hunt had attended with Sayer in tow.

"No, not that I am aware of, ma'am; and I was promoted to a new role recently. I am a DI now."

Lane asked, "In the Met still? Congratulations."

"Yes, I am still in the Met, with the Art and Antiques Unit in Specialist Crime Command."

Lane nodded then added, "I remember you from the Nottingham meeting. Do you know why?"

She had an authoritative tone; one that Catrin remembered

from the ACPO meetings.

"No, ma'am."

"Most aides to senior officers do their job but switch off from the big discussion, I find. They focus only on their boss's needs. But you, you were taking it all in, I recall."

Catrin flushed slightly. It was true; she had become absorbed in the discussion.

She answered, "I was new then, still learning a lot at that time; it was a good opportunity."

The older woman started to head into the building.

"Well, good luck in your new role. To be honest, I half-expected to see you in a place like this."

"You work here, ma'am?"

"Just visiting; I am seconded to the National Crime Agency at present; a common case brings me here. Anyway, I must get on."

"Thank you," Catrin said, as she too turned, heading out.

For remembering me - and my name. I didn't recall yours at first, just the face. But after two years in so many meetings, it was not surprising.

As she left the building she was hit by the realisation that the working life of a major crimes unit, a homicide team, was not for her despite it being a role that almost all police officers aspired to at some time or other. In the eyes of the public it was the cream of police jobs. She had thought that way once.

Lane said she was assigned now to the National Crime Agency staff, presumably based at their headquarters in Tinworth Street in London. The officer was clearly on the rise. She had not been the first to suggest a similar career 'next step' to Catrin. Others would be leaping at it, she knew.

But more than most junior rank officers, she had a big insight into the politics and power trading going along with the changes in major crime policing. Working as Sandra Hunt's aide had provided that. It was at times a 'dog-eat-dog' activity; the politics of regional jurisdictions versus national approaches. When things went wrong, the search for scapegoats could change the life of an officer overnight.

In taking an assignment like that, you were 'out of sight, out mind' very quickly with the police service you started with. If you transferred back, particularly at short notice with a black mark from some interagency squabble, they tried to work out what you now were; one of 'them' or one of 'us'. Catrin hadn't seen it happen to any officer close to her, but she had been in meeting rooms where, beneath the dry language of management interaction, lives were changed for such reasons.

'Pity about the Ipswich operation; the resources need to be reallocated; we will take Alderson back, find a home for him... somewhere.' She had heard variants on this on more than one occasion.

It wasn't the way she wanted to go. Nor Chris. He, too, had been approached; in his case by the National Cybercrime Agency. He had simply said he was too new in his role at the Met, having just moved from the Devon and Cornwall Police.

"It is important for me to do a good job with my current employer, sir," he said to the senior officer trying to recruit him.

The man had said, "We'll be back for you sometime, Treneer, mark my words. 'Agility' is the name of the game; move with the teams in a national approach..."

He had gone home and told Catrin.

"Last thing I need is that," said Chris.

She smiled. "It would make things difficult."

He put on his serious face. "Difficult? It could create havoc with my five-a-side team commitments!"

Catrin knew that the homicide team investigating the Bindley Woods case was moving fast, keeping up the pace on this enquiry. It was not simply because a body had been found; after all, that death had happened years ago. It was the reality that tomorrow, or the day after, or next week, they would be assigned to another investigation. The chances were that a new one would probably be a fresh death, occurring within minutes or hours of the crime being committed. The team would start the investigation process all over again. The maximum progress had to be made while each investigation was the top priority. For the officers involved it was an all-consuming grind at times.

As she drove around the roundabout bypassing the M5 to head further east for the M40, she realised that this lifestyle wasn't for her. It would eliminate her chance to work with Jean on art and remove that part of her enjoyment of life. She may have risen to the rank of inspector, but she wasn't this sort of police officer.

It was good to know that, she thought.

As she pulled into a petrol station to fill up, she suddenly recalled the last time she had been so sure of 'not' doing something, in a career sense; she had been talking with Chris. They had been driving from Bristol to her parents and she had been sure she would never be working in the Art and Antiques Unit.

25 DETAILS

'Back to my real work,' thought Catrin as she parked in the underground garage at New Scotland Yard.

In her absence, the Art Team had pulled out the files from the Gorton Gallery robbery and re-sorted the materials stored in the evidence locker. They had also started a chronological listing of the elements of the incident from the first 999 call onwards, on a whiteboard.

On a separate whiteboard, Harper was laying out two maps of the floor of the gallery, one showing the 'starting state', before the robbery, labelling the position of each art work on display at the time. On the second floor plan, the 'found' scene as recorded by the SOCOs, the artwork in the gallery was being located and colour coded. The stolen works were listed in red on one side. Other works damaged by the vehicle entry were marked in blue and any items that had been moved or disturbed in the immediate aftermath were being tagged in yellow.

As she entered, Isabelle Howlett was standing next to him.

"We are working out precisely what happened to each artwork, item by item, ma'am, as best we can," said Harper.

Catrin nodded. "Good. Once you have it completed, or anything new strikes you, let me know and we can start the walk-through of the incident. Hopefully I am done now with this Bratby thing."

She went into her office and started reading the Gorton Gallery case reports in detail again, in preparation for the walk-through.

In the course of doing so, Neville Coltrane popped in and said, "Thanks for the heads up on the Kidderminster thing; I talked with Wicklow, brought him up to speed. He is not looking forward to telling the Minister of the complication but he will brief him this afternoon. Any progress here yet?"

He was examining the diagrams.

Catrin said, "We are still sorting it out, Neville. Not yet."

~~

The robbery had taken place on a Tuesday, the first day the gallery had been open after a long weekend. The Friday before, the gallery had also closed early; at lunchtime, the report said. A decision to stay closed on the Saturday and also the Sunday afternoon, both normal business hours, had been made sometime earlier, to give everyone a long weekend holiday. Business had been good of late and the co-owners decided that they all needed a break.

Both Jocelyn Gorton and her brother, with a staff member, had been working that previous Friday morning. The sister left at lunchtime to visit friends in Cambridge. The original investigation had made a routine check and that visit had been confirmed; it included a christening of a god-daughter on the Sunday and Jocelyn Gorton stayed with her friends until Tuesday, when she received a call about the robbery. She headed back straightaway. Gorton had planned originally to return Tuesday evening but the news so upset her, the report said, the husband of the couple she was visiting drove her home in her vehicle, then he took a train back. Traffic cameras around the church where the christening took place and others on the M11 had picked out her vehicle and confirmed both her and the driver.

Russell Gorton had been invited also and had planned to go initially. The mother of the baby being christened was Jocelyn's friend, not his. On the Thursday evening he had cancelled, to stay at the flat that the siblings shared in Davies Mews, a high-end residence a short walk from the gallery. He had called the friends, pleading exhaustion and a sinus head cold.

His statement, corroborated by his sister and the staff member, said he had struggled through the Friday morning at the gallery then went to see his doctor, claiming severe sinusitis pains, asking for a prescription for antibiotics or something to address it. The surgery had confirmed that appointment. There was a footnote saying no medications were prescribed; over-the-counter treatments with rest and hydration had been recommended.

In his statement, Russell Gorton had said he had stayed home over the weekend, only leaving the premises early on the Monday for a security equipment update at the gallery that their security contractor requested.

"Let's leave that until we cover the security coverage aspects," said Catrin.

The only person he claimed that he talked to in person over the weekend at the mews was a neighbour; they met at the bin station in the building, both disposing of rubbish bags. The investigation team had checked that out. She had recalled seeing him; he had sneezed in the place and she hoped that she wouldn't catch whatever he had; he had sounded very nasal during their brief exchange.

Only Russell Gorton had been in the gallery Tuesday morning before the robbery took place; one of the two hired staff was due in early p.m. He had been uninjured, but had been treated for shock after the robbery.

By late-afternoon they had mapped out the locations of the art, before and after the robbery, seeing what had been moved or damaged. The walk-through and re-construction of the crime gave them what they already knew, largely. As they went through it in detail, Catrin played the role of 'devil's advocate'. She had been totally outside the investigation.

'Why? Where exactly? When and who?' were the questions frequently asked by Catrin, as they worked through the events as reported in the files. Isabelle Howlett started forestalling Catrin's questions during her responses. The process had its tedium, its repetitiveness, but by mid-evening they had worked through the incident, re-confirming the accuracy of the original investigation. More importantly, they had identified some items or issues that were now missing or raised new questions; things that possibly should have been followed up at the time.

The most important of these was the realisation that they were basing the losses on the inventory of the Friday before the robbery. They had no independent information on any transactions made the following Tuesday morning, nor information on customers that day. The only evidence they had about the physical inventory was Russell Gorton's statement. 'It was deathly quiet after the long weekend. Other than the postman, we had virtually no one come in and no sales at all. I was glad I gave Fiona (the assistant due in that afternoon) the extra half-day off.'

The other finding that was unexplained was not to do with a work of art; it was a photographic record of an area with white powder marks on the floor near the back of the gallery, away from the damaged area where the taxi came through. It was not solely loose dust, the report said.

Catrin had said, "I don't see why a gallery like the Gorton would allow that during opening time. What was it? There is nothing in the files that I can see to explain it?"

It was eight-thirty p.m. She looked at her watch.

"That's good progress, I think. We will come back at it next week. Let's call it a night."

As they wrapped up, Howlett said, "Mark and I are going to the pub for a bite. Would you like to join us?"

Catrin smiled. "I would love to; I'm starving. Thank you."

She had told Chris that she would be working this evening,

too. Building a relationship with her team was part of that.

It was in the pub, in their conversation on everything but the case, she found out why Howlett had given up her course at the Courtauld Institute to train to be a conservator.

Mark had been talking about his brother's issues with his fiancée and whether or not the wedding was likely to go ahead when Howlett said, "Best that they sort that out before the wedding, one way or another."

"I suppose so, but it is looking a bit 'iffy' right now," replied Mark.

"Suppose so? I know so, don't I?" she replied, somewhat emphatically.

Mark looked at her, then at Catrin; both realizing that their boss would not understand the context of the remark.

In the silence it created, Howlett said to Catrin, "I'm divorced. My husband was in the job and took up with another officer while I was on that leave of absence, training to be a conservator. When I found out… I gave up the course, came back to work, picked up the pieces. Thank God we had no kids."

Harper looked a little uncomfortable; it had been his comments that had started them down this track.

Catrin said nothing for a moment, assessing Howlett.

Then she said, "Are they still here, your husband and the other woman; in the Met, I mean?"

Howlett pursed her lips. "He is; a sergeant in a borough, Waltham Forest. She left the Met and him, went into something else. I don't know what. He and I don't keep in touch."

Catrin said dryly, "Well, if they find a body of a police officer beaten to death with a heavy brass hand loupe, we will know who did it, won't we?"

Howlett laughed. "Not that, ma'am. I like my loupe, I wouldn't want it damaged."

The moment had passed. The comment about 'no kids' complicating the separation struck a chord with Catrin. Not that she had any worries about Chris, she thought, but they had been talking about that subject, having children, only the previous weekend. It wasn't the first time they had discussed it, but they both were realizing that they needed to decide whether they wanted a child; the 'future' wasn't going to be the 'future' forever.

26 EDIE

The following Monday, they continued the re-examination of the details of the case.

There had been separate interviews with regular clients of the Gorton Gallery about the works on display around that time of the robbery. These fragments of information reinforced the composite picture provided by the owners.

"Sales records for the gallery show nothing happened that morning before the robbery, supporting Russell Gorton's claim," said Howlett, looking through the business records.

Catrin said, "And security tapes of the day?"

Harper said, "I recall that, I read it … here."

He pulled out a document and leafed through it as Howlett said, from memory, "The system was down. It had been out for a day and a half and was only fixed by the Thursday night before the long weekend. There is correspondence with the security firm showing that the Gorton couple were anxious about it, given the holiday and their plans to be away, so the security company installed a new unit on the Thursday. It was apparently working satisfactorily on the Friday morning. Then they had a reset problem of some sort after they closed."

Harper was now reading the notes and picked up the thread.

"There was no motion sensor coverage or video of the entrance area to the gallery for the whole weekend, only the entry alarm active on the front door. The follow-up showed that it was a module failure in the new equipment and that was attributed entirely to the security system supplier. If the robbery had occurred over the long weekend, they would have been very exposed, from an insurance viewpoint; but it wasn't. The security firm contacted Russell Gorton early on Monday, once the fault had been spotted at their end. Gorton went over to open up and meet their technician who installed yet another unit and tested it. As of Monday morning, they were fully covered again; long before the robbery."

Howlett said, "That was what led to the news coverage comment about a security system failure, but it was mis-interpreted. From the camera covering the entrance, no-one appeared to enter the gallery on the Tuesday morning, as Gorton said, other than the postman."

She looked at Catrin, then said, "We are going to look at the video again ourselves, I see, aren't we?"

Catrin smiled. "Yes we are, but we will speed it up a bit."

It was 10.40 a.m. on the Tuesday morning on the recording clock when they saw the blur. No-one came into the gallery but a face pressed firmly against the window by the door, distorted by the glass.

"Strange," said, Harper. "It's a woman; she is looking for something."

Nothing else showed up, other than the postman, until the crash itself when the man in black came running directly at the camera, it seemed, arm extended and then the image disappeared. They had sprayed black paint on the lens; some of it had hit nearby art.

Howlett came up with the idea.

"Media coverage," she said. "In the off-chance the woman who looked in the window was seen by others in the vicinity, who commented to the press. Long shot, I know…"

Harper said, "Let's check also with the gallery and other

galleries in the street; see if they had a woman looking in their galleries that way on the day."

That was how, by the following day and after more checking, they found Edie Cummings.

~~

"It is good tea, this."

Catrin said, "I am glad you like it, Mrs. Cummings."

"Edie, please. Everyone calls me Edie other than my mum when she was alive. She called me Edith."

"Well, Edie, I am just going to go over the information you gave to DC Howlett this morning and we are going to record it, you understand?"

"I'm not arrested then?"

"No, you are free to go whenever you want, or stay and drink your tea and… I think DC Howlett will even see if there are some sandwiches made, after we finish."

The older woman was in her fifties, they knew now, but looked considerably older. She looked down-at-heel but was not a street person. Edie was clean, had her hair combed; the clothes were old, but in good condition.

"So," she said, "what do you want to know?"

Catrin replied, "We would like to know just what happened when you went past the Gorton Gallery and looked in through the window. That's all."

"On the day it was robbed, right?"

"That's the day."

Cummings shifted her shoulders, settling down to tell her story again.

"I did what I always do. I look in through the windows of all the galleries, see if there are any changes I can spot. If there are, I go round the back."

She stopped.

"I am not going to get into trouble am I? It's just stuff thrown away?"

Catrin smiled at her encouragingly. She could see the

wariness.

"No, Edie. We are just interested in what you saw, not what you took. You take discarded items away from the bins if they are useful, don't you?"

"Yes, well… If there are changes, the things they put out are often useful. Packing, broken frames, stuff I can use. Sometimes there are old canvases, even; rubbishy stuff, but I can use part of them sometimes. It's all useful for my own work; the things I make and sell."

She paused.

"I go down to Trafalgar Square mainly, mooch around there and sell them on the steps. Not by the National Gallery; they won't let me there, these days. People will give a few quid for a little piece of handmade craft art. I do quite nicely some days."

She looked worried.

"You aren't going to tell the social or the tax people that I don't declare anything, you know, as income; that's the word."

Howlett said quickly, "That is not relevant here, Edie, so don't talk about it. Just what you saw."

"At the front or the back?"

"The back first," said Howlett, wanting to get on.

"There were empty boxes of white stuff messing up the things they put out. Some plaster and gesso. Acrylic gesso, the modern stuff, not like proper gesso with rabbit glue."

Her brow furrowed as she worked out how much detail to give these people.

"That's like a base for oil painting. Do you know what it is? You put it on the bare canvas. Well, it made a hell of mess of some good wood thrown out. It doesn't come off easy, I tell you, gesso. I had to sand an' scrape."

Catrin said, "You are sure of the day and the time, Edie?"

"You bet. By the time I took them back to the place when I stash things for later and started again, the road was blocked off and a taxi was sitting in the window of the same place. Even more of a mess then; but I couldn't get to any of it - not steal the paintings obviously, just take some of the bits from the rubbish."

Howlett said, "And at the front beforehand, what did you see to make you go around the back?"

"You mean, what did I see before the taxi hit the building?"

Catrin said, "Yes, when you looked in."

"Not much. It all looked the same inside as the last time I looked, to be honest. I wasn't hopeful of anything round the back. Other than the painting in the corner, the one with the island."

"What about it?"

"It had gone."

They were going through it one more time, to Edie's evident annoyance.

"Well, apart from the art facing the front; the 'stoppers' - you know, to get people looking."

She looked at the detectives as if she was about to lecture them on gallery exhibition technique.

"The eye-catchers, to make 'passing trade' stop. I always use one of my 'English roses' myself. It often works, stopping the foreigners as they are going by. I paint the 'Sir Winston Churchill' rose a lot. That gets them, soon as I say the name.

"That day they still had the two paintings in the raffle thing; the fundraiser for whatever, right in the centre of the gallery, facing the window. The others, well, they are at right angles, on the walls. So you are seeing them sideways, or at an angle at least. You follow?"

"Yes," said Catrin.

"So the island one wasn't in the same location. It could have been moved. Then of course, when it was over, the taxi thing, I mean, God knows what was where."

She paused.

"My tea is getting cold."

Catrin thought for a moment. She decided to revisit the statement Edie had made about the back of the building.

"At the back. The white stuff on the discarded wood; the plaster or gesso. Do you still have any of it, or the wood pieces? Frames, were they?"

Edie looked at her calculatingly.

"No, the frames are gone, recycled in my art. But the powder, it's technical."

Catrin looked directly at her.

"Well, try me. I will ask if I get lost."

Edie nodded. "Plaster washes off after soaking it a little, you see. Gesso is a sod of a thing to get off once it sets. It's the acrylic in it. Harder than plaster and it sticks."

"Gesso? You are sure?" asked Catrin.

Edie Cummings nodded. "Course I am. I still have the tub with some left. It's hard; I should have thrown it out... but I didn't yet. There was an empty tub of plaster and one half-full one, and a smaller tub of gesso, nearly empty. I took the half-full one and the gesso tub."

Catrin said, "Off the record at 11.27."

She switched off the recording. Her eyes were gleaming, looking at Howlett, who was seeing the same thing, she thought.

"Edie, PC Howlett is going to take you for more tea and a snack. Have what you want. On me. And thank you for your help. And then PC Howlett and another person from forensics will take you home and collect the tub from you. And we will need your finger prints, if that's OK. Not for any reason other than checking which are yours and which are someone else's."

Edie's face changed to an expression of protest, that then disappeared as Catrin said, "And they will stop off and buy you a new tub of gesso. Won't you, DC Howlett?"

Edie said, "Can I have a sandwich then; in the canteen?"

She was looking a little more calculating now as she picked up that her information was of value. "And will you want me at the trial of the robbers, to talk about the stuff at the back?"

Catrin replied, "We are a long way from anything like that, Edie. But thank you for your help."

She stood up, gathering her folders, showing they should leave. But Edie was immovable.

She said, "It's just, where I sell my art, I get moved on a lot.

No street licence, so… I wondered if someone could have a word. One of those street trading officers even took my pictures away once, the bugger. Confiscated them, all my hard work. Coppers aren't so bad, they just tell me to pack up and move, but the trading officers are like 'little Hitler' sorts. They should get proper jobs not harass 'enterprennairs' like me."

Howlett was hiding her smile as best she could.

"Entrepreneur, Edie?"

"Yes, I take cast-off stuff and recycle it into works of original art and beauty. The young people understand. They buy it like hot cakes sometimes; I can't make enough. One even told a Little Hitler to leave me alone once; bought both my pictures and told him to bugger off."

Catrin, was smiling. She said, "And where do you go to sell your art?

"Generally Trafalgar Square, or around Billingsgate and up towards St. Paul's, depending on where the tourists are; they go for them, the young ones, as I said."

Carin looked at her, putting on an expression of firm negotiation.

"How about I get you into Spitalfields Arts Market, with no hassle there? If I can fix that?"

Edie wrinkled her nose.

"It's a bit out of the way, out in the sticks. I like to be closer to the Thames. I tried it a couple of times near there, but not… you can get me inside, without being hassled?

Carin said, "It will take some fixing, but I will do it."

She gave the impression it was her last and best offer.

"Fair enough, Inspector Sayer. That would be very much appreciated, at least for rainy days. And in return, I will be happy to be a witness for free; you just say."

As they walked out, before Howlett took Edie for her sandwich, she whispered to Catrin, "And at least we will know where to find her if we do need her."

Catrin nodded. "If it's raining, true."

She hadn't the heart to tell Edie that being called as a witness was not exactly discretionary, if it was needed.

As she watched them leave, Edie said to Howlett a little imperiously, "We can stop at Cornelissen's for the gesso; they sell quality stuff. And I will look round the back -

Howlett said, "You are getting a sandwich and tea, then we can get your gesso in Jackson's."

When Catrin briefed Coltrane he couldn't help but laugh.

"First Bratby, now Edie Cummings, your very own Gulley Jimson. I could see her tearing around Cornelissen's creating mayhem, from what you say."

L. Cornelissen & Son was a high-end art supply shop near the British Museum that had been in business since the mid-1800s.

Catrin smiled at thought. Coltrane's reference to Jimson was to a fictional eccentric artist. The producers of the film of the book about Jimson, 'The Horse's Mouth', had hired Bratby to create paintings specifically for the film. She couldn't get away from the man.

Then he turned serious.

"It could be that something happened at the gallery before the robbery, but what? Edie seeing that Seal Island had been moved; you spotting marks of what could be gesso or plaster on the floor that were not there previously; and now left-over gesso found outside. Nothing substantial, really."

So she shared the idea that her team had come up with.

"Well, we do have this idea, Neville. But it may not pan out."

27 RUBBISH

When she had finished outlining her team's brainstorming conclusion, Coltrane said, "Let me get this straight. You are suggesting Seal Island was stolen separately from the other five works. It was taken down over the weekend and encased in something which prepared it to look like part of the debris from the damage inflicted during the robbery. That somehow the Gorton siblings disguised it as rubbish using, in part perhaps, gesso and plaster daubed over some sort of casing, covering it. Is that right?"

Catrin said "Yes Neville, it's a possibility, a theory. The Bierstadt work is not that big. If it was disguised, it could have been moved out in the rubbish. It was a real mess after the taxi went through the front.

"We don't have the details sorted out. Howlett is with Bertie Wells trying to work out how it could have been executed. Harper is tracking down the contractor who did the removal of materials after the SOCOs finished; we need to talk to them. I have a call into the SOCO team lead for the forensic activity at the scene, but she is out on-site on a case, her voicemail says."

She added, "It would mean that the Gorton couple orchestrated it; Seal Island, the theft of the other paintings, the robbery, the damage to their shop. Complicated, but not impossible. We really need now the time sequence of events after we took control of the scene; our focus had been entirely on the pre-robbery days and hours."

Coltrane nodded.

"Interesting theory - and that's all it is at present, despite the gesso and this woman's observations. But I don't see why they would do it that way. If they could get five paintings out by theft, why not the sixth?"

Catrin said, "We don't know; other than limitations on the capacity of the escape vehicle. The images from CCTV weren't clear on the exact number; nor were the witness statements consistent. But you would think they would load the taxi with the Bierstadt in preference to any of the others they took, from a value viewpoint. We can't explain that flaw in our argument, either. We are just connecting the dots."

Her boss looked at Catrin, worried. "I wonder what the SOCO team will think of this suggestion. We should talk to them first, I think, Catrin, before we do much more."

In four hours they found out what the SOCOs thought. Catrin and Neville Coltrane were summonsed to Chief Superintendent Bob Matheson's office. Already seated at the table was his counterpart heading the Forensic Services Unit, Nigel Drummond and, beside him, a woman Catrin didn't recognize.

The introductions were made and Bob Matheson said, "I understand that a rumour is out there that the SOCOs at the Gorton Gallery robbery missed a disguised painting somehow. That a valuable painting slipped away in the building rubbish?"

Coltrane said, "The idea was discussed this morning, sir; it is no more than a possibility, at present. Whether the owners, the sister and brother, could have used materials there to cover and disguise the painting before the robbery."

"Worthy as that is, as an idea," Drummond responded, "it would have been a courtesy if someone had spoken to us first. Corinne received an irate call from the CEO of the specialist contractor who cleared the debris after the incident. A DS Harper was asking him questions and he put two and two together. He called us, a bit put out. The contractor does other work with similar security status both within the Met and for the City police and it worried him.

"It was our arrangement, under our control, not the gallery or the insurers, albeit that it was later billed to the insurance company. The scene was still designated as a crime scene, but it wasn't exactly a good idea to have Old Bond Street closed for very long, as you can appreciate. Corinne?"

The civilian forensic scientist pulled out a USB memory stick and placed it on the table.

"I was the site supervisor throughout, from the first call until the designation of the site no longer being an active crime scene. Apart from my deputy covering some portions of time, my teams were on scene in shifts for two fourteen-hour days, with me there for the main shift each day.

"The front of the building where the taxi went through was glass, stone and brick and a little lumber and metal from window framing. Immediately inside were some damaged display units and paintings. We took the structural items apart completely as part of the process. These files categorize everything removed from the site, front and back, including photographs. It provides the description and the dimensions of everything, as each piece was added, painstakingly, to the dumpster."

She pushed it across to Catrin.

"I assure you, DI Sayer, the painting did not leave the site in the manner you are now investigating."

She sat back. Her chance to speak seemed to have dissipated her earlier image of being the affronted party.

After a silence, Neville said, "Well, thank you for -."

Catrin interrupted him.

"I am sorry, it's my fault. You are right; I should have come to the SOCO team first, before I did anything else. I didn't. The possibility seemed reasonable, based on new evidence and I got caught up in following the lead. I asked DS Harper to follow up with the contractor. DCI Coltrane's first comment to me was actually along the lines of your concern, so all I can do is take responsibility for acting too prematurely."

She knew she was blushing heavily at her error.

Chief Superintendent Matheson said, "Thank you, DI Sayer, for that. Nigel?"

The forensic chief nodded, "It's sorted now. And thank you, Bob, for fitting this in so quickly. Corinne, we should go."

He stood up, as did the SOCO. She smiled at Catrin. "It's OK. It's as well to check everything."

Catrin nodded, attempting to smile but failing and soon found herself with her boss and his own superior.

Matheson said, "Sayer, chin up. Keep at it. We need to find this painting, Neville says. So full marks for leaving no avenue unexplored. You just happened to fall across Corinne Gilbertson; probably one of the best in their bunch. Next time, talk to Neville or me when you get a lead before implementing it, if you can. It's still early days for you in this role."

"Yes sir, I will. Thank you."

He turned to Coltrane. "I think that's it; we didn't need the defensive barrage."

Coltrane smiled and stood up; Catrin jumping up also, getting the signal but also her expression querying Matheson's last remark.

Matheson said, as he picked up his desk phone handset, "The Barking betting shop robbery. There were four SOCOs assigned to the site. At one point a CCTV camera caught five of them there; one was leaving with a case. If the officer managing the outside security hadn't noticed, he would have walked off with quite a bit of cash. None of the four noticed; each was lost in their own task.

"If you want to steal mail, steal a post van to take it away in… if you want to steal money hidden on an investigation site…"

Catrin said, "You need a security uniform, a police uniform… or a SOCO suit. No one would bother."

"Precisely. Back to it."

He spoke into the phone, "Millie, send in the next ones..." as Coltrane and Sayer went out through his door.

In the corridor, Catrin said, "Neville, I am sorry for the mistake."

He looked at her and wrinkled his nose.

"Let it go, Catrin; that was what Bob was saying. You made a decision. That's what leaders do. Hopefully most times they are right; sometimes they are wrong. It goes with the job."

He was thinking as they walked to the lift.

"Seal Island wasn't found in the gallery. It wasn't in the rubbish and it's not in the Acton haul. Unless the Nahigians tell us where it is, we are out of luck. I think it must have gone in the getaway taxi after all and has already been sold off. The Americans will have to mourn the loss. That's all there is to it."

"We will tell them during the conference call on Friday."

28 GALLERY

Catrin was back in her office.

"We are going to revisit the Gorton gallery together. Mark and I will interview Jocelyn Gorton. Isabelle, you look around, see if anything gives you inspiration while you have the crime scene photos in your mind as a reference. We are looking for anything that was missed; anything. What, I don't know, but if you see it…"

The sister had been due back at work that morning and Isabelle had verified she was in the gallery.

Howlett said, "And we have another case request just now, ma'am, while you were out; not through DCI Coltrane, direct from Sussex Police."

"Sussex Police - wasn't that where the Alzheimer's case - ?"

Howlett said, "Yes; but from a different station. About a stuffed dog painting that was stolen."

Harper was containing himself and Catrin burst out laughing. "A stuffed dog, that's a 'collectible', so send it to Antiques!"

"No," Harper said, "It's a nineteenth century painting of a work by a famous taxidermist of the period. It belongs to local banker; quite influential I expect, for them to call on us again. It was very lifelike, I gather, by a Victorian artist who

213

specialized in painting such things."

Catrin rolled her eyes.

"This is one of yours, I take it, Howlett?"

Isabelle said, deadpan, "In the past, yes; but you did say you were reviewing assignments, so perhaps Mark or yourself would like to go looking for a stuffed dog in Bognor Regis?"

She looked at Harper, an amused smile on her face. He shook his head, grinning.

Catrin looked at her DC. "Not this time, Isabelle; it's all yours. Arrange a visit if it can't be done remotely; but not before we three have finished the gallery visit and get prepared for the coordination videoconference this week. We need to get all of us thinking this one through."

~~

As she looked around on arrival, Catrin saw that the Gorton gallery was similar in size to 'Liz's Place', the gallery that sold her own art. But that was off Fulham Road, just west of Harrods, rather than in Bond Street, the heart of the high-end art market. Catrin knew that Liz Marshall had looked into this carefully as she set up her fledgling business to bring new British artists to the market.

Her gallery had to be located where she could attract customers, but with lower overheads. The current location overlapped the Knightsbridge and Kensington areas, but brought in an informed client base living further west; people who wanted British art by living artists without paying Bond Street prices.

The Gorton gallery had done very well, though, according to its books and, surprisingly, it seemed to do at least as well if not better after the theft.

What wasn't stolen, ironically, was the painting by John Bratby. Catrin was taking in the work as she waited for Jocelyn Gorton to finish with a customer.

The plaque by the painting gave the details. Len, the father of the current owners, was a contemporary of Bratby and both had studied at the Royal College of Art. They had been painting in Italy at the same time. In Bratby's case, he was on a bursary, in Len's case, his mother's indulgence. While the time there was unnerving for Bratby, as he found it did not stimulate his art, for Len Gorton it was transforming; he loved the place and spent much time there afterwards.

Bratby returned to the UK and developed his own styles and artistic responses that came to be called the forerunner of 'Kitchen Sink Realism'. Len Gorton painted in Italy, increasingly turning out more derivative than original works, he realised; competently executed but without any real identity he could call his own. He stopped painting and, using an inheritance, opened the current gallery.

In establishing the Gorton, he did not forget his friend John. He gave display space to works by Bratby that, at first, did not sell. Later, they sold like hot cakes; except for this one Catrin was looking at, which was not for sale. It had not been purchased, apparently; it had been a personal gift; a portrait of the artist's first wife.

Howlett moved next to Sayer.

"Another Bratby, ma'am."

"We will be falling over them soon, Isabelle. DCI Worsley used to call this team the Goya-chasers. I will have to correct her on that."

Howlett laughed.

"I am not going to tell you the names we called the ACU at the beginning; it was nowhere near as polite. But I like this one. I remember it from the initial investigation."

Catrin looked. "But the frame and the matt?"

She pulled a face so that only her colleague could see. If anything, the dark mustard mat should have set off the vivid colours of the work but tonally it was wrong; too dominant. A different mounting for the work was needed overall, particularly as the plain, rough-wood frame seemed weak, out of balance with the matt and the painting itself. It really needed reframing completely.

"Three detectives, I am surprised. Is there anything new happening regarding our robbery, Inspector?"

Jocelyn Gorton was in her forties, looking too thin for her height, but very stylish; her dress, her designer hairstyle and her very even, deep tan. Catrin doubted that it was the result of a lot of time outside in Dubai playing tourist or working; more likely it came from carefully controlled exposures at a the hotel spa.

"Yes, Ms. Gorton. We are re-examining the case in detail and neither DS Harper nor myself were involved during the initial investigation. And we have now recovered the two McKinnon paintings during another investigation, as well as the three other works you lost."

The woman's face transformed, she looked happy; then it clouded over. "But not 'Seal Island', I take it, from what you said?"

"No, not that painting. And there are no leads to it at present, unfortunately. So we begin again. I would like you to take us through your own movements and those of people you were in contact with in the week leading up to the robbery."

Gorton said, "But I have given my statement already. In fact, this officer, DC Howlett, was present when the other inspector interviewed me."

Catrin persisted. "Nevertheless, we are going through it again - with everyone."

She was judging the reaction of the woman. But after a grimace, Jocelyn Gorton said, "Where do I start?"

They walked her through the time period again, getting largely the same answers. Variations they noticed were not significant and could well be explained by the passage of time. On two occasions they pointed out the differences. She blushed, correcting herself.

"I am not making it up, Inspector, honestly. I am trying."

"It has been two years, Ms. Gorton; it is understandable."

At the end, she talked about coming back to the gallery

after the police tape was removed to meet with the insurers and builders; dealing with her brother's shock and her own.

Catrin led her to talk about the damage and the clean-up; something not covered in the original investigation. Gorton went through the repair stage; the temporary boarding of the front, the planning and repair of the front wall and entrance.

"Was there damage elsewhere?"

"Well, the lights; the vibration unseated several joist mounts for lighting so a number of lights were out."

"But no more structural damage?"

"No, thank goodness."

"On the photographs we saw some marks along the floor on the back wall. Did you notice them?"

She showed her a photograph taken from the SOCO database.

"Actually, yes I did. They weren't present on the Friday morning before I left, but they were there once we got back into the gallery, after the crime scene designation was removed. But after the robbery, it didn't register that much, it just got lost in everything else. Is it important?"

Catrin shrugged. "We just noticed it during the review, that's all. We have no idea, really."

She changed the subject.

"And Mr. Gorton; when will he be home, for us to speak to?"

The woman looked a little saddened.

"Frankly, I am not sure. It was part of our discussion there last week. He wants to make Dubai our primary site now; I don't. We didn't agree on it. He has found someone who would share these premises. He wants to sell up and lease back some display space. Financially it makes sense; people are always after property here. But this is where our father started the business and I don't want to lose that."

She paused, thinking.

"Somehow it doesn't seem right to transfer control of the gallery here."

Catrin waited for more. Isabelle Howlett was walking

217

around, half-listening to Harper and Sayer doing the interview, taking in the works on display. She had just returned again to the Bratby painting.

Gorton looked up, past the two officers.

"We are going to have further analysis of the business options by a consultant. It may come down, perhaps, to us separating our business interests entirely. While I supported the Dubai development, it was always to me ancillary; a new growth area, not a replacement. But with Russell, it has become dominant."

She noticed Howlett.

"In fact, the only concession I made to him last week was to have our father's painting by John Bratby relocated there; an appeasement, in a sense. I have ideas for redeveloping our displays in that area anyway. It seemed to satisfy Russell in the short term; a step along the road he wants.

"But when he is heading back here, I can't say. He has made no plans to return at present, I regret to say. He likes the life out there."

She smiled at the two officers.

"Sorry. Family matters that don't really affect you. I am wasting your time."

Catrin said, almost as an aside, "Surely part of the value for the new gallery is to have this location also? To attract top artists from the region who will want to have their works displayed for sale in London."

Jocelyn Gorton smiled ruefully. "Almost my exact words, Inspector. He claimed a simple contractual arrangement would suffice, but my lawyer is not so sure; we are checking that. But why make it more complicated than it currently is?"

Catrin suddenly had a thought. "Do you know, or can you tell me, if he is developing other partner arrangements for the Dubai location - or another addition?"

The gallery owner looked at her, re-assessing the detective, it seemed.

"He hasn't said that, but I suspect that he is doing so. He made a comment about 'expanding east in the future - India, he thought - but couldn't consider having three galleries. He would need external financing for that. It took a lot of our resources setting up the Dubai gallery with a local partner, an Emirati national. Everything in the Emirates works that way. All foreign businesses there need a local partner."

Her voice chilled as she finished. Catrin thought that was clearly a point of contention between the brother and sister.

Howlett called over, as she approached the desk.

"Who did the matting and framing, Ms. Gorton? I meant to ask during the earlier interviews."

She meant the Bratby. She avoided looking at Catrin as she spoke.

Gorton smiled.

"My father himself, early on. He did some mounting of contemporary works he showed back then. But he wasn't that good at it, to be honest. Which is where your question came from, I think.

"But being modern art, you can get away with a lot. Part of the reason I agreed to Russell moving the painting to Dubai is that we always disagreed about re-mounting it. The matt and frame are not suited to the painting, I maintain. Russell always insisted it should not be changed. It is an altar for him; a memory of our father, not a painting."

Howlett eyed her boss; that was the answer to her earlier observation.

Catrin wasn't really focusing on the Bratby and its framing. She was now wondering how they would get to re-interview Russell Gorton in a timely manner - and whether DCI Coltrane would authorize a visit to Dubai for that purpose.

~~

As they drove back to Scotland Yard, Catrin's mobile rang; it was DI Merton's number, from the West Mercia team. She connected as the other two went quiet.

"Catrin? It's Alan Merton."

"Yes, Alan; I am driving at present, I won't be in the office for half an hour or so in this traffic."

"Well, I am just following up on the discussion you had with DCI Hendry. We have now identified the victim, a former prisoner in Wilson Green, the same location as the man Edwin Ashe. We have a list of people at the prison - prisoners and staff there during the week they overlapped. Could you review it against your own investigation of that painting for us? Just in case?"

"Happy to do that. Send it over."

"The email is on its way now. Let us know if anything strikes you as interesting, if you would."

They closed the call.

"They are moving along, ma'am," said Howlett.

"It's a homicide team," said Catrin, "And they seem to be moving a little faster than we are on this case, I agree."

Her phone beeped. She had a new email.

In the office she opened up her laptop; it was easier to view the list there. The body in the grave was a man called Ian Kendrick, a member of a gang in Birmingham with a long prison record. He had been in Wilson Green at the same time as Edwin Ashe; in his case, for three years of a seven years sentence, not a week on remand. Kendrick was granted parole a year after Ashe's death.

Her eyes stopped three-quarters of the way down the list of other prisoners in Wilson Green the same week as Ashe, focusing on one name. Michael John Farrell, sentenced to six years for robbery, with a previous sentence for armed robbery and assault; a repeat offender. He spent his last sentence in HMP Birmingham, at Wilson Green. Previously, he was incarcerated at HMP Dovecote, in Staffordshire, a category B facility; part of it in secure confinement. He was released two years after Ashe's death.

Not a common name, Farrell. She was about to go into the system and search him out, then something stopped her. She knew she should call DI Merton right back; but she didn't. She sat there, thinking back to the conversations with Noel Richards and the people in Tregynon, recalling the man at the church dinner.

After a few minutes she called Chris, checking what he was doing. Fifteen minutes later she was closing up her system, heading out.

"Harper, brief DCI Coltrane about today's discussion, if you would, when he gets back. Ask him about the possibility of interviewing Russell Gorton in Dubai. I am taking the rest of the day off; something has come up. I will see you both sometime tomorrow."

With that she was out the door.

As Howlett checked the shared printer later, she found a page uncollected; a confirmation of a reservation for tonight at the Maesmawr Hall Hotel in Tregynon for a Mr. and Mrs. Treneer. She worked it out and decided to say nothing, just putting the page in her boss's in-tray, face down.

Mark had just headed over to Coltrane's office once he saw him return. Howlett decided to call her contact in the Surrey Police, to see about setting up a quick trip down to Bognor Regis. It would keep her out of the way, she decided. She would be chasing a painting of a stuffed animal if the flag went up that her boss had absconded back to Wales.

29 CONFESSION

On the drive up to Powys, Chris complained lightly about the fact that being a chauffeur was not part of his job description. Catrin fired back that the Audi was more computer than car; he should be happy. And it was a romantic evening away with his wife, if anyone asked.

"Promises," he said, trying to cheer her up; she was looking quite absorbed, worried now she had made a decision to go to Tregynon first and see Farrell, rather than simply call DI Merton. She argued to herself that she was 'following up on their own investigation, started by Minister Richards', but she knew it wouldn't wash with either DCI Hendry - or, indeed, DCI Coltrane. Her last instruction, from Matheson, was to run new ideas past one of them before acting. And here she was, heading back to Wales.

In truth, she needed to think through what she was doing and didn't want to do that while driving. She knew she had to be back in the Met tomorrow if, for nothing else, the Task Force coordination videoconference in the afternoon. They had to give them the bad news on the Bierstadt. The failure to make progress with the location of 'Seal Island' was with her team, so she should be there.

In the end she called for help, leaving a voicemail message

with Inspector Meredith in Newtown. They were near Warwick when the Powys officer called her back and Catrin took her time explaining the developments.

"Are you sure about this, Catrin? The cleanest thing is just to report back to the West Mercia team, isn't it?"

"No, I am not sure about anything, Carole; that's part of the problem. But I will need to get back to them sometime today; I can't hold off too long. And I don't want to leave a track in the database searches before I do, just in case."

There was a silence.

Meredith said, "How about I get Seren Fowles to call Farrell, innocently? She could set something up at the church with him. I am sure she can come up with a reason. If not, she can find out where he will be this evening."

Catrin thought that was a good idea.

She asked, "In fact, whatever happens, can I borrow her and Constable Morrissey this evening? To go with me. They know the place and the people."

Meredith responded, "He is on duty and Seren will be OK with working late, I hope. And there is strength in numbers, from what you say. But I can't see John Farrell getting violent with us. It would be quite out of character, despite his size."

"I think so, too. But you never know. If it is the same man, he has a record that includes violence."

~~

As it worked out, Deacon Farrell was going to be at St. Deiniol's Church anyway that evening. He had a meeting with some youth members there, due to finish at 8.00 p.m.

PC Fowles said, "I just left it that I would drop by, ma'am, around the end of the meeting. He said that would be good; it would force the meeting to closure, as sometimes they went on a bit. I just told him I had someone he may want to speak to. He assumed it was a person in need of help and I didn't deny it."

She and PC Morrissey had arrived at the hotel in uniform together as Catrin and Chris were finishing a quick supper. It was now 7.45 p.m. Chris could see that his wife was nervous about this course of action she had instigated; she knew she was out on a limb.

Catrin said, "I will follow you over in my car but the three of us will go in together."

Alone with Chris in the lobby afterwards, she said, "Watch the football or whatever. I will call when I am done."

She kissed him.

"See you soon."

He countered, "You should be very careful. No risks, right?"

Then more humorously he said, "A nice romantic hotel in Wales with my wife and… she is dumping me, heading off with other police officers for the evening."

She whispered, "Later. And you need to rest anyway; you're the chauffeur; you are driving me back early tomorrow."

Then she was out into the night.

~~

When they entered, the meeting involving Farrell in the church hall had just about finished and half a dozen teenagers were preparing to leave. John Farrell took in the appearance of the detective from London and the two local officers in uniform. The expression on their faces told him everything.

"Let's go into Reverend Crouch's office; he is not back yet. You wanted to talk about something, Seren, and seeing that Inspector Sayer is back here, I have a suspicion what that is."

Catrin said nothing until they were in the office with the door closed. She sat opposite Farrell with Fowles next to her. Morrissey stood to one side. He wanted to stay on his feet, just in case, he had said outside.

Catrin said, "When I was here last time, Deacon Farrell, just before we were leaving, you found out that I was an art crime detective. You gave me a look which I took to mean you would like to talk further, but then you changed your mind. So now is the opportunity."

He said, "You mean about the painting that Judith had; the one you came to look into? Yes I gave it to her. I had a similar one given to me, but I sold it for charity. Penance paintings, I think of them as."

Catrin asked, "How did you come into possession of these paintings?

He thought a moment.

"Can I talk with you alone?"

Sayer shook her head. "Fowles and Morrissey are police officers; this is their jurisdiction, not mine - and I have already shared my suspicions with them and their inspector. I asked them to accompany me because you know each other. It won't get easier than this. In fact, it will get harder once I call in others, which I will be doing."

He nodded, understanding now that there was something more significant to this issue.

She said, "Did you get them from Edwin Ashe?"

He shook his head.

"I got them from a man called Ingelsby, Colin Ingelsby, now deceased. He delivered them to me the year before he died. I went to his funeral in 2012. When he gave me the paintings he knew he was terminally ill. He asked me to keep one myself and give the other one to Judge Richards, as he had found out I knew her."

"You knew Ingelsby from HMP Birmingham, Wilson Green, I take it."

He looked at her, realizing that she knew a lot about him.

"From before, in fact. We served time together in HMP Dovecote. We both had other lives."

"Catrin said, "But you knew Ashe and this Ingelsby from your time in Wilson Green; correct? You were all there at the same time"

He nodded, "Of Ashe, more than knew him. He wasn't there long. But yes. I know his story."

"So you are aware of the Ashe signatures on the Bratby

paintings, and the reason for them?"

He paused.

"All too well. Yes I do. But… there is a letter, sealed; it is in my flat in Newtown. Perhaps we ought to get it. It was given to me by Ingelsby, for something like this, he said. If something occurred because of the paintings."

Catrin shook her head.

"It will be retrieved at the right time, by the right people; the team investigating the death of a man called Ian Kendrick, another former prisoner in Wilson Green at the same time as you. His body has been found buried in woods in a golf course near Kidderminster. Buried, in fact, with a Bratby painting with the same 'Ashe' signature. But you know about that too, I take it?"

She had phrased it carefully, leaving it open, the interpretation.

It was as if a bucket of ice-cold water had been poured over the man. After a moment he bowed his head and prayed silently. Then he looked up.

"About the painting, yes; I knew there were three. I thought Ingelsby had kept the third himself. About Kendrick; no."

He paused.

Catrin stood up.

"Mr. Farrell, I am not interviewing you. I am not the investigating officer. I just wanted to confirm that you were involved, the person who brought the Bratby painting to Judge Richards."

He nodded.

"It was me, yes; I took it along and surprised her, told her the story of Edwin Ashe, the one… you will hear in due course, I suppose, from others. She saw her role in the death of the young man and it became a bond… a strange but very spiritual bond between us. That is why she kept the painting."

Catrin's curiosity got the better of her. She said, "Judge Richards only remanded Ashe; he was in Wilson Green just a week, yet he comes out and kills himself. And now you, this man Ingelsby and Judge Richards all share some common guilt

- why?"

He sat motionless.

Then he responded, "People have gone now; it's just us until Reverend Crouch gets back. Can we get a cup of tea? I will tell you in the kitchen. And James can sit down, too. I am not running away. Then you can make your call. Will you do that?"

As they returned to the hall to go through to the kitchen, Catrin saw three people, two teenagers and a young man who couldn't be more than twenty, sitting there waiting, looking concerned.

The older one said angrily, "We saw you go in with John and wanted to wait; to make sure everything is alright. John?"

He was looking at Catrin and Seren suspiciously. Morrissey moved a step closer.

"Everything is fine, Kevin," said Farrell, but his face belied his statement to all of them.

"He's a good man," said one of the teens, "You should leave him alone!"

"Katy, now don't cause any trouble; please. Just go," said the deacon.

They looked angry, upset, Catrin could see: both at Seren Fowles and James Morrissey. They would know them through the church, at least by sight, she realised. She didn't want this meeting to go off the rails and for anything stupid to happen; she was far enough out on a limb already.

So she pointed at some chairs across the room and spoke in Welsh.

"Let's sit down. Why is Deacon Farrell a good man?"

As she moved over, she said to Farrell and Seren Fowles, "You lot can make that tea."

John Farrell and the two local police officers were left standing as the detective from London sat down with the young people from St. Deiniol's church.

For ten minutes she listened to the onslaught of reasons as

they talked across each other, bursting to inform her; things they knew personally, things they had heard. How they had found out all about him, on-line, knew his record, what he had done; but it didn't matter now. What really mattered was the person they knew, the man that helped others. One of them, Kevin, said he would be back in Stoke Heaton or dead on drugs if it wasn't for John Farrell. His comment, thought Catrin, came over as simple fact, not the hot passion of the other two. She thought that there was probably some truth in that.

Catrin took it all in, the intensity, the sincerity; the bond that had built up between these young people and the clergyman.

"He is the most genuine adult I know, he is a really, really good man," said the girl Katy, choking back tears.

Once the energy had spent a little, Catrin held up her hand and stopped them.

"I believe you," she said, softly. "I just have some questions for Deacon Farrell. Some other police officers away from here are likely to have some, too. But I believe you. Now, you need to leave us to talk, it has to be in private. That is the way it is."

They stood up. The girl impulsively ran over and gave John Farrell a hug and, after a second the other two, in solidarity, did the same before trooping out.

Then they were alone again.

Farrell said, "I didn't know they knew so much about my record."

But his face was reflecting the surprise that, knowing it, they were so supportive of him.

Seren Fowles said, "Young people and the internet; they can find out anything."

There was a sudden lull as John Farrell realised that DI Sayer wanted to get back to the business at hand.

"You suggested tea?" said Catrin.

30 INGELSBY

Farrell closed his eyes, said a short, silent prayer as his mug steamed a little in front of his face. They didn't push him.

"I work with people coming out of prison because I understand. I was in them myself, more than once. A violent, angry man, then."

He glanced at each officer in turn.

"There are no lone warriors in prisons, DI Sayer; that's Hollywood fiction. There are structures, rules within; what works, what doesn't. Tough guys alone don't last. Believe me, it doesn't work that way. You choose your group; you live by the rules; prison rules sometimes, prisoners' rules always. I was high in the heap of my lot. The man in the grave, Kendrick, was of similar status in his. We were similar personalities but different allegiances. Colin Ingelsby was lower down in Kendrick's lot, until I took him in, gave him protection. That was after Kendrick had him beaten twice."

He was assessing the reaction but seeing nothing from the officers.

"Ingelsby was gay, but he was not a predator. Ashe wasn't gay, but was put in a cell with him. And he was a beautiful-looking young man. The paintings of him as a boy show it; even in those crude sketches, don't you think?"

He paused. Catrin didn't answer his question. She wasn't there to discuss art.

He continued, "People use handsome or other words for men but … it was not wrong to use the word beautiful about Edwin Ashe. It was Colin who said that about him, to me; when he brought the paintings over."

His face lost the look of recalling past memories and he grimaced.

"Now Ian Kendrick was not gay but he was a predator, sexually and in other ways; intimidation, control of others. And Ashe was a target. Being good looking and young in a men's prison is a big liability."

He looked down at the table, deciding what to say next.

"For want of a nail - the old nursery rhyme, you know? That was the sort of sequence leading up to Edwin's death. I was a part of that 'for want of' to be truthful. The start though was his own doing, from his own lips.

"Ashe was in his early thirties but looked in his twenties; some people are lucky like that whereas me…"

He smiled ruefully. They knew what he meant.

"Edwin had been to university twice, dropped out or failed each time; it wasn't his money paying, it was his parents who financed him. Drugs were part of the issue, I gather. Then in his late twenties he got a job with a company, nothing special, but it gave him some independence. He and a woman he fell for at work came up with a scheme to defraud their employer of quite a bit of money. He was in Finance, she was in Purchasing; they forged signatures, invented suppliers, jigged around inventory numbers. How? What? I don't know. Ashe wasn't denying it in Wilson Green. In fact, Colin told him to shut up about it. But the man was scared; we all are, first time in. He was trying to act so tough. Newcomers often do."

He paused, distracted.

"Do you understand what I am saying?"

Sayer said, "He was frightened, good-looking and other men wanted him sexually, including Kendrick?"

"Kendrick in particular. He was a right bastard. Come to think of it, so was I, in my own way, back then. Of course, Colin Ingelsby fell in love with Ashe. But he never touched him, despite sharing a cell for a week. For him it was primarily romantic love, I would say. Ashe was oblivious, I heard; he just saw that Colin was being helpful and friendly."

Catrin said, "Did Kendrick molest Ashe, then, during remand?"

"No, not then. What I heard was, it was intimidation, a threat disguised as a promise. He had two of his people bring Ashe along to his cell and he told him how attractive he was and, once he came back after his next court appearance, he would be his; lock, stock and barrel. 'Just a heads up', he told him. 'There would be benefits, so think about it. Get used to the idea'.

"That's what Colin told me; and I believe him."

"Why?" asked Catrin.

"Because Colin came to me and asked me to help, pleaded with me, in fact. Ashe had gone back to their cell, scared stiff, and talked to his friendly cellmate, so Colin came to me. He wanted them both to be part of our lot."

"Gang, you mean?" said Catrin, "We are talking about gang structure, not social groups, aren't we?"

She disliked his obliqueness on the description.

He looked down at the table and nodded.

"I didn't see any profit in getting involved, so I told him no. I was all about self-interest in those days, believe me."

His head came back up. Catrin saw his eyes were wet with tears.

"Later, after Ashe's death, after Colin's beating the first time, I told Kendrick to lay off him. It was causing too much trouble in the block. Then Colin went after Kendrick again, so Kendrick had him beaten worse. I couldn't allow that. Not for me, with my status."

He looked at his own thumb, the deep furrow in it.

"I was just about to crush the end of Ian Kendrick's ring finger in the door jamb. He had to hold it there while I questioned him, knowing I was going to slam it. It was his punishment."

"That was it. I crushed his finger, as promised, but didn't hurt him more than that. I had threatened that, too. I was a different person, then."

He held up his thumb, smiled a little grimly. "Prisoners' rules; don't break them."

Catrin's mind suddenly went back to the visit to the exhumation site. She thought of the channel through the grave, the discovery of some finger bones but not others on his left arm.

He looked at her, questioningly and she shook her head.

Then she asked, "Left hand or right, do you recall, in the door?"

"His left; he was right-handed. We were being generous."

Seren Fowles was absorbed in Farrell's confession. She shook her head and intervened.

"I can't believe you would be like that, John; knowing you now."

He half-smiled, half-grimaced in his nervousness at the revelation.

"I was, God forgive me. I did a lot worse, Seren."

He took a deep breath, started speaking faster, wanting to get through it.

"That's it. Colin Ingelsby was released, full of repentance and religion. I had little to do with him, to be honest. He had 'got religion' as one of my people said after Ashe died. But now I know it wasn't that; whatever he had, it wasn't that, whatever group it was he joined. By his release he was quoting verses of the Old Testament about punishment for sins. We thought he had gone off his rocker.

"About a year before my own release, I went to see the duty chaplain one day, a rabbi; something I wanted to wangle that he saw through anyway, but as he said 'no' to my request he looked at me. 'You should let it all go, John', he said. That was all. I had no idea what he was talking about, I thought, but a week later I went back and asked him.

"We talked. A month later I was done; totally exhausted with my life as it was, so I went to him again to ask for help. I started along the path I am on now. A wily old Jew led me to God and even helped me to understand Christianity."

And arrange his first suit after his ordination, Seren suddenly realised, thinking back to her discussion weeks ago with the Rector's warden, Gordon Lewis.

"In 2011, Colin came to see me, he had looked me up. I was working near Kidderminster and studying for the role I now have. We talked about life in general and then he said he had a request. He was at peace with his role in Ashe's death now."

Catrin asked, "He believed Ashe killed himself because of the threat from Kendrick, then?"

Farrell nodded, "Colin always thought so. But it was only part of it, I think. It was everything; being caught, his forthcoming trial; the disgrace. His parents were wealthy; he had no reason to steal. It was the parents that had commissioned John Bratby to do the studies of Edwin in his early teens - not finished paintings; something to choose from."

Catrin said, "Preliminary sketches?"

"That could be it. They were going to commission a painting of their son based on the sketches but Bratby ended up in a disagreement with them; it never happened, I gather. They paid him for the sketches; that was all."

Catrin had read that Bratby could be cranky with clients; she could see the scenario that Farrell described. When he fell into obscurity later in life the painter was drunk on both alcohol and egotism around his past glories. He probably charged Ashe's parents outrageous prices for the sketches.

She asked, "How did Ingelsby come into possession of the sketches? Ashe was only in Wilson Green for a week."

John Farrell laughed then looked at her seriously.

"Inspector Sayer, you don't know much about prisons, obviously! A week in one can seem like a lifetime. In fact, a day can. Colin was into the 'Art Therapy in Prisons' program, one of the things seen as mollycoddling inmates by the hardliners. It was part of the anger management and violence reduction programs; take it out on paper with paint or pastels, not with fists in the block."

He shook his head. Catrin hoped he wouldn't go off at a tangent on prison reform issues. She had to call Merton now, pretty quickly.

Farrell continued, "Colin persuaded Ashe to go with him; just the once during the week he was in. Ashe left him the paintings in the note he left behind in the car, I suppose, because he knew Colin enjoyed art. His parent's honoured the request. Sometime after the funeral they came along to the prison to visit Colin and brought the paintings, to thank him for being a friend to Edwin in prison. They had no idea, of course, of what really happened. Colin made the best of it saying how he liked Ashe and had tried to help him. But he knew better than to tell his parents any more than that.

"He kept the paintings only for a day in his cell then asked for them to be put with his personal items for when he was released. It was too painful, he told me later."

Farrell paused, reflecting.

"Colin said that Edwin had no idea that he had fallen for him; but I wonder about that. Ashe was not a naïve teenager. The fact he left him the sketches, thought about it in his final hours of life makes me think otherwise."

Catrin asked, "And Judge Richards? I can see why Ingelsby would think you and he might warrant a penance sketch, or whatever they are, but why her? Because she sent him on remand rather than give him bail? She was doing her job, that's all."

He nodded.

"He should have had bail, though. She was having a bad day, she told me. The prosecutor said Ashe had pushed a police officer during his arrest; that was enough to sway her; a violent act. In fact, Ashe had tripped on a curbstone and lost his balance, falling on the man. The prosecutor was just mining the arrest report; a fast read, that sort of thing, looking for anything he could use. Fraud, disposition to anger and hitting out."

"Judge Richards was through the hearing in no time flat. When I talked to her, she recalled it vaguely, partly because Ashe was so good-looking. She said it had occurred to her that he would have a difficult time inside, with those looks, but still, she sent him in.

"Colin had asked us to reflect on our roles and put the paintings to good use. He had done so with his, he said. But he didn't explain anything further. I didn't ask him."

Nor will I do that with you, thought Catrin. DCI Hendry will be asking what you know about that.

Farrell continued, "Later, I went to see him at the hospice. I had not long been ordained, so I asked him if he wanted to tell me more, unburden himself now, not later, if that was what it was. He smiled, was quite bright about it, really. 'No, he was fine now', he said.

"He wanted me to hold a letter for him; to open after his own death if anyone should ask about the ownership of the paintings. His friends at the church he belonged to had it. They would send it on in due course. It could help sort things out, if needed. It sounds like it will be, doesn't it? For want of a nail, as I said."

He sat back.

"That's it. I gather I will need to speak to other police officers looking into Kendrick's death?"

Catrin said, "Yes. I will call them now. And your own 'Ashe' painting?"

He looked suddenly surprised.

"I don't have it any longer. It was sold in 2013 in an auction in Shrewsbury, to help pay for my car, my Astra outside. I needed a better vehicle to do my work here. I have the details at home somewhere."

They were interrupted by the office door opening after the briefest knock. Reverend Crouch entered, seeing them together. He took in the uniforms and the stranger.

"Well, John - and Seren and Jim, we have a visitor, I see."

The momentary silence was broken by Fowles. "This is Detective Inspector Sayer, from London, Simon."

From the tone of voice and the identification of Catrin's role, the priest caught on; then he looked at John Farrell, confused.

Farrell asked, "Could I have five minutes with Reverend Crouch?"

Catrin nodded, "I am going to call DCI Hendry in the West Mercia Major Crimes Unit now. I will be outside."

Her glance to Fowles and Morrissey made it clear that they were to stay.

As she stood up, she suddenly asked, "The golf course at Kidderminster, the one by Bindley Woods; do you know it?"

The look on Farrell's face showed he understood.

"I used to work there. The body must be in the coppice, then. I told Colin Ingelsby about the course, how lovely and quiet it was in the woods; that people didn't go there."

Then he realised how it would look, how involved he could appear to be. Catrin turned and left the room. She had gone as far as she could, she felt.

31 REPORT

For some reason, Merton's mobile phone didn't connect; perhaps he had a life outside work after all, thought Catrin. It was a Detective Constable Siyal who answered Catrin's call to the 24-hour number for the West Mercia MCTF. Just as he spoke the wind picked up through the trees outside the church and she had to concentrate; she could hardly hear him.

"This is DI Sayer, Metropolitan Police. Is DI Merton available?"

She walked back along the path, moving into the lee of the church entrance. The conversation would echo in the empty church if she moved back inside.

"No, he is off-duty this evening, ma'am. You came up for a morning, I recall; the Bindley Woods case."

"Yes, that's correct. And that's what I am calling about, to report the location of Michael John Farrell on your 'possible associates list' from the prison. DI Merton sent it to me for review. The man is now using the name John Farrell and is currently in Tregynon, near Newtown, a deacon at the church there, St. Deiniol's. I am actually there now. He has information pertaining to your enquiry."

Siyal said immediately, "Is he in custody?"

"No, not formally. But two local police officers are with

him and I will arrange for others to secure access to his home. I assume DCI Hendry's team will handle any interview, custody or searches."

"Yes, they will, I expect, if you are correct. I will call DI Merton right now and let him know. We will send over a team or let you know what we want to do. He can reach you on this number, I take it?"

Her mobile had shown up on his call display.

"Yes. I need to get back."

She closed the call but decided, for some reason, to stay outside. She wasn't sure why until Seren Fowles appeared. Seren saw the London detective tucked away in the lee of the church wall, hiding from the wind.

"John asks if he can stay here until the other police officers come; in the church, praying, rather than go to the police station. Reverend Crouch has said he would stay, pray with him too, and James and I can watch him. I don't think he will be any trouble but… do you want him taken into the Newtown Station, ma'am?"

Her look said she was unsure what Catrin would want.

"Fowles, it's your patch. Clear it with Inspector Meredith and tell her I have no objection. But ask her to send someone to secure access to John Farrell's home."

"And you ma'am. What will…?"

"I am going back to my husband at the hotel once I have the call back from the West Mercia people, if I can. I don't think it will be long. I will wait here, for the storm from Hindlip to break."

She looked out across the churchyard.

"I am sorry, Seren."

Fowles looked at her; she knew what Sayer meant.

"Ma'am, I think you have handled this very sensitively. But why not wait inside? You could use Reverend Crouch's office."

They looked at each other as Catrin's mobile rang. She looked at the display.

"The heavy mob. Go call your boss."

"Sayer," she answered.

"DCI Hendry; I am with DI Merton. Where are you?"

Catrin replied, "Outside St. Deiniol's Church in Tregynon, near Newtown. Deacon John Farrell is inside, with two police officers and his priest. He was in prison with Ashe and Kendrick. He also gave the painting I was chasing to Judge Richards."

"Have you cautioned him?"

"No sir. He volunteered information that he gave the painting to Richards. He has been with his priest in the church from shortly afterwards. The locals will send officers to secure access to his home. But he can explain the link between Ashe and the man Kendrick. He seems co-operative."

"Stay there, Sayer."

"I have to leave by morning, sir. I have an important case commitment in London tomorrow afternoon."

"I will be there in an hour and a half… Just stay put."

The line went dead.

Catrin got off the phone as Fowles was winding up with Inspector Meredith.

"She's OK with it, Catrin, unless you or the others say to take him in."

Catrin said, "The West Mercia team is on its way here. Let's leave Farrell and the minister alone, other than you two watching. Actually, go back and ask Reverend Crouch to step out for a moment, if he would, please. You and Morrissey stay with Farrell. Tell Reverend Crouch he can go back directly afterwards, but I do need a word."

Within two minutes the priest was outside.

"DI Sayer, I understand what is going on. John has been explaining, but I don't think…"

She interjected, "I don't want to know anything from you, Reverend Crouch."

He looked at her, perplexed, as she continued.

"Deacon Farrell is experienced in the world of arrests and so on. He is going to fool himself that he can handle this alone."

"Yes, he says he just wants to explain…"

"No!" said Catrin, more sharply than she intended. "Now get on to someone; the bishop, whomever and get the best criminal law solicitor you know for him; convince him of that. In fact, John Farrell probably has better knowledge of the right people locally than you - or I. But other police officers will be here in a little over an hour and a half. At least have him represented by then."

The church minister looked at her, absorbing the intensity of her message as she calmed down.

She added, "The detectives from the Major Crimes Unit will be very experienced, you understand?"

He nodded.

Catrin said, "This is a possible murder investigation. They will go through him and his possessions like a dose of salts. It will be very thorough and any reasonable grounds for suspecting that he was involved, or that he had knowledge of the crime before or after the fact, will have him back in the prison system. He needs the right kind of help; right now, whether he wants it or not."

She looked at him, seeing that he now understood the seriousness of his deacon's position.

Crouch said, "I will call the bishop. He will know best."

"Reverend Crouch, spend time with him as you want, but he must stay in the presence of the two officers until our colleagues arrive. Now, if I may, I will go back in and find somewhere to wait. You will need to use your office, no doubt."

He looked at her. "Well, we are all at the front of the church now. Go back to the kitchen; make yourself a hot drink; you look like you need it."

32 PLASTERED

The first thing Inspector Meredith had said to Catrin on her arrival at St. Deiniol's was, "They woke up the people in Carmarthen, told my headquarters they were coming. I said I would come over to assist."

She was looking at the church carefully. DS Pryce had arrived a couple of minutes ahead of her and found Catrin in the kitchen.

"Carole is on the way, Catrin," was all he said then.

She put down her cup and said, "Let's go outside and wait for her - and them."

She was second-guessing herself now, having talked to Chris to update him on the developments, unsure when she was likely to be back. He wanted to come over.

"Just in case he loses it. You should have someone with you."

"Farrell is with the two officers you met."

Chris said, "Not him. The DCI coming over."

"Hendry's not going to arrest me, or anything, Chris... you stay put. The locals are here."

When they were outside the church, Pryce said to Meredith, "Are you going back in, to take over in there, ma'am? It's our patch."

"No," said Carole Meredith, "I will stay here. I am just looking where we need to lay the red carpet for the West Mercia team's arrival."

Pryce had just come back from having a cigarette further out in the church grounds. It was close to the projected arrival time of the Major Crime people so Meredith sent him inside to check the status. He reported back in a minute.

"The two clergy are praying together and talking quietly, one or the other. Fowles and Morrissey are at the back, sitting watching them."

Meredith said, "And?"

"Morrissey was comforting Seren, I think. She had been crying a bit, I think."

"On duty?" Meredith said, po-faced.

Catrin smiled. "She likes the deacon, it appears."

Carole Meredith said, "I got that impression."

"But she's young," said Pawl Pryce, "not hard cases, like you two."

He smiled and it gave Catrin her first bright moment of the evening.

"Truculent and pushy, your sergeant, Carole; needs reigning in a bit."

Meredith was just about to respond to Sayer's banter as Pryce said, "It looks like them, I think; several vehicles."

The moment of levity was over.

They were in convoy; two cars and a crime scene van. As they arrived, the wind suddenly dropped.

"Here they come," Pryce said unnecessarily, the smell of smoke from his breath now passing across the two women.

The cars parked. The SOCO van switched on its blue flashers as it stopped, probably to protect itself from the non-existent traffic, or marauding local livestock, or... simply following procedure. 'Great' thought Catrin, just what we need, flashing lights. As the West Mercia team got out of the vehicles, she could see that there were three detectives with the SOCOs; Hendry and Merton with a younger female detective, probably a DC. They exchanged brief words among themselves then, as they got closer to the church door, Alan Merton asked Catrin, "Is he still inside?"

She nodded. DCI Hendry just stared at her, waiting to see if she had anything to report. Catrin chose not to speak; he would need to fire the first shot, she decided. It was less than a second; then the three newcomers entered the church without another word. Catrin and the two Powys officers waited outside.

A minute later, Reverend Crouch came out, after which the three detectives and Deacon Farrell emerged, followed by Fowles and Morrissey. Catrin saw that they hadn't handcuffed him, at least.

Merton and the female officer took Farrell in one car, heading back towards Newtown and then on to Hindlip, Catrin assumed.

DCI Hendry walked over and said, "DI Sayer, a word please, if you would spare a moment?"

He turned to walk away, but Catrin didn't move.

"This is Inspector Meredith and Sergeant Pryce, sir," Catrin said.

He looked at them, nodded and then came over for formal introductions before he resumed his intent to question Catrin.

"The officers in there just happened to be at the church when you arrived, is that it, Sayer?"

Before Catrin could reply, Carole Meredith said, "They are members of my team and members of this church, sir. They are getting married here. They probably popped in to talk about the arrangements and found DI Sayer here."

Hendry gave Sayer a look as if, 'that didn't answer the question'.

"And you just happened to visit today, right?"

His question was to Catrin.

Pryce said, "DI Sayer used to live down the road, sir."

That was stretching it, thought Catrin; an hour's drive to Aberystwyth. She wasn't sure that the Powys officers would be helping with their dissembling comments.

She said, "I wasn't sure if the Farrell that I met here was the man on your list, so I came and checked first."

DCI Hendry said, "From a long way down the road; London. I should give you some stick over this, holding back, Sayer. But I won't unless something comes out that you have in any way compromised the investigation. Understood?"

He looked at the two local officers.

"Could I impose on you to get an officer to direct my team in the van to Farrell's flat? Lead them over? And put an officer on watch at his car; I gather it is in the car park. We probably need to impound it for forensics; I will decide after the preliminary interview."

"Certainly, sir," smiled Meredith, visibly co-operative.

The priest looked on from a few feet away, waiting.

He said, "I had better go and lock up the church." He then paused before adding, "Thank you, Inspector Sayer."

She knew what he meant; he now understood the seriousness of the issue for his deacon. His comment and Meredith and Pryce's support brought home that she had been right. This was a small community in Wales, not the big city.

DCI Hendry said, "Sayer, before you head back to London, take a walk with me, please. Country air is good for us even if it is nearly midnight. Goodnight, inspector; sergeant."

Catrin looked at Pryce and Meredith and smiled, then fell into step alongside the tubby tyrant. He was exaggerating; it wasn't long after 11.00 p.m.

"My team thinks I should jump all over you, but I am not going to. You had a suspicion that Farrell was involved but sat on it until you drove up and sorted it out. I am not sure what DCI Coltrane will say to you. I called him. He had no idea you were here, did he?"

"No, sir."

"He tells me you have a big item tomorrow, some international case."

"Yes, sir."

He looked at her.

"Yes sir, no sir, Sayer. Is that it?"

She looked at his face and realised that in fact, she could talk to him, one-on-one, for some reason.

"I wanted to be sure. This is a small village. The man is clearly involved in 'good works' as they say. The last thing was to have all this -"

She indicated the cars, the SOCO van, the blue lights flashing.

"- roll through without foundation."

He looked at her.

"You come from a village yourself?"

"No, from Pontypridd, a small town. But like here, people know each other. It will be the talk of the community tomorrow and... I wanted to be sure, that's all."

The senior detective stopped suddenly and turned to face her.

"Staying at a hotel, I take it?"

"The Maesmawr Hall Hotel, yes. My husband is there; he drove up and will drive back, while I sleep. He is a computer tech with the Met. We will leave very early tomorrow. I can sleep in cars and on planes."

"You had better head back, then. Thank you for the help. I will let DCI Coltrane know by email that it was appreciated; perhaps that will help you out of your hole, a little."

"Thank you, sir."

He smiled knowingly. "You also got what you wanted though; didn't you? How Judge Richards came to have a painting by this artist Bratby with a new signature plastered on it; it was a part of the reason for coming up, wasn't it?"

Catrin nodded, "Yes, to be truthful, it was a big part. And the signature wasn't plastered, it was painted."

He seemed happy with that.

"We are taking Farrell back to Hindlip. I will let you know anything relevant to your investigation that comes out of the interview. He has a solicitor lined up, Merton says. The man already called; fast that. Goodnight."

His face showed his suspicion as he turned away, heading back to his vehicle.

She said nothing, keeping her hopes to herself, just calling after him, "Can you let me know? Not simply about the painting; about Farrell, too?"

He said without turning back, "Yes, you deserve that. DI Merton will be in touch."

Catrin drove back to the hotel, expecting to go up to her room to see her husband. She found him in the bar, talking with a sales rep. They were watching football together on television.

"Gavin, this is my wife, Catrin. She has been visiting people here," he said.

The sales rep smiled. "I just got here a few minutes ago. There must be something going on near the church; police cars were there with blue flashing lights. Did you see it? Chris gave me the highlights of the game so far."

Catrin smiled. "Yes, I did. I think I will head up to our room; leave you two to the match."

Chris stood up. "Goodnight, Gavin. It was nice talking to you."

"Is everything OK?" he asked, when they were out of earshot.

She nodded. "As well as could be expected."

She smiled at her husband and took his hand and then put her arm around his waist. In a few hours they would need to be on the road, to make an early start back to London. She had seen a text come in from Neville Coltrane and decided it could wait a while.

~~

Catrin woke near the M5/M42 interchange suddenly, having dropped off to sleep again almost as soon as they left the hotel, shortly after 5.00 a.m. It must be the lights of the motorway, she thought. 'Painted not plastered' was front and centre in her thoughts, chasing her into consciousness.

"Do you want some coffee," said Chris. "I will look for a place -."

"In a minute, thanks. Something just came to me; it must have been what Hendry said to me last night."

She pulled out her mobile, checked the time and phoned Howlett.

"Isabelle, are you awake?"

Chris could hear a murmur from the phone.

Catrin said, "Check the dimensions of the Bratby in the Gorton gallery, the unframed painting size, not that ugly outside frame. And get out your kit, your paint-testing kit again. I want you to go and test the paint on it. And check the back."

"My kit, ma'am? Are either of us fully awake?"

She laughed and stopped as her boss's message came through.

"You think that the Bratby painting is covering Seal Island. Or the current painting is a fake, painted over Seal Island. But that would damage it, I think…"

Catrin persisted, "It's an idea and it needs checking. The plaster, the gesso, what was that for, we asked? And if turns out to be fresh oil paint on top, that is one thing. If you get an idea that the painting is the original, but the back is not, that's another."

Howlett caught on immediately.

"We need a warrant and Bertie should do it properly in the lab."

She paused.

"And you are right; it could explain the gesso and plaster. It fits with someone working on a painting there, although I am not sure how."

Catrin said, "Get on to Harper now and work out how to do it; to check it out this morning. I will call DCI Coltrane and brief him as soon as I finish this call. If it's a crazy idea, you and Mark shouldn't carry the flack if it goes belly up. And he is after my blood anyway for…"

She stopped, realizing she had said too much.

Howlett said, "You went up to Tregynon, I know; I found the hotel reservation print-out. You forgot it. I put it face down in your inbox."

Her voice changed tone, suddenly sounded excited. "The dimensions are close, ma'am, I have just been checking as we talked…"

Catrin said, "I will call Coltrane. The two of you do what the boss tells you. I am on my way back now. And we have the Task Force conference call this afternoon, our time."

33 CALIPERS

The clans had gathered around the tables in their various locations, as each could see on their monitors. Catrin noticed that Walkley was the only FBI agent without a paper cup or a water bottle in front of him. Perhaps it was an order from David Klintz.

She had arrived back at Scotland Yard to find her area empty; her art team and Coltrane were still over at the Gorton Gallery. She knew they were there, having been kept in the loop by Harper. He had called again just five minutes after they turned off the M25.

"We are now bringing Jocelyn Gorton in for questioning, ma'am, but I don't believe she was aware, to be honest. She almost collapsed when it hit her, I think. You and DCI Coltrane will interview her, he says, before the Task Force call."

~~

Coltrane had met Howlett, Harper and Bertie Wells at the gallery as it opened, Bertie looking smart as usual and Isabelle looking harried.

She said to Bertie, anxiously, "You are going to do the

check, not me; right?"

"If you say so, Isabelle. It will be fine."

"Thank God for that," she said, "The last thing I need to do is start rubbing away at Seal Island, if that's what it is."

Coltrane led them in and his first act was to advise the owner that they were waiting on a search warrant that would arrive shortly, but they would appreciate her co-operation now. Harper thought Jocelyn Gorton was unnerved and a little flustered; she was surprised but wasn't looking guilty. The young assistant, Nina Templeton, just looked frightened by the police presence.

Coltrane said, "We have reason to believe that the painting 'Seal Island' may be on the premises and we are asking for your co-operation to let us check. Once we have served the warrant, of course, we won't need to ask."

Gorton said, "I don't know what you are talking about."

Coltrane pointed at the Bratby, where Wells and Howlett were now standing.

He said, "We think it is under there. The Bratby has been re-mounted over Seal Island."

The co-owner shook her head emphatically.

"You must be joking, that's our father's... it has always been here! And we would have spotted it during the clean-up and re-hanging; just check the back."

She looked at him, confident in her position.

"Bratby scribbled something on the back, in ink, to my father; the date and location they were together in Italy, not when it was painted. It's quite characteristic and I remember seeing it there as they took it down after the robbery. We had all the paintings removed during the clean-up, obviously."

The two Met staff carefully lifted the painting down. Wells examined the back and then called over to them.

"The rear looks to be the Bratby canvas, Neville. It has the personal inscription," he said.

Gorton jumped in, "I told you."

But Bertie continued, "Except the back canvas look to be a slightly different weave, at first glance, from what I see on the front. We will need to take the painting to the lab before we do any more."

With that he contradicted himself, delving into his bag for something and bringing out a ruler and a large bow caliper, which he slid around the outer frame to measure precisely the thickness of the mounted canvas in several places. As he fiddled, he muttered something about lasers being more precise but less mobile. After various measurements he gave a sigh - of satisfaction or disappointment, Howlett was not quite sure.

Wells said, "It's this peculiar frame and the unevenness of the Bratby impasto surface that disguises it, but I think the actual thickness of the mounted work is about an eighth to three-sixteenths deeper than it should be, comparing it with the stretcher depth supporting the canvas."

He looked at Neville.

Then he added, "Inches, of course; it's an old caliper and ruler."

The two men exchanged glances.

Neville said, "But it wouldn't work, the original Bratby surface…"

His voice trailed off as he realised what Bertie was implying. From Isabelle Howlett's face she was already there. Mark looked apprehensive and Jocelyn Gorton and her assistant looked totally bewildered.

Gorton said, "What do you mean?"

They all went over to examine the back of the painting. Wells pointed out the differences then produced a pair of long forceps from his bag of tricks. He reached into a corner joint of one of the stretcher bars and carefully removed a small off-white particle.

Looking at it closely, he said, "Plaster or, more likely, dried gesso to me; and it is recent. Certainly more recent than the alleged age of the Bratby, I would say."

Coltrane said, "We will need to take this painting and ask you to accompany us, Ms. Gorton. DS Harper will stay and interview Miss Templeton then lead the search of the premises for additional evidence."

The assistant said sharply, "I only started here three months ago!"

Harper said, "Then you can look after the gallery while Ms. Gorton is helping our enquiries, no doubt. Unless you want to close up?"

He looked at the owner. She was standing there, stock still.

She ignored his question and said, "I asked, what does this mean?"

Neville said, "We now think - at least our expert thinks - the Bierstadt is covering the Bratby on the frame, not the other way round. Then it has been painted over in some way, resurfaced, after which a copy of the Bratby has been reproduced carefully on the new surface. And to be able to do that, to retain the original at the back for the ink inscription, it was probably stripped flat to the canvas, we suspect. The back of Seal Island is now snug against the stripped work given to your father by John Bratby; that painting has been ruined."

As she realised the situation, she said, "Russell wanted it in Dubai, I told Inspector Sayer. If… How could he?!"

She burst into tears, shaking her head, understanding at last.

Coltrane turned to Howlett and Wells.

"Check it, now; the surface."

His voice was such that Isabelle didn't demur to Bertie Wells. She pulled out her 'kit' and tested the surface in the same way as she had demonstrated to Catrin in Wales.

As she finished she looked at Bertie who nodded at her and said, "It appears to be oil paint, that's clear. It is covered by a hardener of some sort but is softer underneath, meaning it was painted very recently, within the last few years. This is not the original."

~~

After an hour and a half of questions at Scotland Yard, Coltrane and Sayer concluded that Jocelyn Gorton was probably not involved. The scam had been orchestrated by the brother and had fooled even her. A big point was the issue of how she could not spot differences in the original painting and the replacement. Her answers rang true.

"Every art work after the robbery had to moved out and dusted or cleaned, as a result of the smoke released during the robbery, the broken glass and the building damage. We weren't in the gallery; neither was the art. By the time all the repairs and new lighting were installed - we chose to do some lighting upgrades - everything seemed a little different."

She then looked bewildered.

"That was the only art work not for sale in the whole place for so many years. Visitors look at it and we explain it but, the truth is, I rarely looked at it critically. It had been there so long, it was a fixture."

Somehow that resonated with Catrin and she could see also that it was a turning point for Coltrane, as he sat back in the chair.

Her solicitor drove her home.

When they came out of the interview room, Coltrane said, "I was going to give you hell over going back to Wales - well, going to Wales without telling me why. But now I can only say I am glad you did. Without it, it seems we wouldn't have had the breakthrough. Just because DCI Hendry said 'plastered' and you corrected him?"

She nodded. She was looking along the corridor at Howlett, who had just come back from the lab, waiting for them to emerge from the interview room. She looked angry and miserable.

"Seal Island should clean up nicely; that's the good news. It had a protective layer of heavy varnish. Some water-based flexible plaster compound had been applied over that to make a flat base. Then a thin layer of canvas was added for texture and bonding. Bertie thinks, at that point, it was like a new bare canvas, ready for gesso and the Bratby copy. Nothing is sticking to the original, at least in the test area they are looking at now."

"And?" said Coltrane.

"When we looked at the x-ray images, it was exactly as Bertie had predicted. They stripped the Bratby work flat, trimmed it to the edges, just to keep the back appearing unchanged and reduce the thickness. We will know more once the restorers take both canvases off the frame."

They were now in the corridor heading back to Art and Antiques. The women's washroom turned out to be fortuitously located. Howlett left them, walked in without another word. Through the barrier of the closed outer door, they heard the stall door slam hard.

Coltrane looked at Sayer. "Isabelle really likes John Bratby's art," he remarked needlessly.

~~

Klintz brought the conference call to order.

"So, let's do the updates. We have nothing new here, I hate to say; we are still desperate to establish a solid link from our end. So who would like to start?"

Coltrane jumped in.

"David, we believe we have located Seal Island. What state it is in, we will need to see."

He summarized clearly and effectively the work of the morning.

Klintz pursed his lips.

"Well, Neville, you have made our day, I think."

"Perhaps. As I said, the painting has been overpainted. All we have done so far is preliminary, but the x-ray work assures us that it is Seal Island. It will now be a matter for owners, insurers and whomever to decide on its restoration once we completed our forensic work. I want to find out who did this job."

He paused and looked at his two colleagues, Sayer and Madder. "The idea came from DI Sayer. She was on another case up north at the time and a comment from an officer there made her think of the possibility of the plaster mask. Catrin do you want to add more?"

Catrin shook her head, indicating she didn't want to speak, but suddenly she said, "It just came to me, out of the blue, the possibility of the Bratby work hiding the Bierstadt."

Klintz said, appreciatively, "That's what it takes sometimes, DI Sayer; actually, at the best of times in this game. We will wait to hear more offline from Neville. Gerhardt?"

The German started the update on their team's developments. The French could be heard still talking sotto voce about Seal Island, arguing about whether it could be fully restored.

Catrin's personal mobile beeped and she took a quick look. It was an email from Cathay Pacific airlines, flagging that her request for their economy seat upgrade to premium seating, with its extra leg room, had been confirmed. She had used her frequent flyer points for the request and the approval policy only allowed confirmation 72 hours prior to departure. She was suddenly shocked to realise she was only three days from flying out to Hong Kong.

In her panic about all the work she had to do, she suddenly thought of cancelling the trip and immediately felt bad; it wasn't just a holiday, it was Li's wedding.

Just then Neville Coltrane spoke up.

"We will have to look at gathering evidence, of course. It could take some time."

She looked at Klintz as he responded.

"Well, Seal Island is one thing, a great recovery, but I know the people in Washington will be burning to know how we will bring this guy Gorton in."

Catrin realised that she had switched off as they were talking about the process to arrest Russell Gorton, now in Dubai. Jocelyn had said in the gallery that it must be him, as shocked as she was about the discovery. But they had no evidence at all at present.

PART 3

DUBAI AND BEYOND

34 WEDDING

They appreciated the extra leg room in premium economy on the twelve-hour flight from Heathrow to Hong Kong. Flying on Cathay Pacific brought back memories for Catrin of her first visit, years earlier. She talked excitedly about it to Chris on the flight. After the turmoil of work, the reality hit her that they were finally on their way to see Li and the exotic city again.

She remembered travelling in first class, two compartments ahead of them; a gift arranged by Enlai Lin. Now they could see only into business class - and then only briefly as the curtains between sections were closed once they reached their cruising altitude. She put it out of her mind; this was fine. She had enough space and her husband was with her this time.

It was going to be a welcome break after the tensions and challenges of settling into her new job.

~~

After the brief panic attack in the videoconference call, it had sorted itself out nicely. Neville was adamant that the focus now went back on the Acton warehouse inventory and into breaking the silence of the people in custody.

"Yes, we need to go after Gorton, but we don't have infinite resources. We will flag it to Major Assad in Dubai. He is the cultural artefacts detective we know there; Jerry's team covers art crimes as part of their mandate. I doubt Russell Gorton will be flying back to the UK once he hears about Seal Island being discovered. And we will flag to Interpol that he is a 'person of interest', so if he chooses to fly somewhere else, we will be on to him; or the Americans will."

"Jerry?" asked Harper. It didn't sound an Arabic name.

"Well, he has other names, I know. But that's what he was called at school."

From the tone of it, Catrin thought it wasn't a school in Dubai that Neville Coltrane was talking about. Harper just said 'Ah', knowingly.

After the conference call and review with Neville, she sat down with Howlett and Harper, focusing them on the job of documenting the discovery of Seal Island properly and lining up the work priorities for the week ahead. She knew she would need to work Saturday herself, but the office would be quiet. On Sunday she would sort out things for the trip to Hong Kong.

When she left for her holiday, she felt everything was as organized as it could be.

It was the Monday, just before she and Chris left for Heathrow, that an email came in from the West Mercia team, from DI Merton. John Farrell had been extensively interviewed and had 'assisted with enquiries' but no charges were currently pending against him.

The case had now been downgraded in priority. Kendrick's cause of death remained unknown. One of Colin Ingelsby's fingerprints - a partial - was found on the painting retrieved from the grave; at least one which tied in as a 'possible' once they knew the identity of the alleged perpetrator. They had verified Ingelsby's death in 2012, as Farrell had described.

A man matching his description had been seen talking to Kendrick in Wolverhampton outside a Ladbroke's betting shop. It was as close a link as they could find, dating back to 2010; Ian Kendrick had not been seen again.

There was only one additional piece of information giving some insight, a report of interviews with members of the Stoke-on-Trent Revival Assembly where Ingelsby had been a member. They spoke well of him but thought he was a little unbalanced, with a passionate focus on convincing one particular sinner of the error of his ways. But the name of the person he had in mind was never shared with them.

How Kendrick died remained a mystery. That 'a person or persons unknown', but probably Ingelsby, had buried him in Bindley Woods was a conclusion that the police would bring to the coroner's inquest, but the rest of it was conjecture.

~~

As the aircraft began its descent into Hong Kong, Catrin realised she was entering what was acknowledged to be the centre of triad operations worldwide. Not that she felt at risk. She had diligently carried her sidearm for over two years and, ironically, she was now unarmed. It just felt strange, in that sense.

The last time they had seen Li and James Hoi together in person was at her own wedding. The happy couple was waiting for them on their arrival at the airport. Catrin thought that Li had lost weight, despite her worries expressed on Skype calls.

Li said, "Jean and Melanie arrived yesterday after a long layover in Amsterdam; a plane delay on their routing. Jean seems fine. Melanie had been raring to get out and see the sights, she said beforehand, but now has bad jet lag; she is sleeping again. I introduced Jean to Miele Yau this morning; they are talking pottery stuff. But you will want to rest yourself?"

Catrin nodded. "For a little while, to settle in at the hotel, then freshen up. Then you and I are going for the fitting, right?"

For her bridesmaid's dress.

James said, "It's on the master plan; that's right. Chris and I will talk; I want him to meet my best man. He's into football, too."

The 'master plan' also called for a casual dinner that evening with James, Li and the visitors from the UK at a restaurant in the harbour. By the end of dinner, Catrin and Chris were ready for an early night.

Back at the hotel, as they headed to the lift, Melanie said, "I am wide awake, ready to go out and about…"

Jean just looked at her. "You will be doing it on your own if you do. And if you fall asleep when we go out looking round tomorrow, I will pinch you until you…"

The following day, after a morning and lunch playing tourist, Catrin, Jean and Melanie got together with Miele Yau. She came over from the university to the hotel and, after being introduced to her, Chris left them to talk. He had decided to use the hotel gym then go for a swim in the pool.

Melanie said, "For a guy who spends all his time at a computer, he likes to keep active, despite the time change. I am worn out by the tourist bit."

Catrin said, "I am surprised he hasn't found a five-a-side team to drop in on while we are here."

They focused on Miele; the student realizing that this was her time to speak up; her interview, in a sense. From their meeting yesterday, Jean had said that the young woman was knowledgeable and appeared enthusiastic.

Catrin said, "So how did you decide on us, so to speak?"

Miele said, "The article about you both in Ceramics Review magazine, about a year ago. I mentioned to my aunt that, when I was studying in London, I would visit your pottery and try to meet you. Grandad was in the room. He looked at the article and I could tell he knew one of you from somewhere. So I asked him."

Catrin and Jean exchanged glances.

Jean said, "Neither of us has ever met your grandfather."

Miele responded, "I know. That's what he said, too. He

thought that Enlai Lin had mentioned your name, Catrin, as a friend of Jian Li, is what he told me."

She left it hanging for a moment then changed the subject. Catrin had not discussed Michael Yau with Jean or Melanie, so she hoped the young woman would not go further on that line of thought.

"But that's not the reason. It seemed strange that Grandad was aware of you, I know, but my interest is in the partnership; actually the three of you, in a sense. I want to produce ceramic art. I have ideas, have taken classes and I have learned to make pottery myself. But -."

She paused.

"I have some health issues. Some periods I am good, some less so. I am a Type 1 diabetic and I have some other related issues that can leave me almost without energy at times, for days. And making pottery is hard work, as you all know. So the fact that you two -", she pointed at Jean and Melanie, "can run a successful pottery and you two -", the fingers moved to Jean and Catrin, "- can produce innovative ceramics together is what I want to learn more about, too. I need to find a partner myself - probably here, in time, and start my own studio - and I want to do that right.

"But a year in London, studying at RCA will help and, if you will allow it, working with you at the Cwmbran Kiln while I am there will help me too."

She pronounced 'Cwmbran' precisely, and it sounded correct, Catrin noticed. She must have checked it out, not wanting to make an error in front of them.

"I will do whatever you want... and I don't need pay; it's a part-time internship I am looking for, something to mesh in with my studies."

She wasn't pleading but her voice made it clear that this was very important to her.

Melanie said, "Someone who wants work, for no pay; I think we can handle that."

Jean was looking at Catrin, a little concerned.

She said, "Well, if you have ideas for ceramic pieces you

would like to realise, we can help. But Catrin is the key in terms of new design; it's her thing. And she works full-time; she is a police officer. Her time at the Kiln is limited and sometimes irregular."

Miele's eyes dropped.

"I know, and I understand the concern. But I am a student; that's all, so I will have classes, a lot of my time committed anyway. I won't get under your feet. I can learn from you and from Melanie."

She looked at Catrin. "I want to make it on my own merits in life, to be an artist but also be financially independent."

Catrin realised that she was acknowledging to her obliquely that the family was linked to organized crime. She wasn't apologizing for it, just saying it was not her world as she looked forward. For Catrin, that more than anything else swayed her decision.

She said, "I think we can manage it; I look forward to it."

The student's eyes lit up as she couldn't stop herself from pumping her hands out and saying, "Yes! Thank you."

After Miele left, Melanie said to her partner, "You looked a little worried about making that decision, I thought. She seems very nice; I think she will fit in."

Jean said, "I was, for a while, mainly about her expectations of help from Catrin."

She looked at her friend, "With you only working at the Kiln on Saturdays, I meant."

Catrin just smiled. If these two friends knew the real reason she had her own misgivings, they would be even more concerned.

~~

The wedding day went according to plan despite Li's own worries. The Methodist church in Kowloon that her family attended was crowded with guests and church members. Some had known Li from her being a baby; others present had known James Hoi as long.

They had the rehearsal there the afternoon before the event, with Catrin getting an insight into the layout of the building she had heard about from Li on earlier occasions.

At the end of the rehearsal, Li pulled silently on Catrin's arm to indicate that they should break away, leaving people enjoying juice and tea, chatting before a dinner hosted by the groom's parents.

She led Catrin down a corridor saying, "We can't take long."

Through a door… and Catrin found herself in a sanctuary; the church's own columbarium, a wall with rows of small doors containing the cremated remains of the dead. Li took Catrin's hand and pointed to one, clearly the Yeung family location, with two older nameplates and a much newer addition saying 'Han Shen Yeung'. Her brother.

She held on to Catrin as she said, "It is a long way from Bangor and our first meeting. This is where Han's remains now rest. Each year we come here, to tell our story, the recent history of our family, in a sense. I thought you would want to see."

They stood there, silent. Catrin found her eyes pricking, wet with tears, recalling the pathology unit in Bangor, the first and last sight - and one quite-horrific, for her - of Han Yeung. Then, more peacefully, she recalled the sail out on the Menai Straits with Li, to the point where Han's body had been dumped… and the days around then which gave her this special friendship with a woman from Hong Kong.

In the distance they heard a call for Li as the door opened and her father stepped in, saying quietly, "I thought you might be here."

He said nothing else but his face showed his pleasure that his daughter had thought of this, at such busy time in her life.

Catrin was now watching carefully Li's parents as the newly-married pair left the church in the first limousine, with her maid of honour and the best man. They were heading to the Regal Oriental Hotel, where the wedding reception would be held. The arrangement was that she and Li's parents would travel in the second limo; the third bridesmaid would travel with the Hoi parents in the third limo.

Miele had taken charge of Chris, Jean and Melanie, in terms of travel to the reception. From what Li had told her, Catrin thought they would probably find themselves in one of Mr. Yau's Mercedes, her friends blissfully unaware that it was owned by a triad boss and her husband unlikely to mention it, she was sure.

Daniel Yeung and his wife, Eh-Meh, were happy, she could tell, but suddenly in the quiet of the vehicle they looked at each other and, unspoken, Daniel pulled out a leather wallet sleeve from his inside pocket, which he opened and they looked at together. Then, realizing that they had left Catrin out of their special moment, he turned it to show her.

"Han," said Catrin, "It is the photo we used in the search in Wales, in his uniform. And the other photo must be your parents, Mr. Yeung, I think?"

He nodded.

Eu-meh said, smiling through tears, "They will be happy for Jian Li today. A happy marriage and good fortune."

Catrin looked again at the portrait of Han in his uniform, looking serious and confident; a third officer on a cruise ship.

Daniel said seriously, "Thank you again for all you did to find him; and for being such a good friend to Li, across the distance."

At which point, Catrin started crying too, glad that Chris, not part of the formal wedding party, was travelling with others.

There was only one hiccup at the wedding reception; an elderly relative of the Hoi family had fainted, throwing events into confusion for several minutes. Once sorted, the speeches and meal went well. Several people were becoming loud and a little merry and Catrin was keeping her eye on Li; she and her bridesmaids were to leave and change together before the final round of conversations and goodbyes.

James and Li had rented a larger sailboat - indeed, they had taken lessons in large craft sailing in preparation for their honeymoon. It would begin, they decided, not in a hotel but on the vessel in a marina in Hong Kong harbour. They were sailing the islands south of Hong Kong. It was in the formal speeches that Mr. Lin had surprised them with an additional wedding present; the use of his own yacht for a further week, for the couple to sail back instead.

"Extra vacation time, but with my crew also, this time!" he joked.

~~

Miele came over to Catrin and Chris with an older couple in tow. As Catrin took it in she realised that this must be Michael Yau and his wife, as Miele did the introductions.

Suddenly she was lost for what to say, thinking back to the events over the years, both good and bad, that had occurred as a result of this man's involvement with Li's life; things she knew about but could never share with others. And there was his role in addressing her problem with Nam Wu, which Li had not explained at all and which she could never acknowledge.

In the end, she shook hands formally with them and said, "It is a pleasure to meet you."

A waiter hovering behind them held out a tray of glasses; champagne flutes and one flute with a clear sparkling liquid.

Michael Yau said, "Soda water, Mrs. Treneer, for a toast. And to thank you for agreeing to help Miele while she is in London."

Miele said, "It's Sayer, grandad, Catrin's surname as an artist."

Catrin took the glass as the others took the champagne, thinking that Miele's grandfather was well aware of her maiden name. He just smiled at his granddaughter and nodded.

"A toast to…?" she asked.

Yau said, "To the bride and groom again, of course, that

their wishes be fulfilled; that Miele's wishes to fulfil her artistic life be successful and... what would you wish for, Mrs. Treneer?"

It came out of the blue, the request.

"What to wish for, for me... health and happiness, perhaps, as for everyone."

Then Catrin looked into Yau's eyes as she spoke again.

"Perhaps for a peaceful life for all; for me, one in which I do not need people thinking about a threat that I believe no longer exists, anyway; to be free of it entirely."

He looked at her a little quizzically at first, as did Miele, apparently unaware of the context of the comment, that police forces in the UK and Malaysia still believed that the death threat against Catrin existed. Then he nodded, understanding. He raised his glass again. Mrs. Yau's face remained blank.

"To all those things, then," he said, encouraging them all to take a sip of their drinks.

As they put the partially emptied glasses back on the tray he said, "Well, Inspector Sayer, we will have to see what the future brings, won't we? It is indeed a pleasure for me to meet you at last."

The maid of honour came up and touched Catrin on the shoulder, then whispered, "Time to change."

She pointed at Li and James, moving now towards the door with the best man and the third bridesmaid. Both bridesmaids smiled at the Yau's as Catrin said, "We must go. I will see you in a bit, Chris."

Saved by the bell, thought Catrin. But she had noticed his use of her business name and rank as he said, "We will have to see what the future brings."

And, she realised, he was even aware that she didn't drink champagne, or any alcohol at all.

~~

There had been two photographers at the reception, taking shots of the wedding party and guests. It would have taken someone with a security mindset to analyze the pattern of their work and see that, outside the wedding party, anyone who spoke with Mr. Yau for any length of time was being photographed.

If Catrin was still thinking like a security aide, she may well have spotted it. As a bridesmaid enjoying the wedding, she missed it completely.

35 STATEMENT

It was at the end of the short holiday, as they waited in the departure lounge of Hong Kong International to go home, that Catrin switched on her business mobile for the first time since leaving London. No message had come to her personal phone about a need for her to contact her office. In fact, this was no different than the two years working with AC Hunt. Holiday leave had not been interrupted then, either.

It was only during her time with Worsley's Art Crime Unit that a message would arrive to that effect. The unit was a small team and, unlike Art and Antiques, with its structured focus on art recovery, a violent crime suddenly involving the ACU was less predictable in the response required, the timing, or the people resources needed.

She saw the email from DI Merton in the middle of the headers and opened his message.

DI Sayer,

As per my earlier email, Michael John Farrell was interviewed and released the evening after we took him in for questioning. Other than his role in transferring the art to the subject of your own investigation, he played no role, we think, in the death of Ian Kendrick. His formal statement is attached

for your review; DCI Hendry said you would want to see it.
Alan Merton

Catrin downloaded the attached document as Chris nudged
her. "It looks like the boarding gate people are arriving to start
the process. I am off to the loo; watch the bags and then I will
come back and do the same, if you want."

After the dinner on the aircraft, as Chris settled into a
movie, she finished reading the document she had
downloaded.

My name is Michael John Farrell. I am an ordained deacon
of the Church in Wales and I work in the Newtown area of
Powys. I have been employed there for three years.

Prior to my ordination I studied theology, initially part-time,
before a final year at a seminary, full-time. During this period I
worked at Bindley Golf Club in the landscape and course
maintenance department and served pastorally at All-Saints,
Kidderminster. I had prior experience of similar work at the
same golf course much earlier, after leaving school. They re-
employed me during my studies.

Prior to my studies, I served sentences for crimes I was
convicted of at HMP Dovecote and HMP Birmingham,
Wilson Green. I met Colin Ingelsby at Dovecote. At Wilson
Green I met him again and also became acquainted with Ian
Kendrick. I knew of, but had no contact with, Edwin Ashe.

Ingelsby and I discussed various aspects of our lives in both
prisons. I believe at some point I talked about my work at the
golf club and the grounds, stating that the coppice that was
part of the golf course complex was a peaceful area; it had no
public right of access and only golfers searching for balls were
likely to go into the edges of the woodland, other than
maintenance or Department of Forestry staff.

On 12 October 2009 I received a phone call from Colin
Ingelsby asking for my help. I was then studying for the
ministry and engaged in the support of people leaving
institutional life. I met with him accordingly at the Grazing

Cow pub near Telford. It was one of only two meetings with him after our period of overlap at Wilson Green prison. The second was at the hospice where he passed away. We were not friends or regular acquaintances.

At our first meeting, Ingelsby reminded me that he had been left a bequest of three oil sketches by Edwin Ashe, another man who was imprisoned on remand for a short period. He told me that the paintings of Ashe were by John Bratby, a British artist, and may be worth something if sold at auction or through a dealer.

He informed me that he was 'saved' as a born-again Christian and did not want the money himself. He wanted people involved in the death of Ashe, as he saw it, to receive them and reflect on their role leading up to Ashe's death, then do with them as they wished. He asked me to keep one myself and deliver a second painting to Judge Judith Richards, who, he said, had unfairly withheld bail for Ashe, leading to his imprisonment on remand. That had been a major component leading to Ashe's decision to end his own life, he stated.

He showed me the two paintings and I saw that the signatures were 'Ashe'. When I asked him about this, he said the name of the person in the picture was more important than that of the artist. I took it he or someone else had altered the sketches by adding the name but did not question him further about this change.

I presumed he kept the third painting himself.

Before the second meeting at the hospice on 9 February 2011, I had been ordained as a deacon. I asked him if he needed help. I did not see him alive again although I did go to his funeral. Other aspects of that second discussion I consider 'privileged' by faith and my ordination vows, to be between a member of the clergy and a person seeking spiritual help.

After the first meeting, I went to see Judith Richards and explained the request, giving her the option of whether or not she wanted to receive the painting. Ingelsby had provided hand-written notes confirming his own ownership and his wish to transfer one sketch to each of us. She asked to see the sketches and after discussion, said she would keep one, but had no need for a copy of the note, which I retained. The remainder of our discussions I consider 'privileged' by faith and ordination vows between a member of the clergy and a person seeking spiritual help.

Signed: M J Farrell

Catrin saw it was a minimal content statement, the least that Farrell could get away with and appear co-operative, probably heavily managed by the solicitor provided to him. She tilted her seat back, catching out of the corner of her eye some violent action on her husband's video screen; he was lost in his movie.

She thought that DCI Hendry's team must have pieced most of it together, as best they could. The investigation would now be filed, she expected. Without a cause of death they had only the suspicious nature of the burial and the link with the painting owned last by Ingelsby.

She wondered if Ingelsby had killed Kendrick by premeditation or by accident. She found her mind mapping out what should be done next and suddenly saw that she was treading into areas she had better stay out of. As she closed the documents and saw on her mobile the original email, below it was a note from Miele Yau, wishing them a safe journey home and looking forward to meeting again in London.

She closed her eyes. Next thing she knew it was dark, her throat was dry and a blanket was around her, presumably put there by Chris, who was now fast asleep next to her. She had slept for four hours.

~~

At the same time, a man in a building on the River Thames at Vauxhall Cross was examining a number of documents. His colleagues could see he was getting excited about something and knew better than to ask him about it. It wasn't the first time that Stephen Drew had done this. He was a very experienced case officer and, in the area of commercial and financial espionage, they were a long way away from the 'action' people. A little excitement was to be enjoyed.

The building was the headquarters of the Secret Intelligence Services, SIS, formerly known as MI6, and the file he was repeatedly reviewing included photographs from Jian Li's wedding, a transcript of the interview during Miele Yau's application for a student visa and the summary of known information on a Detective Inspector Catrin Sayer.

But for the last half-hour he had been lost in an examination of the on-line images of art works by Sayer and her creative partner, Jean Hughes. He had just written a memo to a junior staff member, without explanation, to ask for an expert critical assessment of the art.

He paused before reading another document and decided to contact the key person at Scotland Yard he needed; a Commander Craig Barlow, the head of the organized crime operations of the Metropolitan Police, called Trident.

It was finally time to act, he decided.

36 STRIFE

When Catrin returned to work on the following Monday, she walked straight into a beaming DCI Coltrane getting ready for the Monday briefing.

"Catrin, all went well? Good holiday?"

"Yes, Neville. The wedding went very well and we had a nice time. And here?"

"Trouble and strife, trouble and strife as the cockneys say," he explained needlessly, but she saw he was in a happy mood. Catrin may be from Wales but she had been living in London for a decade, so he had no need to explain Cockney rhyming slang; in this case, wife.

He continued, "In the form of Jorge's wife, to be specific. Once Kristoff was released on bail last week and her husband wasn't, she became rather angry with Kristoff's wife on the phone; and of course, we recorded it. We will go through it in the briefing. And you will be doing the interview with Kristoff; we are bringing him back in today; you will be a new face for him and his lawyer. And our colleague from France, Inspector Talon, arrived yesterday evening; Gitan will be in the interview, too. I have a cunning plan, as someone once said."

~~

Catrin entered the interview room with Gitan Talon. She could see that both Kristoff Nahigian and his solicitor, a man called Salter, were surprised. The French detective was obviously not one of the regular team and Nahigian hadn't seen this female officer since the police walked into the warehouse to make the arrest.

"I am Detective Inspector Sayer, Mr. Nahigian; I lead the art investigation team here. This is Inspector Gitan Talon, with the French police, our counterparts there."

Kristoff Nahigian said, snippily, "Getting into this a little late, Inspector, aren't you?"

Catrin ignored the comment and noticed the brief expression of disapproval on the solicitor's face turn back to a neutral mask. He simply asked for the details of the French officer's unit and Talon passed over a business card.

Catrin said, "Just listen, Mr. Nahigian."

She pulled out a small recorder on to which they had transferred the relevant section of the phone tap.

Gabriella Nahigian's voice caused a look of surprise on her husband's face. As the content of the call unfolded, Catrin could see the mix of controlled concern and annoyance fighting with his attempt to remain impassive.

When she switched it off, he said immediately, "That had better be legal."

"It was quite legal, Mr. Nahigian. We can give the court the appropriate documentation and, of course, her solicitor also will want it, in due course. But hear from Inspector Talon, also."

The French officer's English was accented, but good. "Mr. Nahigian, I am going to tell you about something that we believe you already know; the status of your counterpart operation in France. The warehouse near Paris is already closed after a raid at the same time as the one on your premises, with Mislav and Laurin arrested. We deliberately didn't go near the Lille warehouse although we knew about it. We are ready to do so; in fact, we will do so very soon."

Nahigian shrugged but said nothing.

Catrin spoke up. "As we will arrest your wife; charge both her and Jorge's wife with criminal involvement in the Acton operations."

Kristoff Nahigian shook his head firmly. "You can't do that. They may know about our business; they are our wives, but they aren't involved. Come on, they are our family!"

Catrin said evenly, "The recording gives us a basis to charge them and, although we haven't gone after them yet, who knows what will come out of their arrests?"

He realised what was happening.

"No; no deal. You don't understand. If I talk I am dead -."

Catrin interrupted him. They had planned it that way.

"Actually, I do," Catrin said, with some venom. "I have had a death threat against me on two occasions; the last being two years ago. I know exactly what it's like; which is why we are not after chapter and verse from you. To do that, even if you chose to co-operate, Mr. Salter would want you and your family in witness protection: immunity, new identities; the works. And you are not prepared to accept that, we know. It's not off the table, by the way. It was DCI Coltrane's original offer, which you refused. But it's not what we are after at this point."

She spoke more softly, trying to appear conciliatory.

"We want something you know, something about the French operation, something perhaps that they aren't even aware of you knowing - but the crucial thing is that it has to link to the USA end. A person. A shipment. A location of an item that went through that route. We are open to ideas. But it has to be useful to us and the Americans and it has to be right now."

She could see his expression changing. He was listening carefully, more engaged.

"The pay-off for you is that we drop any arrests of Gabriella and Jana based on what you have heard. Nor will we go after them on anything specifically related to the Acton warehouse. That doesn't mean they get a free ride on anything that may come out separately. And anything you give us will be off the table in the prosecution case against you, your brother and the other two, as evidence of your guilt; it won't be used against you or your people here."

Catrin let it soak in a moment.

"We never go back on a deal like this; ask Mr. Salter."

She stood up.

"Immunity for your wives for the Acton operation, at least. Nothing seen as giving you a deal; nothing appearing blown at this end. But it doesn't wait; it's live now. Inspector Talon's operation will start soon, which will be the best opportunity to bury the leak in the confusion in France. We will leave you to it, to talk about it. Mr. Salter, you understand that you can't leave this room or make a mobile call, or send a text until this is closed, one way or the other?"

The solicitor said, "Clearly. You will be watching us, I am sure."

Catrin said, "The signal is blocked from here anyway, right now."

It took them twenty minutes before the lawyer waved to the camera, signaling they were ready. Once they were re-seated, Salter spoke first.

"Two small items. One for each wife, in a sense. Individually they are no big deal but together; you can piece it, make it work. A location of a pair of 17th century vases from Flanders stolen in 2008 now in the home of a US citizen in Virginia. Secondly, a travel itinerary of a French citizen who we think will not be known to you, who met with the American to secure the deal. We won't give you the shipment details but you have two people to go after, and a link between them."

Talon said, immediately. "That's not enough. Give us the work involved now, the name."

Kristoff said, "All I know is that there are two Limoges vases, matching, with decoration copied from works by David Teniers the Younger. Seventeenth century, as Mr. Salter said, but valuable."

It was clear that Gitan Talon knew of the stolen works and the value of the pair. He looked at Catrin and nodded.

She said, "One more thing -."

Nahigian snapped, "That's it. You are getting what you asked for."

She smiled, shaking her head.

"It's not about your involvement; it is about confirmation of your non-involvement in something. You had the two McKinnon's in the Acton warehouse with the other three paintings from the Gorton Gallery job. But we have Bierstadt's 'Seal Island' now, stolen at the same time, as you will know. Am I right in thinking that the Bierstadt was never an item of discussion with you, not on your radar? And don't just say 'yes' for the sake of it, please; we will get there by other means very soon, I assure you. So don't make this whole deal backfire by tainting it. I just want to save time."

Nahigian smiled back. "No comment on the McKinnon's or the others, they are not part of the deal. But Seal Island. We had no involvement, to be honest. Never saw it; no-one talked to us about it; we never touched it."

He sounded emphatic and the confidence didn't appear feigned.

She nodded.

"I think we have a deal. I will just check with DCI Coltrane and Inspector Talon will do the same with his counterparts. If so, we will be back in a minute or so. Then we'll get the details and you both will need to be here while things are set in motion in France."

The lawyer suddenly looked alert. He passed back Talon's business card; he suddenly realised it would be a liability. Then he said, "I wonder, Inspector Sayer, could you have DS Madder and -."

Catrin said, "We thought of that too. DS Madder and DC Nkrumah are standing by to interview you about some of the items at the warehouse, ones that you have not been co-operative about in the past."

Talon said, "And probably won't be co-operative about now, I suspect."

They stood up and left as Madder and Nkrumah walked in.

The officers started the recording equipment and Madder said, "Sorry, Mr. Salter, to keep you waiting. Something came up…"

The interview recording, with its time stamp, could be something which Salter might need for his client, in due course. His lawyer would be able to confirm that at the time of the raid in Lille, Kristoff Nahigian was being interviewed yet again on the Acton warehouse inventory and had said nothing at all.

Outside, Neville said, "I think we are on. Give them five minutes then knock and confirm. Get the main details and, Gitan, you and Eric can talk. We will leave it to him to send out the information to David Klintz; it should appear to come from France."

The Frenchman nodded, "Yes, Chief Inspector."

He pulled out his mobile and moved away to talk with his colleagues.

Neville said to Catrin, "The throw in at the end; Seal Island?"

She looked at him. "We have spent weeks trying to chase down connections between this group and the Bierstadt. As we said, the Gorton Gallery robbery was a professional operation, but I think we are going in the wrong direction. We need to look at connections Russell Gorton had with people capable of carrying out the robbery. Subsequently we can investigate how the McKinnon paintings ended up at the Acton warehouse. I don't think the Bierstadt robbery involved the Nahigian brothers at all, as Kristoff just confirmed.

"When Gitan gets off the phone we will head back in and sort out the deal."

~~

Later, Nkrumah had been listening quietly as Catrin brought Harper and Howlett up to speed on the West Mercia case.

"They let the deacon go after questioning. Apparently the

pathologist can find nothing in the corpse to indicate foul play and the tissue analysis and pharmacology show nothing untoward. Whatever he died of will remain a mystery unless new evidence turns up. The case has been classified as an improper burial of human remains, so the West Mercia Task Force has finished with it, really. They have more important things on their plate."

Her team members just nodded. Nkrumah, though, said, "That's disappointing; an unsatisfactory finish, isn't it? The man was probably murdered, then dumped."

Catrin smiled. "It happens, Derek. There isn't always a cause of death established. If you want that satisfaction, join the drug squad; from experience I can say you will always have a cause of death identified with the bodies."

"Or Trident, gang crimes," said Harper, with a grin. "They can tell whether holes are caused by bullets or knives."

He was smiling at the younger officer. But Catrin was silent, suddenly shivering at the mention of organized crime, as if someone was walking on her grave.

~~

It was later in the day. Catrin was feeling the effects of her long travel day returning from Hong Kong and now being back at work, but she didn't want to leave early; she had a lot to catch up on in her in-tray.

Almost reading her mind as he popped into her office, Neville Coltrane passed her a large sealed envelope, as he closed the door.

"That time of year; performance development reviews. I had Caldwell draft up interim report notes for Harper and Howlett before he left. You have only had leadership responsibility for a month or so, I know, but you will do their interviews. I will be happy to see either officer about anything arising that they feel is undeserved or unrecognized, due to the transition.

"And, of course, I will be doing yours, with input from AC

Hunt. You had her review last year, so you know she is thorough."

Catrin said carefully, "She is that, Neville."

She had thought of it some time ago, as part of her promotion responsibilities, but in the mêlée of her recent assignments, it had skipped her mind totally. Now it was real; she would be assessing her people.

"There is too much to do, isn't there?" asked Coltrane, rhetorically, as he walked out.

A few minutes later Catrin left the office for a file she needed and Harper was looking at her carefully. He said, deadpan, "We were talking, Isabelle and I, whether you were open to bribery or not."

She looked at him, then realised. "Yes, the envelopes are flying around. It's that time. They should computerize it."

He laughed. "No way! It would be too easy for any of us to get in and destroy the evidence."

As Catrin smiled, picking up the file, she thought that Harper's review would be straightforward. Howlett though, she would struggle with the recommendations.

But she had higher priority things at present. Tomorrow they were going to visit the Gorton Gallery again, to see if they could get anything useful out of Jocelyn Gorton, now that the dust had settled.

37 SCRAPBOOK

"My solicitor has advised me not to speak with you without her being present, Inspector Sayer," said Jocelyn Gorton.

She paused for a moment then seemed to need to explain herself. Catrin and Harper didn't ask anything, they just waited.

"My outburst about the discovery your colleagues made here, the disappearance of our Bratby and ... Seal Island being here, well; you can understand, I think? My comment, blaming my brother. I jumped to conclusions. I have no basis for them."

Catrin said, "Of course, Ms. Gorton. I quite understand."

She turned, looking at the wall space that had been freed up. It now hosted a diptych, a scene of Canary Wharf at night, abstract but identifiable. It certainly improved the overall image of the gallery.

Catrin added, "We, of course, have informed all the appropriate people about the recovery of the stolen paintings. They are quite delighted. The Herron family is very pleased to hear about Seal Island - and its potential to be restored."

Jocelyn Gorton nodded emphatically.

"I know, both Cheryl McKinnon and Mr. Herron's wife, Celia, contacted me. In that sense it was a great relief. The Herron couple had been so generous in loaning the work and… I understand the police in the USA told them you think I had no involvement in the disappearance, which helps a great deal. Thank you for that."

"FBI," said Harper, "the Federal Bureau of Investigation is the agency involved."

Gorton smiled at him. "Well, whoever it is. I do appreciate it."

She looked as if she wanted to talk further, but was aware of her legal advice. She just stood, looking uncomfortable.

"She said, "DC Howlett is not with you this time?"

"No," said Harper, "She is on another case… in Bognor Regis, actually."

Catrin studied the diptych and said carefully, "She would probably be happy not to come back anyway; she particularly likes John Bratby's work, including your painting, as you saw."

Gorton said, "Funnily enough, I didn't like it much; it was too… familiar. Until it was gone. Now I do."

Her voice had developed an icy edge to it. Catrin turned to face her and walked closer.

"Have you been in contact with your brother, may I ask?"

Jocelyn shook her head.

"I tried. He won't talk to me or answer emails. My solicitor had a call from a lawyer in the Emirates saying they are authorised to act for him on business matters concerning the gallery. All communications about separating the businesses are to be conducted through them. I think I told you, we had been discussing - before all this - the potential separation of the two galleries into completely separate businesses. Well, I think it is a lot further along - in a process led by him and, to be honest, in sentiment from me, now. I am catching up, in a sense.

"But I am talking… and I shouldn't."

Catrin said, "Then, could we make an appointment to meet with you and your solicitor; soon? We do have some more questions."

Gorton said, "I'll call her right now; see if we can do this straight away."

Clearly, thought Catrin, the sister wants to talk about her

anger at the whole mess her brother had brought on them.

The lawyer's office was closer than Scotland Yard, so they went there; a modern, Scandinavian design inside, bright and efficient, in an exterior that looked two centuries old. Catrin filed away some design ideas she saw there. One fine day, given the money…

She began, "Jocelyn, the case is a lot clearer for us now. The criminals that possessed the five other paintings from your gallery were not involved with the robbery, we believe. They just received them, to be sold on illegally in due course. Whoever committed the robbery at your gallery was linked to the Bierstadt concealment. The team was highly organized, experienced at an almost military-style operation and, we believe, your brother worked with them. Another person was involved, too; the artist who made the changes; the Bratby stripping, the re-mounting of Seal Island and its subsequent over-work with the Bratby copy. It must have taken time by a talented artist or restorer, a forger in effect, even if he or she worked around the clock. It takes a lot of expertise.

"We also know that the Bierstadt was not in its position in the gallery on the Tuesday morning of the robbery. When the work was conducted to conceal it with the Bratby painting, and by whom, remains unknown. Our thinking is that the switch was made during an intense operation over the long weekend. That was why your brother cried off joining you on your visit to Cambridge; it was not due to illness.

"We are re-evaluating whether the down-time on your security system over that weekend was a module failure or not; whether, in fact, it was caused by the thieves or your brother somehow."

Catrin watched the woman; clearly she, too, had been mulling over the mechanics of what must have happened at the gallery, to enable the switch to be made.

"Did your brother have the contacts; people you know of who could do either the robbery or the technical work?"

Gorton replied quickly, "Not that I know of."

"Did he have the skills to do the fake himself?"

She paused.

"We shared the same home, as you know, in Davies Mews. Your people have searched it; twice now. There are no materials to do this at our home or at the gallery. You know the conservator we use regularly and I am sure you have checked him out. But I would say, no. Russell studied art at the Slade, but did not keep active as an artist once we took over the gallery. I haven't seen him paint for years, so I would say no. Someone else did the alterations."

She paused then said slowly, "You may want to check people he knew back in his student days. He has a scrapbook of some description, with names and photos and... it is still at the flat."

She suddenly glanced at her solicitor, to check that what she had just said wasn't inappropriate. Jocelyn Gorton has some ideas about how it happened, but it was intuition and she didn't want to go too far with that.

"We will; thank you."

Catrin thought it was time to move on to the other question that had been puzzling Coltrane.

"The Dubai development, the start of the second gallery there. How did that come about?"

They sat back and listened to the story of how a wealthy client of the gallery who was English but now resided in Dubai had brought along a friend, an Emirati, who had suggested the idea. It had never occurred to Jocelyn but she listened attentively, more out of politeness than any real interest. But after they left, she found out Russell was hooked already.

"The Gorton Gallery, Dubai; sounds exotic, does it not," she recalled. "I was happy enough with the Gorton Gallery, London, at the time. I wish we had simply turned the man down, politely."

Catrin didn't mention that it was DCI Coltrane's idea to chase up who would want to receive a stolen Bierstadt painting. During her week in Hong Kong, Howlett had been given the task of checking - with the FBI, with other galleries in London and with Customs and Excise - any known collectors of eighteenth and nineteenth century American art who were based in the Emirates.

Howlett had said, when briefed, "There are far too many American painters in that period, Neville!"

Coltrane just said, as he walked out, "I know, Isabelle. Restrict it to the Wild West, horses, cowboys, mountains…"

They now had a list of seven wealthy people in Dubai; five Emirati, two other nationals, who had sizeable collections of such paintings and sculptures, works by Frederic Remington, Thomas Moran and, among others, Albert Bierstadt.

38 PERFORMANCE

The search of the Davies Mews flat, for the third time during this investigation, gave them Russell Gorton's scrapbook from his university days. It provided some interesting photos and comments. Nothing overtly peculiar or bizarre; no statement by a group of students saying, 'Let's get together in twenty years or so for a reunion and knock off a place in Bond Street; steal some paintings'. But Catrin's team delved into the memories, photos and names. Mark spent a day with the records people at the Royal College of Art looking at old files, after which, they knew they were on to something.

A detailed review provided two lists; a larger list of friends from the university days and a short list of five people that Russell Gorton was close to at the time. Background checks on four of these led nowhere, but the fifth name came up trumps, a woman called Sylvia Henshaw. It was the Germans who came back with the key link.

"We have nothing on her, but her name came up in conjunction with a theft from a schloss near Weiden four years ago; a number of paintings. She was a girlfriend of one of the accused, we understood."

They were on a conference call in response to an email from Gerhardt Amsel back to Catrin.

"What happened to them?" asked Coltrane, "Are they inside?"

He looked at Catrin, his expression hopeful. There was a moment of silence then Gerhardt said, "Unfortunately not. They were found not guilty, but we know they were. We understand that Henshaw and Baum, one of the men, broke off their relationship shortly after the arrests. Whether that was linked to the crime or to the prosecution, we cannot say. It may simply have been an agreement to avoid unnecessary visibility for her, if she, too, was criminally active."

Catrin was glad that they weren't on a video link. Coltrane was smiling at the news about Henshaw's link to art crime, which wouldn't have gone down well with the morose tones from the Germans.

She asked neutrally, "How many were there, on the theft at the schloss?"

"Three," came down the line.

No-one had missed the number being the same as the number of thieves entering the premises during the Gorton Gallery theft.

"Can you send us the details, Gerhardt?" asked Coltrane solicitously, understanding the German's embarrassment.

~~

Sylvia Henshaw had no criminal record and nor was she suspected of any involvement in criminal activity in the UK previously. Indeed, from what they could piece together initially, she led an exemplary life after college, working at Colman Fine Art Restorers in Paddington. She had been in a relationship after university with one of the men in the photograph of Russell Gorton's college friends, Derek Lambley. Four years later she took a maternity leave after a baby was born and subsequently returned to Colman's, where she had worked ever since.

The couple had separated acrimoniously when the child was three, with Lambley gaining sole custody of the child, for whatever reason. He married someone else two years later. It was around that time that Henshaw spent a lot of time in Germany.

"It's not enough," said Catrin to her team. "We can't go chasing after Henshaw, or talk to her ex, without a more solid basis for doing so. All it will do is alert them to the fact we are on to her. We had better wait on Gerhardt."

The German team was checking on the whereabouts of the three men in the Weiden job at the time of the Gorton Gallery robbery. It took a few days but the Germans were diligent. Two of the men could not be accounted for in their usual haunts during the week around the Gorton Gallery robbery; the third man had been at his mother's funeral that day.

"Are you sure he went?" asked Harper, on the call.

Gerhardt replied frostily, "Even criminals have mothers; of course he went. But we asked others attending anyway, to be sure."

He sounded quite affronted that this British officer would malign the man on this point.

Howlett was staring at the whiteboard. "So the numbers don't add up. Three men went into the gallery during the robbery. They could have recruited someone locally. In any case, someone else was driving the getaway taxi; someone who knows about driving in central London, not a visitor."

Gerhardt said brightly, seeing a chance to recover some ground, "So you will be reviewing surveillance recordings again, I hope? This time for a larger area of Bond Street for the days before the robbery. There was probably a rehearsal, I would expect."

He knew that this would be a demanding task; hours of checking for a needle in a haystack. It quite perked him up.

In fact, it was easier than it seemed. They left it to the people who managed the traffic monitoring, particularly the ANPR system. The Automatic Number Plate Recognition system was usually used for tracking licence plates of suspected criminals and to identify specific vehicles involved in a crime.

It had identified the getaway taxi, but had missed locating it in time for an interception after the robbery. The driver of the escape vehicle knew exactly what to do to slip between the weak spots in the monitoring system.

Catrin said, "We don't have a plate; what we need is a pattern analysis. We want to know of any vehicles repeatedly passing south on Old Bond Street, perhaps slowing unnecessarily around the point where the taxi turned into the gallery."

She waited for the reaction. What she got was silence. Then one of the techies said, "It will take some time; we will need to talk to the people in PCeU."

The e-crime unit of the Met; where the expertise on computer systems resided, and where Chris Treneer worked.

He smiled. "In fact, you could put a good word in with that husband of yours; they are always too busy over there."

"I will go and see him right now," said Catrin. "I will even talk to his boss. He owes me one from the time I did that job in Cornwall; it's payback time."

Two days later Traffic came back with the identification of a white Opel Zafira belonging to Adam Kerrigan, one of the other men in the scrapbook photograph. It had driven past the gallery, southbound, three times around the same time of day as the robbery for two days running, including the Tuesday a week before the robbery.

Kerrigan had not worked professionally as an artist after college, it seemed. He was now a chauffeur for an agency providing a high-end limo service to Lufthansa for VIP clients. He knew the traffic routes around London intimately; a job which would make him a good getaway driver, if he had the nerve for it.

Later, at home, Chris said, "It seems that we pulled a rabbit out of a hat, the traffic boys and our lot." He was grinning as he spoke.

~~

Allan Jones

"So what have we got?" asked Coltrane, wanting a summary he could use with others.

Catrin was reporting succinctly on the developments at the morning briefing of the Art and Antiques Unit.

"A former college friend of Russell Gorton who is a conservator seems to have links to people in art crime - at least in Germany. A member of the same group of university friends is a professional driver in London. His personal vehicle was traced to show him doing surveillance of the route the taxis took in the approach to the Gorton job."

Her boss grimaced.

He said, "We haven't established a link between the conservator and Gorton, though. Nor have we with the chauffeur. He could argue that he had a number of reasons for shuttling around Bond Street. I see the link but it is too tenuous."

There was a silence.

Howlett said, "We could go back through the street tapes now; not for cars, but for people on the street around the time the Zafira was seen. Perhaps Kerrigan - and others involved - parked and walked back through it."

Coltrane nodded as Mark Harper visibly shuddered; the thought of more hours watching computer screens clearly didn't agree with him. Coltrane smiled and looked at Catrin.

He said, "Nkrumah, you and Howlett do that; tag team and take breaks to keep your sanity... but Bertie, you have something too, I think?"

It was obvious that Bertie Wells did have something new to add. He looked at Catrin apologetically, signaling that he should have told her in person first.

"We finished the forensic work on the painting and then moved on to the surrounding matt and the frame. In the frame we found a thread of cotton snagged in a splinter - and we found blood on both the splinter and the cotton - the same type, the same DNA. If we could get a sample from anyone who was a suspect for the Bratby-Bierstadt forgery work, we could tie them in or rule them out. This woman Henshaw, for example."

He paused, waiting for someone to comment.

Howlett said, "Conservators wear cotton gloves. You are suggesting that the person who did the switch on the Bierstadt pricked her finger, like in the fairytale."

"Him or her, we don't know yet," said Bertie.

DCI Coltrane raised an eyebrow and looked directly at Catrin.

She said, "Well, perhaps Mark and I should pay Sylvia Henshaw a visit. He can charm her; I saw him charming the niece of the couple who own the Tompion."

There were some smiles and comments, as Mark looked at his boss, wondering what to say; he didn't seem to hold the same level of confidence in his smooth-talking as she apparently did.

Before he spoke, Catrin said, "Well, it's that, Mark, or working with Dennis on the street tapes…"

"I'm with you, ma'am," said Mark quickly.

"Just as well," said Isabelle darkly, "I would get blood out of her one way or the other. I bet you she was the one, Bertie; there is no 'him or her' about it."

Coltrane closed the morning briefing with a reminder that the performance reviews were due very soon.

"I don't care about solving crimes," he said, tongue in cheek, "what I like most is making sure the paperwork is neat and tidy and that you all get two levels of promotion in a month from now, with big, fat pay raises, all because your performance development reviews were all so wonderful."

The groans filled the room.

~~

With Mark Harper the performance review went mainly to plan. They agreed easily on aspects of strong performance and in areas he needed to consider; they identified a couple of courses he should take to address these and improve his chances of promotion. Catrin told him that he would also get some of the US liaison action, as opportunities unfolded.

For his part, he made the point that she had been too involved in 'irregular' issues like the Tregynon case since joining the team for him to truly say how she was doing, but he felt that it was 'so far, so good'. He liked her style of team leadership and the fact she was no slouch about art.

His final comment was, "I liked the way you didn't react to Madder's thing on day one, ma'am. It could have given him some grief, I know. It means you think about colleagues and team members."

With Isabelle Howlett, it didn't go to plan; at least the review did not to Catrin's plan; more to Howlett's, she thought afterwards.

After the introduction, she asked Howlett for her first thoughts on the period they had worked together, a preliminary to sharing her own thoughts.

Howlett actually sounded like a big sister as she spoke.

"Ma'am, I know this is meant to be formal, but I want to speak openly; can I do that?"

Catrin nodded. "That would be good, yes."

"You are trying too hard, Catrin."

Catrin's surprise was evident. Part of the review was, in fact, to ask questions about her performance as a team leader from the perspective of the person being appraised, but that was not at the beginning of the protocol.

Howlett clarified her comment.

"With me, I mean. Since you joined and we went up to Tregynon, when you wanted to get me out of my rut, I suppose; it was rather obvious, you know? Like, I am sure you will raise it; do I want to finish my conservator course? Do I want other duties which may advance me towards promotion? The truth is I want what I am doing, what I have been doing for years. That's it. I like my job."

She watched her boss's reaction then went on.

"You are all-singing, all-dancing, so to speak; a model of

career progression, doing really well. You could go far in the Met unless the politics screw it up. They probably will; it happens to others. But I'm me; not you."

Catrin thought of the response. "Team's change, jobs change, Isabelle. It's just the way it is. Art and Antiques grew larger and then shrunk a bit; every team in the Met faces that. I think that I, and Neville, would want to see you make progress in your career during such changes."

Howlett smiled, as if she wasn't being understood.

"Ma'am; I like what I do. If the Met changes the unit, or my job, or I don't like my boss, or if they move Neville and screw it up, then I would go. I am not in it for the 'twenty-five and a pension'. I would probably go to the private sector, do the same thing for a consulting firm at better pay. It's not like I have to, but that's what I would do. But I like being in this job."

"You want DCI Coltrane to remain the boss, then?"

She nodded.

"I am from Oxford; a local townie, not the university lot that Neville was part of. I have no airs and graces. The boss is one of those people who may have been born with a silver spoon in his mouth - and may well now have a drawer full of gold ones - but he is completely above class consciousness. He is happy with me in the team and I am happy with him being the boss - and he knows art; in that he is one of the best.

"Don't get me wrong, I like working with you too, to be completely honest. You also know about art."

She paused, then said suddenly, impulsively, "I will tell you something in confidence. The first time I heard your name was from Neville, years ago when you joined the ACU. He came in and said to Caldwell that ACU now had a new member who had a real eye for art. Caldwell was still wincing from Keith Marshall's defection to the ACU, as he put it. He seemed to miss that Marshall left with a reason and a promotion.

"So Phil asked who it was. Don't remember her name, said Neville, but she is good. Was buried in Brixton in uniform, comes from Wales by the sound of her. Phil had attended

Wadham College, as did Neville more recently, you know?

"Caldwell made a comment that was dismissive and I remember Neville's face, the look. Somewhere between annoyance, disbelief and disdain. What mattered to him was that you had talent and artistic understanding. There are other examples. But I like the man."

"I do too," said Catrin, suddenly.

She recalled clearly the event Howlett was talking about; her first proper day with the Art Crime Unit after the Bangor stint, in which she had an undercover role. They had been in the lab with Bertie Wells, looking at a painting by Maxim Garin that had been recovered from a botched smuggling operation. Neville had asked her opinion of it, testing her. DCI Worsley had commented later that she had passed some sort of threshold; she had not received an earful of Coltrane's own interpretation correcting her before he left.

Later, she realised as she wrote up her notes that her review of Isabelle Howlett's performance and her recommendations were not that dissimilar to those made the year before by Philip Caldwell. It wasn't what she set out to do, but that was the reality.

39 SWAB

In deciding on the strategy for approaching Sylvia Henshaw, Catrin was taken back two years, to a meeting with a suspect in the Stubbs investigation, Ryland Cronin. She had played a plodding, detail-oriented detective. She recalled having to work hard to appear obtuse without overplaying it, to get Cronin to slip up.

She said to Harper, "You just have to appear harried and frustrated by your pedantic boss, then be nice to Henshaw. It will come naturally."

Mark said carefully, "I will try my best, ma'am; to be nice, I mean."

She looked at him. "The pedantic boss bit isn't a problem, then?"

"I think I will manage that," he responded enigmatically.

Sylvia Henshaw was easily recognizable from her college photograph. Her hairstyle was unchanged; a short, almost masculine cut of dark hair, now without the blonde top-knot of her college days. She was still trim, a small woman physically, but with a sense of energy about her. In fact, she was just heading out to a yoga class when they arrived at her flat in a small block in Wimbledon. Catrin explained that they needed 'a few words with her' regarding her friend Russell Gorton.

"Now?" she said, "Can't it wait? I will be done in an hour."

Catrin said woodenly, "We would like to do it now; we have a lot of his friends on our list and we are already in the area. If you don't mind...?"

Sylvia did, but they were police officers, so she put down her sports bag and let them sit down in the living room. She didn't offer them tea or coffee.

Catrin pulled a tattered manila file from the worn, government-style briefcase she had borrowed from Laura Bainbridge. It contained a set of papers and an A4 writing pad with several pages containing a long list of names, some checked off, some not, some ringed in red ink. She had asked Howlett to concoct it. The only name in there that mattered was Henshaw's. Taking longer than necessary, she checked it off.

She began, "So you and Russell Gorton were friends at university?"

Sylvia said, "Yes; there, and for a few years afterwards casually, but we lost touch. You know how it is."

Catrin looked as if she had no idea how it was.

"So when did you last see him or speak to him?"

Sylvia looked puzzled. "I have no idea; it has been over a decade since we lost touch, as I said. Actually, thinking about it, I do know. At a party about four years ago; totally out of the blue, we met up. I spoke to him there, but we didn't follow up. We were each with other people."

Mark nodded as if he understood, at least. Then Sylvia thought it was her turn.

"What's this about, then? With Russell?"

Catrin said woodenly, "His gallery was robbed about two years ago. Paintings were stolen."

Henshaw responded, "I know about that, it was in the papers."

Catrin said, "Well, we have traced the paintings. Some were in a warehouse, but one was handled differently, a Bierstadt seascape. It was overpainted to look like the Bratby painting that they had in the gallery, the one that belonged to their father. It had been 'kept on ice' there, hidden, and was about to be shipped out to the Gulf."

Catrin watched her carefully as she revealed the detail. The woman's face betrayed nothing. But she noted, despite her being a conservator, she didn't ask about the Bierstadt; had it been damaged? How did they do it? The sort of technical questions that arise during an interview with professionals to which the police officer generally can't respond.

Sylvia just said, "But I still don't see - ."

Catrin said, "We are talking to everyone Russell Gorton knew who has artistic capabilities to paint the fake. People he studied with; people he worked with over the years, conservators he has employed; anyone relevant, in fact."

Sylvia said, disbelievingly, "Now that will be a long list; he has been in the art world since college. And I resent the implication - ."

Mark said softly, "It's just routine follow-up, Miss Henshaw."

Henshaw's eyes were on the file open on Catrin's lap, the long list of names and the number of pages in the folder.

"We have to eliminate people from our enquiries," continued Mark, soothingly, conveying he was not too happy with the way the investigation was going.

Catrin said unsympathetically, "Which is why we need to get this done. We have another two people to see this afternoon. So can I establish your whereabouts on the day of the robbery?"

She gave her the date.

Henshaw "I have no idea, offhand. I will look it up."

She went over to a laptop on the table and pulled up a calendar file.

"Tuesday, a Tuesday; here it is. I was working. I had a contract that week fixing a painting for Swindon Central Library; I went to see it in place before it was sent to the studio where I work."

She smiled, pleased at the ability to respond.

Catrin continued, looking at her pad, writing away, "And the week or so before, particularly the weekend?"

Henshaw responded, "I can't help there. It says nothing in my calendar about the weekend, so I assume I was around here. I had a family birthday the following weekend in Slough. I remember that, and it is in the calendar. But the weekend before, no. Not a clue."

"So you have no alibi," said Catrin, stonily.

Mark let out a soft hiss as Sylvia Henshaw said, somewhat truculently, "I didn't know I needed one, to be honest, for life in general, I mean."

Catrin persisted, "Could you paint a Bratby copy in a weekend, then? Hypothetically speaking?"

She was goading her; it was plain to both Henshaw and Harper.

Henshaw gave an angry sigh, waited a moment and then said carefully and calmly, "I am an artist. I suppose I could, given the right materials but the truth is, I don't know. You don't know until you try and then achieve what you want to do, you see? It's art, not checking bloody lists of names. Now, I have spent enough time on this… whatever you are doing. And I have missed my class."

Catrin said, a little defensively, "We are eliminating people from our enquiries. Someone faked the Bratby painting on top of the Bierstadt; we think it may be someone Russell Gorton knows."

Henshaw said promptly, "Well, you can count me out. I don't know what you are talking about. I haven't even visited the gallery."

Catrin responded, "It would be helpful to eliminate you on fingerprints and DNA; we have a ton of those from the robbery files, you see; employees, clients, building workers. It's a lot to go through."

She tried to make it sound a task that any bureaucrat would be happy to tackle; steady work for months ahead. She knew she had to be careful not to overdo it, though.

Sylvia Henshaw looked at her and paused. "I don't have time to go trotting into police stations, waiting to get ink all over my fingers. Frankly, I am amazed at this… wasting taxpayer's money chasing anyone and everyone who knows Russell. Why do you say he did it anyway?"

Catrin started to speak. "We can't go into -"

Mark cut across her, sounding at the end of his tether.

"Miss Henshaw, you don't have to visit a station. I have the finger printing kit here and a swab for the DNA. It will take less than two minutes; then we can get out of your way and you can get on with the day."

His tone was apologetic as he looked at Catrin, apparently irritated by his boss

Catrin was looking at him, annoyed at the interruption, the clash being observed by Henshaw as a silence descended.

The woman said, "Fine. Let's do it."

She smiled at Mark, letting him know she thought he had a miserable boss to work for.

They expedited the DNA work. Two days later, they had a firm match between Henshaw and the blood on the Bratby frame.

Catrin asked, "Do we pick her up; see what we can get out of her?"

Coltrane thought for a moment.

"We will arrest Henshaw and Adam Kerrigan at the same time. But you won't be here. I think you and I will be in Dubai as they are brought in. It is time to talk to Mr. Gorton about how he screwed up the perfectly good art gallery business he had going with his sister."

~~

In the end Coltrane decided to send Catrin and Mark Harper to Dubai. He wanted to go himself but he had conflicts; other meetings he couldn't miss.

He said, "I know a conservator at Al Fahidi; we met in

Paris last year. It would be nice to visit the museum and also see Jerry again."

Catrin asked Mark as they left his office. "Al Fahidi?"

"It's a fort, ma'am, now converted to a museum. It has artefacts going back over the different civilizations in the region."

"The Acton haul is blessing and a curse," Coltrane had said.

Mark Harper thought the complexity and size of the Acton prosecutions was a blessing; he got to go with his boss to Dubai.

In the briefing after the next Task Force conference call, where Coltrane brought everyone up to date and announced his intentions, he said to both of them, "But do take the time before you see Gorton to look around with Assad. After the meeting, of course, the shock value will give you no time; you will need to be back on the overnight flight. With him, I hope. I would give you an extra day out there, if I could, but with everything going on, you had better get back."

He mused, "A drawn-out extradition request will not go down well with the Foreign and Commonwealth Office so if we can avoid it, I would be very happy. And I certainly don't want to leave it to the Americans."

David Klintz had offered to send Walkley over to get Gorton, using US embassy resources and influence, but that had been headed off by the other Europeans, It was a turf war; it may be the Middle East but to them it was a European matter.

"Dubai is just around the corner for us, David," said Neville, trying to be diplomatic after the Germans had been quite candid about jurisdiction.

"It's an overnight flight from Dubai to London or Paris, same as, in effect, for us," said Klintz, sounding a little annoyed at the rejection. "And it is our Bierstadt that the man screwed around with."

In the end Neville Coltrane said, "We can handle it, David.

I am sure that my team can bring to bear the international dimension. It is, after all, our national we want back from there; a crime committed on our patch."

~~

Catrin was working at her desk later when an unexpected visitor turned up, knocking on the door frame as he entered.

Inspector Terry Entwistle said, "Do you have a moment, Catrin?"

He didn't wait for an answer, just closed the door and sat himself down. Catrin hadn't seen Entwistle to talk to for some time. His specialty was Asia-based gangs, including triads, with criminal operations in the UK. Entwistle had been the primary link with the Royal Malaysian Police in the aftermath of her visit to Malaysia more than two years ago.

"Something up with the Malaysians? Should I be worried?" asked Catrin, straight off.

He shook his head then said, "Yes and no. Not about Nam Wu. That's the good news. We believe he is dead."

Catrin said, "Why - and when? And how?"

"I can't say. All we know from the Royal Malaysian Police is that the Wu family had a gathering two days ago for a funeral of an octogenarian grandmother. As is usual at their funerals, photographs of other family members who have died, particularly those who died recently, are placed in honour on a dais, for flowers and other tokens of remembrance to be placed there. They are sure Nam Wu's photo was there; they had someone attend."

"Does Sergeant Farra know?"

"I believe so; they said they were informing him also. I know you are still in touch with the Farra family. I see no reason why you can't mention it, but give it a while, just in case."

"Well, that's good news; for me, for us," she said. "RMP still see it as a personal vendetta against us by Wu, not a triad issue?"

Entwistle nodded, "Nothing has changed there, as far as we are aware."

His face changed, so she said, "And the 'no' part, Terry?"

"You need to take this as a 'heads up'. I probably shouldn't be mentioning it, even. So…"

He touched his nose, in the time-honored signal for 'off the record'.

Catrin nodded.

"We had a request from our contacts in SIS… for all information on the Ten Dragons triad linked to the Malaysian incident, plus all known Ten Dragon contacts in the UK and Hong Kong that we are aware of. I know the contact at Vauxhall Cross quite well; we have shared information over the years. I was all ready to co-operate - until he also asked for information on you and any triad contacts that you had encountered, in cases you had worked on."

His gaze was steady, neutral.

"I asked him if the requests were linked and, somewhat reluctantly, he said, 'yes'. I told him to file it formally through senior channels. I don't provide information on colleagues to … what's Jack Taylor's phrase?"

Superintendent Jack Taylor, Worsley's boss, was from Yorkshire and was known for his occasionally colourful phrases.

Catrin said automatically, although her mind was elsewhere, "His 'slimy friends'… MI5 are his 'slippery friends'; I think it was that way around."

She looked at him, thinking what to ask then realizing she couldn't really ask him anything.

"Terry, I appreciate the 'heads up'. Just so you know, I was in Hong Kong recently, for a friend's wedding. I don't know if, for some reason, that triggered something."

Entwistle said, "I can't say more. I get the impression that someone higher up in SIS has also been in contact with our boss, Commander Barlow, already. I say that only from his reaction when I updated people in my shop earlier this morning. And that is just a guess.

"If this becomes official I can't talk to you about it, of course. But then I haven't talked to you about it anyway, have I?"

She nodded as he stood and opened the door, leaving without any further comment.

She called after him, "Thanks for the news about Wu."

But her mind was elsewhere. Why was SIS interested in her?

40 DUBAI

They arrived in Dubai International in the evening, after a day-long flight, descending into the redness of the setting sun. Suddenly they were in darkness, flying more slowly in the approach sequence into the airport, the view increasingly dominated by the kaleidoscope of lights and skyscrapers; illuminations far brighter, Catrin felt, than the lights over London. The dominant feature on the skyline, by far, however, was the Burj Khalifa, the tallest building in the world.

Fortunately they were met by local officers and hurried through immigration to a Blue and White Toyota Land Cruiser for the drive to their hotel.

The following morning they had breakfast there with Major Jerry Assad, to explain the plan. He was a local, an Emirati, a very pleasant middle-aged man who spoke well of Neville.

"We went to the same school; well I went there for a year while my father was in London, at the embassy, a little before Neville's time."

Harper said, "Charterhouse. The tie." He pointed a finger. But he knew already that DCI Coltrane was an Old Carthusian.

Assad asked, "And you were at …?"

"City of London. I used to walk to school, it was that

close."

Assad nodded, recognizing the name, a fee-paying boys' school located on the Thames near St. Paul's Cathedral. Catrin noticed that neither of them brought up Pontypridd High School.

After the preliminaries, Major Assad listened carefully, asked a few innocuous questions and offered any support he could. Somehow Catrin felt he was laying it on a bit; that he knew the whole thing anyway from Coltrane. As Assad had said, they had good relations and they were 'old school chums'.

She said, "We need an arrangement to catch him cold, sir, preferably at his gallery. However, if he is not at that location or otherwise available, it causes a problem. We know he is in Dubai at present; you confirmed that to DCI Coltrane."

Assad smiled broadly; he was clearly pleased to find a way he could be of direct assistance.

"Inspector Sayer, please allow me to organize this aspect. By the sound of it you want to give him enough time to make the right decision, but not too much. You don't want him to try anything foolish. But even if he does, he will not be leaving without our authority, I assure you.

"I will arrange an appointment with Mr. Gorton shortly beforehand, making it for me, I will say. He will have no choice, of course. He will also be accompanied by his lawyer here, I am sure. I suggest around 4.00 p.m. would be the right timing.

"Which leaves us most of the day for me to host you both in a tour of our city and, as Neville suggested, a visit to the museum."

Later, a Mercedes with a driver took the three of them to the mall where the gallery was located, arriving at the agreed time. It was a modern thriving shopping facility at the main floor level, with more specialized shops and galleries at higher levels. As the escalator reached the third floor, the small front façade of the Gorton Gallery was visible.

She glanced at Harper. He too had seen it and had, unconsciously, taken a deep breath. Catrin tried to conceal her own nervousness. A lot would be riding on the conversation over the next thirty minutes.

They recognized Russell Gorton from his photo as they walked in, but not the Emirati in the dark suit talking to him. In contrast, Major Assad knew the man and greeted him cordially in Arabic and then made the round of introductions.

The lawyer was introduced as Mr. Mohamed Ghadir.

Russell Gorton said immediately, "Major Assad, I will, of course, answer any questions that you may have, but I decline to answer questions from these British police officers."

He looked at Sayer and Harper. "I'm sorry, but you wasted your time coming here."

Assad said nothing but looked at the lawyer, clearly unhappy with the statement. The lawyer shook his head, a sign indicating that he had counselled a different stance for his client. The exchange of looks told Catrin a lot; the two Emiratis had talked earlier, it was clear. Neville had said it was a different world here; the locals controlled everything, in a sense. Every business had an Emirati partner and they sorted things out between themselves, no matter what any foreigner thinks. Assad had been confident about setting up the meeting with Gorton because he had made sure his lawyer was in the loop.

Catrin spoke up.

"Oh, it's not wasted, Mr. Gorton, thank you," she said. "We are inviting you to return to the UK to be arrested and face charges."

Breaking his own position statement, Gorton said, "Charges; for what?"

Catrin said evenly, "For robbery, including the theft of a Bierstadt painting, among others, and sundry related matters, such as filling Old Bond Street with smoke. It caused mayhem, respiratory problems for people nearby and it made everyone's windows dirty."

She had deliberately moved over to a nearby painting as she

spoke, apparently giving it her full attention as she continued.

"We had hoped to ask our questions here, but will happily wait until you are in custody in the UK. This is really nice. Is the artist local? How much is it going for?"

He looked at her, astonished, as she looked back at him.

Get him off-balance right off the bat; that was the key, Coltrane had told them. If the meeting is in the gallery, one of you go after his art, either praise it or damn it, it doesn't matter much which; he is so close to it emotionally. After announcing our intent, it will pull his mind in two ways at once. That should help.

Gorton said, "I don't understand. In any event, I want no further discussion -."

Major Assad said, "Mr. Gorton, you may choose not to answer any questions posed by these officers, but please hear them out. This is Dubai. I would encourage you to be polite."

He looked at the lawyer, who nodded at Assad and whispered something to Gorton. Catrin took it to mean that he should not deliberately annoy the Dubai policeman.

She said, "You don't understand? My questions about the work of art, or about the wish to arrest you? Mark, show Mr. Gorton our picture."

Mark Harper pulled out his smartphone and showed Russell Gorton the Bierstadt 'Seal Island' image, a shot taken in Bertie Well's lab at New Scotland Yard. The lower corner of the Bierstadt was visible with the edges of the covering work, the copy of the Bratby painting. Between the two, the sandwich layer showed nicely.

She said, "We have nearly all of it, I think. Warrants were issued this morning for the men who did the Hackney Heist, the diversion you fixed for the main act; two German nationals and your friend Adam Kerrigan. I am waiting to hear if Kerrigan is in custody yet. There was another person we haven't identified yet, but in time we will, I am sure.

"We have also arrested the artist who did the work to cover

Seal Island and charged her yesterday; another of your friends, Sylvia Henshaw."

After Gorton absorbed it he said, in disbelief, "And you invite me to come back to face related charges?"

"Yes," said Catrin, "we think it is in your best interest. Support your friend Sylvia; help her out. She was a former girlfriend, after all."

His look was dismissive. 'So what?' it implied. What he said was, "I don't know what you are talking about."

Good, thought, Catrin; the lies have started. She walked back to face him.

"Conservators generally use cotton gloves while working, as you know. And that rough wood frame on the Bratby, the one your father made, has splinters; in fact, one stuck in Sylvia Henshaw's hand. Forensically, we were fortunate; the splinter didn't break off, you see. It just penetrated the glove, pricked her and absorbed some blood. And the glove left a cotton thread, with the same blood. Henshaw agreed to give her fingerprints and a DNA swab when we first interviewed her. She was confident, you see - then. As you are now."

Catrin paused.

"Henshaw probably even complained to you about the frame at the time she did the work."

He muttered something indistinguishable dismissively, but his eyes showed she had hit home. Then, looking at the image on Mark's phone he said, "Someone hasn't done a good job on this; it should come clean, I would have thought."

He was changing the subject. She could see he was carefully choosing his words.

Gorton added, "Whoever did this would have obviously have made sure that Seal Island would be recoverable, cleanly and completely, wouldn't they?"

Mark said, "Actually, the conservators are going very carefully at this point. The underlying layer was a plaster composite of some sort, removable by water, covered by the new canvas layer and gesso. Then on top of that there is the painting of the Bratby copy. A sandwich. But a sandwich with hairline cracks going down through it. Do you need me to explain it more clearly?"

His expression was somewhere between innocent and challenging.

Major Assad said, "Perhaps you should do so, sergeant, just out of professional interest, so to speak."

Assad was not looking at Gorton, but at the man's lawyer.

Harper continued, "X-ray analysis showed some cracks of varying depth that must have occurred after the layers were added. So some paint and gesso migrated down, how far, we don't know; and the gesso appears to be stuck firmly to the Bierstadt in several places. So they are working very carefully. It will take some time."

Catrin added, "Of course, the owners are quite distressed that the painting is not yet 'out of the woods' after its mistreatment. There is some pressure on the FBI to act."

She looked at Major Assad, then at the lawyer. The implicit question was, did they really want the Americans making a fuss about Gorton with people in Dubai?

Russell Gorton said, "I don't… It would be …"

He stopped. He was caught between his knowledge of the technique used to hide Seal Island, presumably carefully tested by Henshaw and himself in advance, and his need to say nothing. Catrin could see his anger rising.

"It's a set-up. But I won't play. I don't want to talk with you any further."

He turned away, ready to terminate the discussion.

Catrin said, "The news releases tomorrow morning will include a press statement about the challenges encountered during the restoration of Seal Island. The owners will express their concern about the extent of any damage. We, of course, will issue a warrant for your arrest and inform Interpol and the Dubai authorities formally. Then the bureaucrats will take over regarding the extradition request. We do have an extradition treaty with Dubai, you know."

He turned back and looked at her. "And I have very powerful connections here. I am a success here; I have had no trouble with the law, as Major Assad will attest."

Catrin went for the planned clincher; a two-part hit.

"We worked out the costs of the Gorton Gallery theft, approximately, and will be checking bank accounts. We get the impression that the operation was not cheap and, with it, one assumes there is a significantly higher pay-off to the people involved. We have found an overseas account for Henshaw with over three hundred thousand pounds in it, deposited around the time of the robbery. A lot of money for one player in the team."

She paused, making sure that she was focused only on Gorton as she said the next sentence.

"So we think someone was prepared to pay a much higher price to secure the Bierstadt than its market value of three million dollars; a collector with lots of money. It will take some time, but the Germans and our financial people will track the money flows, at least some of them… It would be so much neater to just close it out with you, Sylvia and your band of merry men who used the taxis, wouldn't it?"

Harper was watching the effect of the remark as it registered with the lawyer. He knew immediately that they had succeeded; Gorton would be on his way home. Whoever the buyer was, the person would want this line of enquiry shut down fast. But he enjoyed Catrin giving the second part of the finale.

She said, "Then of course, there is the religious aspect of the painting."

The lawyer's eyes also showed Harper that she had hit a mark with that one, too.

Gorton said, "Seal Island - what do you mean?"

"Not Seal Island, the Bratby painting that was stripped. The church."

He burst out laughing. "Church? It was a head and shoulders of Jean Cooke, his first wife. They were my father's friends. The painting contains her, a Corn Flakes packet on a table and a dilapidated window behind; it is hardly a religious painting."

"A window through which you can see a church," said Catrin. "Remember DC Howlett? She loves Bratby's paintings. She is talking to some art academic she knows about writing an article for a journal, about the loss of the painting and its significance. After all, John Bratby did the huge crucifixion painting at Lancaster University. It is controversial, I know, but a religious painting, nevertheless. He featured churches in other paintings - such as his painting of the Church of Ascension at Dartmouth Row, Blackheath."

She looked at Gorton, her face inviting his response.

He said, "As I recall, hardly any painting by him had religious overtones. It wasn't his thing. Portraits, a lot of his second wife, nude, were his thing. They wouldn't sell here, as you can imagine. You are barking up a wrong tree there, Inspector."

He was trying to sound confident, arrogant even, but there were cracks in the veneer. Catrin ploughed on.

"DC Howlett will be looking at the Dartmouth Row painting today, coincidentally."

She looked at Gorton's lawyer.

"It is owned by the Foreign and Commonwealth Office, in Whitehall. The curator there is very accommodating. And you are right, Mr. Gorton, relatively few of Bratby's paintings feature churches."

"Which is why destroying even one of them is… significant," added Harper.

Catrin had returned to examine the painting she had been looking at earlier.

To no-one in particular she said, "Your contacts here, your supporters, are probably religious men, Mr. Gorton, devout."

Catrin glanced over to Major Assad; it was the signal for him to speak.

He looked at Gorton but they all knew his words were for the lawyer.

Assad said softly, "Even if someone in the Emirates had

been interested privately in Seal Island, should it have arrived here, they probably would not like a… taint of this nature being associated with its past. But you probably know that, living here."

From his expression, she gathered that Assad knew exactly who in Dubai was interested in acquiring the Bierstadt. She also thought that it would be highly unlikely that they would be brought into that confidence.

Russell Gorton stood there, taking it all in, particularly the exchange of expressions between the local art detective and his own lawyer.

He said, "So what happens now; you are going to ask them to hold me?"

He nodded at Assad; making clear who 'them' were.

"No," said Catrin, "We are going home, tonight, on the British Airways flight. There is a business class seat reserved in your name; not paid for, of course. Just the reservation.

"If you are on it, then we will arrest you in London. And how much is this worth?"

She pointed to the painting.

"Outside a police officer's pay rate," he snapped back.

"Probably mine, I agree," said Catrin. "Pity. Goodbye Mr. Gorton."

As they moved to the door, the gallery owner said, "Amazing; so British of you. Why don't you think I will simply pick up sticks and go somewhere else?"

Harper responded.

"Because as soon as you do, no matter where it is, the Americans will be after you, as an Interpol-flagged fugitive. They have contacts just about … everywhere, don't they, ma'am?"

"Yes," said Catrin, recalling the conference call and the efforts of Klintz's team to be involved. "And the FBI is really keen to send people over. You don't want the life of a fugitive, Mr. Gorton. Believe me, it will be no joy. Get the best deal you can, if you can; serve your sentence and get on with your life."

In her mind was the phrase 'black helicopters'. In hatching this plan, every time the Americans were mentioned, either Howlett or Harper muttered the phrase. It was a running joke. She had told Harper not to say it in Dubai at all. Walls have ears.

They looked at Jerry Assad and the three police officers walked out, the local detective saying something quickly and softly in Arabic to Gorton's lawyer as he turned to leave.

Outside he said, "I think that went well, Inspector Sayer."

Later, they had dinner with Major Assad before he arranged a ride for them to the airport. Catrin thanked him for all his help and hospitality and promised him a dinner in return in London; Assad visited the city regularly. Coltrane had told her that she needed to start developing her own international relationships, so this was a good start.

Catrin thought that they should monitor Gorton until flight time but Coltrane overrode it.

"Don't bother; he will realize he has no choice. It is more important that you build a relationship with Assad. Part of your new job."

In the British Airways executive lounge at the airport, Gorton walked over to them, holding a whisky glass.

"I suppose this is no surprise."

He sounded normal, but there was a sense of disappointment and anger, suppressed.

Neither Harper nor Sayer responded directly.

Catrin said, "I take it that you have contacted your solicitor in London already? It would be advisable to do so."

"Oh, yes. He is all prepared."

He smiled.

Catrin watched him carefully. He thinks he has negotiation room; Gorton must be hoping to come out of this with a deal. He hadn't listened carefully enough to her message at the gallery.

There would be no easy deal, Neville had said; nor could

she give any hint of one. The politics were too dominant. Mr. Herron had loaned the Bierstadt in good faith and a powerful American diplomat wanted his due; the maximum gaol time for the person who had betrayed his trust.

Somehow, in his self-confidence, Gorton had not seen that. But it wasn't her place to address it, just to get him back to the UK. And it wasn't up to the Americans anyway; it was an issue for the CPS and the High Court system.

BA 0214 left at 1.50 a.m., on time. The seating reservations placed Russell Gorton by the window and Harper in the adjacent aisle seat. Catrin was across the aisle.

The only minor disturbance was as they dimmed the lights after dinner. Gorton had consumed a cocktail and several glasses of wine on the flight, his last for a while he knew. He started to give a sarcastic discourse on the life and loves of John Bratby a little too loudly for some seated around him. Harper told him quietly but forcefully to drop it; they all needed to get some sleep.

At Heathrow, DCI Coltrane met the flight with the Airport Police. He wanted the privilege of arresting the gallery owner himself. Catrin saw that Howlett was with him; she wanted to come too, apparently, to join the party. From the expression on her face, Catrin was glad she had Harper and not Howlett with her on the flight. Gorton's discourse on Bratby on board and Howlett's love of the artist's work would not have been a good mix.

They took him into a secure area to arrest him and place him in handcuffs.

DCI Coltrane said, "We have been contacted by your solicitor already. He will be at your first interview at Scotland Yard."

He paused. "Did you call your sister?"

Gorton shook his head. He looked weary now, not angry. It was more than an issue of a night on a plane.

Coltrane persisted. "Would you like to do so now?"

Russell Gorton's response to the offer was a mix between a smile and a sneer. "So you can enjoy listening in, no doubt."

"No," said Neville, simply. "You can speak in private. You have my word on that. The reason you have avoided doing so in the last weeks is over with now, isn't it?"

Gorton thought about it and shook his head. "All in due course, but I can't do it now."

"Tell me," said Coltrane. "Did you like the Bratby at all?"

Gorton grimaced. "I hated the damn thing, despite what I said to Jocelyn and others. Always did. But then I had no love for my dad, either, despite him leaving the gallery to Jocelyn and me."

He turned, looking at Howlett and said, matter-of-factly, "You liked it, I know. I knew that before your boss here rubbed salt in the wound about it in Dubai. I even remember you looking at it after the robbery."

Isabelle Howlett looked imperturbable. She was an experienced police officer and would not give the man a chance to gloat, if that was what this was about. She couldn't tell.

"Are we ready, sir?" she asked DCI Coltrane.

He nodded, turning to the two uniformed officers. "You can take him away now."

When he was out of sight, Howlett offered her team members a lift back to the office.

"Take Harper, if you would, Howlett," said Coltrane, "I will take DI Sayer with me, give her more work to do."

Harper groaned. "For us as well, sir, no doubt."

When they were alone, Coltrane said, "Let's go. I just wanted to talk, a preliminary to doing your performance review later this week. Did you get enough sleep on the plane?"

"I did, actually; for an overnight trip, thanks. I was going to say, I am now sure that Gorton had a client for the Bierstadt in Dubai, as we suspected. It was pretty obvious from the exchanges between Gorton, his lawyer and Jerry Assad. But I doubt we will hear that from Gorton's lips."

Coltrane responded. "No, he won't say. It's the carrot and stick thing. He will end up with a top-notch barrister here; people back there will pay, ensure his gallery thrives and look after his interests - providing he looks after theirs in return. The mad idea for the robbery probably came out of the whole 'new venture' thing."

She could tell he was assessing how attentive she was.

She asked, "But why would an Emirati - or some other rich person living there - go wild and get involved in the theft of a US painting? Bierstadt is hardly top rank."

Coltrane laughed. "Because the man liked it, wanted it and it wasn't for sale, I suspect; and it was owned by an American diplomat. Who knows?"

He continued, "It's been more than a month now. Are you happy in your new position? And are you happy with your team? Your reviews seemed fair. We can talk about them and your recommendations back in the office, another time."

She thought a moment.

"Yes Neville, I am. The Tregynon thing as I started the job was a little out in left field, but this trip to Dubai chasing the Bierstadt theft has brought home the reality of the role. And I am learning about people management and leadership.

"Investigating art crime with Art and Antiques is not quite the same as my work previously with the ACU. I knew that, in principle. Now I am experiencing it in practice. But the team work and the international dimension; yes, I like that aspect. And your thoughts, Neville; how am I doing?"

He nodded unhesitatingly.

"With me, it's fine. I am happy with my decision in putting you in the position. You are doing well; clueing in on the Bierstadt, for example. That sense of pulling things together and seeing a new angle; it's exactly why I wanted you as a member of my team."

He paused.

"Let's leave the detail to the review. Now, the 'Madder trick'; the Van Dongen test he tried on your first day. I didn't take him to task about it. That would have been counter-productive. But are you two getting along?"

Catrin said, "I acted like it never happened the day after-wards. He has been alright with me since then, so I think we are getting along."

They were outside the building. An airport police car was parked behind Coltrane's Bentley, watching it. Coltrane gave the officer a nod and opened the doors.

As they climbed in he said, "Good. We have decided to promote him to Inspector, leading the Antiques Team. I have a meeting with him this morning to let him know. You and he will be equal rank, so it is important you work well together."

'Message understood' thought Catrin. Her boss would doubtlessly be giving Madder the same message.

As they set off, she asked, "And the additional work?"

They pulled away from the lights to go through the tunnel on to the M4.

Coltrane answered, "The case work can wait until we get back. I will, however, set your targets to include within the next quarter, I think, a visit to David Klintz and the FBI team; some first-hand contact on cases we have in common. It means a trip to Washington.

"Walkley will be taking you down to their range, I expect, seeing as you were AFO trained. You can bond; shoot targets, break bread and spill coffee on the same table."

He was sounding serious but his eyes were looking amused.

She answered, "I will stick closer to Agent Klintz."

She sighed, settling back into the comfortable seat of the luxury vehicle. Despite what she said about sleeping on the flight, she could happily drop off in the Bentley; not that she would ever do so.

"Klintz can probably get me into any gallery in DC to see art that is either on display or in storage."

41 CONSEQUENCES

"What's up?"

Chris was watching her, she saw.

Catrin answered, "Too much on my mind, to be honest…"

He said, "For the last few days before Dubai and these last two days, now you are back, you have been carrying the weight of the world on your shoulders. Even with your work, you get intense, but not depressed. You are sitting holding that sketch pad but doing nothing with it."

She thought for a moment. "Let's go out, take a walk and get some air. That might help."

"Suits me," Chris said, switching off the television.

Catrin knew there hadn't been physical surveillance. And that wasn't through any arrogance associated with simply being a police officer. She had been specially trained in the subject of spotting watchers - countersurveillance - when the news of the death threat from Nam Wu had first been raised. It had been hurried, intense; but she had subsequently received more advanced training for her security role with Assistant Commissioner Hunt. It was intrinsic for her to monitor those around her, but in any case she had been checking more carefully during the last week. However, if SIS were using electronic surveillance, she had no idea.

They walked west, picking up Quaker Street then headed across the Arts Market to Bishopsgate. This walk would lead them back through Petticoat Lane. It was a regular exercise route they used. During it she told him what she knew, based on the 'heads up' from Entwistle. Chris was the only person other than Jian Li to know the history of Michael Yau's involvement in removing the death threat by the Malaysian triad member.

She said, "SIS must have established a link between Yau and me, or Yau and Li. They may have found out that I was informed about Yau's involvement in stopping Nam Wu and think I am compromised in some way. If so, they will go after me - or have the Met do something. It will ruin my career; that's what worries me. I've done nothing wrong, Chris, but…"

He thought about it as they walked.

He asked, "They haven't done anything yet, as far as you know?"

"Not that I am aware of. Probably when I am called into someone's office then taken to an interview room… then I will find out. But I can't talk to anyone about it, that's what's frustrating. I don't even know if my phone and computer are bugged."

Her husband said, "Catrin, you could be right… and also wrong. It's SIS. They may know something or they may want something from you, to do something for them. I don't know what but… that's the way they work, I gather. If they just had information on you they thought to be suspicious from a security perspective, they would inform the Met and leave them to handle any follow-up and disciplinary aspects."

Catrin thought about that aspect for a moment.

"I am an art detective, not someone to be involved in any intelligence activity. Besides, I have Jian Li to consider. Anything which links her to triad information is placing her at similar risk; or, at least, potentially blighting her career as a lawyer. Lawyers have obligations…

"Damn! I knew in my gut when Li told me that she had gone to see Michael Yau two years ago and asked for his help that it could all backfire. I think it may do so. And I can't talk to her about it. Not that I should, but even if they raise this with me, I can't talk to her. It would just make things worse."

He smiled at her.

"That's the least of your problems. If you want to talk to Li, I can fix it as something totally untraceable."

"There you go; now I am compromising you. See what I mean?"

He put his arm around her shoulders.

"It will work out. You are a good person, my love, a good police officer. People know that."

She was crying now, the strain of keeping it to herself for a week had been overwhelming her.

Chris said, "And if it gets really bad, you can call in Evelyn from the Federation."

Catrin laughed and cried simultaneously at memory of the Police Federation solicitor, Evelyn Carter, a tornado of a defense counsel she had worked with during the Police Scotland review of her conduct years ago.

"Oh, Evelyn! She was a terror last time, during the Scottish thing with PIRC."

"See," he said, "it's not all dark."

~~

Catrin and Neville did the interviews with Russell Gorton. He was denied bail despite turning himself in. They were told that, other than the solicitor, he accepted no visitors in the first week, during the period of the main interviews.

He was candid about his role in organizing the robbery, the failure of the security system and the concealment of the Bierstadt, but wouldn't comment on the roles of others. They didn't push him too hard on that; they had enough to secure a conviction, the CPS said. While much of the evidence on the other participants was circumstantial, Sylvia Kershaw had broken down at her third interview with Catrin and Mark, admitting her own part in it. She had been motivated by the money and her wish to win Russell back, after all these years.

Catrin asked, "So were you and Russell in a relationship again, once he made the approach to involve you in the Bierstadt robbery?"

She shrugged. "We started one; well, we had sex - twice, in fact. Hardly a relationship. But I could tell at the first date that he had no real interest in me. It was all business for him. But I hoped…"

In contrast, Gerhardt said the Germans admitted nothing and denied having any involvement, despite Adam Kerrigan's information. His interview was one for the books.

Catrin had left that one to Mark and Isabelle, in part to share the workload and evidence preparation. But she was watching the session on CCTV.

Mark said, "So it was boredom; that was the reason you became involved in a robbery?"

His voice reflected that he was somewhat incredulous.

Kerrigan ignored the tone, just nodded matter-of-factly until Howlett pointed at the microphone.

He said, "Yes - and, you know, I used to be the stirrer in the old group at RCA, causing ructions, the life and soul of the party. Now I just… drive around London. Don't even do anything artistic anymore. So when Russell asked I said yes."

He looked earnest. "It took some nerve to go through with it, though, on the day."

"I bet I did," said Mark, encouraging the flow.

"The Germans, Dieter and Tomi, it was like business as usual, no sweat; but me, my heart was in my mouth."

"How do you feel now?" asked Isabelle.

"About doing it, you mean? I shouldn't have, I know, but funnily enough, it seems alright; it woke me up in a sense. Got me out of my rut. I spent some time on holidays abroad with my money, got out of London."

He sighed. "I'm not happy about what will happen after the

trial, naturally, but, part of me feels more alive. I asked Sylvia out, see if we could start something… she is thinking about it. She knows Russell isn't interested in her."

He looked intently at Mark.

"I should have asked her years ago, looking back. We could be good together."

Mark was thinking that the man could have done all of that by improving his social life, not robbing a gallery; he wouldn't go to prison for asking a woman out on a date. The interview was turning into gossip corner.

He said, "So the thing with Russell being in shock, it was a put on?"

They wanted to build more on Gorton's case.

Kerrigan laughed. "It was real enough. He knew it would happen, of course, but you have a two-ton black cab come through your wall, it scares the … well, he was shocked. We just got on and did our bit, left him there."

He paused. Then he looked at his solicitor, an older man who seemed happy enough with Adam talking his head off.

"I'm not telling them the full names of the Germans; I can't do that. It wouldn't be right, would it?"

Coltrane walked into the observation room at that point.

"How's it going?"

Catrin said, "Fine with Kerrigan. He and my team are chatting away. I think his solicitor is just letting it happen, will use it in sentencing mitigation. He did it out of boredom, apparently, to prove he was still the life and soul of the party with the old gang from RCA."

Coltrane laughed then looked at her. "You seem a bit down?"

Catrin said, "I think we will be spending the next few months preparing for court, with this crew and the Acton warehouse lot. Not doing more investigations, just preparing the CPS and ourselves as witnesses."

He nodded. "Not months, but there will be a lot of that, for certain."

Catrin wasn't sure yet what to say about the news that Terry Entwistle had imparted, but that was what she had been thinking about as Coltrane walked in.

He sat down, watching the interview with her as it unfolded. Compared with the Acton warehouse sessions with the Nahigian brothers, it was like walking into a noisy pub after the quiet of the British Library Reading Room.

After a while, he stood up.

"Well, that's going along nicely. You have the reception at Liz's Place on Thursday evening, but I can't go, unfortunately. Sorry about that."

Catrin was caught off-guard by the sudden change in topic; from the case to her artistic life, one of the occasional social/marketing events organized by Liz Marshall. In this case, it featured art by Jean and herself. It was an invitation-only event, for people in the art world, some art press and collectors of work by the artists featured. Jean and Catrin found themselves doing one of these, often with another artist from Liz's 'stable', once or twice a year. This time, they were the sole art focus; Liz felt the interest level and the number of pieces available for sale would be worth it.

"Oh, that's fine, Neville. I know life is busy."

Coltrane, as a member of an influential and wealthy family involved in sponsorship of the arts, had more invitations to events than he could possibly handle, she knew. The Coltrane Foundation support for various activities in the field of visual arts guaranteed that. But it was typical Neville, to acknowledge and apologize for not being able to attend.

"Have you invited any of the team?" he asked.

She hadn't, it struck her. Then she realised why it hadn't occurred to her; it could seem as if she was showing off to the people in Art and Antiques. She still felt the fragility of settling into the team.

"No, I haven't, and it's a good point; thanks for flagging it. Normally I leave all the invitations to Liz, but I think I will mention it, start with Mark and Isabelle; invite them along."

He stood up, on the point of leaving.

"I might transfer my invitation to Kit Madder; unless you want to invite him directly yourself?"

She got the point; relationship-building.

"That's a good idea; I will do it directly; thank you again."

He nodded as he left, apparently satisfied with both the interview progress and the opportunity to enhance team-building.

42 ACCIDENT

It was Chris who spotted the news item in an internet search the same afternoon; he called Catrin.

"I just saw something on the news; an accident involving one of those officers in the Newtown area we saw at the hotel, PC Fowles. Someone ran into a police car, despite it being stopped with its lights flashing. I will send you the link now."

She opened it immediately, despite being in a meeting with Harper and Howlett. The person injured had been described as 'Seren Fowles, a young police officer in Newtown'.

She looked at Howlett. "The young woman who helped us, Seren Fowles, is injured. She had been out of the vehicle and got back in but didn't have her seat belt on while she talked on the radio; It was rear-ended and - a head injury."

Howlett shook her head. "Will she be alright? She is engaged to that other officer we met, I recall."

"It doesn't say."

There was a pause; Harper sat waiting patiently. Then they got back to work.

She followed it up that evening on the internet. The following morning she decided to call Newtown police station from the office. She was quickly put through to Inspector

Meredith.

"It's not about work, Carole. I heard the news about Seren. I wanted to pass on my sympathies and wasn't sure..."

"Catrin, thank you. We have had so many calls; it is really helpful for us here. They airlifted her to the Walton in Liverpool and she is through the surgery, we understand. They specialize in head injuries. We hear that she will make it through, God willing. They can work wonders these days with rehab."

"And Constable Morrissey?"

"Not good. It has hit him hard, as you can imagine. He and her mother are there now, in Liverpool. They had set the wedding date and he had just accepted a new job, down at Carmarthen, a bit more glitzy a role."

"He seemed very keen."

"Well, that's on hold for now. Seren is his priority and all the family is around here. Everyone is doing what they can, of course. Her church is responding wonderfully I am told, looking after things for them. It's hard on everyone really."

Catrin said "I really liked her, short as my visits were."

~~

The preparations for the reception at Liz's Place the following day took over Catrin's mind. She, Jean and Melanie met up with Liz Marshall at a bistro across from the gallery.

"I have to get my horses into the paddock looking clean and fresh for the punters; it helps the sales enormously," Liz said.

Her husband, William, rolled his eyes and looked across the table at Jean.

"Not exactly helping her cause, is she?"

Jean smiled. "It must mean Catrin and I have pedigree; we are thoroughbreds, even if we come from Pontypridd," she parried, knowing William disliked discussion of such subjects. It had been at the same bistro, Sandi's, about two years ago that it slipped out that William was from the aristocracy.

Liz asked them about what they would talk about at the 'opener', a theme around their more recent works, and how they worked together.

"Ironic, really," said Melanie, "that Miele is arriving in two weeks; it would be right up her street hearing the talk and the questions after. I told her I would try to capture the interesting bits."

"I doubt that Liz will let you trot around recording the event and taking mug shots of the guests with your phone camera," said Catrin.

"I don't see why not," responded Melanie, looking across to Liz to gauge her reaction. "The crowds at these things are often snapping photos of the works and taking selfies with the artists. Remember that photo with the tall guy?"

Jean grimaced at the recollection. She had spoken for both herself and Catrin that evening; Catrin had been pulled away with Assistant Commissioner Hunt somewhere, at short notice. A man a lot taller than Jean had put a long arm around her shoulders and snapped a shot of them together. Jean, not welcoming the uncalled-for embrace, had hunched her shoulders slightly, trying to smile. The resultant expression, complete with gaping blouse front, was a nightmare image flashed to Jean and Melanie briefly by the ace photographer, pleased with his work. It had been the butt of Melanie's humour for days after.

"Perhaps he will send it to Ceramics Review," she had mused afterwards. "Catrin would love to see it."

The following evening, prior to the event, Catrin went along to the Kiln so that she could share a taxi over to Liz's Place with Jean and Melanie. Normally she would travel by Tube or in her car, but it had become a ritual now; when they dressed up for these events, they took a cab. Even though Catrin now had an assigned vehicle, she didn't want to break the tradition.

As they paid the taxi on arrival, Melanie said, "I just had a brief glimpse of Miele Yau from the back. She was going inside; or, if not, it is someone very much like her."

In fact, it was Miele Yau, in the company of an elegant, older Chinese lady, obviously from London on listening to her English. Catrin had little time to talk to Miele before the opening, when she and Jean were expected to speak for about fifteen minutes.

All she heard was that Miele had suddenly decided to bring forward her arrival to London by two weeks after hearing about this evening.

"I got off the plane this morning," she said, beaming at them about her sudden decision.

During the talk, as people sipped their drinks, Catrin and Jean went through their prepared points. Most people were watching them or looking over at art they were referring to; either items for sale or works purchased by others and loaned back for the event. Catrin felt that someone was particularly focused on her. Her surveillance and counter-surveillance training told her not to take such a feeling for granted.

A 'sixth sense' is not simply intuition, she had been taught. The mind can handle subconsciously the inputs of very complex social interactions, crowd movements and group dynamics. If you have a sense of being watched, it is probably that something is happening. If you have either visual input, aural or both telling you something is not quite right, don't ignore it.

In this case, she sensed it was a man in the rear of the loose group of on-lookers and as her eyes swept the audience she took in that he was a well-dressed Caucasian, looking to be in his fifties.

He didn't turn his head, a classic giveaway; he simply defocused and stopped staring, blending in with the group as a whole. He was someone who knew about surveillance techniques, perhaps, she thought. Catrin was then distracted further, seeing a familiar face - Isabelle Howlett. Behind her were Harper and Madder, together looking at one of the works on sale.

In wrapping up their talk, they took questions. Some were relatively pedestrian but one from an American woman, a collector of their work, had them thinking and looking at each other. Jean opted to go first.

"You ask about changes in mood in our works reflecting, perhaps, significant changes in our lives. As you said, Catrin is also a police officer. She has experiences in that role that affected her art. I know you two discussed it at a lunch one time.

"It was interesting, though, that you also picked up on changes in form and textures of the worked clay in the same way. I am gay; my partner Melanie and I have had both very positive and very negative reactions to that statement over the years and in my case, it has certainly affected my mood, how I work with clay on a particular day."

She was looking at Melanie as she spoke.

"But I have always had the strength of my partner and the love of my family and friends to help me through - and here, in London, we are happy. It wasn't always so. That plays back at times in my work."

She looked at Catrin, indicating she should take over.

Catrin said, "As Mrs. Kowalski said, in my case events over my police career have affected my art. Not many bad ones, fortunately, and one very good one; I met my partner, my husband Chris, on a case in Cornwall. But art is only partly about skills, technique and practice; at its core is the emotional inspiration of the artist. When something serious or traumatic happens, you have only two choices; you stop producing art until you get back on an even keel or you use art to help deal with the emotional turmoil that ensues. I choose the latter, as it helps me. It's different work that develops, sometimes for a period, sometimes longer. But some of our clients like it, I know."

She was watching Howlett's head bob up and down vigorously; Isabelle clearly agreed.

Then she saw the 'stare' guy from earlier, and again she

felt… something; a *frisson* of disquiet disturbing the moment.

Afterwards, Miele Yau was full of her pleasure at the decision to come to London early, prior to the start of term.

"Seeing you two explaining your work together was worth it; I am so glad we talked in Hong Kong and I can't wait to see the Cwmbran Kiln and spend time with you there."

She would be staying with Mr. and Mrs. Lui until term began, she said, introducing the woman with her. They were friends of her father. After that, she would move to a student residence. Catrin wondered if Mr. or Mrs. Lui were part the world of the triads. The woman looked well-dressed and self-assured, talking with Jean and Melanie about the works available.

Melanie said, "A hall of residence? It must be a private one; RCA doesn't have its own student residences. Private ones are expensive, I think."

Neither Miele nor the Chinese lady said anything, as Jean glared at her partner. Catrin just thought that, given Miele's family situation, money would not be a problem.

Liz walked past, working between clients and was introduced to Miele. Jean explained that the student would be working with them during her time in London. Liz was enthusiastic, particularly talking with Mrs. Lui beside her.

"Are you still pleased with your purchase, Mrs. Lui?" she asked the woman.

"Yes; and so is Miele," said the older woman, smiling.

Catrin then realized that one of their works for sale had been bought by the woman.

Melanie said, "Mrs. Lui bought it last week, but agreed with Liz and William to leave it until after the event tonight."

It was one of the higher priced items that they had available at present; clearly the woman had money, whether or not she was triad-linked. On impulse, Catrin quickly looked around as Miele kept talking. There was no sign of the man who had been looking at her earlier.

Later, after the event, there was another ritual. They absconded to Sandi's Bistro with William, to leave Liz supervising the caterers and cleaners. It was the way Liz liked it; to get everyone else out of the way as she restored the gallery to a state where it could open the following day. As they were leaving, Catrin asked Liz about the attendance at the invitation-only event.

Miele, Liz said, was the guest of Mrs. Lui; having bought a recent Sayer-Hughes piece she was invited, of course, and encouraged to attend. Regarding the unknown man, Liz said, "I don't know; perhaps you need to ask William; he may know. He handled some of it."

At the bistro, over the excitement of the sales and relief that the event was over, Catrin raised the question again.

William said, "I don't know him, but he collects Meissen I was told by a mutual acquaintance from my old haunts, Noreen James."

William used to work in the City, in the finance sector; exactly doing what, Catrin didn't know.

"He wants to start collecting modern ceramic works and heard about the event. I told Noreen to invite him along. He came, but she never showed up."

Catrin asked, "Did you get to talk to him, then?"

William replied, "Not really, with all the people there. He looked the 'establishment' sort to me."

Catrin thought, he seemed that to me, too; and he was more interested in watching me than looking at art. Establishment meant government departments, Whitehall and - her mind moved inevitably but reluctantly to - security and spooks. The SIS interest.

43 TREGYNON

Over the next few weeks, Catrin and her team were busy, as predicted, preparing the Crown Prosecution Service for the initial stages of the proceedings against the Nahigians and others. She and Kit Madder found themselves breaking the news to a distraught collector in Birmingham; two sculptures he had bought in good faith from a friend who had hit hard times were, in fact, stolen. They had been sold to the friend at a knock-down price and sold on at fair market value. While the friend wasn't involved in the robbery, he was knowledgeable enough to know that their origin was suspicious, yet he still turned a large financial profit from the sale. It wasn't the financial loss that hit the man most, it was the betrayal.

On the way back they stopped in at a home in Milton Keynes. Some of the jewelry recovered had finally been traced to them, which was the good news. The bad news was that the wife's ex-husband had been the thief. He had always been a suspect and his alibi had finally been broken.

"We parted on reasonably good terms, I thought," said the woman.

The day before, Isabelle Howlett headed off for some holiday time with her aunt on Canvey Island just as the Bognor Regis 'stuffed dog' painting was located by the locals; she left the office pleased as punch with the closure of the case.

Three weeks after the news about Seren Fowles, Catrin had a 'thank you' note from James Morrissey, for the card and flowers she had sent. At the bottom, in almost childish letters, was scrawled Seren's name. Fowles had been discharged from the specialist neurosurgery unit in Liverpool back to the Newtown Hospital and had made good initial progress, Morrissey informed her. She was now home, receiving outpatient care and specialist therapy. It had been nearly a month since the accident.

How many times must he have written that news update on cards, she thought; and helped Seren add her own name?

Over the next few days her mind kept going back to the supper at St. Deiniol's, for some reason she couldn't quite pin down. It bothered her. Then she recalled the discussion outside the church; Seren's question about whether she and Isabelle were artists and the comment about a painting of the church. So she phoned Mason Carrington, the watercolour artist and her sister-in-law's partner.

"I have a big request of you. I want you to fit in doing a painting for me of a church in Wales, near Newtown."

Carrington paused. "OK. But why, can I ask?"

So she told him. He was soft-hearted; she knew he would say yes.

An hour later he called back.

"I looked on-line, at the pictures of St. Deiniol's."

"It's pretty, isn't it?"

"Yes it is, it will be a good subject. But I am not painting it unless you come up and paint also."

"Why?"

"Because you need to do this. You have the emotional energy to do it. It will help me paint, having you there, and I think it will help you to be there. You know I am right."

Catrin thought about it.

"I will come up, but not to do a watercolour of the church.

I will sketch and prepare for a ceramic piece based on the altar screen inside. I quite liked that and it will work well, as a design. I'll do that as a gift for the church if you do the painting for Seren Fowles. A deal?

Mason said, "So if it's raining, I am the one to get wet, while you stay dry?"

Catrin laughed. "Something like that, yes; I will call out from the doorway with a megaphone, 'More burnt umber on the lower left', that sort of thing, to help you out."

He said loudly to Chris's sister, somewhere around the house in Falmouth, "Jen, Catrin wants me to do a painting for free, no less, drive to the back end of Wales to do it and she will give me tips on how to get it right!"

Catrin heard the shout from a distance; Jen's voice, "So what's stopping you?"

~~

In truth, she hadn't thought about John Farrell when making the impulsive decision to return to Tregynon. She raised it at the end of the phone call with Reverend Crouch, to get his permission to do the painting and to sketch inside for the ceramic piece she planned. He was delighted, of course, with the proposal and offered any help she needed.

She asked, "And Deacon Farrell? How is he now? I know that they didn't press charges."

He paused before responding.

"Not doing too well, to be honest; the experience seems to burden him. He is still working actively with people in need, including released prisoners; 'his people' as he calls them. He has the energy for that. But there isn't the same peace in him anymore. I work with him on it as I can. He will be around, no doubt, when you visit."

They stayed again at the Maesmawr Hall Hotel. Both Chris and Jen came with them for the fun of it, Chris making comments to his sister about her bravery in leaving Cornwall.

As much as Mason was all over the place for his work, his sister hardly travelled anywhere.

They arrived in the early evening, in separate vehicles from different directions but only twenty minutes apart, expecting to be on their own at the hotel for dinner. The plan was to go to the church to meet people the following morning.

But the word had got around. The hotel knew all about it. Reverend Crouch was there within an hour of their arrival to say hello, followed by three women and a young man asking for Mason. They were members of the local watercolour society and wanted to meet him and ask if they and other members could observe while he painted.

Carrington said warmly, "Bring your things; paint with me, it will be more fun."

PC Morrissey turned up shortly afterwards, in uniform. He was on duty, but wanted to tell them that Seren hoped to see them tomorrow afternoon; she was excited to know Catrin was back to do an artwork, a ceramic for a fundraiser for the church.

"That was all we told her, ma'am. I have been on pins and needles she will find out about the painting, with so many people knowing."

Behind Morrissey, Catrin saw Mason smile at someone referring to her as 'ma'am'.

"It's Catrin, James; I am not working. We will be round to see her tomorrow, so you don't have long to go with the secret."

The following day at St. Deiniol's, the weather turned out to be excellent; a blue sky and clouds, with long shadows on the foliage and stone as they started. Mason got straight into it, surrounded by a lot more members of the watercolour society than had turned up the previous evening.

Catrin said to him quietly, "I'll put my megaphone away. If you need help, just ask one of these people."

He gave her a baleful look, then a smile.

"Go do some work yourself, troublemaker."

As she walked away she heard Mason talking to his impromptu class.

"And no real wind, the bane of plein air watercolour painters; it dries the paint too fast, as we know. Now I have chosen this spot, not the most obvious, but it ..."

Catrin was sketching the altar screen, making notes on colours she wanted to bring out in the finished piece, working out the sequencing she would discuss with Jean; how it would be layered, the firings it would probably need. She had said to Reverend Crouch that they may want to put it in an auction at a future fundraiser.

He looked at her. "I have been looking up your art on the internet, Catrin, as have others here, who are quite excited. I doubt we will do that; auction it, I mean. I don't want the wrath of the congregation. There could be another dead body if I did; mine, on these grounds, not in a golf course near Kidderminster."

The people of St. Deiniol's were there. Food, tea and coffee were laid out in the hall, enough to feed an entire art class, which was just as well with Mason's following. Chris and Jen were chatting with them all, nibbling away; in part for the pleasure of the event, in part to let Mason and Catrin have the breathing space to get on and finish.

At one point Catrin said to Reverend Crouch, "And John?"

He shook his head. "I did tell him."

It was only as she was taking a break to get something to eat herself that her eyes took in the ever-present set of homemade items on sale, the charity fundraiser she had seen on her first visit. Then it hit home that she would need to see John Farrell sometime now; she had no choice. She bought one of the items before going back into the church, looking at the altar screen for the final time. It was there she made her mind up to seek him out after the trip to see Seren Fowles.

They decided in the end that only Catrin and Mason would go with James Morrissey to the house; too many people would overwhelm Seren, he said. She still gets confused easily, even when she is at her best in the day.

But when they got there she was sitting in the living room in a chair, dressed nicely and alert, talking to her mother. Clearly Seren was pleased to see Catrin and she slowly picked up that Mason was the watercolour painter, 'her sister-in-law's man'.

She asked to see Catrin's 'pictures', the ones she would use to make the 'plate with the altar screen pattern'. Her speech was irregular, some words were fine but anything beginning with the letter 's' slowed her down. Catrin could see the frustration it was causing her.

Seren said, "Jim told me that you would only have a drawing of it at this stage."

Catrin smiled at her. "We have something for you first. Well, Mason does."

They brought out the painting of St. Deiniol's, fixed to a mount that the artist had brought with him from Cornwall, just to set it off.

Jim said, smiling at his fiancée, "The Rowan Gallery in town will frame it properly; they offered, for free."

Then there was little talk as they watched her face, taking in the scene, lost in it; then the tears.

44 FARRELL

As Catrin and Mason left later to pick up Jen and Chris, still at the church, Catrin saw the solitary figure standing across the road. John Farrell.

She passed the car key fob to Mason.

"I need a moment; or longer, perhaps."

She took something from her purse and put it in her pocket, then walked over and offered her hand to the deacon. Farrell shook hands hesitantly, not the vigor in his shake that was her recollection from the first meeting.

He said, "Simon came for me; made me come in the end, but I didn't want to intrude. It was a wonderful thing you did for Seren and are doing for the church. Thank you."

Catrin asked, "How are you, John? I have been thinking about you. How did it go with the West Mercia people?"

She knew it from an official perspective, but not from his viewpoint, sitting across the interview table.

He said, "They took me in, of course, as you saw. I expected that. They kept me overnight in Hindlip and released me the following evening. There were several sessions, a lot of questions, repeating things; you know the drill. The fact that Colin Ingelsby used the woods by the golf course I worked at was a big thing for them, even with his letter explaining that."

He paused. "The solicitor was good. I didn't know him, the Bishop did. I hear that you had something to do with that."

He looked at her but she said nothing.

"The cells at Hindlip brought it all back. I could deal with the issues of imprisonment of others because I understood it and they could see I had been through it. But I had forgotten I was free, I suppose, in those meetings. To go back in and be locked up, to be a murder suspect this time was a different thing; it raised old ghosts. I don't sleep well at night now.

"It's not even Kendrick's death, or what he did that haunts me. It's the memory of life in prison, that other world. We, I mean, ordinary people, put others away and say they deserve it. But deserve what? To be detained, to be in a disciplined environment, to work towards rehabilitation if they can, that's right; I understand that. But the jungle in there; the pecking orders, the mistreatment of one prisoner by another and no way to get help; it's like another world. One I left behind; one I try to help others leave behind. But it took one night in the cells to bring it back vividly; too vividly."

He paused, sighed; then he smiled at her.

"I will get through it. Working with others helps. But what I came for was to thank you, not only for what you have done for Seren and St. Deiniol's but also for the way you handled it with me. At least it softened the blow a little."

Catrin looked at him.

"It's been a while now, John. And if you are still struggling, you should get help. People like you are lousy at asking for help, as am I. We like to give it, but we also like to cope on our own."

He replied, "I have my faith and work; and my church -."

"And if your religion isn't doing it for you, seek help elsewhere. Look, I thought I didn't need psychological counselling after this -"

She pointed at the scar on her cheek.

"But I did. While I find peace at St. Paul's, it was a psychologist who initially helped me most."

They had been walking slowly and, without discussion, sat down together at the bench by the bus stop. Catrin could see Mason in the car up the road, talking on his mobile.

She said, "Talk to Simon about finding a counsellor, perhaps."

He pursed his lips, giving it some thought.

Then he said, "Your turn; why St. Paul's Cathedral? You have a lot of choice of churches in London."

Catrin replied, "It was a place I was taken to by chance and where, unexpectedly, I found some peace after the injury. Facial damage for anyone is … well, for a woman, particularly. I hadn't planned to go; someone took me and the experience there was transforming. So I kept going."

She paused.

"But it is also a place I can hide in, in a sense; big enough to be invisible. My last boss at the Met is heavily involved there; the committees, the politics. I can't make sense of half the jobs that the clergy and other lay people have, but I don't have to."

He smiled. "It's a cathedral; it goes with the role, canons and deans and so on. At least you knew what a distinctive deacon was, at our first meeting. Most wouldn't."

"On that note," she said, "You bring me nicely to the other reason I wanted to see you. It came to me this morning and so I looked something up earlier on my mobile - about canon law."

He looked at her, wondering why she should be checking out the rules and regulations of the Church in Wales. She took her hand from her pocket and passed over the small, hand-made cross; two sticks, notched at the overlapping join, bound together with twine.

"One of Anne's hand-made crosses. All paid for. Take it as a present, a token of your recovery."

He looked at her but said nothing, sensing that there was more, as she held his gaze.

She went on, "In the ground, I can see something like this cross coming apart, you know? The cord will rot away. Then you are left with two sticks that could easily be separated, moved by animals. And then all you might find after a time is a stick with a strange notch cut into it. So my question is… based on what I read… do you have an 'irregularity'? I think that is the word."

He shook his head, finally understanding what she was getting at. His voice was tentative, feeling her out. "An 'irregularity' as in the language of canon law? A permanent impediment to a person being ordained, in this case?"

She nodded and waited.

He went on, "Such as the impediment about premeditated homicide? No, Catrin, there are many things in my past, but not that. Distant past or more recently."

He was looking into the distance, it appeared, but she saw he was really looking into himself.

She said softly, "It only clicked when I entered St. Deiniol's earlier. I saw the fundraising items for sale again, as they had been at the dinner the first time. Then I remembered seeing the single piece of wood with the notch. It was in the items that the forensics team found at Kendrick's gravesite."

She paused. "Ingelsby was weaker physically when you met him, I think. He couldn't carry a heavy weight, could he?"

Farrell said carefully, "I see where you are heading, but no; he was more than up to the task of dealing with … He used to be a powerful man."

As you still are, thought Catrin.

But he said, "All I gave him was a gift, one of the crosses, when he came to see me."

She persisted, saying "And did you give him the location for the grave?"

John shook his head. "Do you know the range of things men talk about in prison, Catrin? Silly question, I suppose. You have to look on the bright side as much as possible, look back on the good times. I don't know how many occasions I talked about that golf club and the woods, just enjoying… nature, being alive."

~~

John was thinking back to the night that Colin Ingelsby had turned up with the paintings. Colin had been so earnest in his desire to see that John and Judge Richards received the Bratby sketches; his grand plan shared. He explained the need for redemption to a theology student as if he was talking to a child. John could see his zeal; now with hindsight, his mental instability. At the time it had seemed the monologue of a man who had spent a lot of time knocking on doors, cold-calling God's message to the sinner. Now, it was clearly a deranged obsession.

It was impulse that had made John give him the cross; a message of simplicity and a common bond in Jesus, he thought. Colin took it, said thank you, putting it into his jacket pocket without giving it more than a glance.

Then he was gone.

Looking into the deep recesses of his mind, from days when he trusted no-one and was alert for people wishing him harm, John Farrell knew that something bad was happening, even then. Ingelsby hadn't mentioned Kendrick at all and he must feature somewhere in this plan. The closest Colin came to it was an oblique reference.

"The third painting is being put to good use, John."

For Ingelsby's own redemption, or what? John had wondered about that. Later, after the news about the body being found, he knew for sure, but he admitted to himself that he also had reason to know well before then. But, following up and reporting his fears to the police; he couldn't do that. If his worst scenario was true, it would put Colin Ingelsby back inside.

After Ingelsby's funeral, he had received a letter forwarded from the man's church with a sealed envelope marked 'confidential - John Farrell only'. He opened it to find a similar envelope folded in half, sealed also. It was inscribed, 'For the police; if they ask; don't open.'

They had served prison time together; had separate but similar careers which understood the value of a sealed document containing no fingerprints or DNA. It was then that

John Farrell was absolutely sure that Ingelsby had gone after Ian Kendrick.

He had been in two minds ever since. Part of him wanted to try to find out, see if Kendrick was around, alive and uninjured. The other part rebelled at the thought of getting back in contact with people he had known back then, particularly those who still bore him grudges.

But the police only showed him that note at the insistence of the solicitor. They had just told him that it was a confession, appearing to vindicate him. That was during the early stages of the interviews at Hindlip. As DI Merton had said, "It doesn't mean you weren't involved, does it, though? We don't take it as gospel, so to speak."

The detective seemed quite pleased with his choice of phrase or his irony; which one, Farrell wasn't sure.

But the questioning continued.

~~

Catrin thought that Deacon Farrell, lost in his thoughts for a moment, looked as if he was about to open up and talk more. She reached out, touched his arm, getting his attention and said softly, "Not to me, John. Like last time, I don't want to know. Share it with… whomever; Reverend Crouch or someone you can trust. Unburden yourself. I just wanted to know if you had a hand in the death or burial of Ian Kendrick."

He shook his head again and choked, 'Not me', the tears starting to run down his cheek. The cross slipped from his hand and Catrin deftly stopped it falling on the ground and passed it back.

She looked at him, assessing the man still. After a moment she reached a decision and pointed at the car.

"If giving him the cross wasn't in your statement then it will probably mean a round of further interviews if someone spots the link sometime in the future. If they clue into it from other sources, that is. It's not my case and it's no crime to give a person a wooden cross, is it?

"I have to go; I shouldn't keep the great artist and my family waiting. But take care of yourself. Your work is valuable; so are you. Love yourself a little more. Bye now."

He said, "Goodbye Catrin; thank you. Safe journey."

He stood up with her as she rose from the bench then sat back down as she crossed over the road and climbed into the vehicle. In a moment, John Farrell was alone at the bus stop, lost in thought as a bus pulled up. He waved, indicating it was not one he was waiting for and it pulled away.

He wiped his eyes, blew his nose and headed for Seren's house. He thought he would drop in, see how she was doing and look at the painting of St. Deiniol's while he was there.

Catrin had what she wanted to know. However Kendrick had died, it wasn't, she believed, at John Farrell's hand. That he had suspected or worked out earlier that Ingelsby must have been involved was self-evident, if for no other reason that the burden of guilt he appeared to carry now.

By rights she should have reported her suspicions earlier today to the West Mercia team once she made the connection at St. Deiniol's. But, sitting there, drawing the altar screen, she made up her mind that 'enough was enough'. She didn't think Farrell would carry out an act of vengeance, but he might help a dying man; give him the time to finish his own life in freedom rather than be hauled back into the prison system he so detested. But she had needed to be sure, so it was good that John Farrell had turned up when he did.

After she got back into the car, her fellow painter gave her a funny look.

As they drove, he said, "You have a strange effect on people, Catrin, making them burst into tears; that's two within the last hour."

She pulled a face at him. "I'll start on you next, Mason. Be careful."

They had just arrived back at the church. Hearing the car stop, Chris popped his head out the door, called back and then three people, Chris, Jen and 'almost indecipherable Irene', as Catrin thought of her, came out of the hall door.

Irene said, "I was just telling them, like I told you at the dinner that time, you should come back and live in Wales, not stay in London. Now these two, in Cornwall, well, that's fine; it's a sensible place. This young man needs fresh air, the Welsh countryside, I think."

Catrin looked at Chris.

"I take it that Irene has told you about her visit to London?"

Chris said, "In great detail, yes. Thank you Irene, for being such a good host to us. But we must go; we all have long drives to get home."

Jen was saying something along the same lines. Both of them seemed ready to fly out the gate at high speed. Chris hurried over to Catrin as Jen and Mason swiftly walked to his Range Rover. Reverend Crouch came outside and called, "Catrin, did Deacon Farrell find you?"

"Yes, Simon, he did. We had quite a nice little talk, thank you. Goodbye."

She got back into the Audi with a sigh. "Time to go."

Chris laughed, "Back to Irene's hell-hole. How was it with Seren Fowles?"

She thought for a moment as she stopped to turn at the junction.

"She is looking good and she loved Mason's painting. In fact, it all went very well; the whole thing, really. I am glad we came."

"So was Irene," said Chris.

Catrin's mobile rang and she connected the call on the speakerphone. It was Jen, with Mason saying something in the background.

"We thought we would stop off in Pontypridd, at your parent's, Catrin, to put them in touch with Irene. We can tell your mother how much Irene worries about you living in 'that place'. They could become friends."

They laughed as Catrin thought of a response.

"It won't work. My mum now talks about me being an international art detective, going all over the world. I'm important now; I have to be based in London."

Mason's voice came over the line. "She would probably convert Irene, tell her London is fine; say she should come and visit you, see London properly. In fact, we could suggest it … both of them, together, staying with you two, sleeping on your sofa bed; they will take over the living room for a week or so."

For the next while, the banter between them lifted Catrin's spirits. It really was time to head home; get back to her work and her art. She said as much to Chris and he agreed.

She was in high spirits as far as Banbury; then she got a call from Neville Coltrane sounding upset.

"Catrin, not good news, I am afraid. I think the Acton warehouse prosecution is collapsing around us. I know you have today off, but I want you to come in as soon as possible. I need to brief the team but wanted you and Kit to know first."

"I am near Banbury, Neville; I can't be back for a couple of hours, but will head straight in. But… why?"

Chris was listening, quiet.

"The Nahigians are gone, they have 'done a runner', as they say. Jorge finally got bail yesterday morning, with an electronic tagging bracelet on his ankle, I found out yesterday evening. Kind of them to let me know, I'm sure.

"At two in the morning the tracker alert went off as Gabriella Nahigian called in, all excited; she had knocked a cup of tea over Jorge's leg and the bracelet, she claimed. It had scalded him and she was driving him to the Central Middlesex Hospital, not waiting for an ambulance. The monitoring contractor went through the alert procedure, sending a surveillance car to the home. The borough sent a car with two officers to the hospital, to be sure, but there was no sign of Jorge or his wife, or Kristoff or his wife Jana; they have all vanished. The bracelet is not registering and hasn't been located. The search is on but…"

He sighed.

"They offered to put their homes and business premises up as surety, I recall," said Catrin, "so it wasn't small change, if the court took Jorge up on that. They did for Kristoff, so if he has breached the bail conditions, he is walking away from much of his UK assets."

"I know," said Neville. "I am calling a briefing session in half an hour. See you when you get in."

The line went dead.

45 BARLOW

It was Gerhardt Amsel who came back with the first insight about the disappearance on the following Thursday. "We had a call from Pavel Ciprian with the Trupele de Carabinieri in Moldova. Do you know him, Neville?"

"Of him, but we have never been in contact," Coltrane responded.

He had Vicky collect Catrin and Kit Madder, bring them into his office while he talked with the Germans.

"Gerhardt, I have asked Catrin and Christopher to join me; I will put this call on speakerphone now."

They went through the round of 'hellos'. Gerhardt had his 'number two', Heidi Schmidt, with him.

"It appears that the Nahigians have been seen," said Neville, "Gerhardt?"

"They are in Moldova, in an estate south of Chisinau, the capital, according to local sources there. At the country home of Emilian Ionel, a thief and all-about crook, part of the Romanian Mafia lot. We think he is the lead figure that they have been hiding, been silent about, during your interviews. He must run the show."

Kit Madder was checking his mobile. "Moldova is outside the EU; a Type A, Part 2 extradition treaty," he whispered.

"Needs to have the Secretary of State involved."

Neville grimaced. He said to the Germans, "I doubt that we can send Catrin to invite them to return for arrest this time. I don't think that it would work with them."

He took a deep breath.

"Gerhardt, I take it you will report on this at the Task Force call and give any details?"

The German responded, "Yes, I will. We are after Herr Ionel for other reasons, so this adds to our list. You will file international warrants for the Nahigians?"

"Oh yes, we will. I doubt the Foreign Office will be too active on this one though, so I am not sure how much political pressure we can bring to bear on the case."

There was a chuckle from down the line, a different voice followed by a murmur.

Gerhardt said, "Heidi says we should let the FBI loose on it."

Coltrane laughed. "Let's wait for the conference call; check their level of interest."

When they finished the call, Catrin said, "Kristoff couldn't have told Jorge about the deal we made, could he? Kristoff is the real brains of the pair, that's obvious. A deal is a two-way thing; we said we wouldn't prosecute Gabriella and Jana in exchange for the Limoges vases and the US link to the group in France. But the Task Force knows; including the Americans and Germans."

Neville said, "We can't do anything with that, Catrin."

She responded, "I know. But if Gerhardt or David Klintz was to leak it to the Moldovan police, or it reaches this man Ionel, Kristoff Nahigian would probably be buried on the man's estate, not be enjoying the high life there. He is in a bind."

A silence descended on the trio.

Madder said, "I am not sure, even then. Kristoff could brass it out; say trading a foot soldier and a client was more important than having their wives charged and perhaps detained; it would complicate even further their escape plans. It could work. Clearly they were planning to flee as soon as both brothers got out of gaol."

Coltrane finally said grimly, "And if they were prepared to lose their assets in the UK, it means they have probably no plans to return; they have got all the value out of the Acton business they can. Time to move on."

He sighed. "I think all we can do is stick to protocol. We will issue new arrest warrants for Jorge and Kristoff and inform Interpol, but not charge the two wives; hold to our side of the agreement. Leave it to others to sort this out."

He now seemed resigned to the collapse of the main elements of the case.

"We will have to see what CPS make of it, what can be salvaged. I doubt that they will proceed to trial in absentia. In any event they will go ahead with the charges against Malkovich and Smyth; minor players, I know. They will only get light sentences, but CPS will want to do that to get the facts on record."

It was two hours later that his anger broke. Catrin, just returning from another meeting, could hear him through the closed door of his office. Kit Madder had just emerged, shaking his head.

"He is on to the chap in Immigration; you know, the one who complained about Neville not being 'European' enough when he said the Nahigian's entered the UK illegally far too easily. Apparently they got out as easily, Neville is telling him. The four of them just waltzed into France on the Eurostar on fake British passports, purportedly claiming to be two brothers and their wives from Dunfermline."

He was having a hard time keeping his face straight, despite the raised voice coming through the door.

"Kristoff probably didn't know," he added.

Catrin said, "That Coltrane is a Scottish name, and Neville's roots go back there? No, I doubt it was even on his radar."

Madder said, "It was when Neville asked how anyone

speaking with an Armenian accent could be mistaken for a Scot that I had to get out. I think the immigration guy must have stuck it to him."

~~

They had left the Acton warehouse surveillance equipment in place all this time - just in case someone of interest turned up there. Given the developments, they took the decision to finally pull it out. The technician who installed it was sent along to retrieve it with Nkrumah.

Madder said, "Thank them for their help then get out of there. Mrs. Lehman will talk your hind leg off, given half the chance."

"About art crime; one of those?" asked Dennis.

"No; about timeshares in Portugal."

"I don't know anything about them," said Dennis. "My two sisters and I have enough on our hands keeping up with the rent on our flat in Hammersmith."

Madder smiled. "Just tell them we are very grateful and get back here."

Vera Lehman was pleased to see the young officer and his silent colleague.

She said, "We saw the news item about the arrests. And, of course, the hit squad going in to arrest people that morning was the talk around here for days afterwards; all those vehicles and flashing lights."

"Tactical Unit," said Nkrumah, correcting her automatically as he waded into the official 'thank you'.

There was a noise upstairs as Andy Lehman came hurrying down.

"Guess what, Vera? I just heard from Tom taking out the camera that Detective Nkrumah's sister is studying astronomy at Queen Mary's. Now isn't that a turn up for the books? What year is she in?"

Dennis felt as if he was on the wrong side of the interview

table, given the intense stares of the Lehmann's. 'Be grateful' he had been told.

"She is in the first year of a Ph.D. programme, but I don't know what she does really, it is quite... complicated stuff, I gather."

Andy Lehmann's expression was making it clear that Nkrumah wasn't getting off that easily. They had hosted the police equipment for months now; he wanted his reward.

Tom, the 'not silent enough' technician, came down carrying his cases, taking in the scene in the living room. He got the impression that they weren't leaving just yet.

The following morning Nkrumah was recounting the visit to members of the unit when Coltrane came out of his office.

"Catrin, could you step in, please?"

She left them, smiling at the story evolving, but on entering Coltrane's office she saw from his expression that it was nothing to smile about. His look was serious, showing his concern.

"I just had a call from Bob Matheson. We are to go up to Commander Barlow's office, right away. I don't know the reason; just that we have to head up there. And right now."

When she and Coltrane arrived on the top floor of Scotland Yard, they were shown straight in to the commander's office. Catrin recognized the senior officer for Trident, the organized crime group of the Met, from her previous role working with Hunt. He always came over as 'Mr. Imperturbable' on everything, at any meeting she had seen him at. Not someone who sought the limelight but always prepared, measured, capable.

He sat back in his chair, his eyes on Catrin, monitoring her.

"DI Sayer, I have a proposal I want you to consider carefully. Basically, I want you to help us from time to time; to work with Trident and other government departments dealing with security issues. Not for us, I should say; not change jobs. I wouldn't want to take you away from your role here; just ask for your help on occasions that arise regarding a matter of importance to, as the phrase goes, the 'national interest'.

"However, it is more logical to start with the background reason for approaching you."

He looked at the notes in front of him; or pretended to, Catrin thought.

"Our colleagues in SIS are in an operation to break into a triad group based in Hong Kong called Four Square. I think you have heard of them?"

Catrin responded, "I have come across the name. I read a lot about triad activity during the period I was under threat from the Ten Dragons group."

Barlow smiled. "I think you have more than read about them; you were chatting away not that long ago with one of their key people."

From his file he produced a photograph. It nicely showed Catrin in her bridesmaid's dress talking with Michael Yau at Li's wedding. He placed a second photo on the table showed the group drinking a toast together. She looked at them, then turned to look at Coltrane who was staring at the photographs, his face impassive.

Catrin said, "This man was at my friend's wedding, yes. He is a friend of her father, Daniel Yeung, I believe."

"Indeed," said Barlow. "And this man's granddaughter is now in London, studying art and, I understand, you and your artist friends are mentoring her. Is that correct?"

Catrin just nodded, taking in that a lot of background work must have taken place besides the surveillance work that provided the photographs.

Barlow said, "It gives our people opportunities, routes of access perhaps. Four Square is a very difficult group to penetrate."

He smiled at her then turned serious, focusing on Neville Coltrane.

"DCI Coltrane, I think that gives a flavour, so to speak, of the type of support we are going to request, to accommodate our needs for some of Inspector Sayer's time. If you could leave us now?"

He was smooth, very pleasant but the tone of voice left no doubt; Catrin's boss was being booted out.

Coltrane looked at Barlow, obviously not expecting to be so curtly dismissed.

"If you would, Neville," said the commander quietly, his face fixed, unreadable, "then someone else will be able to join us. A matter of 'need to know'; you understand?"

Coltrane stood up, looked at Sayer and said, "I will see you back downstairs, Catrin, when you are finished here."

As he turned and headed to the door, Barlow said to her, but clearly aimed at Coltrane's back, "I must also emphasize, DI Sayer, that as a signatory to the Official Secrets Act, you are instructed to discuss what you are about to hear with no-one other than myself at this stage. Understood?"

Coltrane turned back and looked at Sayer. Catrin suddenly felt very much alone as she said, "Yes, sir; I understand that."

Then he opened the door and exited, passing without a word a man who was waiting to come in. Facing towards Barlow's desk, it took Catrin a moment to realise that someone else was entering the room, approaching the vacated seat.

As she turned her head, she came face-to-face with the man who had stared at her in the reception at Liz's Place; Mr. Establishment, the man she was sure understood surveillance techniques.

"DI Sayer, this is Mr. Drew with SIS at Vauxhall Bridge. Now, before we begin, shall we have some coffee, to get to know each other a little better? I have seen you with AC Hunt in the past, of course, and have familiarized myself with your file. As has Mr. Drew."

Almost on cue, his admin assistant knocked and entered carrying a tray with a coffee thermos, cups and saucers.

Barlow was sounding pleasant. Catrin got the impression that this man Drew knew quite a bit about her already, probably a lot more than in her personnel file. What that meant for her, she suspected, she was about to find out very soon.

EPILOGUE

"American Modernists, DI Sayer?"

Catrin looked round from the painting 'Metropolitan Port', by Joseph Stella, to see the person who had spoken softly to her from behind, realizing from the voice that she knew who it was. The man was in casual clothes but still appeared smartly dressed. She was visiting SAAM, the Smithsonian American Art Museum in Washington D.C.

Catrin was in Washington for a meeting with the FBI Art Team, the relationship-building exercise identified by her boss during her performance review.

"Agent Klintz! Or do I call you 'Mr. Klintz' off-duty? How did you know I was here?"

The FBI agent smiled. "Not detective skills, in this case. Coincidence, but not totally unexpected. I had a meeting here this morning - not work-related, I should add - and decided to stroll around after it finished, wondering who I would run into that I know. Recalling that you and your husband were flying overnight Friday, it wasn't too much of a surprise to find an art detective playing tourist in an art museum at the weekend."

He scanned the room.

"Where is your husband? Perhaps I could meet him? And off-duty, it's David."

Catrin smiled. "It's Catrin, then. He should be about half-way along the Mall, taking too many photographs. It's a lovely day for it. We are meeting up for lunch then he is heading for the Air and Space Museum. I said I would go to the Hirshhorn to see the new art, but I may just tag along with him instead. Less to do with work, more for the fun."

Klintz said, "Work? That doesn't start until tomorrow!"

"I study works of other contemporary artists when I can. It makes me think, inspires ideas for my own art. The trick is to be inspired to be original, rather than become derivative."

Klintz' expression made it clear he had clued in. "Right! You are a ceramicist, I recall. And DS Harper, your colleague?"

"He is in Connecticut, visiting friends from university for the weekend. He should arrive at the hotel this evening."

"Ah, yes. A Yale man. And DCI Coltrane is still tied up in internal meetings, I was told."

Catrin said, "Yes, he couldn't get away to attend this time."

Klintz paused, a little unsure what to do next as Catrin glanced at her watch.

She said, "I will need to leave in about ten minutes, to meet up with Chris. Would you like to walk with me and meet him, or wouldn't that be convenient?"

He thought for a second. "How about we meet up with him half-way? There is a restaurant I like that we could go to on Ninth Street. If you could text him, perhaps, I would be delighted to invite you both for lunch there. No shop talk or art talk, unless your husband is interested in art."

Catrin nodded. "That would be very nice, thank you. He is a computer guy; e-crime. He likes football; I mean soccer."

Klintz said, "So we won't talk about those topics, either. Soccer I know nothing about and computers…"

He wrinkled his face then changed the subject.

"The Bierstadt 'Seal Island' was restored fully, after all, we just heard. It took them some time but the Herron family is delighted. If the State Department diplomat is delighted with the result, so are the higher echelons of the Bureau with me."

Catrin smiled, "It was almost my first case with Art and

Antiques; well, an offshoot of the Acton warehouse thing, but a success for my team."

"Indeed. It must be the highlight of the year, in a sense."

Catrin thought back for a moment.

"Yes, well one of them. Not that anyone gets a lot of highlights and, of course, the failure to get the Nahigians to trial so far hasn't helped."

Klintz nodded sympathetically, "But we made other arrests in a lot of places; buyers, smugglers and thieves."

Her mind had gone back to Seren Fowles' face looking at the watercolour of St. Deiniol's Church, then her memory jumped to the walk across the road to talk with John Farrell, the sight of him standing there, looking hesitant. Not everything that was success for an art detective could be tied to a recovery of a specific painting. She had her own highlights associated with this new role, tied to a wild goose chase to small village in Wales.

And there were lowlights too. Her mind suddenly went to Stephen Drew of SIS and she momentarily lost her appetite for both art and food. There had been a number of occasions over the last months when this feeling had hit her.

"Shall we go?" was all she could say.

NOTES

The Metropolitan Police do have an Art and Antiques Unit within Specialist Crime Command, established back in 1969. Its staffing and functions reflect a focus on art crime in London as well as an international liaison but the structure and activities described here are entirely my own creation. The separate 'Art Crime Unit' in the Met described herein and in previous novels in the series has no real-life counterpart.

There are a number of churches named after St. Deiniol in the Church in Wales, but not one by that name in Tregynon or Aberhafesp, Wales.

John Bratby (1928-1992) was an important British artist, the founder of 'kitchen sink realism', something of an eccentric, self-promoting rebel. He provided the art for the film 'The Horse's Mouth', notably taking six weeks to paint a large mural on a brick wall. It's only use - to be knocked down by a bulldozer in a single 'take' during the filming. Again, I took liberties; in this case with his art and fictitious relationships. It is estimated that Bratby produced over three thousand paintings.

Alfred Bierstadt was a noted German-American artist (1830-1902) who produced a prolific range of landscape paintings across the USA. Included in these are several paintings of seals off the west coast, one of which, 'Seal Rock' is in the Smithsonian Museum. As far as I am aware, he did not produce a painting entitled 'Seal Island'.

My thanks go to my wife Gill and my friend Jack Soule for pre-reading the drafts and making editing suggestions. Any remaining errors are entirely my own, of course.

ABOUT THE AUTHOR

Allan Jones lives in Ontario, Canada. He was born and grew up in Merseyside, England. By profession an industrial chemist, he worked for many years as a consultant on international chemical regulation. He has lived in or travelled to most of the regions featured in the Catrin Sayer novels.